"Luck's devotion to historical accuracy shines again. . . . *Rimfire Bride* warms the heart."
—*RT Book Reviews*

"Exciting . . . A must-read. Sara Luck is truly a talented storyteller. . . . You feel as if you are there in 1882."
—*My Book Addiction Reviews*

TALLIE'S HERO
A *Publishers Weekly* Top 10 Romance for Fall 2012

The dangerous American West is no place for a genteel British novelist fleeing a scandal . . . but one plucky lady embraces the spirit of Wyoming—and captures the heart of her new hero, a daring rancher with big dreams of his own.

"The Wild West retains its appeal in *Tallie's Hero*."
—*Publishers Weekly*

"Steamy Western romance."
—*Fresh Fiction*

CLAIMING THE HEART

As the Texas and Pacific Railroad expands across the wild frontier, a spirited young woman experiences the triumphs and tumult of building a part of history . . . and loving a track man bound to a politically powerful family.

"Terrific . . . An enjoyable nineteenth-century Americana tale."
—*Genre Go Round*

"Fast-paced, engaging."
—*Romantic Times*

SUSANNA'S CHOICE

Sara Luck's "promising debut" (*Romance Views Today*)!

In a dusty Nevada mining town, an aspiring newspaperwoman crosses paths with a wealthy entrepreneur from San Francisco, and everything changes—including her own uncertain destiny.

ALSO BY SARA LUCK

Susanna's Choice

Claiming the Heart

Tallie's Hero

Rimfire Bride

Marci's Desire

Hearts Unbound

Hearts Afire

Available from Pocket Books

A FAMILY FOR MADDIE

SARA LUCK

Pocket Books
New York   London   Toronto   Sydney   New Delhi

Pocket Books
A Division of Simon & Schuster, Inc.
1230 Avenue of the Americas
New York, NY 10020

First Pocket Books paperback edition January 2015

POCKET and colophon are registered trademarks of Simon & Schuster, Inc.

For information about special discounts for bulk purchases, please contact Simon & Schuster Special Sales at 1-866-506-1949 or business@simonandschuster.com.

The Simon & Schuster Speakers Bureau can bring authors to your live event. For more information or to book an event contact the Simon & Schuster Speakers Bureau at 1-866-248-3049 or visit our website at www.simonspeakers.com.

Cover illustration by Aleta Rafton

Manufactured in the United States of America

10 9 8 7 6 5 4 3 2 1

ISBN 978-1-4767-5378-2
ISBN 978-1-4767-5380-5 (ebook)

To Sheri Jack,

thanks for all that you do for us

A FAMILY
FOR MADDIE

PROLOGUE

Borromeo Catholic Church, St. Charles, Missouri
Fall 1869

Josiah Case Williams stood at the window of the sacristy, looking out over the backyard of the church. The once-golden trees had shed most of their leaves and stood with mostly bare limbs, allowing Case a relatively unobstructed view of the Missouri River. As there had not yet been a hard frost, goldenrod continued to bloom, adding a flash of color to the brown carpet of leaves that lay on the ground.

Case smiled when he saw his mother's youngest sister jump out of a wagon, not even bothering to tie up the horse. His aunt was running for the door, darting between the assembled carriages, surreys, and buckboards that were parked in a nearby open lot.

Without seeing any of the owners, Case knew which of the vehicles belonged to whom, having worked on each of them at one time in his carriage and wagon shop. It was in his shop where he had first met his bride-to-be, Mary Beth Sullivan. He could remember the day she had pulled up in her "lady's phaeton," with its black body and big yellow wheels.

"Mr. Williams, can you do something about this thing?" Mary Beth had asked in a most disgusted tone as she tucked her bright red hair under her bonnet. "Look at me; I have mud all over."

Case had stepped to the side of the carriage and with his finger wiped a smudge of dirt off her chin.

That was all it had taken for him to know this was the woman he was going to marry.

She was not the most beautiful girl in St. Charles, but as he and his best friend, Theodore Dawes, often remarked, she was undoubtedly the most beguiling and impetuous person either of them had ever known. When Mary Beth and Case were courting, they'd often asked Ted to go with them to dances and picnics. A favorite game the two of them had conceived was to make a wager—the payment of which was a kiss—regarding which unattached girl Ted would take home.

Case had to admit he was a little upset that Ted had turned him down when he'd asked him to be his best man. He'd said he wasn't going to be in town, but Case was almost positive he had seen him earlier that day.

It didn't matter, Case thought, turning from the window and checking his watch. It was past time for the wedding.

"It's just like Mary Beth. She's late." With a crooked finger, Case tugged at the collar of his uncustomary starched shirt, and then adjusted the jacket of his tailcoat.

"Getting a little nervous?" Zeke Peterson asked.

Like Ted, Zeke was a good friend, and he had readily agreed to serve as Case's best man.

"What makes you think that?"

"The way you're pulling at that shirt."

"At least I'm not pulling at these pants," Case said as he looked down at his legs, which seemed to be poured into the tight trousers. "I can't believe I let Mary Beth talk me into wearing this getup."

Zeke laughed. "You'd stand on your head and whistle Dixie if she asked you to do it. She's one lucky woman."

"No, I'm the lucky one." Just then the organist began to play. "Sounds like that's our cue. Are you ready?"

"I should be asking you that. All I have to do is make sure I have the ring," Zeke said, as he put his hand down into his jacket pocket and withdrew the gold band.

Case took a deep breath and let it out slowly. "Then let's go."

The two men left the sacristy and each took up his position as they awaited the entry of Mary Beth and her maid of honor.

The organist continued to play, awaiting her signal to start the wedding march, and everyone in the congregation turned toward the swinging doors, which were still closed. The people in the church began to grow noticeably disquieted, and the priest made a motion with his hand, suggesting that the usher open the door to hurry the bride along.

When the doors were swung open, Alice Stokes was standing in the narthex, with tears streaming down her shocked face.

"She's gone!" the maid of honor shouted. "Mary Beth just ran away with Ted Dawes!"

"What?" Case gasped in disbelief. He hurried down the aisle taking long strides. When he reached the door of the church, he threw it open just in time to see Ted Dawes's buckboard racing down the street. On the seat beside him was a woman dressed in wedding finery. As he watched, the woman tossed her veil into the wind, and from the color of her fiery red hair, there was no question it was Mary Beth.

Case, still wearing his wedding attire, was sitting alone at the back of the Brown Dirt Tavern. His dark hair was disheveled; his jaw and chin wore the stubble of twenty-four hours without a shave; his tie was gone, his collar askew, and his suit well wrinkled. A half-empty bottle and a half-full glass of whiskey sat on the table in front of him. Lost in the amber liquid swirling in the glass, Case didn't notice the man who approached.

"Well, I'll give you this, Case Williams. You're certainly the best-dressed drunk I've seen in a while," the man said.

"I'm not nearly drunk enough," Case replied. Looking up, he saw a man with a high forehead and a dark Vandyke standing over him. He put his foot on the rung of the chair opposite him and pushed it out.

"Charles Broadwater," Case said.

Case took another drink.

"How long do you plan to stay here?" Broadwater asked.

"Until I'm drunk."

"All right, and then what?"

"I haven't planned that far ahead."

"That's some ambition."

"What do you mean? You were at the church—you know what happened."

"Yes I do, and so does everybody else in town."

"Why in the hell did he do this to me?" Case asked, taking another drink. "I thought he was my friend."

Charles laughed, amused that it was Ted Dawes and not Mary Beth that was causing this self-flagellation.

Case filled the glass that was now empty and pushed it across the table. "Hell, Charles, are you going to just stand there, or are you going to sit down? Or will you have a drink with a cuckolded bastard?"

Charles sat, pushing the glass aside. "I believe you have to have a wife before you can say you were cuckolded."

Case nodded. "Thanks, Ted, you saved me from that embarrassment." He lifted the bottle in a mocking toast. "I can't wait to get out of this place. I've been watching the river. Which boat do you think'll get to New Orleans the quickest?"

"I was thinking that might be what's on your mind. Are you dead set on going south?"

"North, south, east, west—what difference does it make, just as long as I never have to lay eyes on that woman again?"

"That's good. Would you consider coming west with me?"

Case laughed. "To Last Chance Gulch? That's mighty decent of you. Now that everybody knows the gold's almost played out, you want me to go dig in the mountains so I can show Mary Beth what a damned fool I really am."

"There are more ways to strike gold than dig it out of the ground," Charles said. "I could use a good man working for me. If you could come up with a little capital, I'd even take you on as a partner."

"And what kind of business would I be getting myself into?"

"Freight. That's how I'm going to make my fortune. Every ounce of freight that gets to the Montana Territory comes up the Missouri River, but when it gets to Fort Benton, that's where it stops. And from there it's loaded on wagons and taken all over the Northwest," Charles said. "I bought out the Diamond R Freight Company last spring, and I plan to make it the biggest freight line in the Montana Territory. Case, I need someone I can trust who knows wagons, and who knows more about keeping a freight wagon rolling than you do? It looks to me like you coming back to Helena with me would solve a problem for both of us."

Case took another drink, this time draining the bottle. "Let me think—icicles hanging on my nose in Montana, or pretty girls hanging on my arm in New Orleans? Now, let me see." Case tilted his head while squinting. "I just can't make up my mind— what should I choose?"

"All right, just be like that, but I'm serious. I'd like to have you as my partner," Charles said. "I'll be here a few more days rounding up capital. You know where my ma lives. Come see me when you sober up."

ONE

Battery Kemble, northwest Washington, DC
1875

This morning eight riders were gathered at Battery Kemble field for a steeplechase. Madelyn McClellan was the lone female, and it was her time to ride. Mounted on a filly, she leaned forward, patted the horse on the neck, and whispered into its ear.

"We're the only two ladies out here, so let's show these men a thing or two, shall we?"

Maddie slapped her legs against the sides of her mount, and the horse burst forth like a cannonball.

Maddie loved the feel of a powerful horse and the sensation of speed. When the animal leaped over the barriers, she felt as if the horse had wings, and all she had to do was pull back on the reins and the horse could sail out over the city.

She continued around the two-mile course, crossing the finish line in four minutes and fifteen seconds.

"Miss McClellan wins!" the timer shouted. "Her time is the fastest of the day."

"That's not fair, she's a woman, she doesn't

weigh as much as any of us," one of the other riders complained.

"Don't be a sore loser," said Sergeant Mark Worley, the army NCO in charge of the stables at Battery Kemble. "Miss Maddie, congratulations. It was a great ride."

"All I did was sit in the saddle," Maddie said. She patted the horse on its neck again. "Dame Eleanor did all the work, didn't you, girl?"

"It takes a team," Sergeant Worley said. "Rider and horse."

Maddie dismounted, handing the reins to the sergeant. "Thank you for letting me ride the best horse in the whole stable."

"Think nothing of it," Sergeant Worley said. "Dame Eleanor knows when it's you on her back. And besides, she won, and that will put her in a good mood all day."

Maddie patted the filly as the horse whickered and nodded.

"See what I mean?" Worley said. "Now there'll be no living with her."

"You will give her an extra ration of oats, won't you?"

"I promise I will, but Sergeant Cornett will be taking care of Dame Eleanor after tomorrow."

"Oh no, where will you be?"

"I'm leaving Washington," Sergeant Worley said, a broad smile crossing his face. "I've been assigned to an army post out West."

"I guess I should be happy for you, but I'm not— and I know Dame Eleanor won't be happy either." Maddie slipped the horse a cube of sugar. "Will you tell this new sergeant that I'm not like most of the other women who come down here?"

Sergeant Worley laughed. "I'll pass on the word— no gentle Nellie for Miss Maddie. She wants a spirited horse."

"Where have you been?" Diana McClellan asked when Maddie walked into the front entrance hall of her home. "Did you forget? We're expected to attend Mrs. Delano's reception this evening."

"Since I'm late, why don't you go without me? I hate these functions and you love them," Maddie said.

Diana closed her eyes and clenched her teeth. "Why do you do this to me? I don't know why I even try to make you acceptable. You have thirty minutes—now get dressed."

"Didn't you once say that if a woman can get herself ready in half an hour, she has no business going out in the first place?"

"Well, will you at least try to make yourself presentable?"

Diana was Maddie's older sister, and no two sisters were ever more dissimilar. Maddie was athletic and tended to meet men on an equal footing. Diana, on the other hand, was every inch the "proper" lady.

The two sisters did have one thing in common: both were quite attractive. Maddie's cobalt-blue eyes were set above high cheekbones in a face of almost perfect symmetry, but she seemed totally unconscious of her own looks. She often wore her light-brown hair hanging in one long braid, simply because it was easier that way.

Diana, on the other hand, knew exactly what she must do to accent her beauty, and it showed in the clothes she chose, how she wore her hair, and the way she deported herself. Her eyes were brown and her hair, which was nearly black, was swept up in a loosely wound chignon.

"I can just imagine what you were doing," Diana said. "You smell like horse."

"Some men like that smell," Maddie said, further irritating her sister.

"Well, not the ones who will be at the reception. There'll be dancing tonight, so dress appropriately."

"I hate doing that kind of stuff."

"Of course you do. You'd much rather be out riding, and I daresay you were riding astride, like some common farm girl. You know that isn't at all ladylike."

Maddie and her sister had one or more variations of this conversation almost on a daily basis, and she stood without comment.

"Don't just stand there. We're going to be late as it is," Diana said as she stomped off to the parlor.

The purpose of Mrs. Delano's reception was to raise money for the District's exhibition for the centennial celebration to be held next year in Philadelphia. As the year progressed, each of the wives of President Grant's cabinet took it upon herself to compete for the honor of raising the most money for the cause. Tonight's reception was being held at the Willard Hotel, and Mrs. Delano had announced that her fund-raising scheme was for gentlemen to make a donation each time they danced. The woman who brought in the most money was to be recognized at the end of the evening.

Maddie and Diana had barely set foot inside the ballroom when a young army lieutenant approached them.

"Miss McClellan, I've been waiting for you. May I be the first to add my name to your dance card?"

"Why, thank you, Lieutenant Kirby, I would be delighted to dance with you," Diana replied, flashing a smile that she knew would accent the dimples in her cheeks. She retrieved a booklet from her pocket and handed it to the lieutenant. "Make sure you make a generous donation. You know it is for a good cause."

"Of course. I'm going to try my hardest to see that you win the contest."

"I'd like that," Diana said as she cast a glance in Maddie's direction. With that one look, she had challenged her sister.

Maddie watched as Diana walked off with Lieutenant Kirby. This was one contest she was sure she wasn't going to win.

She wasn't at all jealous of her sister's popularity with men, though she was envious of the ease with which Diana could turn on her charm. She was sure that she would never be able to do that, as she approached a bevy of women who were seated together. Maddie worked her way into the group, content that she was now invisible.

When an intermission was called, Diana curtseyed and smiled at her last dance partner. Looking around the room, she spotted Maddie and headed toward her.

"The point of this event is to raise money by dancing. How much have you raised?" Diana asked.

Maddie had no reply.

"I thought so. Now get out here. You will dance."

"Yes, ma'am," Maddie said as she gave her sister a mock salute.

"Stop that," Diana said as she pulled her away from the women. "Do you want to wind up like your cohorts there? Look at them. Every one may as well be wearing a sign that says Spinster, and you were right in the middle of them. Is that what you want?"

"I'm twenty-three years old. I hardly think I'm an old maid yet."

Just then a gentleman approached, and Diana's demeanor changed immediately.

"Are you available, Miss McClellan?" the man asked.

"Which Miss McClellan?" Diana answered. "I'm afraid my card is filled, but my sister is free."

"I would be honored," the man said, offering his arm to Maddie. "I'm Captain Jason Gilliland."

"And I'm Maddie McClellan."

The two stepped out onto the dance floor, and within minutes Maddie was swaying to the music. For the rest of the evening, she danced with multiple partners, and she questioned why she had been so reticent. Secretly, she was thankful Diana had forced her out on the floor, but she would never admit that.

At the conclusion of the evening the band played a fanfare. Elizabeth Delano, the wife of the Secretary of Interior, stepped out in front of the bandstand. She was also the president of the Ladies'

Guild for the Capitol Exhibit for the Centennial Celebration. The dance tonight had been her idea, and though she had done none of the labor in getting it produced, she had monitored it from idea to fruition. She raised her hand to call for attention.

"Ladies and gentlemen, I am pleased to report that as a result of this gala tonight, we have raised one thousand, one hundred and fifty-seven dollars to be used in making the Capitol exhibit at the Centennial the most glorious of them all."

The applause was generous.

"And now," Mrs. Delano said, as she twittered nervously, "I want to announce the winner of the contest."

Maddie looked toward Diana, who was beaming proudly.

"The young woman who brought in the most money for the cause was . . . Miss Antoinette Delano. I am very proud of my daughter."

"Sure you are," someone yelled from the back of the room. "Just like you're proud of your son, who's giving out all the bogus contracts to his cronies."

The room grew quiet as the man's words registered with most of the men and several of the women who were in attendance. It was well known in Washington circles that Secretary Delano's tenure in office at the Department of Interior was riddled with scandal, much of which centered around his son, John.

"Oh dear," Mrs. Delano said, clearly flustered.

"Do you think the band could play one more piece?" Maddie called. "I'm not quite ready to go home."

Mrs. Delano was clearly grateful for Maddie's request. "That's a wonderful idea, my dear. Let's have a lively tune for our final number."

The White House, office of
President Ulysses S. Grant, Washington, DC

March 22, 1875

"Is there no end to the perfidiousness of those who are sworn to serve the people but wind up stealing from them?"

There were only two men in the president's office, which was on the second floor, southeast corner of the White House. President Grant had asked the question of Edward Parmelee Smith, commissioner of the Bureau of Indian Affairs.

Grant held a match to his cigar and continued to talk between audible puffs as he lit the cigar.

"When Jay Gould and James Fisk tried to corner the gold market, I thought it couldn't get any worse than that." The president's head was now enwreathed by aromatic smoke. "But no, my own vice president was right in the middle of Crédit Mobilier, and my private secretary was taking graft from the whiskey ring. Edward, do you know how that makes me look? There's no way I can run for a third term."

"The people don't blame you, directly, Mr. President," Smith said. "If they express any opinion at all it's that you show too much loyalty to friends and associates who often betray that trust."

The president pulled his cigar from his mouth

and turned to face Commissioner Smith. "And now you're telling me the next scandal is going to involve my Indian policy."

"Some are saying that, sir."

"Some? That's not good enough. Where are you getting this information?"

"Several of my agents are sending communiqués that are somewhat troublesome."

The president dropped into a nearby chair, glowering. "Give me an example, and name names."

"All right, sir. I recently heard from my Blackfoot agent, John Wood.

He says the Blackfoot have no head chiefs right now, and they have become disorganized and spiritless. The different bands are at the very least unfriendly, and some are downright hostile to each other. They appear to have no purpose in life other than to trade buffalo robes and peltries to the traders—in exchange for whiskey, I might add."

"Stop," the president interrupted. "A drunken Indian might be bad for morality, but that's not a scandal."

"According to John, the scandal is how the Indians have become so dispirited. He says it's because of the greed of evil white men who have reaped immense profit from illicit dealings with them. Too often the Indians are being cheated by the very people who should be serving them—by the trading posts, and, I'm sorry to say, Mr. President, some of the agents."

"Unfortunately, what you say confirms some earlier reports I received."

"I can't solve this problem systemically, you understand, but I believe I have the beginning of a solution. I would like to send a few good men out as field superintendents. We could position them in the western states and territories to monitor agencies and trading posts."

"All right. Didn't you say this report was from the Blackfoot agent?"

"Yes, sir, in the Montana Territory."

"Then we'll start there. Find a good man and send him to Montana."

"I will do my best."

"Ouch!" Maddie McClellan said as she kicked at a rock that was lying in her pathway. "Why? Why does she have to do that?" She kicked the stone again.

Maddie was on her way to the Smith house, where she was employed as a tutor and companion to the Smiths' nine-year-old daughter, but before she had left home, she had been upbraided by her sister and her mother.

"A lady never speaks out in a public place," Maddie said in a stilted voice as she attempted to mimic her mother. "What was I supposed to do? Let Mrs. Delano embarrass herself, just because of the remark of one ill-mannered buffoon?"

She turned onto the walkway that led to the home of Edward Parmelee Smith, and looking up, saw Samantha waving to her from the window. The door opened before Maddie reached the porch.

"There you are, Maddie. I was afraid you were going to be late," Hannah Smith said, as she grabbed her cape. "You and Sam have a good time."

Hannah Smith was so active in civic affairs that

she was seldom at home. During the war she had worked in hospitals taking care of the wounded; now she was involved in several church and civic charities, especially those that benefited Indians.

Maddie enjoyed tutoring Samantha, who was called Sam, and was soon lost in the lessons and thus able to put her irritation out of her mind. They worked on math and geography, and then came reading. This was the part of the lessons that Sam liked most, and because Sam enjoyed it, so did Maddie.

"Do you think Cinderella and the prince really got married?" Sam asked, after they finished reading the Brothers Grimm fairy tale "Aschenputtel," the story of Cinderella.

"Yes, I do."

"Why?"

"Because they loved one another."

Sam was quiet for a long moment. "Do you think you'll ever get married?"

"Yes, I do, if I fall in love with the right man."

Just then someone called from the front of the house.

"There's Mama," Sam said, starting toward the sound.

"How was your day?" Hannah greeted as she embraced her daughter.

"Miss Maddie is going to get married."

"That's wonderful news. Who's the lucky gentleman?"

Maddie laughed. "I'm afraid Sam may be putting the cart before the horse a little bit. We were reading 'Aschenputtel,' and then we were discussing whether Cinderella and her prince really did get married when the question of my status came up."

"Oh, Sam," Hannah said, a scowl crossing her face. "It's most impolite to inquire about someone's personal life." She turned to Maddie. "I'm sorry if my daughter offended you."

"Sam didn't mean anything by her question. We were just talking about the story."

Hannah chuckled. "Well, young women—all young women—need to learn proper etiquette. They cannot be speaking out of turn, no matter how innocent it seems."

"Yes, ma'am," Maddie said, as she lowered her gaze. It was obvious Mrs. Smith did not intend Sam to be the only recipient of her admonition.

Hannah turned to her daughter. "Dear, now go to your room and prepare yourself. Your father will be home shortly, and I'm sure he'll want to see you looking your best."

"Yes, Mama," Sam replied, turning and leaving the parlor.

"Maddie, you're doing a wonderful job with her. She so looks up to you."

"I enjoy being with Sam. She is very precocious."

"Perhaps too precocious," Hannah said, handing Maddie two dollars. "I know tomorrow isn't your regular day, but can you come anyway? I have another meeting to attend."

"Thank you, I'll be here."

With the two dollars securely in her purse, Maddie walked home. She knew that the money Mrs. Smith paid her was twice as much as most domestics earned, and it was more than Diana made when she worked as a hostess in the Willard Hotel's tea-room.

Maddie thoroughly enjoyed being with Sam, but she knew her employment was limited. Her long-range plan was to open a school like the one Mrs. Elizabeth Somers had opened in Washington. Mrs. Somers had been asked to tutor daughters of prominent men in the city, and Maddie had been enrolled in her first class. Her thoughts were that perhaps the Smiths wouldn't mind if Maddie looked into inviting two or three more girls to join Samantha in her studies.

When Maddie arrived home, she was surprised to hear her father's voice. She glanced at the grandfather clock standing in the hallway and found it was much too early for him to be home from school. But then she heard another voice and was sure the voice was that of her employer, Commissioner Smith.

Even though she knew it was wrong, she stood motionless as she listened to the conversation.

"You know I don't have any administrative experience," Roy McClellan was saying. "I teach agrarian studies, and I can't see that that would be a valuable skill for what you are asking me to do."

"It's not what you teach; it's where you teach," Edward Smith said.

"Most people don't look at Howard University as the best stepping-stone to a career in government."

"But in this case it is," Smith continued. "Working with the recently emancipated students, as you do, gives you a unique perspective on treating people of a different race with dignity and respect. That is exactly the trait I want my field superintendents to have. Where you would be going, the people are called savages. And whether they deserve it or not, the very word calls to mind a difficult environment."

"That's just it, Edward. Since this would be such a major disruption for my family, I would certainly need Annabelle's approval before I moved all the way to Montana."

"Oh, Roy, I wouldn't expect you to leave Annabelle here in Washington. I intend to station you in Helena, should you decide to take the position. From what I hear from my agents, Helena is a thriving little community. The gold has petered out a little, but the capital of the territory has just been moved there. And if Washington is any indication, that in itself could prove a boon for the economy."

"You've given me a lot to ponder," Roy said. "How soon do you have to have my answer?"

"As soon as possible. But now I need to be on my way."

Commissioner Smith grabbed his hat and stepped out into the hallway.

"Maddie. How nice to see you."

"Hello, Mr. Smith . . . Papa." Maddie looked from the man to her father, knowing full well that the men were aware that she had been eavesdropping.

"This is my daughter, who has not quite learned her place."

Edward laughed. "Don't be too hard on her. She's instilling this very spark of curiosity in Samantha, and should you chose to accept my offer, I will hate to see her leave."

"I'll let you know my answer by the end of the week."

"Excellent. Good day, Roy, Maddie."

"Good day," Roy said.

When the commissioner closed the door, Roy turned to his daughter. "How much did you overhear?"

"Oh, Papa, I haven't been here long. I didn't mean to listen, but when I heard Mr. Smith's voice, I thought I might have done something wrong."

"Never mind, but in regards to the commissioner's offer, I would appreciate it if you did not mention this to either your mother or your sister," her father said, and then he smiled. "I will tell you right now, I am flattered by the offer, and I am going to take the position, but I don't want your mother to know she didn't have a hand in my decision."

"Yes, sir," Maddie said as she hugged her father.

For the last three weeks the McClellans had been living in a suite at the Willard Hotel, because all of their belongings had been shipped to St. Louis. From there, the crates would be put on a riverboat to make their way up the Missouri River as long as it was navigable. When the boat reached Fort Benton, Montana, everything would be loaded off the vessel and onto wagons, to be taken via mule train to Helena. This hope was that the McClellans' things would reach their destination before the family arrived.

On this warm May morning, a hired carriage dropped Maddie and her family off in front of a building that looked more like a church than a train depot. Maddie looked at the clock tower that stood beside the door. They had less than an hour to wait until the train departed.

"Why don't the three of you find a place to sit while I check our baggage through to St. Louis," Roy said. "Don't walk off and leave your traveling valises anywhere."

Maddie smiled when she heard her father's comment. Even though he would never admit it, she knew he was every bit as excited as she was. He was to be a field superintendent for the territory of Montana.

"I'm going with you," Annabelle said. "I want to make certain you don't lay our tickets down someplace and then walk off and leave them."

Roy smiled at his wife. "I guess I am excited."

Maddie and Diana found a place to sit.

"I can't believe Papa is making us do this," Diana said.

"You didn't have to come. He gave us a choice."

"Humph. Some choice. Where was I going to stay when he leased the house to the Jacksons?"

"You could have taken a room in a boardinghouse," Maddie said.

"Absolutely not. How could I have entertained in a boardinghouse? If you hadn't been so keen about going along with this, we could have found a halfway decent flat to rent together."

"Diana, aren't you even a little bit excited?"

"Why should I be? It's going to take us a month to get there, and the last part of the trip we're going to be traveling by mule train. The whole thing is disgusting. I just know I'm going to hate it in Helena."

"No, you won't."

"What makes you think that?"

Maddie put her hand on her sister's and smiled at her. "Because I know you. I've never known anyone who makes friends as easily as you do. Besides, look at it this way. You've already won Washington over. Now you'll have a whole new territory to conquer, and once we're settled I can watch you, and maybe I'll learn a few things."

Diana smiled. "What makes you think you'll listen to me once we get to Montana? You've never paid any attention to me before."

"Well, I didn't say I would be a good student."

"Maybe I can start the Diana McClellan Charm School for Young Ladies."

"Westbound train is now loading on track number five!" someone shouted through a speaking trumpet.

"Here comes Papa," Maddie said, picking up her bag.

"They've just called our train, and your mother's waiting by the gate. Come on, girls, our adventure begins."

TWO

Dearborn River, Montana Territory

The roaring river broke white as it cascaded across the rocks and whirled in pools at the river's bend. The water was cold and pure, and it was for that reason a cabin had been built in a copse of trees near the river's edge.

"Come on, Dandy, don't be shy now," Case Williams said as he prodded his horse into the water.

Case was looking forward to taking a break in his trip back from Fort Shaw. Several of his drivers had gone on a rampage when they had delivered a shipment to the post trading store, and General John Gibbon had thrown the men into the stockade. He wouldn't let them out until someone came to settle for the damages done to the store. Now William Cooper had threatened to take his contract away from the Diamond R and give it to the Kirkendall freight outfit. Cooper was a steady customer, and in order to protect the account, Case had fired the drivers on the spot and agreed to become half owner of the Fort Shaw sutler's store.

Fortunately, another train was on the Carroll road, and Case was able to consolidate the two to get them back to Helena. He knew he should have stayed with the train, but Tom Clary was now in charge, and Case could depend on him to get the wagons home without any foreseeable trouble.

And besides, he wanted to call on Riley Barnes. He had met the man soon after he had arrived in Montana, and he credited Riley with saving his life. On one of Case's first trips to Fort Shaw, he was thrown from a horse and suffered a broken ankle. His horse ran away, and because Case was in unfamiliar territory, he had hobbled and crawled aimlessly until he had become weak and dehydrated.

Riley discovered him and took him back to his cabin, where his wife, Badger Woman, tended to his ankle. Despite the wide difference in their ages—at the time, Riley was seventy and Case was twenty-six—the two men became good friends, and Case always enjoyed his visits.

Case crossed the Dearborn River and began to yell loudly.

"Hey, old man. What's in your pot that you'll share with a tired and hungry beggar?"

At that moment, the door opened and a grizzly old man with a long white beard stepped out holding a rifle pointed at Case.

"You mean you're going to shoot me after all the work Badger Woman did putting me back together?"

"Case? Is that you?"

"It is," Case said as he dismounted and led Dandy up to the cabin that he had helped enlarge. "Is there a place where I can throw down my bedroll, or have the girls taken over the place?"

"You know there's always room for you, my friend," Riley said as he stepped out of the cabin and closed the door. "Case, it's been a bad winter. Badger Woman died back in February."

"What happened to her?"

"It was durin' a cold spell. She went down to the river to fill the bucket, and somehow she got wet. She caught the newmony," Riley said.

"Pneumonia, that's bad anywhere, let alone out here."

"She died within a week. Warn't nothin' I could do for her. When we could get around some, me 'n' the girls took her back in the woods, laid her out on a stand up in a tree so's the wolves couldn't get to her."

"I'm really sorry to hear that, Riley. If I had known, I would have been here."

"I know, but there wasn't no way of getting word to you. I figured Badger Woman, bein' as she was so much younger'n me, would outlive me so as she could take care of the young'uns. Now, I've been left with these five little ones to raise up, all by myself."

"Did you send word to Petah? We send wagons to Fort Macleod all the time, and I can bring her back. If she knew Badger Woman was gone, I know she'd want to come back to help you."

"Petah's man was sent to Fort Pelly."

"Then there's no way she can come. Fort Pelly's over seven hundred miles north. What about Kimi?"

"She's doin' what she can. But she ain't much more'n a girl her ownself. I think she's only about twelve. Besides which, I'm gettin' so old that I can't hardly get aroun' all that much anymore, so she has to do for me, too."

"Nonsense, Riley. You can outwork any two men I know."

"It's my eyes. They're failing me, so I can't hunt like I used to. I don't figure I got all that long left, 'n' truth to tell, if it warn't for me worryin' 'bout what's goin' to happen to the girls 'n' all, well I'm near 'bout ready to go 'n' meet my Maker."

"Don't be so quick to leave your friends, Riley. There are a lot of us who'd like to see you stick around."

"Ain't that much to stick around for. I can tell you for certain, though, that this here country ain't nothin' a'tall like it was when I first come out here."

"How's that? It looks the same to me."

"It's not the scenery I'm talking about—it's the scoundrels that's took over. Now, you take the Blackfoot," Riley continued. "Back when I first come on the Blackfoot, they was a proud people, and rich too, in what counted. They had horses, fur for tradin', buffalo for huntin'. Now they's just a few of 'em that's even left, what with so many of 'em been kilt off by the gold hunters 'n' the soldiers, and if that don't get 'em, then it's the smallpox or, worse yet, the whiskey. Have you heard about what your white government has done?"

"What do you mean, 'my' white government? It's as much your government as it is mine. You're a white man, and you're an American."

"No, I ain't white no more. I left the white race and America back in eighteen hunnert 'n' thirty-five. That was long 'afore that foolish war you folks fought agin' one another. No, sir, I don't consider them folks in Washington to be my government at all. Most especial not with this new law and what they're doing to my people."

"What law are you talking about?"

"White Calf tells me they took back half the land that was s'posed to belong to the people, 'n' they didn't give 'em not a red cent for it."

"That figures. It goes along with what's happening in Nebraska. The government's offered the Sioux twenty-five thousand dollars to give up hunting, and with fifty thousand Indians, that comes to a half dollar apiece. "

"Those bastards in Congress know what they're doin' is wrong. With the buffalo purt' nigh all hunted out, most all the Blackfoot is goin' hungry. You know what the guvmint's doin' about it? They're a-givin' out salt pork that ain't hardly worth eatin', 'n' flour that's all full of weevils. That is . . . what gets to 'em in the first place. Thing is, what with all the cheatin' that's goin' on and whatnot, if there *is* anything that's actual worth somethin', why, most of it gets stole long 'afore it ever gets here. Why, by the time my young 'uns is growed up, they'll more'n likely be the only Indians left in all Montana. 'Course, there prob'ly ain't nobody worryin' none about that."

"Well, don't give up just yet. I know the Bureau of Indian Affairs is sending a new man out to work with the agency," Case said.

"And just what difference do you think that'll make? It'll just be another polecat dippin' his hands down in the pot to take what ain't his," Riley said.

"Onliest reason they keep sendin' more people out here is so there'll be more of 'em to get their hands down into the kitty."

"Maybe this time it will be different. The new man's name is Roy McClellan, and he's going to headquarter in Helena. The Diamond R is handling his freight, and from the looks of the bill of lading, it seems like he's moving a whole house full of belongings. I would assume he plans to be here for a while."

"Well, I reckon we'll find out soon enough. Is McClellan going to replace John Wood?"

"No, he's going to be a field superintendent, whatever that is."

"More'n likely he'll be a swindler, too."

"Let's all try to reserve judgment on him—give him a chance to prove himself."

"If you say so."

Case shook his head. He knew that Riley had already made up his mind.

"Are we gonna just stand here and jaw at one another, or are you going to come in?"

"I'll take that as my official invitation," Case said. "Just let me put Dandy in the shed and I'll be in directly."

Case unsaddled his horse and gave him and Riley's horses each a forkful of hay before leaving the shed. He hesitated at the door to the cabin. He wondered how Riley and the girls were managing without Badger Woman.

Case had been with Riley when he had found Petah and the five little ones huddled in a cave five years ago. Riley and Badger Woman had taken them in, and the love the girls had given had turned the crusty old curmudgeon into a sentimental grandfather.

They were a family. And Case was proud to be a part of it.

He opened the door and stepped inside.

"Where are my hugs?" Case asked as four little girls came running to him.

"Oh, Uncle Case, what did you bring us?" the smallest child asked.

"I've got peppermint sticks for everybody." He withdrew a drawstring leather pouch and began handing out the candy. "Two for Koko, two for Kanti, two for Pana, two for Nuna, but wait, I have two left—where's Kimi?" Case looked around the cabin, pretending not to see the young girl who was standing by the step-top cookstove.

"Hi, Uncle Case," Kimi said. "I heard you and Papa talkin', so I put some cornbread in the oven. It's almost ready."

"Well, would the woman of the house want some candy?"

Kimi smiled, her black eyes shining as she came running to Case and wrapped her arms around him. He was touched when he felt her shudder. So much responsibility for a mere child. He held her until she pulled away to remove the crisp brown bread from the oven.

"You're in luck, Case. I snared a jackrabbit this morning, and Kimi and me made a right good stew. We also put in some of them shriveled-up vittles you brung us, and it's turned out right tasty," Riley said.

"I told you you'd like desiccated food. It just took you a while to get used to eating vegetables, but the girls need them," Case said.

"We like the apples the best, but Papa won't let us eat them every day. He says we'll run out," Pana said.

"You eat all you want. I'll see that the next wagon going north has a fresh supply, and I'll have them left at St. Peter's. You can pick them up when you are at school."

"Are you goin' to sleep here tonight, Uncle Case? 'Cause if you are, I'll get some soft robes laid out for you," Kimi said.

"Why, thank you, Kimi. When are you girls going back to school?"

"I may not be going back," Kimi said. "I've learned how to read and write. And with Mama gone, I need to stay here to take care of Papa."

The girls had been going to the mission two days a week to attend school. The mission was ten miles away, so they would spend the night there, rather than ride back and forth.

"No, you ain't goin' to stop goin' to school," Riley said. "Look how good you girls talk. You want to grow up soundin' as ignernt as me?"

"Riley, your language may be rustic," Case said, "but there is nobody who could ever say that you are ignorant."

Kimi went over to hug Riley. "Uncle Case is right. You are the smartest person I know."

"Hrrumph," Riley grunted, embarrassed by the accolades.

"But your papa is right," Case said. "You need to keep going to school."

It turned cold during the night, and Kimi got up to make certain that all her sisters were warmly covered. They weren't actually her sisters, of course, but she was sure she couldn't be closer to real sisters.

Crawling back into her own robes, Kimi drifted off to sleep, and though sleep came quickly, it wasn't peaceful.

She was cold, and she could hear the gunshots and the screams and cries of the others. She stood there aware only of the red blood, and of the dark, unmoving lumps that lay in the white snow.

"Come, come!" Petah said, grabbing her and pulling her with her. "Come, we must run! We must hide!"

Petah was twelve, Kimi was seven. The others—Koko, Kanti, Pana, and Nuna—like Kimi, were standing in the snow, the numbness of the horrific things they had witnessed pushing out the fear. Nuna and Pana were four then, Kanti and Koko both under two.

"Come!" Petah said. "You take Nuna and Kanti, I'll take Pana and Koko. We must hide before the soldiers come back!"

Petah took them to a small cave on the bank of the Marias River. Kimi knew the cave—she had played in it many times. But they hadn't come to play; they had come to hide.

It was cold . . . so cold.

Kimi was cold, and she pulled the robes more tightly around her, realizing at that moment she was now safe, warm, and with people who loved her. She had been dreaming.

Before Petah left, she had shared with Kimi that she, too, often dreamed of that terrible night. Nuna and Pana had no clear memory of the event, only images and impressions. Koko and Kanti had no memory of it at all.

They were the lucky ones.

When Maddie and her family left the train at Bismarck, in the Dakota Territory, they were approached by a young man wearing the uniform of an army captain. The captain addressed her father.

"Excuse me, sir. Are you Professor McClellan?"

"I am." Roy offered his hand to the captain.

"I'm Captain Tom Custer. My brother wishes to offer you the comfort of his home until you leave for Fort Benton."

"Well, that's very generous of him," Roy replied. "Is General Custer aware that I have my family with me?"

"Yes, sir, we received a telegraph from the bureau. He and Mrs. Custer are expecting you and your family. If you will come with me, I have an ambulance and a buckboard at your disposal."

"An ambulance?" Annabelle questioned.

Tom smiled. "Yes, ma'am. The ambulance, being well suspended, is the most comfortable vehicle in the army inventory."

"Then I thank you, Captain," Annabelle said. "After being on the train so long, my body is a bit weary."

"Have you seen to your baggage yet?"

"I have not," Roy said, as he moved to go to the mound of luggage that was forming on the railroad platform.

Captain Custer turned and signaled to three soldiers who were standing beside two vehicles near the depot. The men immediately moved toward the luggage.

"These men are at your disposal, Professor."

"Thank you, Captain."

"I'll see to your family," Tom said, turning his attention to Annabelle and the girls.

With the luggage loaded onto the buckboard, and the McClellans ensconced in the ambulance, they began to move the short distance to the river.

Looking through the raised sides of the ambulance, Maddie saw that the street was filled with pedestrians who were making their way between wagons and buckboards, while dozens of horses were tied to hitching rails. By Washington standards, the crowd was small, but the noise they were making was overwhelming.

There were shops of all descriptions, from leather goods to millineries to apothecaries.

They passed saloons and gambling halls as well. She saw several soldiers in uniform gathered outside of one, around a young woman who was wearing a garment cut so low that the creamy tops of her breasts threatened to spill out. Maddie felt her cheeks flush as she wondered how any woman could publicly display herself in such a way.

It took but a few minutes for them to reach the

Missouri River, where Maddie saw a boat tied to a wooden dock. The dock was almost submerged by the surging water. The name, painted on the side of the boat, was DENVER.

Captain Custer stopped beside the ambulance. "Ladies you may want to step down while we load the wagons. With the river so near flood stage, there could be a mishap."

"Oh dear," Diana said. "Are we in danger?"

"Not unless the horses get startled," Maddie said. "Then they'll run off the other end of the ferry."

Captain Custer laughed. "The young lady is right. It doesn't happen often, but I would hate to put you at risk."

Maddie watched as Diana put on a performance, a version of which she had seen many times before. She clasped her hands to her chest, and began batting her eyelashes at the captain.

"You won't let anything happen to us, will you?"

"Oh, no, ma'am," Captain Custer said as he dismounted. "I'll personally escort you onto the ferry."

Maddie watched as the captain took Diana by the arm and pulled her aside while the wagons and the rest of the passengers were allowed to board. How could Diana do that? How did she know exactly how to get the attention of a man?

Maddie couldn't decide if she thought it was foolish the way Diana acted, or if she was just jealous because she couldn't do the same thing.

"There it is," Tom Custer said as the ferry approached the other side of the river. He pointed to a group of low-lying buildings scattered about one hundred feet up, beyond the bank. Some were down in a valley, flanked by a long chain of bluffs. A short distance from them, sitting on top of a hill, was another gathering of structures, where three blockhouses were connected by a long, high wall.

"It almost seems like a small town," Maddie said. "I thought an army post would just have soldiers."

"It is like a town. Out here, we have to be pretty self-sufficient."

The boat made landfall then, and since it was such a short distance to the buildings, Maddie asked her father if they could walk. The captain dismissed the ambulance and the loaded buckboard proceeded to the Custer quarters.

Leading his horse, Tom walked with them. They came upon a level plain that at the time was being used for drills. Here, some of the soldiers were marching to and fro, while others were riding horses at a gallop.

The buckboard had stopped in front of a very attractive brown two-story house with a wide front piazza.

"Here it is, folks, the commandant's quarters," Tom Custer said, as he tied his horse to a hitching post. He stepped around and between a half dozen staghounds, none of which even lifted its head.

An attractive woman opened the door and stepped out onto the piazza.

"Welcome to our home, Professor McClellan. I'm looking forward to our visit, especially with your beautiful wife and daughters. I'm Libbie Custer."

"Thank you, Mrs. Custer. I do hope our stay will not be an imposition," Annabelle said.

"Don't even suggest such a thing. How often do you think I get to entertain such enlightened people?"

Just then a man's leg came through an open window, and everyone's attention was focused in that direction.

"My dear, dear Autie," Libbie said, "is that the impression you want to make on our guests?"

"I just wanted to see for myself that this McClellan wasn't George."

Maddie smothered a giggle, as her father was flummoxed by the general's behavior. His unconventional method of arriving on the porch certainly didn't match his larger-than-life reputation.

Libbie took her husband's arm and pulled him over beside her.

"When the colonel gets away from civilization, he tends to forget some of his manners, but Eliza's going to take care of that tonight," Tom said. "She's preparing a wonderful dinner, and we're going to have a delightful evening."

"Colonel? I thought he was addressed as General," Diana said.

"That was his brevet rank during the war," Tom Custer said. "And I was a colonel, but guess who still uses his rank? You didn't hear me calling myself Colonel Custer, now, did you? It's only our egomaniac here who still uses that."

"Egomaniac? Oh, that's mean," General Custer said as he cuffed his brother on the shoulder. "Who goes around here wearing a pair of baubles all the time?"

"Baubles? They're medals of honor," Tom said, "and only me and three others received two such medals in the entire war."

"Only I," the general said, correcting Tom's grammar.

Libbie shook her head. "Now do you see why I'm so anxious to have guests? I have to put up with this all the time."

She came down the steps to take Annabelle by the arm. "I don't believe I heard your name, dear."

Case stayed with Riley longer than he had intended, but he felt he needed to. Riley had said he was slowing down, and Case wanted to see for himself. Unfortunately, Riley was right.

For the entire week that Case was on the Dearborn, he had hunted and fished, trying to get some meat and fish smoked so Kimi would have some food stored to fall back on.

He tried to convince Riley to come back to Helena with him, but Riley thought the girls might be mistreated. They were full-blooded Blackfoot, and many in town were prejudiced against Indians, no matter how innocent they were.

When he reached Helena, Case knew he should go by the Diamond R to let them know he was back in town, but that was the good thing about having partners. Either Charles or George Steell would have everything under control.

Case went straight to his house, which was a foursquare on Madison Avenue, too big for a single man. But in the back of his mind, Case had always thought the girls would wind up with him, and he wanted to have room for them. He had even considered adding additional bedrooms in the floored attic, and after seeing Riley, he believed that time might be coming sooner than he'd thought.

When he walked into the house it was cold, because it had been without heat for several days. He soon had a roaring fire going in the potbelly stove, and he put several kettles of water on to warm.

What he really needed was a bath and a shave before he went anywhere. As much as he loved Riley Barnes, he didn't like to stay at his house for as long as he had on this visit. His hair smelled of smoked meat, and his clothing reeked of bear grease.

Case had just pulled out the wooden bathtub when someone began banging on his door.

"Hell," Case said as he put the kettle back on the stove.

"Where have you been?" George Steell asked.

"How did you know I was back?"

"I've got my spies out. Warren Gillette sent word as soon as you came through Prickly Pear. I would've thought you'd have come by the Diamond R as soon as you got in town—just to see how your business is getting along."

"You and Charles couldn't handle things without me?"

"That's just it, it's just me. Julia insisted that Charles take her to Salt Lake City—says she's got cabin fever and had to get out of here for a while."

Case laughed. "Poor Charles. Julia can really make him jump through hoops."

"You laugh—this could have been you, you know," George said and when he saw Case's expression go rigid, he quickly apologized. "I'm sorry, Case. I shouldn't have said that."

"Six years is a long time, and I guess I really should be thanking Mary Beth. If I'd have stayed in

St. Charles, I'd still be repairing wagons instead of owning three hundred."

"You own one hundred. Charles and I each own a hundred, too," George said. "And now Tom Clary tells me you've bought in with old Will Cooper. Did you commit the Diamond R to owning a sutler's store?"

"I'd sort of thought we'd all be partners," Case said.

"Oh no, not with that old fart. I don't want any part of it."

"All right, then I'll do it myself. By the way, what was so important that you kept a man from his bath?"

"Oh, I almost forgot. The Bureau of Indian Affairs sent a wire asking if we'd send a private coach up to Fort Benton, and Charles said we would. It seems this new field superintendent's bringing his wife and kids. And I'm volunteering you to go with the coach."

"Me? I've been gone for at least two weeks. Don't I have a lot of work to catch up on?"

"You do, but you won't be going for a few days, so you'll have plenty of time to get the stink off. Where have you been, anyway?"

"I was up on the Dearborn with Riley Barnes. His wife died and I felt like I needed to stay with him for a while."

"You mean his squaw?"

"No, I mean his wife."

THREE

After breakfast the next morning, Libbie Custer announced that she and the general would be accompanying the McClellans back to Bismarck to catch the boat. The ambulance was parked in front of the commandant's quarters, and shortly after they were loaded, General Custer rode up on his horse. Tom Custer was not far behind.

"Ladies, are you sure you want to run off with your father? He can civilize Lo without you being there," Tom said. "Libbie's always importing females to stay with her, and I know you'd be welcome."

"I'm sorry, Captain. I'm afraid I don't understand what you mean by 'lo'," Roy said.

Tom laughed. "That's our name for Indians."

"Oh," Roy said, raising his eyebrows. "Is 'Lo' a universal term?"

"It is to anyone who knows the general."

General Custer began reciting a poem, speaking the lines with the finest elocution.

"Lo, the poor Indian! whose untutor'd mind
Sees God in clouds, or hears him in the wind;
His soul proud Science never taught to stray
Far as the solar walk or milky way."

"Alexander Pope," Maddie said, and she added the next two lines:

"Yet simple Nature to his hope has giv'n,
Behind the cloud-topp'd hill, a humbler
    heav'n."

"Young lady, I'm very impressed," General Custer said. "I'll have to admit, our use of Lo is rather Rabelaisian. But such is the personality of the soldier in the field. Some might say we have somewhat of a perverse sense of humor, but that's what gets us through some trying times."

"Sometimes, it gets a little too far afield," Libbie said, "but getting back to what Tom suggested. I'd love to have you stay at Fort Lincoln—perhaps until your parents get established in Helena. Professor McClellan, would you consider letting the girls stay behind?"

Diana smiled broadly, her eyes begging her father to let her stay.

Roy McClellan looked at each of his daughters. One was visibly petitioning him to agree to leave her, and the other was horrified at the thought that he would do it.

"I am honored that you would invite my daughters to spend some time here in your lovely home, but I'm afraid I'm going to need the girls to help me set up our own home," Annabelle said.

"Oh, Mama, please let me stay," Diana pleaded. "Maddie can help you do whatever it is you need."

"You know that Maddie doesn't know one thing about decorating," Annabelle said. "I am counting on you to help make our house, such as it may be, presentable."

"But, Mama—"

"Our family started this adventure together, and we will end it together," Roy said.

"Yes, Papa," Diana said, as she lowered her head much as a petulant child would do.

Just then a buckboard rolled up behind the ambulance. Maddie noticed there was a man in uniform, a woman, and a passel of children, all of whom were moving around restlessly.

"Lieutenant, all ready to go, I see," Custer said.

"Yes, sir," the lieutenant replied, saluting from his seat. Custer returned the salute.

"Professor McClellan, this is Lieutenant Titus Jackson. He's being posted to Fort Shaw, so he and his family will be on the boat with you from here to Fort Benton."

"There's Weasel!" one of the children shouted, and, jumping down from the buckboard, a young boy, not more than four, ran toward an approaching soldier.

"Private Phillips is going to the boat with us," Lt. Jackson said. "He'll bring the team and the buckboard back."

Phillips approached the officers and saluted.

"Climb aboard, Private," Jackson said. Scooting over in the seat, he turned the reins over to the young soldier, while the woman jumped down and scurried to scoop up the wayward child.

Maddie and the others, including Libbie, climbed into the ambulance, and Custer called out to the driver.

"All right, Cobb, let's go."

It took about fifteen minutes for the *Denver* to get across the river, as the ferry was bucking the current. It was headed toward a two-stacker stern-wheeler tied up at the dock. On the side of the pilot-house, Maddie read, emblazoned in red letters and outlined in gold, the name JOSEPHINE.

She wondered who Josephine was: the captain's wife, or maybe his daughter, or perhaps his mother. She smiled as she imagined another scenario. She was the captain's long-lost love; she had run off with another man, and now the captain was forever pining for his darling Josephine.

Just then the water forced the ferry into the dock, and had Maddie not been holding on to the railing, she might have fallen. Instinctively, she looked around to see how Mrs. Jackson and her children had fared.

The harried woman, while balancing one child on her hip, was trying to corral the others to get them off the ferry. She reminded Maddie of a mother duck trying to get her ducklings to line up in a row.

No one seemed to be helping the woman, and as soon as she got the children lined up, one would dart off in another direction, and she would have to retrieve that child. When she returned, another would be gone.

"I think you could use some help," Maddie said as she moved toward the woman.

The woman, her hair frayed and disheveled, looked at Maddie with a grateful expression.

"If you would see to it that Jeremy gets off the ferry, I think I can manage the others."

"Let me guess. Is Jeremy Weasel's friend?"

"He is indeed. I have seven other children, and then I have Jeremy. He's a handful."

Maddie smiled as she found the small boy, who was scrambling up the steps into the pilothouse.

"Hi, Jeremy, I have a feeling you and I are going to become fast friends over the next five hundred miles."

"What's your name?"

"Maddie."

"Do you get mad?"

"Not very often, but I can when boys and girls don't do what I say, and right now I want you to join your mother and get off this ferry."

"Yes, ma'am." Jeremy went to where his mother was waiting and stood patiently until the gangplank was in place.

"Thank you," the woman said. "I don't believe I heard your name."

"I'm Maddie McClellan, and you are . . . ?"

"Lucinda Jackson—but my friends call me Lucy."

When Maddie rejoined her family, Diana had a reproving look on her face.

"You shouldn't have done that. That child will be bothering you until we get off the boat."

"I'm afraid Diana is right," Libbie Custer agreed. "For a four-year-old, Jeremy can get in more mischief than one can imagine. You saw the field mouse that the general tamed. Somehow he got that mouse out of the empty inkstand and took it outside and let it loose. Had a soldier not seen him do it, that mouse would have been a meal for any marauding hawk."

"I just felt sorry for Lucy. She has her hands full with all those kids."

"Yes, she does. Fort Shaw can have Lieutenant Jackson and his whole brood," Libbie added with a laugh.

When everyone was off the ferry, Maddie looked around at the crowd that had gathered at the dock. She estimated that there were at least a hundred and fifty people.

"My, will all these people be on the *Josephine*?"

"Oh, lass, these people aren't here for the going; they're here for the gawking," General Custer said. "The arrival and departure of a boat is quite a source of entertainment."

"Humph," Diana scoffed, "we won't even have that in Helena."

Custer led them over to the gangplank that was attached to the *Josephine*. A rope was stretched across it to prevent anyone from boarding prematurely.

"Oh dear, I hadn't thought that we might not be able to board," Roy said.

Custer held up his finger. "Wait here—I'll speak to the captain." Ducking under the rope, Custer went aboard. A moment later he returned with a rather tall, dignified-looking man who had silver hair and a neatly trimmed moustache.

"Professor McClellan, this is Grant Marsh, the finest riverboat captain on the Missouri . . . or any other western river," Custer said.

"Welcome aboard the *Josephine*, Professor McClellan," Captain Marsh said as he extended his hand.

"I'm pleased to hear the general heap such high praises upon you, Captain," Roy said. "Just watching this river makes me shudder."

Captain Marsh chuckled. "Believe me, the *Josephine* can handle whatever is put before her. The general tells me you're the bureau's new field superintendent for Montana."

"That is my new title," Roy said. "May I introduce you to my wife and two daughters? All of us are excited and anxious to be on our way."

Captain Marsh touched his hand to the bill of his cap in salute. "Ladies, it will be a pleasure serving you, but I'm afraid we won't be getting under way until dawn."

"That will be fine," Annabelle said. "Can you suggest a hotel where we might spend the night?"

"Your stateroom is ready, now. If the loading of hardwood all night long is not too obtrusive, you're welcome to come aboard."

"Thank you, that's a very generous offer, Captain," Roy said. "We'd love to spend the night on the boat."

"Well, now that that's settled, we'll be taking our leave. Professor, Mrs. McClellan, girls," General Custer said as he removed his hat. "Please be assured that when Lo tries to get the better of you, you'll always have friends in the Seventh Cavalry."

"We so enjoyed your visit," Libbie said as she embraced Annabelle and good-byes were said.

"Purser," Captain Marsh called, "please sign the McClellan family aboard; then have one of the stewards show them to their stateroom." Again, he saluted Roy and his family. "Now if you will excuse me, I must get back to the pilothouse."

The McClellans joined a skeleton crew for dinner that evening, which was a hearty meal of ham and beans. When they were finished eating, Roy insisted that his family retire to the stateroom, in order to stay out of the way of those loading the boat.

Maddie tried to sleep, but she was too excited. When she heard the boat's time marked, she left the room quietly, stepping out onto the hurricane deck.

Captain Marsh had been correct about the sounds from the loading of firewood. She looked down at the boiler deck, where a parade of men were stacking what looked like an endless supply of wood. But even louder than the wood clattering as it hit the deck were the sounds coming from the town of Bismarck. She could hear the loud plinking of a badly tuned piano coming from somewhere. As she listened, she realized it was playing the same two or three songs over and over again. The air was also rife with the low rumble of indistinct conversations, occasionally interspersed with loud cursing that was only too intelligible.

She heard a woman's scream, but it was fol-

lowed so quickly by lilting laughter that she realized the scream had not been emitted out of fear.
She also heard what appeared to be gunshots, but
the sounds of the audible conversations were not
altered, and the laughter continued.

A cool breeze came up and Maddie shivered, then
hugged herself. She wondered how many nights she
would stand at this very spot watching the river as
it stretched out before them for many miles. It was,
she decided, a marker, not only of the distance she
must travel, but of her figurative distance as well.
What did lie before her?

The possibilities were somewhat intimidating.

Diamond R freight yard, Helena, Montana

The back end of a wagon was jacked up onto a
stand, and the right rear wheel had been removed.

"It's just like you said, Mr. Williams," the wheel-
wright said. "The felloe is cracked. Like as not, soon
as you get a good load on it, this wheel is goin' to
give way on you. If you'd like, I'll try and bridge the
crack with staples."

"It looks to me like the crack is too deep for that.
You may as well go ahead and replace the wheel.
We can't make money from a wagon sitting on a
block."

"Yes, sir, I'll get right on it."

The Diamond R yard was a scene of what could
only be described as organized tumult—the air was
filled with the shouts of bullwhackers, the bray of
mules, the whinny of horses, and the lowing of oxen
as the wagons were being prepared for the day's

work. Case made his way through the activity, then stepped into the office.

"Good morning," George Steell said when he saw Case. "Anything more than the usual going on out there?"

"Not really. We're going to have to pull one of the wagons headed for Fort Benton this morning. It's got a broken felloe."

"Maybe you'd better put on a couple of extra wagons," George said. "This new Indian field superintendent is on the *Josephine*, and if the amount of freight he shipped to Bismarck is any indication, he'll have so much baggage, we'll need another wagon just to get it here."

"I'll take care of it," Case said. "Is Sam Maclay the wagon master?"

"Yes, he is, and oh, Gib Dooley will be driving your coach."

"My coach? What do you mean?"

"We got a telegram from Commissioner Smith himself. It seems this Professor McClellan is some bigwig back in Washington, and the commissioner wants his wife and children riding in a coach," George said.

"Really now," Case said, rubbing his chin. "Want to make a wager how long this McClellan lasts?"

George laughed. "Case, my friend, I'm beginning to think you've got a problem with gambling. Don't you have a bet on with Captain Marsh?"

"I do, but I'm going to win that one. Grant says he can bring the *Josephine* up from St. Louis in eighty days, and I say he can't do it."

"I wouldn't take that bet," George said. "What's

to keep the captain from lying about how long it takes? You have no way of knowing the exact date he left."

"I know the exact day he left. My friend Zeke Peterson sent me a wire when the *Josephine* passed through St. Charles."

"How much are you going to lose?"

"The bet is two hundred dollars, but I told you, I'm going to win."

"No, you're not. You won't win betting against Grant Marsh. You should have bet on Captain Coulson and the *Far West*."

Case laughed. "We'll see."

Maddie stood on the hurricane deck of the *Josephine* and watched the bluffs slide by on the south bank as the boat worked its way up the Missouri River to Fort Benton.

"Hey, Miss Maddie," Jeremy Jackson called when he saw her. "Can you come down and play?"

"Not right now, Jeremy. Line up your soldiers and I'll come down after a little bit," Maddie called.

"Don't forget."

"I won't."

Maddie looked down at the Jackson children, who were scattered all over the deck. Several of them were playing jacks and ones, while Linda, the oldest, sat reading. Another was near the edge of the boat, just watching the water, much as Maddie was doing.

And then there was Jeremy off by himself. He was lining up his wooden soldiers, just as she had asked him to do. Diana had been right. The child had sought her out on a regular basis, but she wasn't bothered by him; rather, he had helped her pass the time.

"Well, our long journey is nearly over," Roy McClellan said as he joined Maddie by the rail. "Captain Marsh thinks we may reach Fort Benton today."

"It's been quite an enjoyable trip, don't you think?"

"It has, or at least it has been for you and me. I'm not sure about your mother and sister."

"It could have been, if they would've ventured out of the cabin more often."

"I know," Roy said. "I'm worried about Diana. She's been so negative about this whole experience."

"I suppose she could go back to Washington."

"I don't think so. If it was you, I would feel quite comfortable sending you off across the country by yourself. You've always been the more adventurous type. But Diana is a social butterfly."

Maddie made no comment.

"I probably shouldn't have accepted this position," Roy said rather wistfully.

"Papa, that's nonsense. I saw how excited you were when Mr. Smith asked you to come out here. You're just the right person to work with the Indians."

Roy smiled as he put his hand on his daughter's cheek. "How did you get to be so wise?"

"I learned it from you, Papa, and if it will make you feel any better, I'll take it upon myself to help Diana adjust. If I can find some trustworthy gentleman to take an interest in her, you know she'll be fine."

"Maddie!" Roy said as he smothered a laugh. "How can you say that about your sister?"

"Well, it's true."

Just then Jeremy began calling for Maddie.

"You'd better go now. It sounds like your 'gentleman' friend needs you."

Maddie headed for the steps that led down to the lower deck.

"Maddie," her father called, "thank you for this little talk . . . and thank you for offering to look out for Diana. She'll need your help."

Case Williams and Gib Dooley were in Fort Benton, standing at the bar of the River City Saloon, nursing beers and listening to the piano player.

Case and his driver had arrived in Fort Benton the previous evening. The wagon train, loaded with bullion consigned to New York, had left Helena several days earlier, but the coach had overtaken the slow-moving train. Case had opted to stay with the wagons for the rest of the way into town.

"Case?" Sam Maclay called out as he came into the saloon at that moment.

Case turned to greet the wagon master. "Any problems I should know about?"

Sam smiled. "Not unless you figure losing two hundred dollars is a problem."

"You've seen the *Josephine*?" Case lifted his left eyebrow.

"We haven't exactly seen it yet, but we just heard a whistle, and Jonah Singleton swears he can tell which boat is which. He says it's the *Josephine*."

"He's probably right," Case said as he picked up

his glass and finished his beer. "Gib, you may as well get the team hitched up."

"All right. I'll meet you at the dock," Gib said.

It was less than a hundred yards from the saloon to the river's edge, and by the time Case and Sam got there, the boat was in clear view. The *Josephine* was beating her way against the current as she approached around a wide, sweeping bend. Smoke was pouring from the twin chimneys and the engine steam-pipe was booming as loudly as if the town were under a cannonading. With her engine clattering and her paddle wheel slapping at the water, she approached the Fort Benton landing.

"How many days since the *Josephine* left?" Sam asked.

"Exactly eighty days," Case said. "Where's that river ice when you need it?"

"You ought to know better than to bet against Cap'n Marsh; if he says he's going to be here in eighty days, he'll try his damnedest to make it. You know he's the best there is."

"He is that," Case replied. "I've been thinking, if the steam donkeys are in a place where the crew can get to them, I think we should load them first. If we have too much freight, the rest can wait for the next train, but you know how anxious Marcus Lissner's been. He wanted to get his pumps going last fall."

"How many is he expectin'?"

"The manifest says four."

"Four? How much water is he going to divert?"

"Sam—we just haul the freight. We don't care what our customers do with it."

"I'll get the wagons brought up," Maclay replied.

Case nodded, then leaned back against a post and, folding his arms across his chest, watched the *Josephine* maneuver to the dock.

Onboard the *Josephine*

"There it is!" Roy called. "Just around the bend. Do you see it?"

Maddie, Diana, and Annabelle looked in the direction Roy had pointed and saw a small gathering of buildings clustered along the riverbank.

"Oh, Roy, it's so small," Annabelle said. "What have we come to?"

"You needn't worry. We'll be living in Helena, not here in Fort Benton, and I'm sure Helena is much larger. After all, it is the capital."

Maddie felt a surge of excitement over the adventure that lay before them.

"Deck men, fore and aft, stand by to throw out the lines!" Captain Marsh used a speaking trumpet to call down from the pilothouse.

"Aye, Cap'n, standing by!" the first mate called back as two men rushed to the front of the boat and stood side by side, holding the ropes.

"Deck passengers, back out of the way!" the first mate shouted. The scores of passengers who had spent the last few days out in the open moved back at the order but continued to stare anxiously toward the small town where they would be beginning their Western adventure.

One small passenger stayed standing at the railing.

"Jeremy? Jeremy, where are you?"

Maddie heard Lucy's voice, but she didn't see her. Knowing that Jeremy was in the way, and fearing he might get hurt, Maddie hurried down the steps to the boiler deck.

"Jeremy, don't you hear your mother calling you?" Maddie asked as she approached the boy.

"I wanna see," Jeremy said, pointing ashore.

At that moment the boat's engine reversed, and as the paddles began dipping into the water in the opposite direction, the momentum of the boat slowed so drastically that everyone who wasn't braced was in danger of being thrown.

Maddie reached Jeremy just as he was thrown forward and managed to catch him, though it was all she could do to keep herself erect.

"Jeremy," Lucy said, appearing on deck to take the boy from Maddie's arms. "Thank goodness you were with him, Maddie. I don't know how to thank you for all you've done to help me on this trip. Are you sure you don't want to come along with us to Fort Shaw? You'd be able to snag a mighty fine husband there."

Maddie was at a loss for words when she heard Lucy's comment.

"Oh dear," Lucy said, realizing that she might have spoken out of turn. "I'm sorry, Maddie. I shouldn't have said that. It's just that you're not a young woman anymore, and Titus and I have remarked that it's a shame you haven't married. You have to be twenty, or twenty-one."

"I'm twenty-three."

"Then you do need to get married. Look how you've taken to Jeremy. It's time you became a mother."

Maddie was uncomfortable with the direction of the conversation.

"Jeremy is a delightful child, full of curiosity and a sense of adventure. Who wouldn't enjoy being around such a boy?" she asked.

"His sisters," Lucy replied with a smile.

"Ladies, clear the deck," the first mate called, and Lucy, with Jeremy in hand, returned to her family. Maddie went back up the steps to the hurricane deck, which, while out of the way, allowed her an unobstructed view of the boat's landing.

FOUR

Maddie was watching all the commotion of docking the boat when she noticed a man nonchalantly slouched against a post. His arms were folded across his chest, though one hand was raised to his chin. His head was cocked slightly and he was looking at something on the boat. He had dark hair, dark eyes, and a strong chin. And though his clothes were not unlike those of any other man, she sensed a controlled arrogance about him, as if he were out of place here.

"Is this what it looks like? My sister ogling a man?"

Diana's question startled Maddie, because she hadn't realized that her sister had come out to stand beside her, and she hadn't been aware that it was obvious what she was doing.

"Of course I wasn't ogling a man. That's ridiculous," Maddie said trying to recover. "I was just watching all the activity. I think I see some of our trunks already."

"Then if you haven't staked your claim on that man, I think I'll stare at him. How long do you think it will take before he looks up here?"

At that precise moment, Case appeared to look up toward the two women. He waved and Diana waved back, but then they heard Captain Marsh call down to the man.

"Say, Mr. Williams, I seem to have misplaced my calendar. Can you fill me in on the exact date?"

The man laughed a deep rumbling laugh as he shook his head.

"You don't have to rub it in."

"I just don't want you to try to run away before we talk," the captain said.

"I pay my debts."

"I guess he wasn't waving at us," Maddie said with a mischievous grin on her face.

"Well, that's his loss," Diana said, "but don't you think he's one of the handsomest men you've ever seen?"

"You say that about half the men you meet."

"Well, I'm very selective about the gentlemen I want to meet. Wouldn't it be something if he lived in Helena?"

Maddie chuckled. "Diana, just listen to yourself. You aren't even off the boat and you're already thinking about a man. You say you aren't going to like it in Montana, but look around you. How many women do you see?"

Diana looked around at about a hundred people. Except for the few women who were getting off the boat, she didn't see any others.

"My, my, you may have stumbled onto quite a discovery. If this ratio holds true in Helena, perhaps this won't be so unpleasant after all."

Just then Annabelle stepped out onto the deck.

"Here you are. Your father's already gone below to either arrange transportation or to find a place for us to spend the night."

"You can't mean we'll be staying here tonight?" Diana asked.

"We may have to, but I'm praying that won't be necessary," Annabelle said. "For the life of me, I cannot imagine what possessed your father to bring us to this godforsaken place."

"Well, I, for one, am looking forward to being here," Maddie said. "Look, Papa is motioning for us to join him."

By the time the McClellan family was off the boat, several wagons had been drawn up and were being loaded with cargo taken from the boiler deck.

"Stay right here until I find out what we are expected to do," Roy told his wife and daughters.

"If we have to spend the night, I wish I had thought to hold back my satchel," Annabelle said.

"I think I saw our things put in a separate pile," Maddie said. "I'll go down and see if I can get it for you, Mother."

Maddie made her way down to the dock, being certain to stay out of the way of the stevedores. They had formed a human chain, passing one crate to another as they offloaded the cargo into the waiting wagons.

But just as she was ready to step onto the dock, Maddie heard someone on the boat yell, and, looking up, she saw a large, heavy piece of equipment dangling precariously from the loading crane. Then, even as she was looking at it, she saw the cable slip from it, and the big black object started to fall, coming directly toward a man who was standing right in front of her.

Clearly the man hadn't noticed it, and she didn't have time to shout a warning, so she did the only thing she could do. She ran toward him, and with her full weight knocked him off his feet, falling on top of him as she did so.

"Here, what . . . ?" the man shouted angrily.

At that exact moment the heavy piece of machinery came slamming down beside them, smashing a hole through the wagon and crashing to the ground, fortunately falling in the direction of the river, and not toward the two people who lay sprawled on the ground.

The team was startled and tried to run, but the wagon's rear wheel was jammed against the machinery and couldn't move. As a result the mules began braying and rearing up in their harnesses.

"I'm so sorry," Maddie said, looking down into the grinning face of the man she had observed earlier.

"You don't have to apologize, miss. If I would've known you were going to save my life, I would have waved at you."

"That wasn't me; that was my sister."

"Case, if you can get off your duff, help me with these damn mules!" the driver shouted as the mules continued to bray and rear.

"Stay right here, ma'am," Case said as he helped Maddie to her feet. "I want to get your name so I can thank you properly."

Maddie watched as he hurried to the front of the wagon, where he grabbed the harness of the near-side mule, who was kicking violently. By now at least three other men had arrived, and each grabbed the harness of one of the other three mules to help Case and the driver get the two teams under control.

With the mules steadied, Case came back to examine the piece of machinery, which was now wedged in the ground.

"How's the steam donkey, Case?" the driver asked.

"I don't think it's reparable," Case said.

Sam Maclay laughed. "I guess this is why old man Lissner ordered four of these things."

"It's a good thing he did," Case said. "I'd better go find the captain and get some money for Mr. Lissner."

"What about the wagon? I'd say the Diamond R needs about two hundred dollars, wouldn't you say?"

Case smiled. "I think two hundred is just about right."

As he started toward the boat, he saw that Maddie was still standing there.

"Miss, you've got no business being down here. You just saw what can happen."

"Yes, I did see what almost happened," Maddie replied pointedly. "And if I hadn't been here, where I have no business being, you could have been badly hurt. Or worse."

Case smiled. "You do have a point," he admitted, "but I'd feel better if you'd step back out of the way."

"I'll go as soon as I get my mother's valise."

With a polite nod, the man walked away and Maddie watched him climb up the gangplank. She was disappointed that he had forgotten to get her name.

When she walked back up the bank, Diana was standing there with a smile on her face.

"I must say, you certainly picked a dramatic way to meet our handsome and mysterious stranger."

Maddie chuckled. "I suppose it was rather dramatic. But Case would have been hurt."

"Case? He told you his name?"

"No, but that's what the man called him."

"You do know, don't you, that it would have been much better if he had rescued you?"

Maddie turned to her sister with a quizzical look on her face.

"You have to learn—a man looks much better in shining armor than a woman does."

"Are you saying it would have been better if the steam donkey had fallen on me?"

"Steam donkey?"

"That's what that piece of machinery is called."

"Lord help us, only someone like you would know the name of that ugly old thing. That's so unladylike," Diana chided. "For heaven's sake, don't let anyone know that you know what a steam donkey is."

"Diana, really," Maddie said as she turned to find her mother.

"Come to pay me my two hundred dollars, have you?" Captain Marsh asked when Case found him in the pilothouse.

Case shook his head. "Quite the contrary, Grant. I figure you owe me more than two hundred dollars."

"What are you talking about?"

"You didn't hear it? Your crane just dropped a steam donkey on one of my wagons, and I don't think it can be repaired."

"I was down in the engine room, and I didn't hear anything. Was anybody hurt?"

"Just my pride," Case said, as he thought of being saved from danger by a woman.

"How much do you figure I owe you?"

"I think our two-hundred-dollar bet will cover the wagon, but you'll owe Marcus Lissner for the steam donkey."

"I suppose I do," Captain Marsh said. "I'll check the manifest and see how much he declared them for. Will you be staying around for a while?"

"I hope not. Charles is in Salt Lake City, and George is by himself, so I want to get away as soon as I find my passengers."

Grant chuckled. "Did you tell your passengers they'll be riding behind a team of mules, or did you go all out and hitch up the oxen?"

"None of that—I'm ridin' in fine style. I brought a coach."

"A coach? Who's so important the Diamond R sent a coach?"

"I'm picking up the new field superintendent for the Bureau of Indian Affairs."

"Professor McClellan—a damned decent fellow," Grant said.

"I'm glad to hear you say that. Could you point him out to me?"

Captain Marsh stepped up to one of the windows that surrounded the pilothouse and looked out toward the riverbank.

"There he is, up by the mercantile. He's talking to that man in the red shirt."

Case saw the man Captain Marsh had pointed out, standing beside four good-size trunks.

"Thanks. Sam'll be around for a while, so when you figure out how much you owe Lissner, give it to him. Oh, and eighty days is a mighty fine trip. I almost wish I could pay you the two hundred dollars."

"If you feel that way . . ."

"I said almost," Case said, laughing as he left.

Approaching the person Captain Marsh had pointed out, Case overheard the man in the red shirt talking.

"It's goin' to cost you a hunnert dollars. That is, what with there bein' four of you 'n' all."

"Why should the number of passengers matter?" Roy questioned. "I only need one coach whether I'm alone, or if my family is with me."

"Excuse me, sir, are you negotiating for a coach?" Case asked.

"This ain't no business of the Diamond R, Williams, so just get on out of here," the man in the red shirt said. "I got to this here man first."

"Are you Professor McClellan?" Case asked.

"I am." Roy turned to Case and offered his hand. "And how, may I ask, do you know my name?"

"Don't listen to him," the red-shirted man said. "He'll charge you more'n a hunnert dollars."

"I won't charge you anything," Case said. "Your coach has already been hired and paid for, so you won't be needing this gentleman."

"Did you say my coach has already been paid for?" Roy asked.

"Yes, sir, paid for by the commissioner of Indian Affairs. The local Indian agent, Gad Upson, asked that I express his regret that he's not here to meet you. I'm afraid he's been called away."

"I fully understand, but I'm grateful for his consideration." Roy turned back to the man in the red shirt. "My good man, it looks as if I won't need you after all. I thank you for your time."

The man shot an angry glare toward Case, muttered something under his breath, then turned and walked away.

That was when Case saw Dooley approaching with the coach.

"Here comes the coach now. Is this your luggage?" Case looked at the pile of trunks.

"Yes, and I apologize. I'm afraid my wife brought more than I think we'll need."

"It's not a problem. Just get your wife and your children, and we'll start as soon as we're loaded. Oh, and sir, you might suggest that your family take advantage of the privy out back of the mercantile. Your little girls might get antsy before we can stop."

Roy chuckled. "My little girls?"

Case was confused by the laughter. "Did I make a mistake? I was under the impression that you were traveling with your wife and two daughters. Was that in error?"

"No, I do indeed have two daughters, and I'll see to it that they take advantage of your suggestion."

Roy walked away to gather his family, leaving Case to supervise the loading of the trunks into the boot behind the coach.

"Hey, boss," Sam Maclay called as he stepped up to the coach. "What should I do with the damaged wagon?"

"Can you move it?"

"I think so, but the doubletree needs to be replaced before I can send it on the road, and of course the box is splintered, but you saw that," Sam said.

"I hate to hold the train up. How many wagons are loaded?" Case asked.

"At least ten."

"All right. Put Jonas Pippen in charge, and let's put those ten on the road. You stay here to oversee the repair and start the rest of the train tomorrow."

"That's what I expected you to say, so I've already done that," Sam said. "See?"

At that moment ten loaded wagons lumbered by the coach.

"We'll see you in a week," Pippen called down to him.

"Try 'n' keep 'em on the road, Jonas," Case called back with a little laugh, as the wagons pulled past the coach.

"I hope he doesn't have any trouble," Sam said.

"You haven't heard any rumblings, have you?" Case asked.

"I know what's got him spooked," Dooley said. "It's the soldiers, ain't it? You know they went and arrested five men—wanted to arrest fourteen, but the deputy marshal wouldn't hear of it."

"What caused that?" Case asked.

"They say these men followed a band of Assiniboines up in the Cypress Hills, and the Dominion of Canada wants them extradited," Sam said.

"Didn't that take place at least two years ago?" Case asked. "If I remember right, the Indians rode off with a bunch of horses. Did anybody mention that before these men were arrested?"

"Nope," Dooley said, "but it's sure whipped up all the Indians. They was a whole bunch of 'em camped all around the fort."

"Well, it shouldn't bother us," Case said. "We don't go anywhere near the Assiniboines."

"That's what you say, but them Indians move all over this whole territory," Dooley said.

"Speaking of moving, we've got to get loaded before the professor gets back," Case said as he turned his attention to the mound of luggage. "I want to get to the crossing before nightfall."

Dooley looked at the pile.

"I thought you said we was a picking up a man and his wife and two little ones. How much stuff do they think they're gonna need out here?"

"Stop complaining, Dooley," Sam said as he grabbed a trunk and heaved it into the boot.

Case had passed up the last piece of luggage when he heard Professor McClellan's voice behind him.

"Oh dear, I should have been here to help you with all our belongings," Roy said. "I found my wife and my two little girls."

"Good. I want us to get started . . ." Turning, Case saw Professor McClellan with three women. One of them was the young woman who had pushed him to safety when the steam donkey had fallen.

"Oh," he said. "I beg your pardon. I didn't mean to . . . that is, I wasn't told . . ." Realizing that anything else he might say would just make it worse, he grew silent.

Diana extended her hand. "Mr. Case, I'm Diana McClellan."

"Not Mr. Case. Case is my first name. Actually, it's my middle name. I go by Case Williams." He took Diana's hand, and Maddie perceived that he was reluctant to drop it.

"Case." A broad smile spread across Diana's face. "And I'm Diana. I think I'm going to like this country—no formalities, everyone on a first-name basis right from the start. Do you live here in Fort Benton, Case?"

"No, I live in Helena."

"Oh, how wonderful! We might be neighbors, then," Diana said. "I'll be living in Helena as well."

"I know. I've been collecting all your crates of furniture and I do believe you moved everything imaginable."

"What?" Maddie asked. "Why do you have our furniture?"

"I should have explained. I'm with the freight line, and we took delivery of your shipment a week or so ago. We'll be holding it in our warehouse until you decide where you'll be living."

"Good, good, I'm glad to know everything arrived," Roy said.

Just then the boat purser approached the little group.

"Professor McClellan, I hope your trip onboard the *Josephine* was enjoyable," the purser said.

"It was, Mr. Peabody. Indeed it was a fine boat," Roy said. "I guess you'll be returning to Bismarck."

"Yes, sir, just as soon as we can get unloaded," Peabody said. "It's been a pleasure having you and your family aboard."

"Thank you; it was our pleasure to be your guests."

Peabody turned to Case.

"Cap'n Marsh saw that you were still here. If you have a minute, he wants you to sign off on the bill of lading, and I think he has a draft ready for Marcus Lissner. Can you come and get it?"

Case pulled a watch out of his watch pocket.

"What do you think, Dooley? Can we spare the time?"

"Whatever you say, boss man. I can lay the whip to these beauties and make up the time if I need to."

"Sir, don't even think about doing that," Maddie said, stepping beside one of the animals as if she was going to prevent anything from happening. "Horses, even if they are draft animals, don't deserve to be hit."

Dooley raised his eyebrows when he heard Maddie's comment, and he looked to Case.

"Ma'am, a Diamond R driver is not a barbarian. He does not strike his horses," Case said with a degree of contempt in his voice. "Dooley will be cracking the whip very near the lead horse's ears. That sound will be enough to encourage the horses to run faster."

Case turned quickly and hurried down to the waiting boat captain.

As Maddie watched him walk away, she was sorry she had not held her tongue. Why had she voiced her opinion about the driver hitting the horses? Just by looking at their condition, she should have known that the six horses now in the traces had never borne the brunt of a whip. It was quite obvious that her ill-advised comment had irritated Case.

Diana, too, was watching Case. She had a cunning smile on her face, much like that of a cat who has a mouse in its sights. The very thought of Diana toying with Case unsettled Maddie. It was quite obvious that this man would not fall for her sister's conniving ways.

Maddie turned away. How did she know what Case Williams was like? She had only met him a couple of hours ago, but he exuded a kind of strength and masculinity that Maddie admired in a man.

Maddie was disgusted with herself. If ever there was a demonstration of her utter lack of social skills, it had just been on display. By contrast, Diana had related easily to Case; he had held her hand and smiled warmly at her. But what was his reaction to Maddie? If she had to say, it would be irritation.

What was wrong with her? Why couldn't she be more like Diana?

The driver scrambled back to the seat after he had secured the luggage with straps.

"Mr. McClellan, I expect Case'll be here directly, and he'll want to pull out pretty quick," Dooley said. "Since we got all your belongin's strapped down, there's no sense standin' around waitin'. You might want to climb on in and get yourselves comfortable 'fore he gets here."

"Of course," Roy said, as he offered his assistance to his wife.

Maddie could see Case and Captain Marsh down by the river. The driver had said Case would want to pull out quickly. From that comment, she surmised that Case would be returning with the coach.

Maddie smiled as she looked toward the wharf where the *Josephine* was moored. If Case would be returning with them, the obvious place for him to sit would be beside her. If she had the chance, she would try to make a better impression on him than in the two exchanges they'd already had.

As she was watching, she saw Captain Grant hand something to Case, which he deposited inside his jacket. The men shook hands, and the captain laughed. Then Case turned and started for the standing coach.

Maddie moved toward the center of the seat to make room for him, but when he reached the coach, he didn't say a word to the passengers. Instead, stepping onto one of the spokes of the wheel, he swung into the driver's seat.

"I guess Mr. Williams is not going to be riding with us," Annabelle said. "Isn't that considerate of him? I'm sure he didn't want to crowd us."

No one made a comment as Maddie moved back to her side of the coach. She heard the driver call out.

"Heah, team!"

Then there was the crack of the whip, and the coach lunged forward with a jerk.

Case and Dooley rode without speaking, the silence broken only by the clatter of the horses' hooves, the jangle of harness and chain, and the rolling of the wheels. Case stared straight ahead, his hand knotted in a fist as it lay on his leg.

"That sassy little filly got to you, didn't she?"

"Humph," Case grunted.

"I seen the way you bristled when she told me not to be beatin' no team."

"I'll admit she put a burr under my saddle. Why would she even think something like that?"

"Ah, she ain't nothin' but a pilgrim; she don't know no better. Don't pay her no nevermind."

"It just aggravates me when people come out here from the East thinking they're going to teach us some of their highfalutin ways. They think we're all hicks and hayseeds."

"I don't think so," Dooley said. "'Mr. Case, I'm Diana.'" He said the words in a high imitation of a woman's voice.

"Cut it out, Gib," Case said as he slapped at Dooley's arm.

"Seems to me like you ought to be a mite nicer to 'em. I mean, two purty women like that comin' in to town, and them with no husbands in sight. Why, that black-haired one's already got her cap set for you."

"And what makes you think that?"

"I can just tell. I watched the way she looks at ya. I know one thing, if you don't lay claim to her, ever' buck in town's gonna be beatin' a path to her door."

"What if I'd rather have the other one? The sassy one with the pigtail?"

"No, no. Don't go there. She's trouble." Dooley shook his head. "If it's a wife you're a-wantin', you don't want a woman who ain't afraid of nothin'."

"A wife? Don't you think this conversation has sort of gotten ahead of itself? I've just about got Charles and George convinced I'm content with my life the way it is. I sure as hell don't need some woman getting in the way."

"Mark my words. When the right little old girl comes along, you'll be givin' up all your visits to Bridge Street."

"Damn it, Gib, you don't know what I do when I go there. Maybe I'm trying to sell Chicago Joe some more property," Case said. "You know she's buying every vacant lot she can get her hands on."

"That Chicago—she's a smart lady, but she ain't smart enough to get her hooks in you. Now these two . . ." Dooley motioned back to the coach. "I'm bettin' on the black-haired one. 'I'm Diana.'" Dooley began fluttering his eyelashes at Case.

"Don't go betting a month's pay, because you're going to lose your money."

Dooley threw back his head and laughed, then squirted a stream of tobacco off to one side and slapped the ribbons against the backs of the horses. "Heah, team!" he shouted.

FIVE

Maddie looked out the window at the rushing stream of water they were now paralleling. This, too, was the Missouri River, though at this point, she understood it was no longer navigable by the large boats. She found that hard to believe, as the water was barely contained in its banks.

"I can't believe they don't have some better form of transportation than this," Diana said, as she shifted around on the coach seat trying to get comfortable. "Papa, how long do you think we'll be stuck in this thing?"

"I expect we'll be on the road at least two days, perhaps more," Roy said. "Just count your blessings that the Indian agent secured a private coach for us. We could be crowded in with two or three more people."

"That's the only thing that makes this whole thing tolerable," Diana said. Then she smiled. "Well, not the *only* thing," she said.

"Diana, I don't like the way you said that," Roy

said as he squinted in her direction. "What are you up to?"

"Can't you tell? Diana has decided she adores Mr. Williams," Maddie said.

"Girls—that's enough," Annabelle said. "Out here there won't be too many female acquaintances, and you'll need to depend upon one another for companionship."

"How can I depend on her?" Diana asked. "Look at her. Did you braid your hair this morning, or have you even taken it down since we left Bismarck?"

"I don't think that is any of your concern," Maddie said. "I think I'll fit in out here a lot better than you will."

"You'll fit in with whom?" Diana asked. "The tobacco-spitting Dooley or the handsome Mr. Williams?"

"You two seem to be showing an inordinate amount of interest in Mr. Williams," Roy said. "Have you considered that he probably has a wife and a passel of children?"

"Papa, all I said was that he's a handsome man, but if I'm going to make friends with someone, Case's would be the type of friendship I'd like to cultivate," Diana said.

"Mama, it was a mistake," Roy said turning to Annabelle.

"You mean coming out here? I thought you were looking forward to your new position."

"No, I mean bringing these two with us. Diana wanted to stay in Washington and we should have left her."

"What about me?" Maddie asked, an impish expression on her face.

"You, I'm going to have to keep from running off with the Indians," Roy said as he shook his head.

"If I do run off, send Case Williams to rescue me," Maddie said, and then laughed.

"That poor man. I don't think he knows what's coming his way," Annabelle said. "I can't believe my two sophisticated daughters have hardly arrived in the Montana Territory and they're already behaving like strumpets."

"Mama!" both girls said in unison.

"Oh, look, we're overtaking some wagons," Annabelle said as the coach slowed to pass a train of freight wagons.

"Those must belong to the Diamond R," Maddie said. "There's another steam donkey."

"I told you not to ever let on that you know what those things are," Diana said.

"Why not?" Roy asked. "You never know when you might need a steam donkey, and if you don't even know how to ask for it, you'd be in trouble, wouldn't you?"

Maddie laughed.

"Roy, don't encourage her. She's enough of a tomboy already," Annabelle said.

"Hello, Case! Gib!" the driver of the first wagon shouted as the coach overtook them.

Maddie heard Case and Dooley return the greetings, and similar exchanges were offered as they passed the other wagons.

As it turned out, those ten wagons weren't the

only ones they encountered, as soon after, they met a train headed north. Dooley pulled the coach off to the side of the road to allow the wagons to pass. Maddie observed that this train was not like the other one she had seen. From nine to twelve yoke of oxen were pulling as many as four wagons all coupled together. Jangling bells were attached to their harnesses, as one man seemed to be in charge of each set of wagons. Maddie thought this arrangement was smart, because this train was much longer than the Diamond R train she had seen, and yet it had a third as many drivers.

The last wagon came to a stop beside the coach.

"Gib, you be careful crossin' the Sun," the driver shouted. "That river's runnin' awful fast right now."

"Thankee, Dan, I'll be real careful," Gib shouted back. "I take it the ford's out."

"Sure is, but Healey's got the ferry rigged up, so as how you can make it across."

"Much obliged for the information," Dooley said as the coach started moving again.

For some time the McClellans rode in silence. Roy had put his head back and his eyes were closed, and Diana was writing in her diary. Annabelle sat with a tight-lipped expression on her face as she worried a handkerchief in her hand, while Maddie observed the scenery.

It was not exactly as she had imagined it. She could see the mountains of the Great Divide in the distance, but the most significant landscape features were what she knew were buttes. She was surprised by the size of them. Some appeared to be perfectly rounded, while others were oblong or even square in shape.

Maddie felt the coach begin to slow, and she strained to look out the window, thinking they might be approaching another wagon train. But this time the coach pulled off the road and came to a stop beside what looked like a big barn built of whip-sawed lumber.

Case vaulted down from the high box, then stepped up to the side of the coach, and opened the door.

"Folks, this is Twenty-Eight-Mile Spring. We'll change horses here, and if Dutch Jake has some fresh bread out of the oven, we'll get a bite to eat."

Because Maddie was near the door, she was the first one up. Case smiled broadly at her, his dark eyes flashing, as he took her hand to assist her.

"Ma'am, if you'd like to inspect the horses, you'll see that they've not been mistreated."

"I'm sorry, Mr. Williams. I misspoke," Maddie said.

"Misspoke, is it? And now you've misspoke again."

"I beg your pardon?"

"Didn't your sister say that she liked it out here? No formalities. First names right from the start."

"She did say that didn't she . . . Case, but if that is so, then I am certainly not ma'am."

"What else am I to call you? I don't believe you told me your name when you so unceremoniously fell on top of me."

"It may not have been gracious, but if I hadn't reacted as I did, I dare say you wouldn't be standing here right now."

"That is true," Case said with a nod. "But I still don't know your name."

"It's Maddie."

Just then Maddie heard Diana clear her throat.

"Please, Case, will you help me down? My legs seem to be so cramped; I fear I will stumble when my feet touch the ground."

"I'll not let that happen," Case said as he turned his attention to Diana.

Maddie noticed that he helped Diana down by putting his hands around her waist and lifting her to the ground. Diana fell against him.

"Oh, are you all right? Let me walk you to the station," Case said as he led a willing Diana to the building.

Roy was next to climb down from the coach, and then he helped Annabelle to the ground.

"This is so isolated. Do you think we're safe here?"

"You can't think like that, Mama," Maddie said. "We're here and it's going to be a grand experience."

"So you say," Annabelle replied.

When they entered the building, Maddie realized it not only looked like a barn, it *was* a barn. There were stalls for about thirty animals, and an old man was leading a pair of horses that were fully harnessed.

"Folks, if you'll step through that door, Dutch Jake and his missis can rustle you up a bite to eat," Case said.

"I'm famished," Diana said as she returned her arm to the crook of Case's arm. "Will you be joining us?"

"Maybe later, but right now I'll have to help get the teams exchanged."

When they stepped into a dimly lit room that was off from the stable, Maddie guessed that it was about a twenty-five-foot square. It had a hard-packed dirt floor, three tables with chairs, a long worktable, and a wood-burning cooking stove.

A man and woman were present, and the man indicated that they should sit. He brought each of them a tin cup.

"Ain't got no spirits," the man said. "Indians. They'd just pilfer it."

He poured each of them a cup of coffee, which was the strongest Maddie had ever tasted. She tried to drink, but she couldn't swallow the bitter brew.

"Do you have much of a problem with Indians?" Roy asked.

"Naw, not anymore. You see that one over there?" He pointed to the woman standing by the stove. "Since I took me a Sioux woman, ever'body stays clear of this place. Yes, sir, they knows she'll take care of me."

Just then Case entered the room.

"Shappa," he called as he went over to the woman and embraced her. "Is this old man being good to you?"

"Oh, yes. I got plenty good, just for you." She pulled out a round loaf of bread hot from the oven.

"Wonderful," Case said as he bent down to smell the bread. Then he pulled out a little packet from his breast pocket and handed it to her.

"You didn't forget," she said as she took the packet from him and began to untie the string. "You bring me good emptins."

"Just for you, but no booze, just bread. Don't let Dutch Jake get into your yeast." Case pulled a chair up to join the McClellans. "Shappa, do you have any meat to go with your bread?"

Case had squeezed his chair in between Maddie and her mother, and because of the closeness of the chairs, his leg brushed against Maddie's. Instinctively, she pulled her leg away, but Case moved his leg to rest firmly against hers.

At first she was embarrassed, but when he continued to press his leg against hers, she decided to meet him straight-on. Deliberately, she pressed her leg against his as hard as she could. She watched as a slow smile began to build on his face.

And then he moved his leg away.

Maddie was sorry she had reacted as she had. How could it have hurt if he rested his leg against her own?

"What is that smell?" Diana asked, wrinkling her nose as Shappa brought two tin plates and set them on the table in front of Case and Roy.

"Buffalo steak, ma'am," Dutch Jake said as he placed three more plates in front of the women. "You ain't goin' to find no meat nowhere that's better'n fried buffalo steak."

"It's actually quite good, Miss McClellan," Case said. "And you won't find better bread anywhere in Montana."

Shappa beamed when she heard Case's praise.

"It's Diana." She flashed her patented smile toward Case. "I'll try this, but only because you say it's good. Sir, where are our eating utensils?" she asked as she turned to Dutch Jake.

"They's right where God put 'em."

Maddie laughed, enjoying Diana's discomfort. She placed a piece of the meat between two pieces of bread and began eating the sandwich.

When they were back on the road, the coach rolled along without incident, pulling to the side for several other wagon trains. Maddie was surprised that there was so much traffic on the road to Fort Benton. The other three members of her family were resting, but try as she might, she could not sleep. She rolled her head back, but all she could hear was the distant roar of the great Missouri River, and the occasional laugh from either Case or Dooley.

She thought about the lunch at Twenty-Eight-Mile Spring. She had watched Case interact with the Indian woman. He appeared to care about both Shappa and Dutch Jake. She liked that even though Case seemed to be better educated—more sophisticated—than the other Westerners she had met, he was always respectful and courteous.

Respectful and courteous. Well, not always. When he had pressed his leg against hers, that wasn't exactly respectful and courteous.

Why had he done that? Was he trying to provoke her? To poke fun at her? But even more thought-provoking, why had she reacted as she had? It was as if she were a child, not a twenty-three-year-old woman headed for spinsterhood.

Maddie chuckled. Where Case Williams was concerned, she definitely did not want to be thought of as a child.

∽∞∾

They had been on the road for less than three hours when the coach slowed to a stop. Maddie looked out and saw a building similar to the one she'd seen at Twenty-Eight-Mile Spring.

"We'll give the horses a little breather," Case said as he opened the door of the coach. "If you'd like to step out and stretch your legs, we'll be at the Leaving for about thirty minutes."

Maddie knew that "stretch your legs" was Case's euphemism for "find an outhouse," so she hurried to the little building at the side of the stable. When she returned, Case was leaning against the coach.

"Where do you expect we'll spend the night?" Maddie asked.

"We'll stay at St. Peter's Mission, on the other side of the Sun."

"Didn't I hear one of the drivers we passed say there could be a problem getting across that river?"

"Do you always borrow trouble?" Case asked. "We won't know until we get there, and if there's a problem, we'll handle it."

"I have every confidence that you will," Maddie said as she looked around the way station. "Why did you call this the Leaving?"

"Because we're going to be leaving the Mullan road and following the Missouri River down to the Sun crossing. We'll be there in about an hour, but I think you're going to enjoy what you see."

Just then, Maddie's parents and Diana returned to the coach. When everyone was settled, the coach started up again.

True to Case's words, for once the whole family was engaged in looking at the scenery. The

Continental Divide was the backdrop for the varied buttes that rose from the benchland, but the Missouri River was spectacular. The sound of the water as it cascaded down the rocks made it almost impossible to talk.

Finally, they reached the Sun River, and it was frothing with swirling white water. Maddie could see at least forty wagons gathered in front of them waiting to cross, and there were at least that many and more on the far bank. But the ferry wasn't moving.

"Jack, what's going on?" Case asked as he approached the ferryman, who was standing by the ramp to the ferry. "Why isn't anything moving?"

"The line parted on us, and I thought we had it fixed. But then it fell in again and the current unraveled it even more," Jack Healey said. "This here ferry won't be goin' nowhere. Not till the boy gets back and we can get the cable reset."

"Let's hope he can make a quick turnaround," Case said.

"No matter how fast he runs that team, Odie ain't for sure gonna be back 'fore late tomorrow. You may as well pick your spot and set up camp."

"Damn," Case said. "I've got three women with me."

"I'm sorry, there ain't nothin' we can do. We tried to get a wagon across, but the whole ferry plum near swamped. What I can promise you, seein' as you got women 'n' all, is I'll take your coach across first thing, once we get to goin' again."

"Thanks, Jack, I appreciate that," Case said.

❧

Case walked slowly back to the coach. He wasn't in a hurry to get back, because he knew his passengers weren't going to like what he was going to tell them. He was sure Diana would have something to say.

And he was right.

"Surely that man doesn't intend for us to spend the night here, does he?" Diana asked.

"There's little else we can do," Case said. "You saw what accommodations there were at the Leaving and at Twenty-Eight-Mile Spring. We could go back to Fort Benton, but that's close to sixty miles, and you know how long it's taken us to get this far."

"We'll camp tonight," Roy said.

"Papa, you can't mean that. We'll be squatting like a bunch of savage Indians," Diana said.

"You aren't giving it a chance, Diana. I think it might be fun," Maddie said.

"Huh. You'd probably like it if we were camping with a bunch of wild Indians."

"You ladies may sleep in the coach, if you choose. The seats can be let down to make a bed, and while it's not the most comfortable bed, it beats sleeping on the ground. Professor, I'm afraid the ground's all we have for you."

Professor McClellan laughed. "I was in the war, young man. This won't be my first time sleeping on the ground, and I doubt it will be my last. I'll make the best of it."

"The first order of business is to rustle up something to eat. Gib has some hardtack and canned meat in the boot, but we should try to conserve that, in case we're caught up for longer than we think."

"Where are you going to find food, Mr. Williams?" Diana asked.

"Oh, now it's back to Mr. Williams, is it? Gib, toss me down that Greener, will you? Then get a fire going and heat up some water."

The driver tossed a double-barrel shotgun down to Case. "Need any extra shells?"

"If I can't get us something with the two shells that are already in it, a few more won't help."

Maddie watched as Case walked down by the river carrying the shotgun low, in his right hand. He was about a hundred yards out when she saw two birds suddenly take flight in front of him. Lifting the gun to his shoulder, he fired twice, and even from here, she could see feathers fly as first one and then the other bird suddenly stopped, as if hitting an invisible wall, and tumbled from the sky.

When Case returned with the brace of ducks, he began dipping one into the pot of boiling water.

"Who's going to help pluck these?" he asked, not expecting an answer.

Maddie stepped forward. "Shall I be the rougher or the pinner?"

Case's deep rumbling laugh rippled through the camp.

"Do you know how to clean a duck?"

"I'm willing to try anything."

Case nodded. "I suspect that's true. Maddie, you're quite a girl."

After the ducks had been roasted over the open fire and the evening meal was finished, Case began preparing for the sleeping arrangements. There were blankets stored under the seats that would provide a short though comfortable bed for Maddie, her mother, and her sister, and there was a piece of canvas that was stretched out from the side of the coach.

"This is it, Professor," Case said as he handed a blanket and a ground cloth to Roy. "But consider yourself forewarned. You can hear Gib's snoring even if we're right beside the great falls."

"Case Williams, you're a telling a tale on me," Gib said. "That ain't true. I can sleep like a newborn babe."

"It's not you I'm worried about."

The day had been too full of activity for sleep to come when Maddie lay on her pallet. She wasn't used to sleeping in her clothing, and she loosened the buttons that fastened her dress and untied the ribbons on her camisole. She considered removing her outer garments, but under the circumstances thought better of it.

But she could unbraid her hair. Diana had suggested that it looked as if she hadn't taken it down since Bismarck. That, of course, wasn't true, but she hadn't let it down for a couple of days, and she was sure she looked like a ragamuffin.

As quietly as she could, she found her satchel, and, withdrawing her brush, she sat in the corner and began unbraiding her hair. She tried to brush the long strands, but in the confined space of the coach, she found she couldn't do it. She knew that her father and the others were sleeping under the stretched canvas on the river side of the coach, so very quietly, she opened the opposite door and stepped out into the night air.

Even though it was June, it was quite cold, and she thought about getting her blanket or even a shawl, but she would certainly awaken someone if she tried to retrieve it.

The fire. It had burned down to coals when the ducks were roasting, but there was extra wood nearby. She could rekindle it and sit by the fire and brush her hair.

She crept across the damp grass. When she reached the fire pit, she added some small branches and peeled off some bark from the wood. Soon, she had a small fire blazing.

"You shouldn't be out here by yourself."

Maddie jumped when she heard Case come up behind her. He put more wood on the fire, then pulled up a log and sat down, leaving room for her to sit beside him.

"You startled me," she said as she took the seat beside him.

"Good." He grabbed a stick and began poking at the fire. "What if I'd been an Indian creeping up behind you?"

"I thought Dutch Jake said there weren't any problems with Indians."

"He said he didn't have any problems with Indians. But that doesn't mean the rest of us don't have a problem now and then."

Maddie's eyes grew large. "Is Papa going to be in danger?"

"I would be lying if I didn't say there's some risk. There isn't any tribe that is one hundred percent civilized, if by civilized you mean living like a white man would want him to. As for your father, it's up to him."

"Why do you say that?"

"Indian agents don't always keep the word of the Great White Father. The government says, move this tribe beyond that river or behind this mountain range and we won't bother you. The land will always be yours in perpetuity, but then something comes up and . . ."

"You mean like gold being discovered in the Black Hills?"

"Exactly. What chance does Red Cloud or Spotted Tail have of keeping the Black Hills for the Sioux when gold is assaying at $19.47 a troy ounce?"

"President Grant told them they could stay there."

"And you believe that." Case turned to Maddie. "Indians can do bad things. Last month a Blackfoot killed John Rock not a hundred yards from where we're sitting." He felt Maddie shiver at his words, and to lighten the mood, he pressed his leg against hers.

"Mr. Williams," she said, as she cocked her head toward him, "is it an Indian I am to fear, or is it the man who sits beside me?"

Case chuckled as he eased the pressure on her leg. "We'll never know now, will we?"

He picked up another piece of wood and threw it on the fire. A gas bubble trapped in one of the fire logs popped loudly, sending a shower of embers to ride the rising heat wave into the night, there to join the glowing orange sparks with the gleaming blue stars which filled the black vault of the sky.

"What are you doing out here, anyway? Is the bed that uncomfortable?"

"It's comfortable enough," Maddie replied. "I just couldn't sleep. Too much is happening, I guess. But I could ask you the same thing."

"I think I was asleep, but I woke up when you walked by."

"Oh, I'm sorry. I tried to be as quiet as possible so no one would hear me."

"I didn't hear you. I felt you."

"You felt me?"

"Yes, it's almost like a sixth sense that you develop when you think you might be in danger."

Maddie looked at Case and smiled, her eyes gleaming brightly in the golden light of the fire.

"Why, Case Williams are you suggesting that I might be dangerous?"

Case was quiet for a long moment, studying this vulnerable young woman before him. For the first time he noticed that the top of her dress was unbuttoned, and the ribbons of her camisole were untied. Her skin gleamed in the reflection of the flames, and though she revealed no more than could be seen had she been wearing an evening dress, he found the moment extremely arousing. Yeah, you are dangerous. Much more than you realize, Case thought.

"No, of course not. That didn't come out the way I intended it."

"Too bad." Maddie's smile broadened.

Case shook his head. "I'm not even going to ask what you mean by that."

"And that's good, because I'm not sure how I would answer your question." Maddie still had her brush in her hand, and she began brushing her hair. As she did so, Case could see the rise and fall of her breast, and because he found the sight distracting, he reached for the brush.

"Let me do that," he said.

Without a word, Maddie turned and handed him the brush. He rose and straddled the log, allowing his legs to rest against her hips.

SIX

This was the first time anyone other than her mother or her sister had ever brushed her hair, and she was surprised by her reaction to it. There was an intimacy to the pull of the brush through her hair, in knowing that the brush was being wielded by this man. She was also acutely aware of his closeness, and of his legs touching her. But it was what he did next that astonished her. Handing her the brush, he took up her hair and began weaving the strands into a braid. For some inexplicable reason, she had not been more aware of his virility than at that very moment. He was obviously confident enough in his own masculinity that braiding a woman's hair didn't bother him.

"How do you know how to braid hair?" Maddie asked.

"Do you think I can't do it?" He pulled some of the errant strands back from behind her ears.

"No, I'm just curious. That's all."

"I've braided lots of little girls' hair," Case said.

"There, I'm all done. I wish I had a ribbon to tie it with."

The words *little girl* stung. She turned to look at him.

"I am not a little girl," Maddie said.

"Believe me, I know you are not a little girl." At that moment he let his gaze fall to her chest, where the loosened camisole gaped open, exposing the tops of her breasts.

Maddie had forgotten that she had left her dress unbuttoned, and her hand rose to close the gap.

Case caught her hands in his.

"No." The word was not harsh or demanding, but a gentle plea.

Maddie lowered her hands, taking his hands with hers. Then she took a deep breath, causing her chest to heave, aware that Case was watching. He moved closer to her, and she wet her lips with her tongue as she prepared for him to kiss her.

But he did not.

He dropped her hands and moved with unsteady fingers to her chest. She thought he was going to touch her and she waited, not knowing what a woman should do in this situation. She was aware that she wanted him to touch her, and yet she also knew that this was the very thing that a woman of lesser morals would allow. She never let her gaze waver from his eyes, hoping she was telegraphing her desire without having to say the words.

As if reading her mind, he cupped her breasts in his hands, and even through the cloth of her dress, she felt as if her breasts were on fire. And then it stopped.

He dropped his hands and, closing his eyes, lowered his head. For a moment he sat motionless; then he moved to her camisole. Taking the ribbons, he began stringing them through the islets, closing the undergarment, and when he was finished, he tied a bow. With that done, he moved his attentions to the buttons of her dress, fastening them, one by one, slowly and deliberately. His eyes were clinging to hers, and her heart was pounding as she could feel an unknown sensation begin to build in her private parts.

When her dress was properly closed, he smiled and, with his hands on her shoulders, pulled her to him. He kissed her, the gentle touch of his lips sending jolts through her body.

He held her gaze for a long moment, neither pulling away nor repeating the kiss. Finally he dropped his hands.

"No, Maddie, I don't think of you as a child."

Maddie smiled as tears began to glisten in her eyes, a reaction that she would never have expected.

He leaned forward and kissed her again, this time on the tip of her nose.

"I think it's time for you to go back to the coach."

Maddie nodded, not daring to say a word. She stood, expecting him to go back to his bedroll as well.

"Are you coming too?"

"I'd better take care of the fire. I'll just sit here for a bit."

"All right," Maddie said. "Good night."

Case lifted his hand. "Good night."

Maddie crossed the grass to the coach. When she

looked back, Case was still sitting by the fire, and she fought the urge to run back and join him.

Case should have walked Maddie back to the wagon and seen to it that she was safely inside. He had warned her about Indians, but with all the wagons that were congregated, danger from a horny bullwhacker was far more likely.

A horny bullwhacker? What about a horny man?

He had felt a pressure in the front of his pants when he had first seen Maddie by the fire, and it was for her safety that he had told himself to go to her.

But that wasn't it at all. He had wanted to be near her, to engage in a conversation that was inconsequential, just to prove to himself that he was not attracted to her. And he would have been successful, if only she hadn't left her dress unbuttoned.

Dooley had teased him about the two women, and Case had vehemently denied that there was any interest on his part. If he were evaluating the likelihood of a relationship with one of the McClellan women, Diana would probably be the one who came out on top. As Dooley had rightly said, she was the more attractive of the two, and he believed she was closer to his age. Even in the worst of conditions, he had never seen her when she didn't look like she had just stepped out of a bandbox.

But Maddie seemed more impetuous. She had not hesitated when she leaped forward to push him to safety. Most would have. And, in the little time he had known her, he had noted that she didn't hold back regarding what she thought or how she felt. She wasn't afraid to speak her mind.

"If it's a wife you're a-wantin', you don't want a woman who ain't afraid of nothin'," Dooley had said.

This line of thinking was disturbing.

What was it that made everybody think a man needed a wife?

Six years ago he might have agreed. He had been ready to settle down with a woman and raise a family, but what had that woman done to him? She'd humiliated him, but he had learned to live with that. What he couldn't accept was how easily she had thrown away his heart. It had been as simple as throwing off her veil.

He closed his eyes and it was as if that day was yesterday—Ted and Mary Beth, she in her wedding finery . . . the buckboard clattering down the street . . . her fiery red hair tossing in the wind.

No, he would never let a woman get that close to him again, especially not a woman who thought she was the Queen of Sheba, like Diana McClellan did. But what about Maddie? Every woman he knew had some angle, some way of manipulating men, but he couldn't quite decide what Maddie's was. It would take some time to figure her out.

Case stood and kicked dirt around the fire. Something made him stop when he saw one log that wouldn't go out.

When he reached the coach, he crawled under the canvas, taking his place on his bedroll. When he was settled, he turned to watch the one little ember shining brightly in the ash pile. He smiled. Could that be an omen?

❧

The next morning breakfast was scant. Along with the ferry, Jack Healey ran a small store with limited supplies and Case noticed that overnight the prices had doubled as more wagons had joined the line waiting to cross.

"It ain't that I don't like Jack," one of the bull-whackers said, "but I don't want to give him that much of my money just 'cause his ferry don't work."

"We can take care of that," Case said, grabbing a Winchester rifle from under the seat of the box. "Dooley, go down to the sawmill and see if you can round up some slab wood. We'll try to get enough meat to take care of everybody here and have some to take with us."

"I'll have the fire laid just the way you want it, boss."

"All right, you, you, and you," Case said as he pointed to three men. "Get your rifles and come with me."

Maddie was alone in the coach as she watched Case and three men ride away, each one holding a rifle. She wondered if some problem had arisen—if Indians were nearby. Hadn't Case told her last night that an Indian had killed a man not a hundred yards from where they were sitting?

At the thought of last night, Maddie's face flushed, and she moved her fingers to her lips. Had he really kissed her, or had she just dreamed it? But then she felt the buttons on her dress, buttoned all the way to the very top. Case Williams had done that, and he had braided her hair. She pulled her hair around to fall from her shoulder, but because she had not replaced the elastic, the strands were loosening. Quickly, she tightened her braid and hunted for her elastic to hold it.

But hadn't Case said he wished he had a ribbon? On a whim, she opened her carpetbag and searched for a ribbon. When she couldn't find one, she withdrew a narrow strip of grosgrain from a camisole and tied it around her braid.

There. If you want to braid my hair again, you'll have your ribbon, Mr. Case Williams, she thought.

Maddie smoothed her brown tweed dress and then attached a clean collar. As she picked up her shawl, she wondered how much longer it would be before she got to change her clothes. She started to step out of the coach, but then she stopped. If Diana saw the ribbon in her hair, especially if she recognized it as her camisole ribbon, she would make some comment that Maddie wouldn't like. She pulled it from her hair and returned it to her bag.

Stepping out of the coach she took a deep breath. She was glad Case had ridden out, because she wasn't sure how she should react when she saw him. Should she be effervescent and friendly, or should she be reserved and embarrassed?

She truly didn't know the answer to her question. Her experience with men, especially men who had kissed her, was nonexistent. She wished she could get Diana's advice, because Diana always handled men with such ease and grace. Seeing her parents down by the river, Maddie decided she would join them as soon as she attended to her toilet behind the ferry station. As she walked the half mile to the outhouse, she made a cursory census of the temporary community that was congregated. There were fifteen wagons in the Diamond R train, and she counted at least twenty men nearby. These wagons, unlike the train they had passed on the Benton road, were pulled by oxen instead of mules. The animals had been turned loose and were grazing on the surrounding bunchgrass that was just beginning to green.

In addition, there were thirty or forty more wagons behind their coach, but these wagons had different markings from those belonging to the Diamond R. She watched as men unhitched their oxen and turned them out to graze, while the mules were kept hobbled. Among all these people—and she estimated that, combined with the Diamond R bullwhackers, there were close to a hundred—she had not seen one other woman besides her sister and her mother.

For the first time since leaving Washington, she felt ill at ease. No one at Fort Lincoln, on the *Josephine*, or at Fort Benton had done anything to cause her to be alarmed, but now, with such a lopsided ratio of men to women, she felt uncomfortable. But she decided she had no reason to be afraid. After all, no man had made any untoward advance toward her.

At that thought, she gasped. One man had! Again, she reached up to touch the lips that Case had kissed. She knew that his move toward her, though it was unsolicited, had not been unwelcome. And even though she had only known Case for two days, she trusted him implicitly.

⁕

By midmorning the hunting party had returned with three pronghorn antelopes—two bucks and a doe. The animals were dressed and the game was put on a spit for the long roasting process. After five or six hours, the entire encampment was permeated with the aroma of cooking meat, and Maddie and several others gravitated to the site.

"Whoa, there, Gurney, ease up on puttin' any more of that red stuff on that meat," someone called when the meat was taken off the spit. "You purt' near put on a ton when they was all cookin'."

"Don't worry about it, we've got a lot of cayenne in this here wagon," Gurney replied. "Ol' man Johnson ain't goin' to miss this one little bit."

"I ain't talkin' about him missin' it, I'm talkin' about you makin' it so hot cain't nobody eat it."

"Ha! You wait till you taste this," Gurney said. "You'll be cussin' your mama out 'cause she never fixed nothin' this good for you."

Seeing Maddie in the crowd, Gurney tore off a piece of the meat and handed it to her.

"We'll let the little lady tell us what she thinks."

"I shot this animal. I should get the first bite," Case said as he stepped up beside Maddie. He took the meat and popped it into his mouth. "I say it's good." Then he pulled off a bit of the meat, making sure there was plenty of the outer crust. He put it in Maddie's mouth.

A big smile crossed her face when she had swallowed the meat.

"It's delicious." And to prove her point she stepped forward and pulled off another piece.

"There ye be, gents. Case and his woman both

say it's good, so we'll have at it just as soon as I can
carve it up," Gurney said.

Case took Maddie's hand and led her away from
the group.

"You did that well," he said as he dropped her
hand. "These men may be a little rough around the
edges, but most of 'em are as good as gold. If they
think you respect them, they'll do anything for you."

"Well, it was easy. The meat is very good," Maddie
said. "Tell me, why did he call me your woman?"

Case looked away for a moment, but then he
turned back to Maddie.

"Maybe someone told them that. I hope you don't
mind. If they think you're my woman, no one will
come near you. I've told my men not to bother you
and your family, and if one of them disobeys that
order, he will be gone."

"I understand."

"Look up there. We're getting company." Case
pointed to a coach approaching the long line of
wagons that had formed. "Let's go see who it is."

Maddie and Case got to the Diamond R coach just
as the new coach pulled up. It had WELLS FARGO
painted in gold across its red body.

"Howdy, Harper," Dooley called from his perch up
on the driver's seat. He squirted a stream of tobacco
as he lowered his feet from the splashboard in front
of him.

"Ain't this ferry fixed yet?" Harper asked. "Dutch
Jake said Odie Butler changed horses and wouldn't
even slow down. Said the cable broke."

"That's true," Case said. "But did he pass you on the way?"

"Can't say that he did."

"Then I'd say it's a pretty good bet he's not back yet."

Harper laughed. "Ye got me there, Case."

"Do you know, did Walt Hughes join up with Pippen yet?"

"Not yet," Harper said, "but Walt will ketch up mighty quick. Jonas must've figured out Odie ain't back yet, cause he's lollygagging around back there. Decided he was tired of hardtack and salt meat and sent a couple of the boys out huntin'."

"How far back was he when you passed him?"

"He hadn't made it to the Leaving yet, but he was close," Harper said.

"Good, then he should pull in sometime tonight."

Just then the door of the coach opened.

"Case? I thought that was your voice," a man said as he stepped out of the coach.

"Dale Hathaway, are you the only passenger?" Case asked as he offered his hand.

"No, sir," Dale said, turning to help a young woman out of the coach. "May I present Miss Annie Higgins, a most delightful young woman on her way to Helena."

"That's good. I, too, have some women on their way to Helena. This is Miss Maddie McClellan. Her sister, Diana, and her mother are here someplace."

"Welcome, Annie," Maddie said. "You're just in time for a feast. Gurney's cooked some pronghorn and it's delicious."

"Miss McClellan, have I met you before?" Dale asked. "And if I have not, where have you been?"

"Washington," Case answered for Maddie. "Her father's the new superintendent of Indian affairs and they just arrived on the *Josephine*."

"Oh, it is my loss. Miss Higgins and I just arrived on the *Far West*. Had we all been traveling together, we would be fast friends by now."

"I'm sure you would be, Dale," Case said as he shook his head. "But now Maddie is right. The meat's ready. Dooley, let Harper edge his coach in between you and the train and come on down."

"I'll wait, boss. I hate to leave the coach with all these jokers around here hittin' the sauce. Ye nev'r know what they'll pull."

"You go on down, Dooley," Harper said. "I'll watch out for ya. You have to be pert near cracked up jest a sittin' here twiddlin' your thumbs."

"Thanks, Harper. I have to admit, I'm a hankerin' for some of Gurney's meat. It's smellin' awful good," Dooley said as he climbed off the coach.

When the five reached the fire pit, there were about twenty or thirty people gathered around, including the McClellans. Jack Healey had brought out a bench, and Annabelle and Diana were seated on it while the others were standing around.

"Here he is. Here's the boss man. Now we can eat," someone yelled.

"You didn't have to wait for me," Case said. "Say, Jack, do you have any utensils for the ladies?"

"I only brought out three," Healey said. "I didn't know we had another lady. I'll see if I can round up another fork and a tin plate." He turned and started back to the store.

"Mr. Healey—don't go," Maddie said. "My mother will let me share her plate, and as for a fork, I've got one. It's right where God put it."

Jack laughed. "Girl, you're a keeper, you know that?"

"Madelyn McClellan! I can't believe I heard you say that!"

Annie raised her eyebrows as she looked at Maddie. "Your sister?"

"Yes, come meet her."

The meat was exceptionally good, and when everyone had eaten his or her fill, one of the bullwhackers brought out a fiddle and began playing music: "Turkey in the Straw," "Buffalo Gals," and "Oh! Susanna," among others.

Maddie was enjoying the camaraderie as everyone, including Diana, joined in the singing.

"Hey, Gus," someone called. "How about 'Wait for the Wagon'? Don't you think that's sort of appropriate since we're all waitin' for Odie?"

"All right, but we're changin' the names a bit. This time it's a nod to the boss." Gus inclined his head toward the four women, who were still sitting on the bench. When he started to play, everyone began singing and clapping their hands in time to the music.

> "Will you come my Maddie dearie to the wild
>   mountain free,

Where the river runs so pretty, and ride
    along with me,
And you shall be so happy with your Casey
    by your side,
So wait for the wagon, and we'll all take a ride."

Maddie wasn't sure she had heard her name in the song, but she was certain she had not heard the names Phyllis or Jacob, which were the ones usually associated with this tune.

"Miss McClellan, you have to answer," Dooley said as he started clapping, and all the men joined him. "You have to. Them's the rules."

Maddie knew the words to the song that was the answer to "Wait for the Wagon," but she was most uncomfortable. She found Case on the other side of the circle and, with a pleading expression, begged him to get her out of this.

But he was clapping just as loudly as the other men, and he had a big smile on his face. When he saw her looking at him, he nodded his approval.

Very boldly, she stood up and went to stand by the harmonica player.

"All right, this is it." And she began to sing in a clear voice:

"I thank you, Mister Casey, but I'm not
    inclined to go,
Your wagon is so clumsy, and your team so
    very slow."

When she finished the words, there was a loud cheer, and several of the men who were standing near Case began laughing and slapping him on the back.

"I guess she told you."

"That little ol' gal's too spunky for you, boss."

"Case! Case!" a man said as he was running toward the fire pit. "Jonas Pippen just rode in on a mule. Come quick."

"Isn't he supposed to be with the train?" Dooley asked.

"Yes, he is," Case said. "Maybe we'd better go see what this is all about."

With the music and the celebration going on behind them, Case and Dooley walked quickly back to the coach, where Jonas Pippen was standing alongside an unsaddled mule. It was obvious he had ridden the animal bareback.

"Boss, we got trouble," Jonas said.

"What's wrong?" Case asked.

"Our mules. They've all been took."

"How'd that happen?"

"Indians. They come in attacking us and Jasper and Clyde was both hit."

"You mean shot?"

"That's what I mean."

"Are they alive?" Dooley asked when he heard the news.

"Yeah, they're alive. Pell was hit in the leg and Cline got it in the shoulder. Bernie Pavlov did what he could for 'em. He got the bleedin' stopped, and we put some coal oil on the wounds, but the bullets is still in there, 'n' we need to get 'em to a doc so he can take the bullets out before they start festerin'."

Even as he listened, Case was assessing what should be done.

"How far back do you think you are?"

"We come past Parker Butte, but I don't know how far we got, 'fore this all happened."

"Dooley and I will be going back tonight. Are you up to coming back with us?"

"You know I am. I ain't leavin' my men at the mercy of those savages. What if they come back in the morning? This time they took all our mules, but what if they figure out what grub we're carrying? They'll be back."

"If they took all your mules, where'd you git this one?" Dooley asked.

"Ah, hell, this is old Dobbin. You ever heared stubborn as a mule? Well Dobbin wouldn't move so they rid off without him."

"Excuse me, did I hear you say your train was attacked by Indians?" Roy asked, as he joined the men.

Pippen looked at Roy with suspicion.

"It was Indians, no doubt about it, and who are you?"

"Jonas, this is the new field supervisor of Indian affairs for the Montana Territory, Professor Roy McClellan," Case said.

"McClellan? Are you the one who sent a boatload full of furniture that we had to haul?"

Roy chuckled in spite of the seriousness of the situation. "That was me, but tell me about the Indian attack. Do you know what tribe it was?"

"Our guy, Stone Eagle, don't think it was Blackfoot. He thinks it was probably Sioux or maybe even

Assiniboine. He didn't get close enough to see no beadwork or nothin', so he can't be sure."

"At this point it doesn't matter," Case said. "Harper, I'd like to commandeer your coach to bring my men back. It's a little bigger than mine, and you're not going anywhere until Odie gets here."

"What about my passengers?" Harper asked.

"The young lady can stay with my wife and daughters," Roy said.

"Thank you, sir," Case said. "And Dale, do you mind sleeping under my coach?"

"That won't be a problem," Dale Hathaway said.

"Mr. Williams, I feel I should go with you," Roy said.

"I understand, but I won't bring the wounded men back tonight, and Jonas is right. The Indians could come back, and there could be shooting."

"I was a company commander during the war. I've seen my share of shooting," Roy said, not with bravado, but with quiet confidence.

Case nodded. "Yes, sir, I suppose you have. Forgive me, I didn't mean to insinuate that you couldn't handle it. Do you have a weapon with you?"

"I do. It's in one of the trunks."

"Good. You can make the call whether you choose to go with us or not, but with your experience, I personally think you would be more valuable here. As you know, Indians don't operate within boundaries, and if they thought they could get away with it, they might attack. . . ." Case did not finish the sentence.

"I understand."

"Good. I don't think the oxen are at risk, but I'll

put some sentries out anyway. And I'll tell the men that you'll be in charge, should it come to that."

"I don't know about that. These men don't know me. Do you think they'll accept me as their commander?"

"Sir, let's hope this is a moot point, but the Diamond R men all work for me," Case said as a matter of fact. "They'll do what I tell them to do."

SEVEN

Case wanted to reach the stranded wagons as soon as possible, so keeping the team at a trot, the three men reached Parker Butte within an hour. By now, the wagons that had been left behind with the steam donkeys in Fort Benton had come up. Walt Hughes, who was standing in front of a blazing fire, heard the approach of the coach and walked out to the road to meet it.

"I thought you might be comin' back with Jonas," Walt said.

"Where are Pell and Cline?"

"We got 'em on a blanket in one of the wagons."

Case climbed down from the coach, then hurried back to check on the men.

"How are you doing?" he asked.

"I can't believe it. I come through the whole war 'n' never got shot one time. I come out here and what am I doing? Drivin' a wagon 'n' I get shot," Pell said.

"Soon as we can, we'll get you boys back to the mission at St. Peter's. Father Imoda will fix you up."

"Pavlov done a pretty good job of it his ownself," Cline said. "I don't think I need a priest."

Case laughed at Cline's comment. "This priest can do more than pray for you. He's a trained physician and he'll know just what to do to get the bullets out."

"You going to take 'em back tonight?" Walt asked.

Case shook his head. "No, not tonight. Odie's not back with the new rope for the cable, so we'd be stuck at the crossing if we did go back. Anyway, I want to make sure the trip is as comfortable as I can make it."

"I'll tell you what worries me," Walt said. "We're carrying a lot of machinery mixed in with other freight, but Pippin's train is mostly supplies. You know—coffee, sugar, flour, beans, cured hams, that sort of stuff. If the Indians know we can't move, they may get the idea to come back and clean us out, and this time they'd bring every able-bodied man within fifty miles."

"You may be right. Palmer Crab's train is waiting on the other side of the river. As soon as I get across, I'll have him bring his oxen to you. He's hauling ore, so we don't have to worry about Indians going after that."

"But what do we do in the meantime?" Walt asked.

"You've got mules. Let's hitch them up to Pippen's train and get them in a defensive position. Then put your wagons on the outside with the mules in the center. Oh, and keep some men on guard tonight," Case said.

"What about you, going back on the coach tomorrow?" Walt asked.

"Dooley and I can handle it. It's only an hour back to the river, and except for the horses, we don't have anything they might want. And if they do, I have my rifle and plenty of bullets."

Back at the crossing, Maddie was still at the fire pit, enjoying the celebration, singing and clapping along with the others as they kept time to the music. Smiling broadly, she glanced at the spot where Case had been standing, but he wasn't there. Making a thorough perusal of the circle, she didn't find him, and now she noticed that her father, too, was gone.

Looking up, she saw the red coach pulling away, and that the horses were being hitched to their coach. Curious and without wanting to alarm Annie, Maddie got up from the bench and went to find either Case or her father.

Seeing her father, she called to him. "Papa, Annie's still down by the fire pit, and that's her coach. They aren't leaving her here, are they?"

"No, no one has forgotten her," Roy said. "Case needed to go back to the train that's coming up behind us."

"Why didn't he take our coach if he needed one, and why is our coach moving now?"

"Mr. Healey said we would be the first to cross the river when the cable is repaired, so I thought it would be better if we got a little closer."

"You decided? Not Case?"

At that moment, one of the bushwhackers approached Maddie and her father.

"Mr. McClellan, we've got the sentries out watching the oxen. Do you think we should put another one patrolling the wagons?"

"No, I think men on the perimeters is plenty. They can signal if anything happens."

Maddie narrowed her eyes as she stared at her father.

"Papa, what's going on? What are you not telling me?"

"Daughter, you ask too many questions. There are some things it's best you not know."

"It's Indians, isn't it?"

"Whatever would make you say that?"

"Because Case told me an Indian killed a man here at the crossing just last month. And now Case has gone back to the train."

"All right," Roy said. "The reason Case left is because a band of Indians has run off all the mules from the train." He paused for a moment before he completed the sentence. "And two men have been shot."

Maddie gasped as she put her hand to her mouth.

"See why I didn't want to say anything? If you're going to react like this, what do you think your mother and Diana would do?"

"I'm sorry."

"Well, don't be, because now I need you. I've offered space in our coach to this young woman who is on her way to Helena. Tonight she'll be sharing your bed, and I'd prefer that the others don't know the real reason. I want you to engage the women in some entertainment of your own choosing. Just don't suggest trouble with the Indians."

"All right, Papa."

There was another loud burst of laughter from the fire pit; then the music of the fiddle began again.

"I guess I should get back to Mama before she starts wondering where I am."

Leaving her father, Maddie walked down to join the other women.

"One more song," Gus said. "I've done wore myself out."

"'Goodnight, Ladies,'" someone yelled.

"That's a good one. It'll be for Case and his woman," someone else said.

Gus looked around. "Say, where is Case? Does anybody know?"

"I seen his woman just git back. She can tell us."

Everyone turned their attention to Maddie, and she really didn't know what to say. Much to her relief, her father spoke up.

"Case was called back to the train, but I think 'Goodnight, Ladies' is an excellent choice."

When the last note died away, Diana turned to Maddie.

"I'd like to know something. What makes these people think you are Case Williams's woman? What have you done?"

"I haven't done anything." That is, nothing except kiss him, Maddie thought. "At least I haven't thrown myself at him like you have."

"If you think I've thrown myself at him, you just watch what I can do." Diana turned and stomped off to where the coach had been standing.

Maddie gritted her teeth. Her whole life, she had accepted her mother's obvious favoritism toward her older daughter: Diana is my pretty daughter; Diana is the smart one; Diana is the neat one; Diana can sing and dance, Diana loves people. Oh, and Maddie can ride horses. She's my baby.

After so many years of hearing this, Maddie accepted her position. It was only in recent years that she had summoned the courage to challenge Diana, but if her mother overheard their sisterly spats, it was always Maddie at fault. Never precious Diana.

And now Diana had laid down the gauntlet. She thought Maddie might be interested in Case Williams, and Diana was determined to keep him for herself. It didn't matter whether or not she even liked him. It now had become a contest.

You just watch what I can do. Those were the words Diana had used. Well, those words could cut both ways.

Maddie found Annie and explained that Case had borrowed the Wells Fargo coach to make a quick trip back to the train and that Annie was to spend the night with them.

"Case would have taken our coach, but he said it would take three men and a boy to unload all our trunks, and he was in a hurry," Maddie said, trying to make a joke. "But now it will be fun. You will be our first guest, even before we get to Helena."

"I appreciate that," Annie said. "When I realized we would have to spend the night here, I was concerned about where I would sleep."

"You would have slept in the coach, dear," Annabelle said. "The seats can be put down, and the bed, while not as soft as a feather bed, is really quite comfortable. Don't you think, Maddie?"

"It's all right, but my sister snores." Maddie laughed.

"Maddie!" Annabelle chided. "I have been so proud of the way you two have been getting along, and now you say something so unflattering about Diana."

"Just be forewarned. She does snore." Maddie took Annie by the arm and led her to the new location of the coach.

"This isn't where we were parked," Annabelle said. "Are you sure this is our coach?"

"Yes, Mama, look at the trunks on top."

Annabelle, Annie, and Maddie climbed into the coach, and Maddie lit a kerosene lantern that was hanging from a hook in the ceiling.

"Thank goodness, there's my bag," Annie said when she saw a carpetbag sitting on the floor. "I'd not want to lose all my things."

"Mr. Williams will take good care of your trunk," Annabelle said. "I'm sure you'll have it back tomorrow."

Annie dipped her chin. "Ma'am, I don't have a trunk."

"Oh, I thought you said you were moving to Helena. Did you send your things on ahead?"

Just then, the door of the coach was yanked open.

"Why didn't you tell me the coach had moved? I've been looking all over for it," Diana said.

Maddie laughed. "This coach is the only one here, and it's now sitting within sight of the fire pit. I guess it would be hard to find if someone is walking around with her nose up in the air."

Annabelle shook her head. "Annie, I don't know where these girls came from. Their manners were certainly not learned at my knee."

"I'm sorry, Mother," Maddie said.

Diana said nothing.

"Shall we play dominoes?" Maddie asked as she withdrew a wooden box from her valise.

"I think that would be good," Annabelle said. "Don't you think dominoes sounds like fun, Diana?"

Diana stared pointedly at Maddie. "If I get to choose the game, it will be old maid."

It looks like it might rain," Dale Hathaway said. "I'm afraid it's going to be a wet night for us."

"Not necessarily," Roy replied. "There's quite a bit of canvas in the back of the second wagon, and Pete said we could use it."

"Yeah," Hathaway said. "Good idea. We can make a tent."

"We can do better than that," Harper suggested.

"What do you mean?"

"We'll stretch some canvas under the coach, then use the rest of it to wrap around the wheels. That'll keep us dry."

"Until the water starts running in from underneath," Hathaway said.

"We can stop that, too. All we have to do is put a trench around the coach, then dig a diversionary canal so the water runs downhill," Roy said.

"Sounds like you've spent a few nights out in the rain," Harper said.

"That I did, when I was with the Fifty-Fourth Massachusetts."

"Damn. Did you Yankees really have enough sense to do that? Or did you steal that idea from the Thirteenth Tennessee?" Harper asked, and both men laughed. "I'll find a shovel and start digging."

"Find three of them," Roy said.

When Roy checked on the women in the coach, he was pleased to see what they were doing.

"This is a fine way you've chosen to while away your time," he said. "Ciphering will come in handy when we get to Helena and you girls start working at the brickyard."

"Papa, that's not funny," Diana said.

"Well, maybe not the brickyard, but you may want to think about finding something to do while I'm out in the field."

"Today's not the day to make a decision," Annabelle said. "I think this is about all the dominoes I can take."

"It's too early to go to bed," Diana said. "What do we do now?"

"We don't know anything about Annie," Annabelle said. "Do you have relatives in Helena?"

Annie smiled. "Not yet."

"Oh, is your family going to come later?"

"No, ma'am, I'm going to be married."

"Married! That's wonderful," Diana said.

"You must be very happy," Maddie said. "Does you husband-to-be live in Helena?"

"I think so," Annie said. "I know that at one time he did, but then he moved to Salt Lake City. When he wrote to me, he said to meet him in Helena, so if he doesn't live there, it must be close by."

Maddie frowned. "When he wrote to you? Do you not know this man?"

"Oh, yes, I've met him. His name is George White, and he was in Ticonderoga six years ago. That's where I'm from."

"Did he live there?" Diana asked.

"No, but I met him when he married my friend Eva."

"He's married?" Diana gasped.

"Not now. She died."

"How sad," Maddie said. "I know you're going to be very happy. It must be wonderful to be in love."

Annie hesitated.

"You do love him, don't you?" Maddie asked.

"Your manners, Maddie. They've slipped again," Annabelle said. "That's not a question you ask a woman."

"Well, Mama, isn't love important?"

"No, dear, you read too much nonsense. The poems Elizabeth Barrett and Robert Browning write to one another are not the way it is when a man and woman live together."

"But you love Papa, don't you?" Maddie asked.

"I respect your father very much and he respects me. That is enough."

"But, Mama, you do love Papa. I know Papa loves us," Maddie continued.

"Maddie, this conversation is over," Annabelle said in a stern voice. "Now, let's put the bed down and turn down the wick. I've had a long day."

"Yes, ma'am."

When the bed was in place, and the lamp was out, Maddie lay quietly. Even though Annie was a small woman, the extra person made it difficult to get comfortable, but that wasn't the only thing causing her to feel disquieted.

Why had her mother been unable to answer the simple question, do you love Papa? She said she respected him, but in Maddie's mind respect was a far cry from being the same as love.

Maddie did read the poems of the Brownings—everyone memorized "How Do I Love Thee, Let Me Count the Ways"—but she liked "Any Wife to Any Husband":

> I have but to be by thee, and thy hand
> Will never let mine go, nor heart withstand
> The beating of my heart to reach its place.
> When shall I look for thee and feel thee
>   gone?
> When cry for the old comfort and find none?
> Never, I know! Thy soul is in thy face.

When a man and woman loved one another, it was a declaration to the world that they never wanted to be apart—*thy hand will never let mine go*. But when she thought about the long discussions she had heard her parents engaged in before they left Washington, it was as if two business partners were discussing what the financial ramifications of the move would be. Never did either of them express any concern regarding what it would be like to be so far apart.

And now there was Annie. When she had asked Annie if she was in love, Annie hadn't answered. Her mother had chastised her, telling her that wasn't a question you should ask a woman. Maddie had seen something in Anna's eyes—uncertainty? Trepidation? Acquiescence? What she had not seen was an expression of love. Was love something that was only found in poetry?

Maddie closed her eyes, trying to calm her troubled thoughts. Maybe she was destined for spinsterhood, because she vowed she would never marry a man just because she respected him, or just because she thought he could provide her with the niceties society demanded. She would only marry for love—whatever that was.

Maddie was awakened during the night to cracks of thunder, as a pelting downpour began. The isinglass curtains did an adequate job of keeping the rain out, but still, trickles of water ran down the inside of the coach, making the pallet wet. Try as she might, she couldn't get away from the dampness, but she thought of her father and the men sleeping under the coach. She willed herself to make the best of it.

It was still raining when she awakened the next morning, and at dawn, Maddie raised the curtain to her window so she could look out toward the river. She wondered if Odie would get back with the cable today, and if he did, how he would go about getting it strung across the river. With the rain adding to the already swiftly running current, she thought that however it was tackled, it would be difficult.

"Are you ladies awake?" Roy asked as he knocked gently on the door.

"I am," Maddie whispered.

"Of course you are. Why don't you come down to our place and join us for breakfast?"

Maddie scurried to get out of the coach without awakening the others. Her father held an opening in the canvas that encircled the wheels of the coach, and she crawled into a surprisingly dry space.

"Good morning," Dale Hathaway said when he saw her. "Your father was wise enough to save some of last night's meat, and Harper rounded up some coffee for us."

"Here you are, ma'am," Harper said as he emptied his tin cup, then poured coffee into the same cup and handed it to her. "I hope you like it black."

"I do," Maddie said as she took the cup. When she tasted the coffee, it was all she could do to swallow the strong brew.

"Maddie's not much of a coffee drinker," Roy said. "I'll just take that, if you don't mind."

Just as Roy reached for the cup, the flap of the tent opened and Case crawled inside. He was soaked from the rain.

"Is that for me? Case asked as he took the cup of coffee from Maddie's outstretched hand.

"I think it is," Maddie said as she handed off the offending drink.

"What can you report?" Roy asked.

"We brought back the two wounded men. Harper, I know this will slow you down, but I'd like to keep them in your coach until we can get to the mission, where the doc can get the bullets out. Dale, will you ride with them to keep them settled?"

"What about Miss Higgins?" Dale asked.

"I'd like to keep her in the Diamond R coach— that is, if the McClellan ladies won't mind."

"We've enjoyed having Annie with us. Of course she can stay with us," Maddie said.

Case reached for Maddie's hand and squeezed it. It was a simple gesture, but Maddie was all too aware of his touch as he continued to hold on to it.

"Good. Harper, you come with me and relieve Dooley."

"Did . . . did anything happen?" Maddie asked, not wanting to voice what she was thinking.

Case smiled. "No Indians, but a couple more mules wandered back. That means we're only missing thirty-seven. I'd better get down to the river and see what I can do to hurry this operation along."

"I'm coming with you," Roy said.

All four of the men hurried out into the rain, and Maddie got back into the coach. By now, the other three were awake and the seats had been reconfigured.

"Where have you been?" Annabelle asked.

"I was under the coach. I had breakfast with Papa and the other men."

"What an indecent thing to do," Diana said. "No proper lady would ever join a group of men like that, especially in such a place."

"Papa invited me, and so I did it. Oh, Annie, your coach is back, but . . ."

"Oh, that must mean Case is back," Diana said as she rolled up the isinglass so she could look out.

"He is. He said that you should stay with us, Annie, until we get to the mission."

"You saw him? You talked to him?"

"Yes, he was under the coach with me." Maddie said the words hoping to get a rise out of Diana.

"Maddie, why are we going to a mission?" Annabelle asked.

"Because there's a—" Maddie stopped herself before she said *doctor*. No one had told her not to say anything about the two injured men, but she thought better of it. "Because we will probably get a meal there, and have a chance to change our clothes."

"I'm ready for that," Diana said. "Wouldn't it be wonderful if we could have a bath?"

"Dear, it's a mission, not a first-class hotel," Annabelle said. Just then, she looked out the side of the coach. "Well, I declare. There's your father out in the rain with no coat. He will catch his death of cold."

Earlier, Annabelle had insisted that Dooley bring one of the trunks inside the coach, and now she began searching through until she found what she was looking for.

"Aren't you glad we have our things with us?" Annabelle asked, as she pulled out a tan macintosh and an umbrella. "I just wish your father would agree to stand under this, but he won't."

"Mama, you know officers never stand under umbrellas," Maddie said with a little chuckle, repeating something she had heard her father say many times.

"Long ago I quit trying to make him stand under an umbrella, but maybe he will at least put on his raincoat," Annabelle said. "Maddie, would you take this to him?"

Stepping out of the coach, Maddie made her way

through the clusters of men, many of whom were gathered under makeshift tents. Some were playing cards while others were talking and sharing a bottle of whiskey.

"Little lady, you're gettin' awful wet out there. Why don't you come get under my tent?" one man called out as he rose from his seat and started toward her. He was stumbling, and Maddie guessed that he had been drinking a little more than he should have. She started to run, and even with the umbrella and her father's coat, she was much more agile than the big, lumbering man was. By bobbing and weaving between the wagons, she was able to evade him, but when she looked around, she realized she had lost her perspective and now had no idea where her father might be.

She continued to wander, getting farther and farther away from the coach, until she reached the river.

It was here that she saw Case. He was walking beside a team of mules as they were dragging cut logs from the sawmill down to the riverbank. His clothes were thoroughly soaked. Maddie thought she should offer him her father's coat, and she moved toward him. When the mules saw her and the umbrella, they bolted, but with much effort, Case was able to stop them.

Looking around, he saw what had frightened the mules.

"Damn, Maddie, I thought I left you at the coach. What are you doing down here?"

"Mr. Williams, you just swore at me. I don't think I like that."

"Well, you deserved it. Do you see any other woman

in sight? They all have sense enough to stay out of the rain."

This comment stung, and Maddie conjured up all the indignation she could muster. She didn't answer him but glowered intently, not allowing her gaze to waver.

After what seemed like several minutes, with neither saying anything, Case let the reins go slack.

"All right. Why are you down here?"

"I'm looking for my father. I want to give him this." She held out the raincoat and umbrella.

"He doesn't really need it. He's inside the ferry office with Jack Healey," Case said as he motioned toward the building. He took off his hat and the water ran from its brim as his wet hair fell in ringlets against his forehead.

Seeing him like that, Maddie felt the anger she had been feeling drain away, and a lopsided grin began to form on her face.

"Then maybe you'd like to use my umbrella."

Case laughed. "I know you're offering the umbrella with the best of intentions, but if any of my men saw me decked out like that, they'd laugh themselves silly."

Imagining the picture, Maddie laughed as well. "Perhaps you're right."

"That's probably the way your father feels, too," Case said, flicking the reins against the mules as he continued to pull the log to where a half dozen or more were already piled.

Deciding that since her father was out of the rain and Case was right, she returned to the coach.

"He wouldn't take the raincoat?" Annabelle asked.

"He's dry enough, Mama. He's in the ferry office."

The rain stopped around noon, and Maddie, bored with staying inside the coach, ventured out. She told herself it was not her intention to find Case, but she did go to the river, where she had last seen him. He and three other men were lashing two logs together to form a raft. They put that two-log raft into the water and joined it end to end with a long string of logs that were already in the water, parallel to the riverbank. She watched for some time, but had absolutely no idea why they were doing this.

Around one o'clock, there was some excitement as a box wagon driven by a team of horses came into view.

"Here he comes!" someone yelled. "Here comes Odie!"

"It's about time he got back!"

EIGHT

The wagon came to a halt, and immediately men started unloading the rope that was coiled in its bed. Rather than taking it to the ferry, they pulled it to Case, stretching it as far as it would go.

"All right, men, start heavin' the rope out onto the floats," Case called. "And Maddie, as soon as you see me on the other side, go tell Harper and Dooley to get the coaches down here. Keep Miss Higgins with you, and tell Harper to come across first."

"I will," Maddie yelled. She hadn't known that Case even knew she was watching, and yet he had asked her to do something. But how was he going to get to the other side of this raging river?

"Men, are we ready?" Case asked. "On the count of three, get 'em in the water."

Maddie watched as the men pushed the logs into the water, but she wasn't prepared to see Case crouching low on the last set of logs. His knee held the rope in place while he poled out into the swiftly moving water.

The river, which even in its normal state was quite rapid, was now in freshet stage due to the heavy rain and melting snow in the headwaters. As she watched the operation, Maddie realized the line of logs would act as a long pivot arm, which would propel Case to the opposite side of the river, all the while keeping the rope out of the current.

The operation was working perfectly until Case, on the far end of the log line, reached the middle of the river. The swiftness of the current caused the logs Case was riding to slip their knots and separate, throwing him headlong into the water. The section of rope on his raft fell in the water as well and quickly went under.

"Case!" Maddie shouted in alarm.

"There he is!" someone shouted, and Maddie saw Case's head pop back up, downstream from the string of logs. The logs were moving rapidly, heading straight for him, and Maddie was afraid they would hit him. As they came to him, though, he went back under water, and Maddie feared he had drowned.

To her relief, she saw him surface again, this time upstream of the logs. Using the current, he started swimming toward the logs.

"He better grab hold of one of them things quick. If he gets swept down into them rocks downstream, he's a goner," one of the bullwhackers said.

Case grabbed hold of the two logs on the end and, making no effort to climb out of the water, simply hung on to them and to the rope.

"Yes!" Maddie said with a sense of relief.

"It ain't over yet, miss. He's still got to land on the other side," Healey said.

Case continued to ride the logs as they pivoted across the river. But now another problem presented itself. Because he had lost the first raft, the arm wasn't long enough to make it all the way across, and there was a danger that it might just sweep back out into the middle of the stream again and separate.

Just before the gate of logs was completely perpendicular with the far side, he let go and started swimming, using the current to help him, all the while hanging on to the rope. Maddie held her breath and prayed that he would make it. That was when she saw four men running down to the river's edge. It was all Case could do to lift one of his arms, and two of the men grabbed that arm while the other two grabbed the rope.

They dragged Case ashore and he tried to stand up but was too exhausted to do so, and he collapsed on the bank.

As Case lay there, getting his breath, the four men pulled the rope back upstream until it was stretched from side to side. Then it was raised to the proper height and secured in place.

"Hurrah!" the men on both sides of the river shouted.

"Folks," Jack Healey called, "this here ferry is about to go into operation."

"Maddie, run back and tell the drivers to get their coaches down here and to put the wounded men first," Roy said. It wasn't until then that Maddie realized her father had been standing on the riverbank beside her, watching the operation as intently as she.

When Maddie reached the two coaches, she called up to the drivers. "Mr. Harper, Mr. Dooley, bring your coaches down to the ferry, and Mr. Harper, you're first."

Dale Hathaway, who had been watching the activity, hurried back to the Wells Fargo coach.

"What about Mr. Hathaway?" Annie asked, seeing her fellow passenger.

"I'll go with the other coach," Hathaway said. "The two wounded men might need help."

"Climb aboard, little lady," Dooley called down to Maddie, "and we'll get goin'."

"Did that man say 'two wounded men'?" Annabelle asked.

"Yes, he did," Maddie said.

"What happened? Was there an accident?"

Maddie could not lie to her mother when she was asked directly, and she thought Annabelle would find out what happened when they reached the mission anyway. "The reason Case had to go back to the train was because Indians drove off all the mules. And two of his men were shot."

"You knew this last night, didn't you?" Diana asked. "Why didn't you tell us?"

"Because Papa told me not to."

"Of course he did," Diana said sarcastically.

"Where is your father?" Annabelle asked.

"He's down at the landing. They've got the cable in place, and we can cross now."

"Finally," Diana said with a long-suffering sigh. "I wouldn't be a bit surprised if it breaks again."

"Let's hope not. You wouldn't be so critical if you knew how hard it was for Case to get the rope across."

"Why did Mr. Williams have to do anything? It was the ferry company's responsibility, wasn't it?" Annabelle asked.

"You're right, but it was Case who figured out how to do it." Maddie described how he had ridden the logs across, only to be thrown off and nearly drowned in the middle of the river.

"Oh, was Case hurt? He's so handsome!" Diana said.

Maddie shot a stunned look at Diana. What did being handsome have to do with being brave?

The two coaches drove down to the landing, to be in place when the ferry was ready.

"All right, Harper, bring 'er on," Jack Healey called. "Slow and easy."

When the Wells Fargo coach was onboard, the boat left the shore. The ferry tended to swing a bit, and to bob up and down, but it was hooked up to the cable Case had carried across, and the connection held.

Once Harper's coach was off the ferry, Case motioned for him to move off to the side.

"How are your patients?" he asked Dale Hathaway when he opened the door.

"A little scratch ain't gonna take me out," Jasper Cline said. "And Clyde here, well, he's so liquored up, like as not he don't even know which way is up."

"Well, then a couple more minutes aren't going to hurt you," Case said. "I want to see how these oxen make it across. They may be skittish without the loads."

The animals made the return trip without incident, so Healey motioned for Dooley to load up.

"You might want to get out of the coach," Roy said when the women were onboard. "You can see more that way."

Those were the words her father had used, but in Maddie's mind, he was trying to put them in a better position to be rescued if something did go amiss. But it was not necessary. The crossing was successful.

When they got to the other side, Case was waiting for them.

"How do you like your first Montana experience?" he asked.

Diana stepped toward him. "I wasn't afraid at all. It was so reassuring to know that you were here to rescue me if something had happened. My sister tells me that you have wounded men. Don't you think it would be better if they were comforted by a woman?"

"These two wouldn't know how to react to a pretty woman like you, Diana."

"Well, we'll just see about that. You'll be traveling with your men, won't you?"

"Yes, I'll be on this coach."

"Then I will be, too." Diana moved to the Wells Fargo coach and got in before anyone could tell her not to.

"Father Imoda! Father Imoda!" Case called, jumping down as soon as the coach came to a stop in front of an L-shaped building. A high-reaching belfry sported a cross, the only indication that the building was a religious institution.

A young man who appeared to be half Indian was working in the nearby garden, and he dropped his hoe and came running when the coach arrived.

"Juneau, where's Father Imoda? Is he here or is he up north?"

"He's here."

"I need him. I've got two men with bullet wounds."

Nodding, Juneau darted off into the building.

A rather small man with dark hair and a beard stepped out of the mission. He was wearing a long black cassock, and he was accompanied by a young woman who was wearing a nun's habit.

"Father Rappagliosi, Mother Raffaella."

"It's so good to see you again, Case. What brings you our way?" Father Rappagliosi asked.

"It's not a pleasure trip this time, Father." Case opened the door to the coach. "I've brought two men to see Father Imoda. They've been shot."

Father Rappagliosi and Mother Raffaella made the sign of the cross. "Father in heaven, bless these men," the priest said.

"They had a run-in with some Indians, and we lost some mules."

"Blackfoot?" Mother Raffaella asked.

"Stone Eagle thinks they were Assiniboine."

Father Rappagliosi shook his head.

Father Imoda came out of the building. "Case, Juneau tells me you've brought me some patients. Are they conscious?" He stepped to the coach.

"Jasper is," Diana said, "but Mr. Pell won't be able to walk. He was shot in the leg and now he's passed out."

"Yes, ma'am. Are you acquainted with the wounded men?"

"No, Father, I am a friend of Mr. Williams."

The priest raised his eyebrows as he looked toward Case. "Juneau, go get the stretcher, and what about you?" he said, addressing Jasper.

"I can walk on my own two legs," Cline said. "I got it in the shoulder."

"Then we'll take care of your friend first."

Pell was put on the stretcher and Dale Hathaway and Juneau carried him into the mission, while Case helped Cline out of the coach. They went to a corner room at the back of the building that Father Imoda used as the infirmary.

Case stood by as the priest looked at Pell. "When did this happen?"

"A couple of days ago," Case said.

"Looks like mortification is trying to set in," the priest said as he took an instrument to probe the wound. "More than likely there are bits of cloth embedded."

Using the probe and a pair of surgical tweezers, Father Imoda removed the bullet from Pell's leg while Cline looked on. Then, using a suction cup, he sucked the pus out of the wound and doused it liberally with carbolic acid.

"That should about take care of him," Father Imoda said as he began binding the wound. Looking toward Cline, he asked, "How about you? Are you ready?"

With both men taken care of, Case went outside to find Diana to thank her for riding with the men. Sitting on a bench in front of the mission, she was brushing her hair, then forming it into a long coiled rope and winding it into a tight chignon. Not a strand was left free. Case smiled. No one would ever be allowed to touch that hair or any other part of her body—not unless it was her idea and she initiated the whole thing.

He thought back to the night when he sat on the log with Maddie and brushed her hair. With Maddie, the action had been spontaneous and without consequence, but instinctively, he knew that wouldn't be the case with Diana—she was much too calculating. Case had been outmaneuvered by one woman, and he swore he would never let that happen again.

"There you are, Case," Diana said as she glanced toward him. "The Sister was so good to lend me a brush. I can't wait to have a long, hot bath and get the dust off."

"She's the mother superior," Case said.

"How can you tell? They all look alike in those long robes."

"Father Imoda thinks Cline and Pell are going to be all right."

"Oh yes. How are the dear men?"

"They're resting. Thank you for taking care of them."

"It wasn't me; it was Dale who soothed them."

Just then, Case heard the approach of the other coach, and he went to meet it.

"You made it, I see."

Dooley squirted a stream of tobacco over the side before he responded. "Well now, tell me, Casey, do you really think I need you sittin' alongside for me to be able to handle this rig?"

Case chuckled. "I wasn't sure, but I knew if the professor was with you, you could do it."

"Mr. Dooley is a fine man," Roy said as he climbed off the box. "The conversation made the time pass quickly."

The door opened and Maddie started to get out.

"Let me help you," Case said, moving to the door.

"You just don't have any confidence in anybody. Not Dooley—not me," Maddie said as she jumped down, but as she did so, the hem of her dress caught on a hook on the side of the coach.

"Now look what you've done," Case said as he stepped over to release her dress. When he looked down, he saw that her legs were exposed all the way up to the ruffles on her drawers. He smiled as he took his time untangling her. She had a habit of exposing those parts of her body that were not intended for public view. And just for the fun of it, he touched her leg. When he did, she jumped, and the action caused her to tear a hole in her dress.

"Now look what you've done," Maddie said.

"Me? What did I do?" Case asked, a look of pure mischief on his face.

"You know exactly what you did," Maddie said as quietly as she could. She tried to get her dress off the hook, but she was only making it worse.

"Allow me, and this time I'm sure I'll get it right." Case lifted the folds of cloth immediately and Maddie stomped off. "Mrs. McClellan?" He offered his hand to Annabelle.

"How are your two dear men? Maddie said they were shot."

"Yes, ma'am, they were, but Father Imoda is an excellent doctor, especially when it comes to removing bullets."

"Oh dear, are they going to live?"

"I think so," Case said. "They're too ornery not to."

Case helped Annabelle, then Annie to the ground. "Come. I'd like you to meet Father Rappagliosi and Mother Raffaella."

"Welcome to St. Peter's Mission," the priest said after the introductions had been made. "And welcome to God's house."

"Thank you," Roy replied. "My family is grateful for your hospitality."

"You are most welcome," Mother Raffaella said. "God's home is always open to His children, no matter what their creed or nationality."

The nun smiled and dipped her head.

"And now, ladies, if you will follow me, I can show you where you may clean up a little, and where you will rest the night."

"Will we be spending the night here?" Diana asked, turning to Case.

"Yes, Father Imoda wants the men to stay overnight, so he can be sure their wounds aren't mortifying."

"You're staying, too, aren't you?" Diana asked.

Case nodded. "Miss Higgins, this layover may be most inconvenient for you and Mr. Hathaway, but Harper has agreed to hold up the coach, if the two of you are amenable to the idea."

Annie smiled. "I'd love to stay if it puts off my arrival in Helena by one more day."

"Annie, what do you mean?" Maddie asked.

"I'm afraid when I think about getting married, I get a little nervous."

"Then, my dear, you are in exactly the right place.

Tonight, when we go to vespers, you can ask God to give you strength," Mother Raffaella said with a broad smile. "Follow me and I'll show you the way to your room."

The nun, Maddie noticed, seemed to be in her early thirties. She was quite attractive, and Maddie wondered about a faith that would be so strong as to bring a pretty young woman to such an isolated place.

"I heard you say 'room.' Where will we be sleeping?" Annie asked.

"You'll be in the dormitory with the children," Mother Raffaella replied.

"Children? What children?" Diana asked.

"The Indian children who live here." Mother Raffaella opened a door that led to a room with a long line of bunks down either side. "Those four beds on the other side of the stove are empty. You'll sleep there tonight. We have dinner at six, vespers at seven."

"Vespers?" Diana asked.

"Yes, evening prayer."

"Do we have to . . . are we expected to attend?" Diana asked.

"Thank you, Mother Raffaella. We will attend," Annabelle said.

As Maddie and the other women followed Mother Raffaella into the building, Case, Roy, Dale Hathaway, and Father Rappagliosi remained outside. Gib Dooley came up to them.

"Case, seein' as we're goin' to spend the night here, me 'n' Harper's goin' to unhitch our teams and turn 'em out into the corral, if that's all right with the padre here."

"Yes, of course, feel free to put them in the corral," Father Rappagliosi said. "You may also feed them some hay."

"Thank you, Father, that's very nice of you," Case said.

"It's the right thing to do," Father Rappagliosi replied. He turned his attention to Roy. "Are you a new arrival to the Territory, Professor McClellan?"

"I suppose you could call me a new arrival. On the other hand, as we haven't yet reached Helena, I haven't actually arrived yet."

"What brings you and your family to Montana?" Father Rappagliosi asked. "You don't seem to be the type of man who has gold fever."

Roy laughed. "You're right about that. My official title is field superintendent for Indian affairs, but I'm not exactly sure what my job will be."

"So, another representative from Washington, and you intend to save the savages from themselves. Is that right?"

"Father, forgive me for saying this, but isn't that more in keeping with what you are doing?"

"I suppose you could say that, but I find I have become very protective of my flock. You say you don't know what your job will be, but surely you were given some guidance from the 'great white father,' as the president is called among the people."

"I'm sorry. I answered your question with flippancy, and it deserved a legitimate answer," Roy said. "My background is in education. I have had a modicum of success in working with our recently emancipated citizens, and I have been charged with employing those same techniques among the Indians."

"May I offer you a word of advice?"

"Most certainly. I want guidance from anyone who has a working understanding of the native cultures."

"Cultures, plural, and that is the operative word," Father Rappagliosi said. "We work primarily among the Blackfoot, but which Blackfoot is it: the Piegan, the Blood, or the Blackfoot proper? They all speak the Siksika language, but each of the three is different."

"There are so many tribes in the Montana Territory, and I am to work among all of them," Roy said. "I'm sure that I have much to learn."

"You certainly do," the priest said. "A good place to start might be with the names our Piegans give to some of the other tribes. The Sioux are the Parted Hair People, the Cheyenne are the Spotted Horse People, the Gros Ventre are the Entrails People, the Crees are the Liars, but the Assiniboine are the Cutthroat People."

"The Cutthroat People? That's the tribe Case thinks ran off the mules."

"The Assiniboine and the Gros Ventre cause the most trouble with our people," Father Rappagliosi said. "That is, if you don't consider what the Indian agents and the army do to them."

"I hope to start an education program. I believe if the Indian tribes are going to survive, they have to assimilate with the white man, and that assimilation must start with the children," Roy said.

"Are you talking about schools?" Case asked.

"Because if you are, what happens to the school that is here at St. Peter's? Will you try and shut it down?"

"Oh no, I would want to build upon what you have already begun," Roy said. "I know that you teach the basics, Father, but I would hope that the agrarian side of education could be expanded."

"I wish you the best," Father Rappagliosi said. "But you must understand that it's going to be difficult for you to win the trust of the people."

"That's exactly why I may request your good offices from time to time. It's my intention to solicit help from as many sources as I can," Roy said. "I want to find out not only what the government thinks the Indians need but what they actually want. And, as nearly as I can, I plan to bridge the difference between those two points of view."

"Good," Father Rappagliosi said. "If that is your goal, I shall do all I can to assist you in achieving it. Now, if you gentlemen will come with me, I'll show you to your accommodations."

"I've been here before, Father, so I know where to go," Case said. "If you will excuse me, I'm going to step back to the infirmary to check on my men."

"Of course," Father Rappagliosi said.

Case could hear singing before he reached the infirmary.

"I know a gal, with a really long nose, her name is Sal, and she has rings on her toes . . ."

The singer was Jasper Cline, and he was keeping time with the music by waving a nearly empty bottle of whiskey.

"I thought Clyde was the only one who had been drinking, but you certainly seem to be in a good mood," Case said.

"Case, have a drink," Cline said, holding out the bottle. "No, you can't have a drink. The good padre here says this is only for"—he paused to say the word very precisely—"medicinal purposes. You got to be shot before you can have a drink. Ain't that right, Padre? You got to be shot?"

"That helps," Father Imoda said.

Cline went back to his singing.

"Sometimes in the moonlight, she dances in the grass, and when she ain't careful, she falls on her . . ." Cline paused before he said the last word and, with a smile, pointed at the priest. "You thought I was goin' to say 'ass,' didn't you? But I stopped just in time."

Father Imoda chuckled. "Yes, just in time."

"How are they doing?" Case asked.

"I believe both will recover with no ill effects, except perhaps a bit of a headache."

"And I'm assuming that's from the bottle, not the bullet," Case said.

"I believe there are times when the Lord looks with favor on the spirits," the priest said. "Many are the times when Jack Daniel's has been my willing assistant. I believe both men will be ready to travel tomorrow."

"Good, I'm glad to hear it."

"You're a good man, Padre," Cline said. "If you ever get to Helena, look me up. Me 'n' you'll go to the Red Star, 'n' I'll buy you a drink."

"Thank you for your kind offer," Father Imoda replied, flashing a broad smile toward Case.

The evening meal was served in a big open room with two extra-long tables flanking each wall. All the men sat at one end of one table and the women and children sat at the other.

Maddie was well pleased with the dinner after eating nothing but meat and hardtack for so many days.

"Juneau does such a good job tending to our garden," one of the nuns said. "We are so blessed to have him with us."

A girl who looked to be no older than ten brought in an oversize bowl and set it before the professor. He helped himself to an ample serving of fresh leaf lettuce, drizzled with a dressing of bacon grease, vinegar, and sugar. Then the bowl was carried to the next man and continued around the table until everyone was served. A much younger child served green onions and red radishes, while another brought in wooden bowls and placed them in front of all the diners. Juneau brought in a pot of asparagus soup and put a ladleful in each of the bowls, and baskets of fresh-baked bread were set on the table.

When the servers were seated a blessing was said, and then everyone began to eat.

The girl who had served the onions and radishes took a place next to Maddie.

"I love the radishes," Maddie said. "Did you help pull them?"

There was no answer.

"Do you work in the garden with Mr. Juneau?"

Still no answer. Maddie was beginning to think the girl didn't understand English, but she was sure she had heard one of the Sisters speaking to the children.

"Do you like being here at the mission?"

It was then that Maddie realized the child was responding to her questions more with facial expressions than with words. By observation, she learned that raised eyebrows meant "yes," and a wrinkled nose meant "no."

It was then that she turned to Mother Raffaella.

"Do the children who attend school live here all the time?"

"We have a few who come in for a few days a week, but these girls live here all the time," she said as she nodded toward the children. "They are all orphans, and this is their home."

"You mean they are nobody's children?" Annie asked.

"Oh, no, dear, I don't mean that at all. They are children of God."

NINE

After dinner, everyone filed into the chapel, where Father Rappagliosi led the service, starting with a reading from the Psalms. Maddie had not attended church since the family had left Washington, and when the prayers were over she wanted to tell the priest how much she enjoyed the service. She found him engaged in conversation with Case and her father.

"Professor, I've been praying about our conversation, and I believe I have come up with a man who can help you, if he will do it."

Case smiled. "Would this man be someone that I know quite well?"

"One and the same, and tomorrow is the day the girls come in to school."

"Does Riley bring them in or do they ride in alone?" Case asked.

"They come by themselves, but perhaps if I sent someone out to his cabin he would come along with them."

"I'll go. I can start tonight."

"I think I'd better send Juneau. If you go to his cabin, he'll have no reason to come back to the mission, and Professor McClellan won't have a chance to speak with him."

"You certainly have aroused my curiosity," Maddie said, interjecting herself into the conversation. "Who is this mysterious Riley?"

"Riley Barnes," Case said. "He's an old mountain man who came to the Rockies more than forty years ago, and for a long time he made a good living. But now buffalo hides are not as plentiful as they once were and the beaver felt hat is no longer fashionable, so he traps for skins that don't bring in as much cash. I'd say he's a little bitter about the loss of his livelihood and about growing old."

"Well, how does he exist?" Maddie asked.

"He does very well, thanks to . . ." Father Rappagliosi looked to Case, but he stopped in mid-sentence.

Maddie was sure she saw Case wrinkle his nose, just as she had seen the little Indian girl do when she had tried to speak to her. She sensed that there was some connection between Case and Riley Barnes, but now wasn't the time to probe.

"If I'm going to ask this gentleman for help, shouldn't I go to him, instead of having him come to me?" Roy asked.

Case laughed and shook his head. "No, no, you don't want to do that. It's best you not approach him alone. Riley doesn't trust the white man."

Roy was surprised by the response. "Oh, I just assumed he was a white man."

"I guess he is one by birth, but he's lived among

and with the Indians for so long, I'm sure he identifies with them more than he does with his own kind. That's why you'd better let him come here if he'll do it. That way, you'd both be on neutral ground, so to speak."

"It sounds like cultivating Mr. Barnes would be an asset for me," Roy said.

"What about the young girls you spoke of? Are they his daughters?" Maddie asked.

"If love makes a child yours, they are his. They are survivors of the Marias River carnage. We are happy to have them with us, but I don't know how long that will be. Now the government has decided that a Protestant denomination will do a better job working among the Blackfoot. So we cannot relocate St. Peter's until the Great Father in Washington tells us we can." Father Rappagliosi was clearly frustrated.

"I assure you, Father, I will try to send your message to Washington once I am settled in," Roy offered. "Or perhaps Maddie should be your advocate. She was a governess for Secretary Smith's daughter and she knows him quite well."

"It would be an honor to have our plea advanced by one as charming as you, my child," Father Rappagliosi said, dipping his head as he addressed Maddie.

"Thank you, Father. It would be my privilege to write on your behalf. How many children are in the school?"

"At one time we had as many as sixty-five, but now we only have sixteen if we count Riley's girls." The priest turned to Case. "I've tried to get that old curmudgeon to let the girls come live with us, but he won't agree to it. And now that Badger Woman has died, poor little Kimi has too much responsibility—taking care of the little ones and taking care of a cantankerous old man, too. It's too much."

"If he comes in tomorrow, I'll talk to him. Maybe between the two of us we can change his mind," Case said.

Just then, they heard the sound of the bell.

"Uh-oh, that's for Maddie," Case said.

Maddie furrowed her brow. "What do you mean, it's for me?"

"You're in the wrong place again. I'll take you back." Case took her hand and began heading for the lamp that was burning at the door by the parish hall.

"The wrong place? How can that be? I'm right here with my father, and what do you mean, 'again'?" she asked as she hurried to keep up with his long stride.

"Were you in the wrong place when the steam donkey fell?"

"If it meant saving you, then the answer is no."

"What about when you scared the mules with your umbrella?"

"They didn't run away."

"And what about when you sat on a log when an Indian could have snuck up on you?"

Maddie didn't answer that question. Was that what he thought? That she was in the wrong place?

"And now, you're the only female who's not safely tucked away in her bed," Case said. "Mother Raffaella is about to lock the door, and then you'd be forced to sleep in the coach again. How would you like that?"

"Would I have to sleep by myself?"

Case stopped short. He put his hands on her shoulders and turned her square to him. In the darkness she could barely make out his features, but she knew he was staring at her.

"Don't ever say that unless you mean it." Case's voice was barely a whisper. He did not speak again until they reached the door.

"Maddie, men are hungry out here, and I don't mean for food. Any man would be proud to have you by his side, but some are not as virtuous as others."

"You mean as virtuous as you."

"You're wrong. I'm not a saint." Case opened the door. "Good night, Maddie."

As Maddie walked through the parish hall there was one lone chimney lamp lit, making her shadow shine large against the wall.

Why did she feel so deflated? She had embraced this new adventure—this new life—with all the gusto she could muster, and yet with every turn she put herself in a position to be reprimanded. By her parents, by her sister, and now even by Case Williams. Why did his rebukes sting the most?

She had always gotten along well with men she had known, whether it was her father's friends, or Mr. Smith, or the men who taught her to handle a horse, but she had always met them on an equal basis—at least, an equal basis in her own mind.

On this trip, she had gone out of her way to be congenial to both men and women on the train, at Fort

Lincoln, and on the *Josephine*. So what had she done to irritate Case? She had let him brush her hair, and then she had let him touch her breasts, but that had not been intentional, and she had been fully clothed. Was that what it was that had disgusted him? Or was it because she had let him kiss her?

And now, what was it tonight that she had done that was so bad? He had said Mother Raffaella would lock the door and make her sleep in the coach. And she had asked if she would sleep alone. That was when his lighthearted banter had stopped.

Don't ever say that unless you mean it. Those were his words. Did he think she was inviting him to sleep with her?

Maddie gasped. That was it! How brazen that must have sounded. She put her hands to her face. How could she ever convince him she hadn't meant that at all?

"Where have you been?" Diana asked.

"I was with Papa and Father Rappagliosi."

"Of course you were. You can't be like everybody else. You have to be right in the middle of everything, especially where there are men involved. Was Case there, too?"

Maddie didn't answer her question. "Tomorrow a man who will be very important to Papa is coming. He's an old mountain man and he's bringing his little girls to school."

"How will that help your father?" Annie asked.

"He's lived with the Indians—with the Blackfoot—for about forty years, and if he likes Papa, he'll help him learn their ways."

"I don't know why Papa would want to do that," Diana said. "He has a job. Indian agents come and go, and I'm hoping he'll decide rather quickly to go back to Washington."

"You didn't have to come," Maddie said. "You were given a chance to stay, and you chose not to."

"And why didn't I? It was because of you."

"Why haven't you ever gotten married?" Annie asked.

Diana was stunned by the question. "I'm not sure I can answer that."

"Has anyone ever asked you?"

"No." Diana said the word very softly.

For the first time, Maddie looked at Diana from a different perspective. Diana exuded an air of confidence and sophistication, especially where men were concerned, but what if inside, that was all done for show. What if Diana was as insecure as she was?

One of the nuns stepped into the long room then, and every little girl rose and stood beside her bed.

"My children, it is time for our prayer for the end of the day. Think about all the things that God has given us, and give thanks. If you have sinned against your neighbor, ask for forgiveness."

With those words every child knelt beside her bed.

Maddie got on her knees too, but she was at a loss. She tried to run down the litany of things that she was thankful for—her parents, her sister, her health—but her mind began to wander. When it came to asking for forgiveness, one face invaded her consciousness. Case Williams. She didn't like for anyone to be upset with her, and particularly not him.

The Sister rang a handbell three times. The little girls rose from the floor and climbed into bed, and not a sound was heard in the room.

Maddy had gone to bed fully dressed. The bed she was in was obviously made for a child. There was barely room for her five-foot-four-inch body to stretch out, and she had to be careful when she turned over, lest she roll off. The bed in the coach had been more comfortable than this.

Would I have to sleep by myself?

"No," she whispered.

She was grateful for the darkened room, because she could feel her face flush with embarrassment. When she had made the comment, she had not been thinking what was now so obvious.

The night by the river was the first time she had ever been kissed, and even now as she thought about it, she could see the fire burning and feel the brush going through her hair. Her hand went to the neck of her dress, the same dress she had been wearing since she left the boat, the same dress the buttons of which Case had closed.

In the dark, she began unbuttoning her dress slowly, lingering over each button as she envisioned Case doing. When she reached the top of her camisole, she found the ribbon and untied it, freeing her breasts to the night air. She touched one bare breast, moving slowly and deliberately. In her mind, it was Case touching her, and that thought caused a moistness to flow from her body. What was happening to her? What had she denied herself?

It was then that she heard her mother stir in her bed.

"Maddie, are you awake?" Annabelle whispered.

"Yes, Mama."

"Did you see a chamber?"

"It's behind the cloth in the corner by the window."

Maddie quickly tied up her camisole and buttoned her dress. All the way to the top. Just as Case had done.

What was she doing? And in a church, at that?

The next morning the Wells Fargo team, the horses fresh from their overnight rest, drew the bright-red coach close to the belfry of the mission. Case, Roy, and Dale Hathaway were already there. Maddie and Diana walked out with Annie to tell her good-bye.

"I just know we'll be good friends in Helena," Diana said. "I hope we live near one another."

Dale Hathaway laughed. "I don't think they'll be any doubt that you'll live close to one another."

"Do you know George White?" Annie asked.

"Yes, I know George. He's a good man," Case said. "He runs the best kiln in town."

Annie glanced toward Maddie with a questioning look on her face.

"I suppose that means a brickyard," Maddie offered.

"No, lime. He came out here looking for gold in the gulch, but he found it in the limestone pits instead."

"Is he rich?" Annie asked.

"He's not a Hauser or a Power, but he's certainly

comfortable," Case said. "Why are you so interested in George White?"

Annie smiled. "Because I'm going to marry him."

"How well do you know him?" Case asked.

Annie hesitated. "I'm going to marry him," she repeated, purposely keeping her answer vague.

"Then you know he's at least fifty years old," Case said.

"Oh, I didn't know that. When I saw him he didn't look that old."

"Annie, are you sure you're doing the right thing?" Maddie asked.

"Why not? If he has money, he'll take care of me."

"Don't you want love?"

Annie shrugged her shoulders.

At that moment, the door opened and Father Imoda stepped out.

"My patients are chomping at the bit to get out of here," he said.

Jasper Cline, with a bandaged shoulder, and Clyde Pell, with a bandaged leg, hobbled out of the mission.

"Thank ya, doc," Cline said, "and thank ya for the spirits."

Father Imoda smiled. "There is another spirit that I usually work with, but I'm pleased that you are able to walk out of here. And if it was Jack Daniel's who helped you do it, I can understand."

"I hate to break this up," Harper said, "but I don't drive for the Diamond R, so you ain't my boss, Case. I gotta answer to Wells Fargo."

"I know," Case said. "I appreciate what you've done. Let's get loaded."

"I'm ready," Pell said.

Annie and Dale Hathaway stood to one side so that the two wounded men could be helped into the coach.

"Dale, you look after these two," Case said.

"You know I will," Hathaway replied as he shook Case's hand. "Professor, ladies, it has been a pleasure meeting you, and I look forward to getting better acquainted when we all get to Helena. And now, Miss Higgins, allow me," he said with a gracious sweep of his arm toward the coach.

Annie hugged both Maddie and Diana. "Thank you for being my friends." Tears were gathering in her eyes when she allowed Dale to help her into the coach.

When everyone was settled, Harper called out to the team, and they were off with a jolt.

"Did you ladies sleep well last night?" Case asked as the coach drove away.

"Yes," Maddie said, not addressing her disquieting thoughts.

"The beds were obviously built for little people," Diana said. "I didn't get to stretch my legs out at all."

"You could have had my bed," Case said.

A bemused smile crossed Diana's face. "And where would you have slept?"

Maddie glanced quickly toward Case to see how he would respond. It was, after all, no less risqué than what she had asked.

Unlike his response to her question last night, Case's answer was without censure. "In the barn, with Dooley and Harper," he said.

Case pointed toward a line of horses in the distance. "Here come Riley and the girls."

Maddie looked where Case was pointing, and saw five horses following single file through the greening grass.

"How many children are there?"

"Five little girls." Case was smiling as he followed their approach.

"Who are these children?" Diana asked.

"I consider them my nieces."

"Your nieces?"

"Yes. When they came to live with Riley and Badger Woman, I felt privileged to be considered a part of the family."

"Didn't I hear Father Rappagliosi say Badger Woman died?" Roy asked. "Surely that old man doesn't take care of five children all by himself."

"It wasn't so hard until Petah left this spring. She married a Mountie and went to the Dominion," Case said. "I know Riley depended on her, but Kimi is doing the best she can."

"And how old is Kimi?" Maddie asked.

"We don't really know. Blackfoot don't set much store in keeping track of ages. All we know is that Riley got the girls five years ago."

"I think it's admirable that Mr. Barnes puts them in school. But it seems strange that he doesn't put them in the boarding school, when it is apparently so close to his home," Roy said.

"Riley may be a cantankerous old man, but where the girls are concerned, he's very softhearted. When you get to know him, you'll understand."

"Here they are," Father Imoda said as the horses turned into the mission lane.

Maddie saw Juneau riding just to the side of an old man with white hair and a white beard as the two led the little cavalcade. Close behind them was a girl whom she would guess was eleven or twelve, and sitting behind her was a child who was much smaller. Next was a pony carrying two girls who looked so much alike, they could have been twins. And behind them was one girl who rode alone. Immediately, Maddie identified with this child.

The others were wearing beautifully beaded dresses made from tanned hides, and their hair had been carefully braided.

The child riding alone had fallen a good twenty yards behind the others, and she was wearing a faded calico dress. Her hair was messy and unkempt. Instinctively, Maddie touched her own braid. While it was braided, it had wisps of hair separating from the main plait.

Maddie smiled. Yes, this child was going to have a friend.

"Why didn't you let a body know you was in these parts?" the old man asked as he slowly dismounted.

"I did let you know," Case said as he extended his hand. "Why do you think I sent Juneau to get you?"

"It's a trick. You want me to meet some government man," Riley said. He looked at Roy with contempt. "Is this here'n the one?"

"It is. This is Professor Roy McClellan."

"McClellan. That's not a good name. Even in the backwoods, we know what you done in the war.

Lincoln had to fire ya 'cause ya couldn't get the job done."

"Sir, I'm a professor, not a general."

"Don't be callin' me no sir. Out here you gain respect by your actions, not your fancy words, so now tell me what you're aimin' to do."

"I want to do what's right for the Indians. And I need your help."

"I'm an old man. I've seen a lot of agents come and go, and each one makes a bigger mess than the one before. You might say you want to do right, but as soon as you get a chance to cheat the Indian, you will."

Roy didn't comment.

"Riley, you're not being fair," Case said. "I've spent some time with Professor McClellan, and I'm convinced that he intends to change things for the better."

"It'll never change."

"You have to at least give it a chance."

"If you're speakin' for him, I'll at least give it a chance."

"That's all I ask."

Case looked over to where the girls were standing. Right in the middle of them was Maddie. She was down on her knees, and the children were touching her hair and her face. How had she made friends with them so quickly?

"Why don't you wear a black robe like the other Sisters?" one of the little girls asked.

"Because I'm not a nun."

"Are you going to be our teacher?"

"No, I'm not. I'm not going to live here."

"Where do you live?"

"I'm going to live in Helena."

"Are you going to live with Uncle Case?"

"No, honey, I'm not."

"How come?"

"Because I have to live with my papa, just like you live with your papa."

"Is he old?"

"Yes."

"Is he going to die?"

"Someday, he will."

"Our mamas died. Our mamas died two times."

"It looks to me like you've made some new friends," Case said as he joined the group. "Did she tell you her name is Maddie?"

"Maddie. That's a funny name. Are you mad at Uncle Case?"

"No, but I have two names. My name is Madelyn and my other name is Maddie."

"Just like Uncle Case. His other name is Josiah." The girls began to snicker.

"Oh, I didn't know that," Maddie said as she looked up at Case.

"There's a lot you don't know about me," Case said as the corners of his mouth began to curl upward. "Did the girls introduce themselves?"

"Not yet. We were just talking."

"This is Kimi, and she's the mother of the family. Koko is the baby, and Nuna and Pana are inseparable. And this is Kanti. She walks to a different drumbeat."

"Don't say that, Uncle Case," Kanti said as she pursed her lips. "I go everywhere my sisters go."

"Of course you do," Maddie said as she drew the little girl to her and smoothed her hair. "That just means you're unique."

Kanti frowned. "I don't know that word."

"It means you're special, and I want to be your friend," Maddie said.

Kanti threw her arms around Maddie. "I like you. Don't you like her, Uncle Case?"

"Yes, I do."

"Then you should make her your *aakii*."

Case laughed with a deep rumble. "Not so fast, little one." He picked her up and hugged her. "We'd better go inside before Mother Raffaella comes after us. Who's going to get to the door first?"

He took off at a run carrying Kanti as the others ran along behind him.

Maddie watched as a knot began to form in her throat. What a beautiful picture Case and the girls made. There was no question of his masculinity, and yet she had just witnessed a side of him that was so unexpected.

Moving away from the building, Maddie walked toward a copse of trees and found a well-worn trail. The trail led to a grotto, where she saw Mother Raffaella sitting on a crude bench in front of a small pool. Not wanting to disturb her, Maddie started to turn away.

"Come, sit with me, my child."

Maddie was surprised that the nun had been aware that she was there.

"I'm sorry. I don't want to intrude, especially when you are in prayer."

"My every waking hour is a prayer," Mother Raffaella said. "I come out here every morning to marvel at God's handiwork and to give thanks. Please, come and join me." She moved over to make room on the bench.

Maddie joined her and for several minutes they sat quietly.

Mother Raffaella broke the silence.

"You are troubled?"

"I'd say more confused than troubled. I don't know who I am or what I'm supposed to do. I've always thought of myself as someone who relates more to men than to women. It's easier to talk to a man, because men talk about interesting things like horses, or politics, or business. It seems like women talk about nothing at all, and they just keep that conversation going on and on.

"But now I'm wondering if I'm wrong. I watch my sister, and she can talk to anyone, especially a man, and they all seem to enjoy it. She talks and they listen. No matter how frivolous the conversation, they listen. I can't relate to men like that. I think men see me as one of their own, a 'hail fellow, well met' so to speak. It's never bothered me before, but now . . ."

"But now you want Mr. Williams to see you differently."

Maddie looked sharply at the mother superior. How could she have guessed that? "Yes. I don't know if he is the right man."

"Don't despair, Maddie. If he is the right man, you will find a way to talk to him. It will all work out."

"Mother Raffaella, did you have a right person before . . . ?"

"It was a long time ago." She smiled wistfully.

"Alexander Cooper. We were to be married, but we decided to wait until he came home from the war—but that was never to be. He was killed at Pittsburg Landing."

"I'm sorry," Maddie said as she placed her hand on Mother Raffaella's.

"I had never known such pain. I thought I would never get over it. But somehow, through prayer, and through dedicating myself to serving the Lord, my heart was healed."

"That's why you became a nun."

"The name Raffaella means 'God has healed.' I chose that name when I took my vows, because I thought it was particularly appropriate."

"Raffaella isn't your real name?"

"It is my real name. It just isn't the one I was born with. My birth name was Elizabeth Bancroft." Mother Raffaella chuckled. "I say the name Elizabeth sometimes, just so I won't forget it. But now, it's almost like Elizabeth is a young girl I once knew."

"Are you happy?"

"My work gives me great joy, especially when I can touch the lives of children. Outwardly, you can't see the pain our girls have suffered, and even though the children who live with Mr. Barnes endured the same tragedy, they are not as scarred. They have known unconditional love—from that crusty old man who wants everyone to think he is so tough and mean, and also from Mr. Williams."

"I saw how Case treated the girls. It was very heartwarming."

"Maddie, I don't know your heart, and I don't know what it's telling you to do, but when it does say something, listen to it. Don't be distracted by anyone, or anything."

"Thank you, Elizabeth. I won't."

Mother Raffaella smiled and then rose from the bench. "Sit here for a while. This is a wonderful place to listen."

Maddie watched as she walked away, wondering why she had called her Elizabeth instead of Mother Raffaella. Then she realized why. It wasn't Raffaella but Elizabeth who had listened to her heart and made the decision that changed her life forever.

People can change; Mother Raffaella was proof of that. Perhaps Maddie could change as well. Perhaps she could put aside her protective shell. Until now she had looked upon Diana's suggestions as unwelcome criticisms. But if she were to be honest with herself, she would have to admit that Diana might be right. She wanted a husband and a family someday, but her challenging personality might be making that impossible.

TEN

After the McClellans said good-bye to everyone at the mission the next morning, the coach pulled out just after daybreak. In spite of the rough road through Prickly Pear Canyon, the change of horses, plus having to stop six times to let freight wagons pass on their way to Fort Benton, they were able to reach Helena in the still light of a late afternoon.

As the coach approached, Maddie could see the town tucked in the valley of a steep ravine. The streets seemed to have no apparent direction, following the course of a gulch for a little while, and then suddenly going around a building or a mound of dirt and leaping to one side only to stop abruptly.

The town itself was a conglomerate of buildings. Some were as modern as anything she would have seen in Washington—built of brick or stone and multistoried, while others were small log cabins, some with sod roofs. There were also several tents interspersed among the more permanent constructions.

As the coach made its way through the melee, Maddie saw oxen and mules hitched to freight wagons and horses standing at hitching rails or pulling carriages. There seemed to be people—that is, men—everywhere. Only occasionally did she see a woman.

The coach eventually stopped in front of the International Hotel, an impressive four-story brick building that appeared to be brand-new. It had an upstairs balcony that doubled as the roof of the downstairs porch. There was a young woman sitting out on the balcony, and as they arrived, the woman walked out to the railing and called down to the coach.

"Diana! Maddie! Hello!"

Case jumped down from the box and opened the door for his passengers.

"I hear someone calling your names," he said, "and you haven't even set foot on the ground yet."

"You're just saying that, Case," Diana said as she stepped into his arms. "No one knows us here."

"That's where you're wrong." He pointed up to the balcony.

"It's Annie," Maddie said as she jumped down from the coach and returned Annie's enthusiastic wave.

"I'm so glad you're here. I'll be right down," Annie said, and disappeared from the balcony.

"Let me be the first to say welcome to Helena," Case said. "I know you're going to be an asset to the town."

When Maddie turned around, she noticed that Diana's hand was resting on Case's arm.

"You have been most helpful," Diana said.

"My daughter's right. We can't thank you enough for getting us, here, Case," Roy said. "And if you don't mind, I'd like to call upon you to give us some direction in finding a place to live. Also, I'm to establish my headquarters here, so I'll need an office."

"I don't think either of those requests will be that difficult to fill."

Just then, Annie came running out the door.

"You don't know how happy I am to see you," she said as she embraced Maddie and then Annabelle. "Will you be living here at the International?"

"I suppose we will, for a while," Maddie said.

"You'll like it," Case said. "It's the nicest hotel in town. Dooley, you see that the McClellans get settled. I've got to get over to the Diamond R."

"I'll take care of 'em, boss."

"And where is the Diamond R?" Diana asked. "In case we need you."

Case pointed toward an open field that could be seen in the distance. "Do you see all those grazing oxen? We're right in front of them."

"That's a long way," she said. "We could let Dooley take you and then come back."

Case flashed a smile. "I'll pick up my horse at the livery right around the corner. Dandy probably thinks I've abandoned him."

Roy extended his hand. "Again, I want to express my thanks to you and the Diamond R."

"It has been my pleasure." Case looked at Roy for an instant and then turned to Diana. "I know this trip has been especially trying for you. All I ask is that you give Helena a chance. I know you're going to love it here."

"That means a lot, coming from you, Case."

Case did not acknowledge Maddie, and it almost seemed that he did it intentionally. He turned and strode away quickly.

Maddie was disappointed, but she covered it up by addressing Annie.

"You'll have to tell us all about Mr. White. Is he just the way you remembered him?" she asked.

Annie chewed her lip, then looked away.

"I've not seen him yet."

"What! Does he know you're here?"

"Yes, Dale went out to Nelson Gulch to where his kiln is, but he's busy."

"Too busy to meet the woman he's going to marry?" Maddie asked.

Annie smiled. "It's all right. It seems it's quite complicated to make lime. If you put too much lime-stone in the kiln and don't fire it exactly right, the whole thing collapses and all your work is done for nothing, so Mr. White didn't want to leave until the quicklime was formed."

Maddie laughed. "You certainly have learned a lot about this business in such a short time."

"I've had a good teacher," Annie said. "Mr. Hatha-way has told me a lot about Helena. Do you know the population is close to thirty-five hundred, and there are only about five hundred women?"

"Just five hundred women?" Diana asked, a big smile forming on her face. "No wonder Case was so nice to me. If there are so few, a single woman can pick and choose who she wants to entertain."

Annie put her hand to her mouth. "Don't say that, Diana. Several of the women entertain—for money."

"That just makes it better for me. A man can recognize quality when he sees it."

At that same moment, just around the corner from the hotel, Case was stepping into Dr. Reece's office.

Dr. Reece was a skinny man with a prominent Adam's apple and thick glasses.

"Good evening, Case, I thought I might see you," Dr. Reece said.

"Did Jasper and Clyde stop by?"

"They did, and they're both healing nicely," Dr. Reece said. "I couldn't have done a better job myself. Whoever took the bullets out knew what he was doing."

"It was Father Imoda."

"Oh yes, the priest up at St. Peter's. He does a good job. You might want to give Jasper a day or two off, but it'll probably take Clyde a week or so to get back on his feet."

"All right, thanks, Doc."

Case's next stop was the livery, where he picked up Dandy; then he rode off to the Diamond R.

When he walked in, he was greeted by his friend and business partner, Charles Broadwater.

"Well, look what the cat drug in," Charles said. "Sam and I thought you went off and left us."

"It was an interesting trip," Case said.

"That's what I just heard. Dooley stopped by before he put the coach away, and of course Jasper and Clyde told me about the Indian raid."

"I hate to think we're going to be sending oxen up to Benton on every wagon, but I don't want to lose forty mules very many times," Case said.

"I'd rather lose mules than men. Down on the Yellowstone, a Sioux party attacked some prospectors and killed one of them."

"Sitting Bull, Crazy Horse, Rain in the Face," Case said. "They're roaming all over the territory, and they're doing as they please."

"I know what you think of Colonel Baker, Case, but somebody needs to do to these Indians what he did to the Blackfoot. You don't find Blackfoot killing and marauding anymore."

"Could it be because there are so few men?"

"I'm sorry I brought it up," Charles said. "So what did Hughes do with his train?"

"I pulled the oxen from Palmer Crab's train and sent them up. I figured it was better to leave ore at the crossing than to leave supplies."

"Ha," Charles said. "I'm sure the mule skinners loved that."

"What's their alternative?"

"Oh, I didn't ask about the professor and his family. How were the little girls?" Charles had a big grin on his face.

"You knew all the time, didn't you?" Case demanded.

"I can't say that I did. When you got the job, I thought they were children, but Dooley says one of them is a real looker."

"I'd say Dooley is right," Case said, a lazy smile crossing his face.

"Uh-oh, has the most eligible bachelor in Helena been smitten?"

"Don't jump to any conclusions and don't tell Julia. She'll be telling everybody she knows I'm ready to tie the knot."

"And what's wrong with that? You've had plenty of time to get over Mary Beth," Charles said. "It's not right for a man to go through life without a good woman."

"I've got plenty of time. You didn't find Julia until you were thirty-three. By your standards, I've got two more years."

"But how often does a beautiful young woman fall in your lap? And since you saw her first, you should get first dibs."

"Don't you think"—Case hesitated, because he truly didn't know which name to supply—"the young woman should have something to say about all this?"

"All I can say is, if you can tolerate her at all, don't let her get away. Not many acceptable ones come our way. You are a successful businessman now, Case. No, I would say it is more than that. You are an exceptionally successful businessman. I think it's time you were married. It will help settle you down . . . and it would be good for business."

"I wasn't aware that I needed to be settled down. And if and when I ever get married, it won't be for business reasons."

"It will be because you are in love with the woman, right?"

"Well, yes, that would seem to be the reasonable approach, don't you think?"

"No, it isn't reasonable at all."

"What in the world would make you say something like that? Are you saying you didn't marry Julia for love? Because I know that isn't true. You love Julia."

"Yes, I do love Julia. But"—Charles held up his finger—"that wasn't the deciding factor. The simple truth, Case, is that love itself isn't reason enough to marry anyone. What is love? It's emotion, right? And emotion, my boy, doesn't go very deep. You need reason as well. You need to ask yourself this question: Will your wife be good for you, personally and professionally? If Julia did not fit that bill perfectly, believe me, I would have never married her."

"That seems to me to be a pretty cold way of looking at marriage."

"Were you in love with Mary Beth Sullivan?"

"What?"

"It's a simple enough question. Were you in love with Mary Beth Sullivan?"

Case hesitated before he responded. "Well, yes, of course. That is, at least I thought I was."

"You thought you were. And so, tell me, how did that turn out?"

"You know how it turned out. I tell you what. You and Julia hurry up and have a daughter. I'll wait around until she's old enough, and then I'll marry her. What could possibly be a better business move than to marry your partner's daughter?" Case teased.

"The hell you will! What makes you think I would want you as a son-in-law? You stay away from my daughter!"

"You don't have a daughter."

"Well, you just stay away from the daughter I don't have, you hear me? I'd better not see you prowling around my daughter, even if I don't have one."

"So much for marrying for business reasons, right, Charles?" Case laughed.

"The very idea of you as my son-in-law makes me shudder," Charles said, joining Case in laughter.

"I'd better go round up the oxen for tomorrow's train," Case said, and, tossing a wave over his shoulder, he left the office. He thought about what Charles had said. Did he really need a wife?

If so, it would certainly not be for business reasons. He had more money than he'd ever hoped to earn; he had Ho Kwan, who took care of his house and garden when he was gone; he had Riley and the girls when he needed a family, and there were more than enough women on Bridge Street to satisfy his sexual needs.

No, he liked his life the way it was. There would be no wife in his future—Mary Beth had soured him on that prospect from now on. He would be perfectly content to live out the rest of his life as a bachelor.

Professor McClellan was able to secure two adjacent rooms for his family, but when the hotel clerk asked how long he would need them, he was unable to answer.

"If we can, I'd like to stay here until we find a place to live," he said.

"I'm sure we can accommodate you. It isn't often that we have three lovely young ladies staying with us." He looked directly at Diana. "If you need anything, my name is Adam Howe, and you just ask."

"Thank you, Mr. Howe," Diana said. "Your hotel is as fine as any we have stayed in during our entire journey."

"We try. Let me show you to your rooms." He grabbed one of the bags and started up the steps. "I believe you are on the second floor, not far from Miss Higgins."

"Wonderful," Diana replied, her smile frozen in place.

"How can you do that?" Maddie asked when they were safely out of anyone's earshot.

"Do what?"

"You know what I'm talking about. Smile all the time. Don't you ever feel like a fake?"

"Of course not. This is the best hotel we've stayed in," Diana said.

"It's because it's the only one," Maddie said, "but that's not what I mean. Every man you see, you act like he's—"

"He's what? Someone special?" Diana asked.

"It's not fair to the men. You know they don't mean anything to you."

"I'm going to marry a rich man, Maddie, and what better place to find one than at a place called Last Chance Gulch? And even though most of the gold mines are already played out, do you have any idea how much money came out of this place?"

"No, I don't," Maddie answered.

"Sixteen million dollars. That's how much."

"I don't believe you, and anyway, how would you know this?"

"Mr. Hathaway was a wealth of information."

"If you knew this, why did you flirt with Case, and now the poor hotel clerk?"

A cynical smile crossed Diana's face. "Mr. Hathaway didn't tell me where all the money wound up. And anyway, what determines if a man is rich? Did you see how many Diamond R trains we met on the way here? Case Williams fits my definition of rich."

"And Mr. Howe?"

"Who?"

"The hotel clerk."

"Oh, I was just practicing," Diana said as she opened the bag the man had deposited in their room.

The hotel had a bathing room, and Maddie was more than happy to wait her turn to enjoy it. True to his word, Adam Howe was doing everything he could to make their stay at the International a pleasant one. The water from Diana's bath had been emptied, and plenty of hot water had been poured into the big copper tub.

Quickly, Maddie stepped out of her clothing and, leaving it in a heap on the floor, slid into the tub.

Settling back, she lay there for several minutes letting the water wash over her body. Closing her eyes, she imagined herself in some exotic paradise, frolicking in a pool with endless warm water tumbling from a waterfall. And stepping out from the waterfall was a man, a Prince Charming.

With a jolt, she sat upright. The man she was imagining was Case Williams, and he was as naked as she.

She took a deep breath and settled back into the water. This was not good. A respectable young woman did not fantasize about naked men. Grabbing the soap, she began tearing off the paper. Stamped on the bar was the image of Aphrodite of Rhodes, and the scent was that of wild roses. She brought the soap to her nose and inhaled the sweet aroma.

Aphrodite, the Greek goddess of love, pared with Adonis the god of beauty and desire.

Madelyn McClellan pared with Josiah Case Williams.

She smiled. It sounded like she was writing an announcement for a wedding.

Wetting the soap, she began lathering her body— first her arms, then her legs, lifting them one at a time from the warm water. When she started on her chest, she noticed that her nipples were erect, having hardened into tight little buds.

Releasing the soap, she cupped her breasts. Thinking back to the crossing, she remembered how Case had touched her. At first she had tried to convince herself it might have been an accident, but as she thought back, she knew that was not true. He had touched her because he wanted to, and then he had kissed her.

Adonis. The statue of Adonis with his male member exposed. Was that what Case looked like? She had never seen a man undressed, and imagining Case's head on the statue of Adonis was stimulating. Her body began to pulsate, a feeling that was heretofore unknown to her.

Picking up the soap again, she looked at the now

fading cut of Aphrodite. The goddess was kneeling on one knee while she spread her hair. Maddie separated her own braid, and the moisture from the room, together with her hair's natural tendency to curl, made her think she could be a model for this famous statue.

Getting up on one knee, she imitated the pose, but when she looked down at her own breasts, they were lacking.

Maddie couldn't help but compare herself to her sister, and the comparison left her wanting. Diana had full, well-rounded breasts; Maddie had small ones. Diana's waist accentuated the flare of her hips and derriere, where Maddie's bottom barely had a curvature. The word that best described Diana was *voluptuous*, while Maddie's form was slender and athletic, some would say almost boyish.

There was no comparison. If Case was interested in either of the McClellan girls, Maddie knew there was no contest. She had lived in the shadow of Diana her whole life, and she had learned to compensate. Instinctively, she developed a separate identity, a personality distinctive from that of her sister, but now she had to ask herself if she had done too good of a job. Would Case—would any man—ever find her attractive?

She stepped out of the tub, with water beads clinging to her nymphlike naked form, completely unaware of what a beautiful picture she actually made.

Case and some of his men were moving oxen from the field into the barn. He couldn't stop thinking about what Charles had said. The last thing Case wanted to do was give up his independence. Charles said he needed to be married for business reasons. The Diamond R was in the business of hauling freight, and because of him, the company had grown exponentially.

How would having a wife improve that?

If he did settle on one of the McClellan sisters, which one would it be?

At first thought, it should be Diana. She was a beautiful woman, one any man could be proud to say was his wife, and she certainly had let Case know she was interested in him by her obvious flirtations. But was there anything beyond that?

Then there was Maddie. He couldn't quite figure Maddie out. She was attractive . . . and if he was honest with himself, he would have to say that in her own way, she was as pretty as her sister. Diana projected her femininity, while Maddie seemed to go out of her way to hide hers.

And yet when he had kissed Maddie, he knew she had responded to him. And even now when he thought about that response, he felt a familiar quiver.

If he'd had to make a choice right now, he would have said he was leaning toward Maddie. There was something about her that attracted him, something that told him she would make him a good wife.

"Hell, Case, get a hold of yourself." He slapped his legs hard against Dandy, making the horse jump forward. "You ain't gettin' hitched—not now—not never!" The sound of the scores of oxen he and his men were moving covered the sounds of Case talking to himself, sparing him the embarrassment of being overheard.

"Case, where are you?" one of the bullwhackers called. "Ain't it about time we put a stop to this here cattle drive?"

"Yeah, I guess I was thinking about something else. Let's put these babes in the barn. Make sure they've got plenty of water before we start 'em out tomorrow," Case said. "We'll leave at first light."

"'We'? You ain't gonna go back up north, are ya? Ya just got home. Don't you ever get tuckered out?"

Case smiled. "Not this time. Anyway, I want to keep Cut Lip Jack in line."

"Ya don't need to be watchin' out for me, boss. I can outride you any day of the week," the man called Cut Lip Jack replied.

Maddie and Diana were in their mother's room, and Maddie was standing at the window, looking down onto Main Street.

"How many more houses will we have to look at before you find one you'll take?" Diana huffed. "We've been cooped up in this hotel for over a week."

"The right one will come along," Annabelle said. "Just be thankful we're in such a new hotel where the rooms are pleasant and the cuisine is absolutely superb."

"Mr. Howe says this hotel should be called the Phoenix instead of the International," Maddie said.

"Why would he say that?" Diana asked.

"Because it's burned down so many times. He

said when we do get a house, we should make sure it's out of the gulches."

"That's good to remember, but right now, I'd like you girls to run an errand for me," Annabelle said as she moved to the desk. "I have several pieces of mail I'd like to post."

"Good," Diana said. "Anything to get out of this room."

Annie joined Diana and Maddie as they walked along Main Street, where one store after another had either just been built or was being rebuilt. Last year's fire had wiped out more than 150 buildings and had cost the community close to $900,000 in damages, but the resiliency of the people of Helena had allowed the city to rise from the ashes. This time, the buildings were being made of stone or brick.

"Do you see all these new buildings?" Annie asked. "All of them need mortar to hold them together, and do you know what makes mortar? Lime. Mr. White is making so much money."

"Is that why he doesn't have time to marry you?" Maddie asked.

Annie shrugged her shoulders. "It doesn't matter."

"You are nineteen and he's how old?"

"Fifty-three."

"That's perfect," Diana said before Maddie could respond. "If he's that much older than she is, he won't care what she does, and if he's rich, he won't care how much money she spends."

"I just can't understand either one of you," Maddie said. "Neither of you ever mentions anything about love. Isn't that important?"

"You silly goose, of course not. Nobody even knows what love is," Diana said.

"I think I know," Maddie said.

"You don't either. It's not what you read in books. Don't you think Mama and Papa have had a good life together?"

"Of course."

"But yet Mama didn't say she loved Papa. Annie doesn't need love—all she needs is a nice home and nice clothes and plenty of money," Diana said. "And if Mr. White insists, she can have his child, but I for one don't want any part of that. If I ever get married, I'm going to put my foot down—no children. All I have to do is think of that poor woman we met on the boat. I know she's not much older than I am, and yet she looked like a worn-out old hag. No, there'll be no kids in my marriage, and Annie is smart to choose an older man, because maybe he won't expect much."

"Surely you don't mean that, Diana. You wouldn't want to have a family?" Maddie asked in disbelief.

"No. I want a man who can give me a nice house and nice clothes and take me to exotic places all over the world."

"I can't believe you actually mean this. It's all about the money."

"Of course! Why else would a woman get married?"

"What about for love? I'll never marry a man if I don't know he loves me."

"Love," Diana repeated scoffingly. "You read too much poetry, Maddie."

"Love isn't something writers just created. Love is real, or else how could they write about it in the first place?"

"You are a hopeless romantic, Maddie," Diana said dismissively.

Maddie didn't answer, but she thought of Case Williams. If she married him, it would be for love, and no other reason.

Marry Case Williams? Where had that thought come from? Maddie felt herself blush and was glad Annie and Diana weren't looking directly at her.

Then, as they approached the post office, Maddie saw the very person who was occupying her thoughts.

"Oh, there's Case," Annie said.

Diana turned quickly. "Where?"

"He just went into the post office."

"Wonderful. Since we're going there too, I'll have a chance to speak to him," Diana said. "There's no doubt Case Williams comes up to my standards."

"Isn't he a little young for you?" Maddie asked.

Diana laughed. "For that man, I'll make an exception. Handsome and rich trumps old anytime."

"What do you do if he doesn't know you want him?" Annie asked.

"That's not a problem," Diana said as a smug expression crossed her face. "This should be a good lesson for both of you. Just watch what happens to our Mr. Williams when I turn on the charm. Follow me."

ELEVEN

When they stepped into the post office a moment later, they saw Case, with a handful of envelopes in his hand, standing in front of the window, talking with the postmaster.

"Why, Case Williams, imagine seeing you here," Diana said, as she approached him. Her wide smile showed perfect teeth as she stared up at him through long eyelashes.

"Diana," Case said, returning her smile.

"Where have you been? Why, it's been weeks. I've missed seeing you." She put her hand on his arm.

Case chuckled. "It's only been one week, and I had to take the oxen up to the stranded wagons at the crossing."

Diana furrowed her brow. "Case, don't tell me you had to do that? I know you could have snapped your fingers and one of your—what do you call them?—would have done your bidding."

"My bullwhackers?"

Diana laughed a lilting laugh. "I love that word. It conjures up such images in my mind."

Case broke the contact with Diana's gaze. Turning to the man behind the window, he said, "I'm sure you've met Isaac Crounse. He's the postmaster here."

"No, sir, I have not. I am Diana McClellan, and I do hope you'll remember my name." She extended her hand.

"I know I won't forget you, Miss McClellan. Are you new to our fair city?"

"I am," Diana said, this time taking Case by the arm. "Mr. Williams made our family's trip so much easier. He got us across the river when no one else could, and he kept us safe from Indians. I don't know what we would have done without him."

"Speaking of your family, where's Maddie?" Case asked.

"Why, Case, she's right over there," Diana said pointing to the door. "And so is Miss Higgins. You do remember her."

Case spun around, disentangling his arm from Diana's hold.

Maddie raised her eyebrows and, without lifting her arm, gave a halfhearted wave.

"It's good to see both of you," Case said, moving away from Diana. "Are you still at the International?"

"We are," Diana said, reinserting herself into the conversation. "Maddie, don't forget to mail Mother's letters."

Maddie smiled. Mother's letters. Diana had never

called her anything but "Mama." Perhaps she thought "Mother" sounded more dignified. She stepped to the window and placed the mail on the counter.

"I have ten letters, Mr. Crounse."

"That will be sixty cents. Are you Diana's sister?"

"Yes, I'm Maddie. Do you have any incoming mail for McClellan?"

The postmaster began checking the pigeonholes that were behind the counter as Maddie watched Case and Diana leave the building. Annie stayed behind to wait for her.

"Well, did we learn anything?" Annie asked.

"I'm not sure," Maddie said. "But one thing is for certain. She walked out with a man and I'm walking out with you." Both women laughed.

When they reached the hotel, Diana was out on the balcony, waiting for them.

"How can you do that?" Maddie asked.

"How can I do what?"

"How can you just go up to a man and start a conversation like that. That isn't very ladylike, is it?"

"Maddie, you don't have to be a shy, gray mouse to be a lady."

"But to be so aggressive?"

"You don't understand," Diana said. "The trick is not to be aggressive. The trick is to present yourself in such a way that it allows the man to be aggressive."

As Maddie thought about what she had witnessed at the post office, she realized that she didn't consider Case's behavior aggressive. What she had seen was Case's attempt to escape.

๛

"Anything interesting in the mail?" Charles asked when he saw Case come into the office.

"Not much," Case said, slitting open an envelope. "I probably need to take a run over to Bozeman. Mrs. Shedd's accusing us of shorting her twenty-eight cases of Kentucky bourbon."

"Well, did we?"

"It was on the manifest, and I personally checked the wagon," Case said. "You know how that woman squeezes a dime out of every penny she touches."

"Just goes to prove my point. There wouldn't be a James Thompson Shedd if there wasn't a Mrs. Shedd behind him. Which reminds me, what are you doing about the McClellan girls?"

"For one thing, I don't call them girls."

"You know what I mean. Have you seen them?"

"As a matter of fact, yes. I just ran into both of them at the post office."

"And?"

"And what? They mailed their letters—I picked up our mail. What else do you do at the post office?"

Charles shook his head. "I guess I'm going to have to take action to get you off your duff, and you know what that means."

"No. Don't get her involved," Case said emphatically.

"It's too late. Julia's already planning a get-together, just a little something to introduce the McClellans to the community."

"Good, have her do it while I'm gone to Bozeman."

"Don't you dare disappoint my wife," Charles called as Case headed for the door.

Later that afternoon, Roy McClellan came into the family's room at the hotel with a copy of the *Daily Independent*.

"Ladies, I think I've found our house." Roy laid a copy of the paper in front of Annabelle. "I just met Mr. Barret, the new editor of the *Independent*. This was the house he was going to take, but his wife found another one she likes better, so it's for sale."

"Oh, Roy, should we buy a house?" Annabelle asked.

"Why not?"

"It makes this move seem so permanent."

Roy was quiet for a moment. "Don't you like it here?"

"I'm not sure. The girls . . . don't you think they'd be happier back East?"

"I accepted this position, and I intend to fulfill my duties in regard to it. If you want to leave, I'll purchase return passage for you tomorrow."

Annabelle took a deep breath. "Let's go see the house."

"Mr. Hoyt, from the real estate company, will be here at three o'clock."

"This is one of the largest houses in town, Mrs. McClellan, right here on Madison Avenue," Mr. Hoyt said. "And with Mount Helena right behind you, why, you've got a beautiful spot."

"I see the fire tower," Maddie said. "Did houses burn up here?"

"Ma'am, when the wind picks up the embers, no house is safe. Earth, wind, water, fire—that's what we've all been promised by God Almighty, and there's not much we can do about it. Here we are," he said as he stopped the carriage in front of a big redbrick house.

"Oh, my," Annabelle said enthusiastically. "You weren't exaggerating, Mr. Hoyt. This house is beautiful."

"Then you'll stay," Roy said matter-of-factly.

"I think so—that is, if Diana and Maddie agree."

It was a two-story house, with round turrets and sweeping porches. It had a portico where a carriage could unload out of the elements, and a carriage house behind a landscaped yard that followed the natural incline of Mt. Helena.

"The carriage house has a nice room over the top, which would provide adequate quarters for a valet, should you want one," Hoyt pointed out.

When they opened the front door of the house, they stepped into an entrance with polished wood floors and wide crown molding. The parlor was off from the hall, a huge room with a hanging gas chandelier and a carved oak mantel over the bricked fireplace. The dining room was large, with a window seat inset that looked out onto a tasteful, though slightly smaller, house next door.

"I say we take it," Diana said before they even explored any more of the house.

"Papa, can we afford it?" Maddie said almost in a whisper.

"If it makes your mother and your sister happy, we'll make do. I understand that it's quite common for people to take in boarders, and Mr. Barret says he'll run an advertisement for free if we'll take this house off his hands."

"Do we really want strange people living in our house?"

"We won't have to immediately, but if we find we can't afford it, that's what we'll have to do," Roy said. "Again, I'm taking you into my confidence. Don't suggest this to your mother or your sister."

"I understand."

"Oh, what a wonderful house this will be for entertaining!" Diana said, taking in the parlor and dining room with a wide sweep of her hand.

This was a beautiful time to be on the Dearborn River. The short grass was green and the cottonwood and aspen had leafed and the water was rippling over the rocks. Riley Barnes was out on his fish platform examining his cage.

He missed Badger Woman. She had always made sure the barricade that drove the fish into the cage was repaired, and he smiled when he saw some spots that were broken. If she were here, she would send him off for more aspen roots and elk sinew, but this year the barricade would not be repaired.

"The little fish have to get through," she would say. "We only want the big ones."

Riley picked up his dip net and lowered it into the four-foot-square enclosure. Today was a good day. Lots of fish.

He would have to help Kimi start the fire so they could smoke some trout. He needed to start laying in a supply of fish now. Lately, he hadn't been feeling that well, and he didn't know how far he could go for game. Small stuff, yes, but his five little girls got tired of eating fowl.

He began pulling the net out of the pen, but it was so heavy he dropped it. Lying on his stomach, he extended his arm into the cold water.

"I'm hungry," Pana said, grabbing a handful of sarvis berries. "Where is Papa?"

"Papa went down to the platform to check the fish trap, but he should be back by now. Why don't you and Nuna take another basket and go see if he has so many fish that he can't carry them all?" Kimi suggested.

"All right," Pana said. "Will you pinch off some biscuits? If we have to wait for the fish, we'll starve to death."

"I'll help," Koko said as she got the crock of sourdough starter from its box behind the stove.

Kimi tried not to let on that she was worried about Papa. She had watched him when he appeared to reel almost like a man who had had too much to drink, when she knew there was no alcohol anywhere near their cabin. He would sit down suddenly and wait, but when he looked at her, it was as if he wasn't seeing her.

"Kanti, go down to the river and get a dipper of buttermilk from the tin," she said. "And check to see how much we have. Mother Raffaella said another cow has freshened, and if we want more, we can have it."

Kanti didn't answer, but she went skipping down to the river with a wooden bowl, so Kimi assumed she was doing as she asked.

Just then she saw Nuna running up from the river. "Kimi, Kimi, come quick. It's Papa. Pana thinks he's dead."

Kimi dropped the sourdough and went running down to Pana, with Koko following behind her.

When she reached the platform, she saw that Riley was lying facedown, and he wasn't moving.

"Please, dear God, please," she murmured, not knowing what else to say. Thoughts were tumbling through her head. Father Imoda. Who would she send to get him? Could Nuna and Pana get there when the sun was already low in the sky?

Running out onto the platform, she knelt beside him.

"Papa! Papa, can you hear me?" she yelled.

When he didn't answer, she took his head in her hands and rolled it over so she could see his face. When she did, he opened his eyes, but he did not see.

"He's alive. We've got to get him to the house. Run and get Mama's tepee travois. It's out by the horse shed. Oh, and bring a deerskin—no bring two deerskins."

Both Nuna and Pana went running up to the cabin.

Koko began to cry.

"Is he going to die?" Kanti asked as she stood just beyond the platform.

"Help me," Kimi said. "We've got to turn him. We've got to roll him up to the bank."

When Nuna and Pana returned with the poles and the skins, Kimi yanked up several of the stakes from the fish trap. Laying them crosswise on the poles, she used the loose sinew to secure them. Then, putting the skin near Riley, she and the girls rolled and pulled until they had him on the travois.

With superhuman effort, the five little girls got him up to the cabin, but they couldn't get him into the house.

"He'll have to stay out here," Kimi said. "Get one of Uncle Case's blankets to put over him."

Kimi and Kanti sat by his side until he seemed to be comfortable. Kimi went back into the cabin and lit a lamp, but it was now too late to fix anything to eat. Taking a skin bag down from a peg, she opened the last pouch of pemmican that Badger Woman had prepared for them. The four girls ate in silence.

Kanti didn't leave Riley's side.

Helena

"I'm going to miss you," Annie Higgins said, as Maddie and Diana waited beside the Diamond R coach that had come to take them to their new home.

"I don't mean to be buttin' in none, Miss, but they're only going about a mile up the road. It ain't like they're moving to San Francisco," Gib Dooley said, as he began stowing the trunks.

"I know, but it's been so much fun having them here at the hotel with me, especially since I don't see Mr. White that much."

Dooley nodded his head and continued with the loading.

"It has been fun, but even I've gotten a little tired of dominoes," Maddie said.

"And old maid," Annie added with a chuckle. "If I have to wait much longer for Mr. White, I'm going to be the winner."

"Don't give up on him," Diana said. "Every day he's out at the kiln means more money you can spend."

"I keep telling myself that," Annie said, "but I came out here to get married, and I'm ready."

"Aren't we all," Diana said. "That is, all except maybe Maddie. She doesn't care a whit about finding a husband."

"Is that true?" Annie asked, turning to Maddie.

Maddie lowered her head. "I suppose not."

Not unless I'm sure he loves me. She didn't voice her true feelings, because she was beginning to think she wasn't like most of the women she knew.

She had to admit, learning of her mother's attitude toward marriage had been most jarring. Watching her parents, it had never occurred to Maddie that they had married for nothing more than convenience. Her father had a housekeeper and a cook, and her mother had a home and an income. If that was all there was to marriage, she was probably better off by herself.

Just then, Annabelle came out of the International Hotel.

"I was just saying good-bye to Mr. Howe. Isn't he the sweetest man?" Annabelle asked. "It's too bad he doesn't own this hotel instead of just work here."

"Would that change his personality?" Maddie asked.

"Of course not," Annabelle said, "but he's not someone I would want either one of my daughters marrying. That's all I'm saying. Now, with Mr. White, Annie knows what she's getting. Any man who works that hard to make a living for his wife is a true gem. When we get settled, you must bring him up to see us."

"Where's Papa?" Maddie asked. "Is he coming with us?"

"Oh no, he wouldn't want to be at the house until all the furniture is in place," Annabelle replied.

Saying good-bye to Annie, the three women climbed into the coach, and Dooley closed the door.

"Good-bye, Miss Higgins," Dooley said. "I saw Dale Hathaway and he said to tell you hello if I saw you."

"Tell him the same," Annie said, as she turned back to the hotel.

When the coach reached the house on Madison Avenue, several freight wagons were already standing out front, and one was under the portico waiting to be unloaded. A black horse was tied to a ring that hung from one of the posts.

"Howdy, folks," Clyde Pell said, as he climbed down from the wagon. "I saw the mister runnin' around, but I ain't seen you ladies since we pulled out at the mission. This is a mighty fine house you've got yourselves."

"Thank you, Mr. Pell. How's your leg?" Maddie asked.

"Thank ya fer askin'. I got me a limp is all, but I been kept in town, fer pert near half the summer, and I ain't a-likin' it. Not one bit."

"It'll do you good to be around civilization for a while," Case said as he stepped through the door of the house and out onto the front porch.

"Case," Maddie said, a welcoming smile crossing her face.

"Welcome to the neighborhood," Case said with a broad smile.

Seeing Case, Diana hurried up to him. "How thoughtful of you to see us to our new home. Isn't it beautiful?"

"Yes, it is," Case said. "I just walked through it, and I think Anton Holter outdid himself on this one."

"Is that who lived here?" Maddie asked.

"No, that's who designed it. It's too bad the newspaper editor turned it down, but I'm glad he did. I'd much rather have the McClellans as my neighbors than the Barrets."

"Your neighbors? Where do you live?" Diana asked.

Case pointed to the house next door. "Right there. You ladies aren't rid of me yet."

"Why, Mr. Williams, whatever would make you think we would want to be?" Diana asked as she lowered her head and gazed up at him.

Maddie could have sworn she saw Diana bat her eyelashes.

"Clyde, Dooley, why don't you help Jack and the boys get this freight off the wagons. Listen to Mrs. McClellan and put it exactly where she wants it," Case said.

"Diana, you come with me and help decide where to put the big pieces. I want to have at least one room presentable before your father comes home," Annabelle said.

"Can't Maddie do that?"

Annabelle laughed. "Are you serious? I said I wanted it to be presentable. Do you really trust Maddie's judgment about where things should go? You know she has no eye for what looks good."

Diana chuckled. "You're right," she said, as she followed her mother inside.

Case had a lazy grin on his face. "Is that right? You have no eye for what looks good?"

"It depends on what I'm looking at," Maddie said, as she walked over to the horse. "I know that this is a fine-looking horse. Is he your personal horse, or does he belong to the company?"

"He's mine. I call him Dandy, because he's a dandy."

"He certainly is beautiful," Maddie said as she began patting the horse's neck. "American saddle-bred, right?"

"Yes, as a matter of fact he is, but how could you tell that?"

"His ears. He's got the hook at the tip. Have you taught him to rack?" she asked, referring to the high-kneed gait that she had seen others of the breed perform.

"No, I haven't," Case said.

"I'll bet Dandy could learn. President Grant's horse is a saddlebred, too, and he's been taught to rack," Maddie said. "I've seen the president ride Cincinnati through Battery Kemble, and it's quite a sight to behold."

"Would you like to teach him?" Case asked.

"I'm not sure I could, but I'd love to try."

"After you get settled in, I'll have to get a side-saddle for you."

Maddie flushed with embarrassment. "I'm afraid I don't use one, much to the disapproval of my mother and my sister."

Case laughed. "Then if that's the case, why don't you take him out for a little run." He untied the horse from the ring.

"Do you mean it? I haven't ridden for so long, and I do miss it."

"Yes, go ahead." Case said, handing her the reins. He stepped forward to help her up, but she had her foot in the stirrup before he could get to her.

She mounted the horse, and as she did so, she displayed a smooth leg all the way up to a pair of ruffled drawers. Case smiled.

"Oh," she said as she pulled her dress down as much as she could. "I guess that wasn't very ladylike."

With that statement, she took off, not down Madison Avenue, as Case had expected her to do, but through the backyard, out by the carriage house, and over the fence behind it. She seemed to be one with the horse as she pushed Dandy to the gentle slope at the base of Mt. Helena.

Case smiled as he watched her ride up the mountain. It was going to be interesting having Maddie McClellan in the neighborhood.

Maddie didn't realize how long she had been gone, as she turned Dandy and headed down the mountain, returning to the portico the same way she had left.

From the sound of the voices getting louder, it was obvious that Annabelle was coming outside, and, not wanting to be caught astride a horse, Maddie dismounted quickly, again showing a long flash of very shapely leg as she did so.

"Case, I would just as soon you not mention this," she said quietly.

"Why not? I thought you were wonderful!"

Maddie rolled her eyes in the direction of the doorway, where her mother appeared.

"I understand."

The two movers, along with Annabelle, approached the wagon.

"This is my husband's favorite chair," Annabelle said, removing a covering to reveal an ornately carved oval-backed armchair. Then, seeing Maddie, she addressed her sharply. "Where have you been, young lady? Your sister is in there right now opening crates, trying to make this place livable, and what are you doing? Keeping Mr. Williams from his work, that's what."

"I'll be right there," Maddie said. She patted Dandy and mouthed the words *thank you* to Case.

"Anytime," he said.

Annabelle, unaware of what had just passed between the two, turned abruptly to Case. "Did I miss something?"

"No, ma'am, everything will be unloaded within an hour."

"I hope so. When my husband gets here, he'll

expect to have things in order. I'll send Diana out to make certain we finish quickly."

"I'm sure she'll be a big help," Case said as he fought to prevent a smile from forming.

Maddie took Diana's place in the parlor, unpacking the familiar items that were to be displayed on the whatnot shelf.

Looking through the window, she saw Diana engaged in an animated conversation with Case. They were both laughing, and Diana was constantly touching him.

And what did Maddie do when she was alone with him? She rode his horse. Maddie closed her eyes and clenched her fists. When she did so, she broke a piece off a Staffordshire figurine she was holding in her hand.

"Damn," she said aloud, "who wants an ugly old whippet in a collection anyway?" She put the broken dog back in the crate, hiding it in the excelsior, hoping it wouldn't be missed.

Finally, the wagons were emptied, and all the major pieces of furniture were put into place.

Diana and Case came into the house together.

"That about does it," Case said. "I'm sorry it took longer than I expected." He looked pointedly at Diana and they exchanged a smile.

"But we did get it done," Diana said.

"You both did a wonderful job," Annabelle said. "Diana, you have been a big help. Thank you, my dear."

"Knock, knock. Is this where the McClellans live?" Roy asked as he came into the house. "I think I came home at just the right time."

"We're just finishing, Professor," Case said. "Your wife and daughters have performed yeoman's duty this afternoon."

"And so have you, Case. What would we have done without you?" Diana looked at Case with adoring eyes as she took his hand in hers.

Maddie couldn't stand it. She very quietly slipped out the door. When she did, she found Dandy tied to the hitching post.

"Hi, boy," she said as she cupped her hand and allowed him to sniff her palm. When he was comfortable, she moved to his withers and began scratching. "I should have brought you something."

"He likes carrots," Case said, coming up behind her.

"I'll have to remember that," Maddie said. "Where can I find some?"

"The garden out back of my carriage house," Case said. "Ho Kwan is my gardener, stable hand, houseboy—whatever I need." Case said.

"Then you really don't need a wife, do you?"

Case laughed, with a deep rumble. "I wouldn't quite say that. Ho Kwan can do a lot of things, but . . . there are some things he just can't do."

"Like what? Can he cook?"

"Oh yes, he's a good cook."

"Can he clean?"

"Yes."

"And he does laundry."

"Uh-huh."

"Then what can't he do?"

"This." Case pressed his lips gently against Maddie's, then drew back, his eyes never breaking contact with hers.

Maddie cleared her throat. "It's still daylight."

A grin of amusement crossed his face. "Is that a problem?"

"It is when my mother is not twenty-five feet away from me."

"But she can't see us."

"How do you know?"

"Because Dandy's on guard."

Case raised his hand to her chin, and he tipped it upward, ever so slightly. He lowered his head closer to her lips.

Maddie was sure he was going to kiss her again, but he stopped short.

"You can ride Dandy anytime you want," he said as he stepped away from her. "I think he likes you."

"I like him, too," Maddie said, her voice barely above a whisper.

With that, Case turned and, leading Dandy behind him, walked to the carriage house that served as a stable as well.

TWELVE

Unable to sleep, Case went to the Diamond R office before daybreak. Something was happening, and he didn't like where it was taking him. His resolve to stay away from any woman he thought could hurt him was being tested. His self-proclaimed declaration of bachelorhood was in jeopardy. How many times did he have to tell people he didn't want a wife?

And yet he did want Maddie. He wanted to take her in his arms and feel her body next to his, to kiss her deeply.

He was fully aware that Maddie had no idea what a suggestive comment she had made when she'd asked what Ho Kwan couldn't do. If one of the fancy ladies had said the same thing, he would have had her upstairs in an instant, but not Maddie.

He smiled when he thought of her galloping off on Dandy, her skirt hiked up above her knee. The night on the log when he had been aroused by the mere sight of her cleavage, she hadn't protested when he touched her breasts and then kissed her thoroughly. He had seen her hair straggling from her braid, and she wore the same dress for days, yet he had never heard her complain.

What kind of a woman was she? What kind of a wife would Maddie make? Why couldn't it be Diana he was attracted to? She was a beautiful woman, all right, but she was so damn shallow that she would be easy to resist. There was only one other woman who was as superficial as she was—Mrs. Theodore Dawes. All he had to do was think of Mary Beth Sullivan Dawes, and his determination to stay single was strengthened.

"Damn, Case, are you feeling guilty 'cause you leave me all the time?" Charles Broadwater asked when he walked into the Diamond R early that morning and saw that Case was already at his desk.

"No, I'm just checking up on you. You're so far behind on paperwork, we're going to need to hire a bookkeeper," Case said.

Charles raised his finger. "And I know just the person. Julie's sister, Nellie, has come home. She's smart and she's pretty, and she'd be a good match for you."

"No."

"Oh, that's right, I forgot. You've got the two McClellan women to sniff out. Did they get moved in to Anton's house?"

"They did."

"Well, that makes it very convenient for you, doesn't it?" Charles asked. "Which one have you staked out?"

Case lifted his eyebrows and then went back to the papers that were spread on his desk.

For the next several weeks, Annabelle and her daughters were busy getting their home in order. One afternoon, while the girls were dusting, they heard the unexpected fall of the door knocker.

"You get the door, Maddie," Diana said as she ran up the steps, pulling a kerchief off her head. "I can't meet anyone like this. I am so unpresentable."

Maddie, too, took off her kerchief, putting it in the pocket of her apron. When she opened the door, she saw two women standing there.

"Would you please announce to the lady of the house that Mrs. Broadwater and Mrs. Fisk are calling?"

"Of course. Won't you come in?" Maddie asked, stepping to one side and allowing the women to enter. "If you'll step into the parlor, I'll get my mother."

"Your mother?" one of the ladies asked.

"Yes, ma'am. I'm Maddie McClellan."

"Oh, I thought you might be . . . uh, never mind. I've heard my husband mention your name. I'm Julia Broadwater and this is Elizabeth Fisk."

"I beg your pardon, but how would your husband have known my name?"

A broad smile crossed the woman's face. "My husband's partner is your next-door neighbor, Mr. Williams."

"You mean Case? Your husband must be Charles."

Now it was Julia's turn to be surprised. "You've met him?"

"No, but Case has mentioned him."

Both ladies looked at each other with what Maddie considered a conspiratorial expression.

Just then, Annabelle came to the door. "Welcome to our home. You ladies are our first callers, and I'm afraid my youngest daughter has quite forgotten her manners. Won't you join me in the parlor for a spot of tea?"

The ladies properly introduced themselves to Annabelle, and Maddie was dispatched to the kitchen. Her mother had some tea cakes prepared, and Maddie included those on the tray. When she returned, Diana had joined the group, and the four women were engaged in conversation.

"We're so happy to have you join us in the new Northwest, as we like to call the Territory," Julia said. "Both Elizabeth and I know how hard it is to make the acquaintance of the more genteel ladies in Helena, so if you would consider it, I'd like to invite you to a soirée at my home on Saturday next."

"How very thoughtful of you," Annabelle said.

"Would this event include gentlemen as well?" Diana asked.

Both ladies laughed. "You really haven't been out and about since you've arrived, have you?"

"We did stay at the International Hotel," Diana said.

"Did you notice that there are so many men, you found yourself tripping over them?" Elizabeth asked. "Of course there'll be gentlemen at her party. Would you want Julia to be forever castigated for not allowing every eligible man in town to enter the competition?"

"Competition?"

"You're an exceptionally beautiful young woman, Diana," Julia said. "I have to ask. Is there some fortunate gentleman back East who has spoken for you?"

"Definitely not," Annabelle said with a chuckle. "And believe me, Roy—that is, Mr. McClellan—and I would like nothing better than to find a wonderful young man for our daughter."

"That's music to my ears," Julia said. "Charles and I are always trying to find a good woman for Case and it seems to me you fit the bill. Beautiful, smart, energetic. According to Charles, the very traits the woman who left him possessed."

"The woman who left him? I didn't know he'd been married," Maddie said interjecting herself into the conversation for the first time.

"Oh my dear, no, no, no. He wasn't married," Julia said as she looked toward Maddie. "But here we are gossiping when that's the very thing we criticize the most when the socially unrefined do it." Maddie felt her cheeks burning. Why had she interjected herself into this conversation?

It was late when Case closed the books in the office, and he was tired. But it was a good tired. The steam-powered fire engine that Seth Bullock had ordered for the volunteer fire department had come in, and everyone had celebrated its arrival. Nicholas Kessler's brewery made the finest beer in the territory, and he had opened the spigots on more kegs than Case could count. After he locked up, he walked around the Diamond R., checking on everything. Tonight would not be a good night for a fire.

He didn't have Dandy with him, and he considered taking one of the stock horses, but it was a clear night. And he, too, had celebrated too much, so he decided to walk home. When he reached Wood Street, he hesitated. It had been a long time since he'd been to the Red Star, and he decided he needed a little male recreation, which was the euphemism the men had for visiting the demimonde.

"It's been a long time," the manager said, extending his hand to Case when he walked in.

"Too busy, Black Hawk, everybody's too busy," Case said.

"All work and no play, Case?" a very attractive woman asked as she embraced him. "You know it's about time for the summer women to go back east. I think Belle's busy, but shall I check to see if Rosa is free?"

"Not now, Joe. I just want to sit for a while. Have Hernando pour me a shot of the strongest stuff you've got."

Josephine Airey, who was known as Joe, laughed. "You didn't get enough of Nick's beer tonight?"

"Maybe I got too much."

Joe walked over to a table and Case followed, pulling out a chair for her.

"What's wrong, Case?"

"Nothing. Everything's going well. Business couldn't be better."

"You know and I know we're not talking business. When a man stops coming in here for as long as it's been since I've seen you, it has to be a woman. Who is she?"

Case looked at Joe and started to give her a flippant answer, but then he got serious. "I don't know.

There are two women who are new in town, and one of them might be the one."

"Is she upper-crust, or middling, or a low, bad woman?"

"Humph," Case said shaking his head. "I don't know what her social position is. She lives with her parents in Anton Holder's house, and that's impressive, but I get the feeling money's not important to her."

"That's a lie. Money's important to every woman," Joe said. "Why else would my girls lie up there on their backs when they could get jobs down at Kleinschmidt's selling knickknacks for sixty-five dollars a month? It's because a good girl like Rosa Diamond will take a thousand dollars back to Chicago when she leaves, and she'll go back home and everybody will think she's respectable. Then next summer she'll be back. And as good as you are, Case, it's not for the sex. It's for the money."

Josephine rose from her chair. "You sit here and you think. This woman's playing you for a fool. She knows you're rich and she'd like to get her claws in you. Just watch out."

Case took a sip of his whiskey, feeling the burn as it went down his throat. He had wondered which of the two McClellan women he was most interested in, and tonight he thought he had been describing Maddie. But what Joe had said could definitely be true.

In Lewis and Clark County, the magistrate's docket could be as full with divorce cases as it was with horse thieving. The common comment was that a man in the mountains couldn't keep his wife,

and the statistics bore this out. One in three mar-
riages ended in divorce.

"Hell," Case said aloud. "Who wants to go through
that? Could be that Mary Beth not showing up at the
altar was the best thing that ever happened to me."

For a whole week, everything in the McClellan
household was put on hold while new dresses were
made to be worn to the Broadwater dinner party.

"Mama, do you think this will be all right?" Diana
asked as she stood in front of the mirror. "I don't
think a princess dress line makes my waist look
small enough."

"We can lace your corset tighter," Annabelle said.

"That won't help. We should have had a break at
the waist," Diana said. "Do you think you can make
another dress?"

Annabelle took a deep breath. "I'd have time, but
it's your father. He didn't want to give me the money
to buy the cloth we have, but I convinced him we
had to be properly dressed if we're going to make
any kind of impression."

"Then could you take the darts out on Maddie's
dress so it would fit me? And if you put a few more
ruffles on it, I could wear hers."

"Yes, I could do that."

"Maddie, you take this one. You don't care what
you look like," Diana said.

"I think your dress is beautiful, and I'll be proud
to wear it," Maddie said.

"Thank you, dear. Do you want to try it on?"
Annabelle asked.

"I suppose I should, in case you have to move the draperies up a little. After all, I don't want to trip."

"Yes, Mama, make sure she can't trip, because if she can, she will, and I'd be absolutely mortified."

Roy McClellan hired a carriage from the livery to take his wife and daughters to the Broadwater home. He had to admit, Diana and even Maddie looked beautiful.

"The guests of honor have arrived," Julia announced, when the McClellans were shown into the parlor.

While they were being introduced, Maddie looked around the room and quickly counted at least a dozen people. She was happy to see that Annie Higgins was there, as was Elizabeth Fisk.

"I believe you have already made the acquaintance of several of these people," Julia said, "but at the risk of not having done so, this is my wonderful husband, Charles, and I'm sure you know his partner, Case Williams."

Maddie thought Case looked extremely handsome in his tailcoat with his tucked shirt, but he seemed to be ill at ease.

"You've met Elizabeth. This is her husband, James Fisk. You'll learn to watch what you say around him, if you don't want it to come out in the *Herald*. He's the editor. And Mr. and Mrs. Hauser, Sam and Ellen. You'll want to stay on his good side, because he's the banker. Then there is Mr. Holter and his wife, Mary. You are enjoying the fruits of his labor, because Anton built your house. And I believe you know Miss Higgins. Her betrothed is Mr. George White. Now, I don't think I missed anyone, did I?"

"What about me?" Dale Hathaway asked as he stepped forward.

"Oh, Dale, I forgot you," Julia said with a chuckle, "but then, I know you are familiar with the McClellans. Mr. Hathaway practices law with Chumasero and Chadwick in the Bently Block."

"I am and I do," Dale said.

"Hold up there, Dale, before you start saying 'I do.' We have two single young ladies and two confirmed bachelors that we're trying to get together, and you're one of them," Charles said, and everyone laughed except Dale, Case, and Maddie.

"There are three single young ladies," Dale said. "Annie and George aren't married yet."

"It's not because of me," George White said. "I'd have been in your office yesterday or the yesterday before that, and Judge Chumasero would've tied the knot good and tight. But Annie tells me she's not ready yet."

Annie was obviously embarrassed, but she didn't comment.

Maddie was glad to hear her friend was hesitating. She was sorry she had not taken the time to visit with her, but if she found an opportunity to speak to Annie in private, she would take it.

"Now that the introductions have been made, if you'll just engage in some chitchat, we'll retire to the dining room when Mr. Evans announces," Julia said as she stepped into the adjoining room.

"Are you the one who rides, or is that the other one?" Charles Broadwater asked as he moved closer to Maddie, a drink in his hand.

"I do like to ride," Maddie said, "but I'm afraid I won't be able to get my own horse for a while."

"The Diamond R has plenty of horses that aren't all driving horses. Have Case pick out a nice gentle one for you and he can stable it behind his house."

"I don't think she needs a gentle horse," Case said as he joined the two. "I told you this lady can ride. She had Dandy going through his paces the first time she got on him."

"Dandy is a special horse," Maddie said.

"Uh-oh, I'm getting the eye," Charles said as he looked over toward Julia. "I'd better see what she wants."

When Charles was gone, Case and Maddie stood together, neither looking directly at the other. "I'm sorry," Case said. "I was told that this was going to be a large reception, where Julia had invited half the town."

"For a dinner party, I'd say sixteen people is a fairly good-size number."

"Not when there are four single people and, as Charles said, the purpose is to get them together."

"Well, we're together. Is this what she meant?"

Case laughed. "I don't think this is what she had in mind. Julia won't be satisfied until she's found a wife for me."

"And you're not interested in that?"

"Absolutely not. I was almost there once, and I'll never get caught again," Case said. "Oh, there's Morgan. May I escort you into the dining room?"

"You may. Who is Morgan?"

"Morgan Evans. He's Charles and Julia's boarder."

"Boarder?"

"Yes, most people in town have boarders. Too many people, not enough houses," Case said.

"You have a big house. Do you take in boarders?"

"No, I'm hoping . . . I'm just saving it in case I need it for something."

When they reached the dining room, Maddie was disappointed when they found their place cards. She was seated beside Dale Hathaway and across the table from Diana, who was seated beside Case.

The next day, Case took Charles's suggestion and rode out to the corral to choose a horse for Maddie. He liked the idea of her riding with him, and he wished she were with him now. He opened the gate and, leading Dandy into the pen, looked at more than three dozen horses before he settled on a chestnut and white pinto mare named Lucky.

"You're a lucky lady," Case said as he put a lead on the horse and moved her out of the corral.

When he got home, it was all he could do to keep from going next door and asking Maddie to go for a ride, but he decided against it.

When he got to the office on Monday morning, Charles was already there.

"Well?" Charles asked when he came in. "What did you think?"

"I had a good time," Case said. "I'm glad Julia made me come."

"Who would have thought that old George White was so good at charades? He came up with 'Sinbad' and 'napkin' and 'coffee,' if I remember right, but how about you? I would never have guessed 'kidnap,'" Charles said. "Do you remember Maddie's clues?"

"I think the first syllable was 'On Stella's foot and hand and arm, my first most daintily reposes,' and the second syllable was 'And Stella's foot and hand and arm yield to my next when she reposes.'"

"And you got 'kidnap' out of that?"

"No, it was her last line, 'Could she be mine by right of capture, I'd dare my whole to win such rapture.'"

"Hmmm," Charles posed. "That's what you ought to do—kidnap Diana. I'm telling you, don't let that girl get away."

Case shook his head. "Get out of here. I've got work to do."

Roy McClellan was in his office, which was barely a ten-foot square, when Sheriff Bullock stopped by to see him.

"Professor, you got a message from Secretary Smith and the telegrapher gave it to me to bring to you," the sheriff said. "I'm not sure what you can do about this, but since you're the field superintendent, they're asking you to come up with a way to get this Bozeman problem resolved."

Roy took the transmittal and began to read. It said that some Gallatin Valley traders had established a trading post just below the mouth of the Big Horn River on land that was claimed by the Sioux. The Sioux considered this land to be theirs and Fort Pease, as the traders called their post, was now under siege.

"Thank you, Sheriff. When does the stage leave for Bozeman?"

"Day after tomorrow."

When Roy got home, he called his family into the library.

"I have some things to tell you, and I don't think you're going to like everything I have to say. First of all, I have to go to Bozeman on Wednesday. I don't know how long I'll be gone, but I don't expect it will be for too long."

"Roy, what's happened?" Annabelle asked.

"There's trouble with the Sioux. They have a trading post under siege. But that's a minor problem where you're concerned."

"What do you mean, Papa?" Maddie asked.

"I've not said anything to any of you, but I am very near the end of my reserves. I went to see Mr. Hauser today to see if I can get a loan, but because we're so new in town and the salary I am now being paid is so low, he turned me down. But because he is a generous man, he said he would not be evicting us from this house for a while in order to give us some time to generate extra income. He suggested we advertise for boarders."

"Oh, no," Diana said. "We can't be reduced to taking in boarders."

"Why not?" Maddie asked. "When we were at the Broadwaters', Mr. Evans was their boarder."

"Mr. Evans? Who was he?" Diana asked.

"He was the man who served us."

"Well, I've contacted Mr. Barret at the *Independent* and Mr. Fisk at the *Herald*, and they're both running ads for us. I expect that you will have accepted a boarder by the time I return. Is that understood?"

"Yes, sir," Maddie said.

Roy arrived at the International Hotel a little before 5:00 A.M. in order to catch the coach for Bozeman. As he was early, he went into the hotel intending to have breakfast, but in view of his current financial situation, he decided he would settle for a cup of coffee instead.

"Professor, you're out early this morning," Case said when he saw Roy enter the restaurant.

"I could say the same for you. May I join you?"

"Of course," Case said, pushing out a chair. "May I buy your breakfast?"

"I thank you, but I'm taking the stage to Bozeman this morning. I don't think I'll have time," Roy said as he pulled his watch from his vest pocket.

Case laughed. "This is your first trip out of town, isn't it? Believe me, you'll have time for breakfast."

"If that's so, then I'll take you up on your offer."

"Good. Zhang Wei, bring the professor a stack of buckwheat cakes and a rasher of bacon," Case said.

Within a short time, the food was delivered and Roy ate heartily while he explained the nature of his trip.

"It seems to me this is a matter for the military," Case said. "I expect the commandant of Fort Ellis will take care of it."

"I'm sure you're right, but when the secretary tells me to go, I have to go."

"Well, don't worry about your family. I'll look in on them to make certain everything is going well."

Roy took a deep breath. "You don't know how much I appreciate that." He hesitated before he went on. "I shouldn't be confiding in you, but you've dealt with me and my family in an honest way, and I trust you. I have to say, I let my emotions control my pocketbook, and now I'm in a position where I have to raise some capital. An ad will run today soliciting boarders to stay in my home."

"That's a very common arrangement," Case said.

"You know my daughters," Roy said. "Especially Diana. She is a most provocative woman, and inviting a man into my home to perhaps sleep in an adjoining chamber is troublesome to me. The ideal situation would be to find a suitable husband for her."

Case swallowed hard, not wanting to hear what he thought the next question was going to be.

"We've both had the privilege of knowing Miss Higgins. Although I don't understand why she hasn't lived up to her agreement with George White, I'm sure when she comes to her senses, she'll be financially secure, and in my opinion that's all any woman can ask for."

Immediately, the words of Josephine Airey popped into Case's mind. *It's not for the sex. It's for the money.* Was he the only person who thought there was more to a man-woman relationship than security?

"I've never asked you this question directly," Roy said, "but are you married?"

"I am not, but if you're offering me your daughter, I'm afraid I'm going to have to decline. I like my life the way it is."

"I can appreciate that. Some men aren't meant to be husbands and fathers," Roy said. "But I do have one request. Would you give your approval for any man who wants to be our boarder? I know it's asking a lot, but I'd feel better if the man my wife chooses is reputable."

"Of course I'll do that, and I'm honored that you would ask me."

THIRTEEN

For the next couple of days, a parade of men came to the McClellan house inquiring about a room. Each name that was offered to Case was turned down. One was known to be a drunkard, another had head lice, while still another was known to be a glutton, and Case thought it would cost more to feed him than he would pay in rent. Case could find something wrong with everyone who came, because in truth, he realized, he didn't want any man living with them. And yet, he knew how important it was to Roy that he find some way to bring in more money.

Diana was outspoken in her objections to taking in a border, thinking that such a thing was "beneath them," and Annabelle was just as opposed, though not for the same reason. She just didn't like the idea of having strangers living in her house.

Only Maddie seemed to grasp the gravity of the situation. One evening, after listening to Diana's complaints about the "low straits" to which they had been reduced, Maddie could take no more of it, so she walked out the back door, sat on the steps, and, folding her arms across her knees, lowered her head. She heard, but didn't see, someone sit on the steps beside her.

"I don't like this either, Diana, but if we're going to stay here, it has to be done," Maddie said.

"What do you mean, 'if you're going to stay here'?"

With a start, Maddie jerked her head up to see Case sitting beside her.

A faint smile crossed Maddie's face. "I thought you were Diana."

"No, it's just me," Case said mimicking a woman's voice as he tried to lighten the situation.

Despite herself, Maddie chuckled.

"Now what do you mean, 'if you're going to stay here'?" Case repeated.

"Papa should have come to Helena by himself. He could be a boarder with someone and he wouldn't have to pay for this big house. If we don't find a boarder or maybe two or three, Mama, Diana, and I should go back to Washington. With the money Papa will save and the money we can earn back there, we can take care of ourselves."

"How would you earn money in Washington?"

"I know I could get my old job back looking after Samantha, if the Smiths haven't already hired someone. And even if they have, I know Mr. Smith would recommend me for another job. Mama could set up a dressmaking shop and Diana could go back to a tearoom."

"A tearoom?"

"Yes, it's place for ladies to gather."

"To drink tea," Case said.

"It's more than that. They drink tea, they visit, they play cards, they talk about books they've read, or shows they've attended. Diana was a hostess at the tearoom in the Willard Hotel and she was very good at it."

"I would expect that she would be."

"And Mama's an excellent seamstress. You may have noticed the dresses we were wearing at the Broadwaters' reception. She made those, so I know she's good enough to sew on commission," Maddie said. "If we go back, we can find ways to support ourselves."

"Is this what your mother and sister want to do?"

"I'm not sure they've really thought about it, because neither one of them thinks ahead very far. But Papa said we had to have a boarder when he got back, and it doesn't look like we're going to have one, so we have to have a plan to offer him."

"What do you think they'll say when you present your idea?"

"Diana didn't want to come here in the first place, so I'm sure she'll want to go back. You have no idea how popular she was. And Mama—I don't think she would mind leaving Papa alone."

"You haven't said what Maddie would think," Case said as he draped his arm around her and pulled her to him.

When he did this, even though she knew he was doing it to comfort her, she felt a quick flash of heat. He had asked what she would think if they had to leave, but she couldn't answer him. She would have liked to tell him she would stay here forever if she could stay with him, but that wasn't to be. His words had been, *I'll never get caught again.* He had made it very plain that he had no intention of ever getting married. Maddie only wished that she were the kind of woman who could make him change his mind.

"You're always the optimistic one, but tonight you look like you're really down. I think I have just the thing to cheer you up," Case said. He stood and pulled her to her feet. He didn't drop her hand until they reached his stable.

Maddie smiled. "Are you going to let me ride Dandy? A ride always makes me feel better."

"No, you can't ride Dandy."

"Oh," Maddie said, a little hurt by the answer.

He opened the stable door. "Step inside."

When she did, Dandy began to whicker and Maddie moved toward him. It was then that she saw another horse in the next stall.

"And who is this?"

"Meet Lucky, and she's a lucky lady, because you're going to ride her if you'd like."

Maddie turned, offering her hand to the brown and white pinto.

"Where did you come from, beautiful lady?" Maddie asked as she moved her hand up to the horse's neck and began patting.

"She's one of the Diamond R riding horses and I'm going to keep her here with Dandy, just for you whenever you want to ride."

"Oh, Case!" Maddie said, throwing her arms around him. "Can we go for a ride right now?"

"I don't know why not," Case said, holding her tight against him as he grinned down at her. "I'll get 'em saddled up. You run and tell your mother you're with me so she won't worry."

The two rode leisurely down the winding street to the business district, passing the Diamond R, where several of the men were leaning up against the corral.

"I do believe it's Miss Maddie," Gib Dooley called when he recognized her. "You're lookin' right smart ridin' astride our Lucky."

"It's good seeing you. We live up beside Case now, so you'll have to call on us when you're up that way," Maddie said.

"Oh, I have a feelin' we're gonna be seeing a lot of you."

"I think it's time to say good night," Case said, as he slapped his legs against Dandy, putting him into a trot.

Crossing the gulch, the two horses climbed steadily to the top of a hill where a wooden tower was standing.

"Case Williams, is that you?" a man called down.

"It is, Fred. We've come to see the sunset."

"It should be a pretty one tonight, but hold on to your horses. I'm going to ring the bell here in a couple of minutes. Time to get the kiddies home."

"All right," Case said, dismounting from Dandy.

Maddie slid off Lucky, and they walked over to a patch of grass and sat down.

"Does that man stay up there all night?" Maddie asked as the bell began clanging.

"Yes, Fred's one of the fire marshals and he just got here, but he'll stay until eight in the morning.

See how the gulches all come together down there," Case said as he leaned over to point to the convergence.

He was so close to her, she could feel his breath on her neck.

"Yes," she said, her voice barely above a whisper.

Case, too, felt the charge between them. With his eyes focused on hers, he continued. "If conditions are just right and a wildfire starts, nothing can put it out."

Both Case and Maddie knew that the fire he was referencing was not the one that burned down buildings, but the one that was beginning to kindle between them. As gentle as the touch of a breeze, he kissed her.

They watched the sun going low, but still above the distant purple mountains. The clouds, now underlit, glowed orange, while the sky turned red.

"Beautiful," Case said.

When Maddie started to respond, she saw that he wasn't looking at the sunset—he was looking at her. She met his gaze without blinking.

Suddenly, and unexpectedly, Case stood.

"We'd better get back. It'll be dark soon and your mother will be getting worried."

Maddie felt a loss when the moment was broken. She rose and went to her horse without a comment.

They rode down the hill in silence. When they reached Main Street, several people were out, and each of them called to Case. He spoke, but he never stopped to talk to anyone.

When they got home, he rode to the stable and Maddie followed him.

"I've been thinking on this ride home, and do you know what I've come up with?" Case asked. "You should turn your parlor into a tearoom."

"A tearoom?"

"Yes. You said Diana worked at one in Washington, and you said she was good at it."

"She was. What made you think of that?"

"Do you remember the other night at the Broadwaters'? I heard Mrs. Hauser say how hard it was for women in this town to get to know one another, and all the other ladies agreed with her. Well, a tearoom would be the perfect place for genteel ladies to gather."

"Oh, Case, yes! This could be the answer, and Diana would love it!" Maddie said, but then her expression changed and she looked crestfallen.

"What's wrong?"

"You can't just say you're opening a tearoom, and it becomes one. You have to have furnishings."

"What kind of furnishings?"

Well, first of all we would need tables and chairs, and then tablecloths and napkins and pretty tea carts and cups and plates."

"Hold up a minute. All those things can be had."

"Not without money," Maddie said.

"If you had the tables and chairs . . . do you think you could make the tearoom work?"

"I know we could!"

"Then you start making plans, and let me worry about getting the tables and chairs."

The next morning, Case stopped in at the Red Star Saloon, where Black Hawk Hensley was sitting at a table playing solitaire.

"Morning, Case," Black Hawk said as he rose from his seat. "What can I get you?"

"I'm here to help you earn more money," Case said, sitting opposite the manager.

"Well, let's hear what you have on your mind," Black Hawk said as he dropped back down in his chair.

"Look around this place. Joe needs to do some renovation," Case said. "You're probably the best gambling talent in town, and yet she only lets you play poker in the Red Star."

"That's true, but she says we don't have room to bring in a faro table or anything else."

"We're going to make room," Case said. "Now help me load up six or eight of these tables and the chairs that go with them. You order up a faro table and one where you can deal twenty-one, and if Joe complains, you send her to me."

"You know she's gonna be mad as hell when she comes in," Black Hawk said.

"It won't last long. When she finds out how much more money she's going to make, she'll build a fancy casino just like they have in New Orleans."

Black Hawk and Case began moving tables and chairs, and soon they had the freight wagon full.

"If you don't mind my asking, what are you gonna do with these?"

"I'm helping a woman open up a saloon," Case said.

"What? Josephine is supplying tables for a competitor!"

"Not exactly. The lady's going to be serving tea and crumpets."

Black Hawk put his head back and laughed uproariously. "Does she have any idea these are coming from a whorehouse?"

"No, and she won't find out unless you go tell her."

Case didn't take the tables and chairs to the McClellans' right away, but instead went down to the foot of Reeder's Alley, where the Chinese lived. He stopped in front of a laundry that was run by Ho Kwan's family.

"How long will it take to lacquer these chairs?" Case asked.

Ho Kwan's father walked around the wagon. "You want the tables painted, too?"

"Not if you can manage to find some tablecloths that might be a little threadbare in places. Of course, they have to be big enough to cover these."

"I can find them," the old man said. A big smile crossed his face. "Maybe the water will get too hot and six table covers shrink. What do you think?"

"I think you have the idea. How soon can you paint the chairs?"

"Two days, three at the most, if we don't get rain."

"That'll be great. Now one more thing. Can you round me up some teacups and some saucers or plates to go with them?"

"How many?"

"I think I'll need at least fifty," Case said.

"This one is hard. I don't think so."

"Sure you can. There are at least fifty laundries on Bridge Street. Get a cup and saucer from each one. They don't all have to be the same," Case explained.

"Oh, I can do that. I have them when you come for the chairs."

"You're a good man, Ho Shao. Ho Kwan will be proud of you."

Ho Shao tented his fingers and bowed his head under the praise.

Before Case left, he withdrew a twenty-dollar gold piece and left it with the old man.

"But Mama," Maddie argued. "Having a tearoom is a much better idea than taking in boarders. I know Papa will approve."

"You are going to turn my parlor into a place of business? Absolutely not. A decent woman doesn't engage in commerce," Annabelle said.

"This is different," Maddie protested. "It will be like a ladies' aid society, only the women will pay for tea. Think of it like that."

"No."

"All right, fine. I'll have Case start looking for a house for us. Maybe he can find something on Wood Street or Bridge, or perhaps Clore."

"Maddie, don't you get sassy with me. I've heard what kind of women live down there, and we don't want to associate with them."

"I don't intend to associate with them; it's just that if we don't come up with a way to make money, living there may be the only alternative," Maddie said, as she tried to impress upon her mother the seriousness of their situation.

"Roy McClellan will never allow that. He'll send us back to Washington before he'll have us live in sight of such immoral women," Annabelle said as she began to cry openly. "You don't know what degradation is until you've . . ."

Now Maddie felt ashamed that she had pushed her mother to tears.

"Mother, I'm sorry. Case told me he's already arranged for the furnishings for a tearoom. It's my fault. I should have talked it over with you before I told him to go ahead."

Maddie left the house and walked next door, hoping that Case was home. When she knocked, Ho Kwan answered the door.

"Is Case here?"

"Oh no, Miss Maddie. He goes to get the furniture today. My people have made them very, very beautiful. No one will guess they come from the whorehouse."

Maddie burst out laughing. "I'm sure no one will guess. We'll be ready for them when he arrives."

When Maddie got home, Annabelle had gone into seclusion in her chamber.

"What did you do to Mama?" Diana demanded. "She's crying her eyes out."

"I suggested we turn the parlor into a tearoom, but she doesn't think we should."

"Maddie, that's a wonderful idea. Why didn't you tell me?"

"I wanted to convince Mama first, but now you see how she's reacting. And the worst part is, the furnishings are going to be delivered this afternoon."

"How did you get furniture? You don't have that kind of money."

"Case got them from . . . some friends of his."

"Then let's start moving what furniture we can. Where do you think we should put it?"

"In my chamber. It's a big room and it has a nice fireplace. If Mama sees that she can have a parlor, maybe she won't be so opposed to it," Maddie said.

"Then where will you sleep?"

"Isn't there enough space in your room? We shared a room when we were little."

"Yes, we did, but it would be unseemly if we shared a room now," Diana said.

"Of course it would," Maddie said. "There's a room over the carriage house. That's where I'll go."

"Won't you be cold out there?"

"There's a woodstove. I'll make do."

At about four o'clock, two big freight wagons pulled up in front of the McClellan house.

"I'm looking for Diana's Tearoom," Case said when Maddie opened the door.

"This is the place," Maddie said as she stepped aside to let Case enter. "But I'm afraid we're going to have to do a little rearranging before we can bring in the tables."

"That's why I brought four strapping men with me. Just tell them what to do," Case said. "Oh, where's Diana? I have a present for her."

"You have a present for me?" Diana asked as she joined the two in the entry hall.

"I do. Jesse, bring the big one."

A large man stepped down from one of the wagons. He pulled out a very tastefully painted red sign with the words DIANA'S TEAROOM. The letters were written in gold calligraphy embellished with fancy black curlicues.

"Oh," Diana said, clearly impressed. "Diana's Tearoom. It sounds so sophisticated, and the sign is beautiful." She hugged Case and gave him a kiss.

Maddie was immediately taken aback by the kiss. It was not the spontaneous "oh thank you" kind of kiss she would have expected, and in that moment, Maddie knew true jealousy.

But why should she feel like that? Since she had met Case, she had been developing a growing admiration for him, and on more than a few occasions, she felt as though he might return her feelings. But he had made clear that he had no interest in marriage.

"Wait, there are more. Abe, get the other two."

This time there was a small sign for the front door, and another to be placed in the parlor.

While Diana supervised Case in the hanging of the signs, Maddie took two men upstairs and began disassembling her chamber. It was quick work to get her things to the carriage house.

The room was smaller than Maddie had thought, and it was not light-filled at all. A knot formed in her throat when she looked around, but she forced it back. If it meant relieving her father of some of his burdens, then this was a small sacrifice she was willing to make. She had hoped her mother would embrace this project, but so far, Annabelle had not left her room, even when she heard the commotion going on just outside her door.

❧

With the signs up, Diana was directing the movement of the furniture in the parlor.

"Maddie, do you think we should move the étagère, or should we leave it here?"

"Why don't we leave it? When we can afford pretty cups, we can display them on it," Maddie said.

"You have pretty cups," Case said. "Wait until you see them."

"Case, what would I ever do without you?" Diana asked. "You are the dearest man I've ever known."

Maddie watched as Diana's eyes grew large and she began an exaggerated batting of her eyelashes, an act Maddie had witnessed many times before. Maddie rushed for the door as the pit of her stomach suddenly began to churn.

Right then, she knew she had lost Case Williams—if, in fact, there had ever been a chance she would have him. She went to the carriage house and ascended the stairs. The decision to move out of the house might have been the best she had ever made. She would make this her nook, her hideaway. It didn't matter what her mother thought, or what her sister was doing, or what happened with Case. She would have her sanctuary.

Maddie worked for an hour getting her bed put back together and arranging her furniture. She was down in the carriage house looking for something that she could use to hang her clothes on when she discovered a rake handle that she thought would work. She was trying to dislodge it from other tools, when the door opened.

"So this is where you've disappeared to." Case stood in the fading light, his frame overpowering the opening. A huge smile was on his face. "Don't you want to come in and see how your project turned out?"

"Does she know whores have sat on her chairs?"

The sound of Case's laughter was infectious and Maddie couldn't help but join him.

"Who told you that?"

"Ho Kwan."

"Poor Ho Kwan. He'll have to go to the woodshed tonight and get forty lashes," Case said, still laughing.

"He'd better not, because I'm out here to protect him."

Case's voice softened. "Who's going to protect you?"

"Do I need protection?" Maddie asked, her voice low and seductive.

"Not from Ho Kwan."

Both Case and Maddie stood for a long moment, neither moving toward or away from the other, until Case broke the silence. "You'd better come in. I think your sister's quite proud of her new venture."

Diana was almost giddy when Maddie and Case walked into the parlor, or what used to be the parlor.

"What do you think?"

"It's beautiful. It really is," Maddie said as she looked around. "Where'd you get the red table-cloths?" She inclined her head toward Case.

"Not where you think. Muquin cut up the dragon just for you."

"Muquin?"

"I don't know if that's her name or not but that's what Ho Kwan calls his mother," Case explained.

"Well then, the tearoom is bound to be a success," Maddie said. "Isn't the dragon all about good luck?"

"It is," Case said, "but Diana's Tearoom is going to make it on its tea and crumpets."

"Oh my gosh!" Maddie's mouth dropped open and she put her hand to her chest. "In all this planning, I never thought about where we would get the food."

"Do you mean you've torn this house apart, and you never thought about that?" Diana demanded. "Case is right. If we don't have something to sell, we can't make any money."

"I still have a little money left from Washington," Maddie said. "I can buy tea and some ingredients for tea cakes, but who's going to make them?"

"I won't be able to. I'll have to entertain our guests," Diana said. "Do you think Mama will bake them?"

Maddie pursed her lips.

"Of course she won't. You're the one who upset her, so you're going to have to do it. I hope you enjoy baking, because if this works, it's going to take a lot of cookies," Diana continued. "And I'm already thinking we should serve a choice of creamed soups and chowder and perhaps some fudge and pralines."

Maddie stomped her foot. "I—can't—do—it—all—by—myself." She said each word emphatically.

Case had been watching this sisterly spat. "May I offer a suggestion?"

Both women turned to him, each one displaying a stern lip and a tight jaw.

"What about Annie Higgins? She's still staying at the International, and I'll bet she'd love to have something to do."

"You're right, Case," Maddie said. "Let's ask her."

"Do you think she can cook?" Diana asked.

"It doesn't matter. I have to have help."

"All right, we'll ask her. When do we open for business?"

"How about day after tomorrow, but let's hold off on the soup and candy."

Annabelle did not leave her room for the evening meal, so Maddie and Diana were in the kitchen deciding what they should eat.

"If I fix something for Mama, will you take it up to her?" Maddie asked.

"It should be you who does it."

"I can't. Not tonight. It's you who can do no wrong in her eyes, and if she sees me, she'll probably start crying again—if she's ever quit."

"All right."

"Diana, will you talk to her? I feel so bad about doing this, but you understand why I thought we had to, don't you?"

"Yes, I do," Diana said, "and I thank you for what you've done. The way to get Mama's approval is if we are successful, and that's up to both of us." Diana moved to Maddie, and for the first time in a long while, they embraced each other.

FOURTEEN

It was a weary Maddie who, with a lighted lantern by her side, walked down the path to the carriage house. The building had the smell of newly sawn lumber, and though she liked the scent, it was somewhat overpowering. She thought about leaving the door open, but the night air was quite cool, so she closed it.

When she reached the upper floor, she realized she had not mounted the rake handle she meant to use as a clothing rack, so her clothes were still on the bed. Moving them, she heaped them on the floor in a corner and then smiled. Her mother would be appalled if she caught her doing that, but at least this one night, she was sure her mother wouldn't be paying her a visit.

Still by the light of the lantern, she began hunting for her flannel nightdress, but when she couldn't find it, she settled for one made of foulard. It was thin, but tonight she didn't care. After she had unbraided her hair, she looked for her brush, but that, too, was not in a place where she could expect to find it. She did find her tooth powder, but she had forgotten to put water in her pitcher, so with her finger, she rubbed her teeth and then wiped them on a handkerchief.

She sat on the side of the bed and looked around. Everywhere she looked, the room was in shambles.

"Why? Why? Why?" Her body began to shake with frustration. "Why does it have to be me? Why can't I be like Diana?"

Maddie set the lantern on the table in front of the window. She would have to remember to get a lamp tomorrow, but tonight, she would keep the lantern burning. She adjusted the wick so that it was at its lowest point, then pulled back the quilt and slipped into bed.

She'd thought she would fall asleep from sheer exhaustion, but her mind wouldn't let her. Tomorrow. What would happen? She had said she would do the cooking—no, Diana had told her she would do the cooking.

Case was right. The success of this venture would stand or fail on the quality of the product, and it was she who had to produce. Closing her eyes, she uttered a silent prayer: *Please dear Lord, let Annie know how to cook.*

Her eyes opened wide and she bolted upright. What was that sound she had heard? Sitting there, she listened intently, until she finally decided it was a tree branch hitting the side of the building. Lying back down, she tried to will herself to go to sleep, but she was wide-awake.

She heard another sound, and this time it wasn't a tree branch. It was definitely the door below. She could hear the squeak of the hinge, but she told herself that if the tree branch had blown against the carriage house, perhaps the wind was strong enough to blow the door open. But then she heard a loud crash. Something was in the building, and her heart began to beat rapidly.

What should she do? Maddie always had an alternative idea, a plan. Quickly, she looked around the room. Was there any kind of escape?

"Maddie, it's Case. Are you awake?"

"Case! You scared the bejesus out of me."

"Well, I wouldn't have if you hadn't left a fool pole across the floor where anybody could trip over it."

Maddie smiled. "Maybe that was my booby trap—just in case somebody came to get me." She heard Case's chuckle.

"My intentions are honorable, madam."

"Then why are you here?"

"Actually, I thought you'd be cold. When I checked on the horses, I didn't smell any smoke, so I brought you some kindling and a couple pieces of wood. Do you mind if I come up and build a fire?"

Maddie's eyes opened wide. She had a smart retort to counter his comment, but she thought better about using it.

"I'd like that very much."

She heard what she thought must be him moving the pieces of wood, and then his footfalls were on the steps.

When he reached her room, he looked around.

"I'm guessing a hurricane came through here."

"I'd say that was what happened."

He moved toward the little potbellied stove and,

bending down, he opened the door. Putting the smallest pieces of kindling on the grate, he struck a match, and in a matter of minutes there was a small flame burning, but the smoke began coming out into the room.

"I think someone forgot to open the damper," Case said as he rose to turn the valve that controlled the draft in the pipe.

"Damn, it must be too big for this size pipe. Do you have any water? I'll have to put the fire out."

"I don't. I forgot to bring any."

"Let me open the window. It won't take long to clear out because I didn't put much wood in the stove. Another thing—don't ever leave a kerosene lantern lit when you're going to sleep." He turned down the wick, leaving the room in darkness except for the glow of the few sticks that were in the stove.

Looking back, he saw Maddie sitting on her bed in a nightdress that left little to the imagination. Her hair was as unkempt as it had been the night at the crossing. He smiled as he thought of that night.

"Your hair is down," he said. "Where's your brush?"

Maddie shook her head.

He didn't know what signal she was sending by shaking her head, but the picture she made was unbelievably beautiful. He moved toward her, and when he was beside her, she scooted over in her bed to make room for him. He knelt beside her and cupped her face in his hands so that he could read her expression. It was an invitation if ever he had seen one.

"Maddie, this isn't a game." His words sounded ragged even to himself.

She boldly reached out to touch him, first the stubble of his beard, then the hair that was falling against his forehead, and finally she traced his lips with her finger.

He caught her hand and stopped the exquisite torture as his lips slowly moved to meet hers.

When his lips first touched hers, it was a gentle caress. Maddie held her breath, not knowing how to react as the kiss deepened and caused her stomach to spiral into a wild swirl.

Case pulled back to look into the midnight pools of her eyes; then, smoothing her hair back away from her ears, he began to kiss her again, this time on her neck. Then his mouth trailed down her chest. Through the thin material of her gown, he saw the buds of her breasts react to her heightened senses, and began to twirl his tongue around first one and then the other.

It was Maddie's turn to stop this time, as she grasped his head and pulled it away. Without hesitation, she pushed out of her gown and let it fall to her waist. Then, lying down she waited—for what, she didn't know, but if it came from this man, she wanted whatever it was.

Case quickly yanked off his boots and, pulling his shirt from his pants, slipped it over his head without taking the time to undo the buttons. He sat down on the bed beside her, but before he moved toward her, he took a deep breath. Slow down, Case, slow down. Get control, he told himself. When he turned to her, she had an expression of wonder, and he knew this was her first time. That realization dampened his ardor.

He couldn't walk away and leave her. This was no ordinary woman. This was Maddie. His Maddie.

How had she done this to him? She had worked her way into his heart not by conniving or manipulating, as most women tried to do, but just by being herself. He loved her. There was no getting around it, but he would never let her know. If he let his guard down now, he would be vulnerable, and if Maddie was not the woman he thought she was and she betrayed him, he wouldn't be able to pick himself up and move on as he had done before.

This one night was hers. He would make it a night for her to remember, but he would leave her maidenhead—her treasure—for the man who would win her heart.

Turning, he lay beside her and began fulfilling his vow.

Maddie felt the rain of kisses that covered her neck, and then Case moved to her breasts. He ran his thumbs over her nipples so lightly that she barely knew he was touching her, except for the sensations that radiated through her body. Then he cupped her breasts and lowered his head, taking a nipple into his mouth. He began to suckle, not demandingly, but slowly, withdrawing and then returning, withdrawing and then returning again.

It seemed impossible to feel both agony and ecstasy at the same time, but that was exactly what she was feeling as he continued his kisses, the rough stubble of his chin brushing against her smooth skin. He rose, then, and, sliding down her body, pulled her gown with him, eventually removing it completely to leave her exposed to the cool night air.

By now what fire there had been was completely out, and Maddie could only see by the light of the moon that was filtering through the window. She felt cheated, because she wanted to know what he was doing, what his expression was, because that way she could know what was in his heart.

But if she couldn't see what he was doing, she could feel it, his mouth on her belly, his fingers exploring her mound. And then she felt his finger slide into that wet cleft, stroking her gently at first and then moving quickly and more urgently, describing circles that grew smaller and smaller until he touched a part of her that started an exciting and delightful quest for . . . for what?

All thoughts left Maddie as she concentrated every force of energy on that one small spot. Then, unable to hold back the gasps of wonder, she felt ripples of pleasure explode throughout her body. She lost all contact with reality as Case moved back up to reclaim her lips. She wound her arms around him, pulling him to her in an effort to savor this moment.

Case realized at once when Maddie reached the summit of sensation, and he knew that she was now his for the taking. His erection strained against his trousers, pushing forward so hard that it was painful. The pressure for release was nearly beyond his control, and he wanted desperately to slip out of his pants, move over her, and demonstrate to her that they had only touched the tip of the pleasure that could be theirs.

He groaned with the pain of withholding. Do it! Do it! His body shouted the words at him. But he knew he wouldn't, he couldn't. There would be no completion for him, whether it was here, with Maddie, or if he left her and went down to the Red Star.

Real completion would mean not just physical release, but total gratification, and that could only occur with a woman who loved him. As he lay beside Maddie, her arms clutching him to her body, he could not dare to hope, nor to dream, that she felt for him as he felt for her.

He knew that he should leave her, but as her breathing slowed, he couldn't do it. The feel of her, the smell of her—these were things he wanted to capture, and in lieu of sexual gratification, he felt her presence as she lay beside him. For the first time since he had left Missouri, he felt contentment.

Was this what true love was?

He closed his eyes and soon they were both sleeping peacefully. For the whole night, he never let her go.

As was his custom, Case awakened early the next morning. Maddie's head was lying on his shoulder and he squeezed her to him, secretly hoping she, too, would be awake. But she smiled and nuzzled closer to him.

What had he done? On her first night out of her father's house, he had put her in a position where her reputation would be ruined. Kissing her gently, he extricated his arm and rose quickly. Grabbing his shoes and his shirt, he went to the door, wanting to get away without waking her. He looked back: she was beautiful as she lay in the bed that was in disarray, in the room that was a shambles. This was a woman worth pursuing.

Tiptoeing down the steps, he came to the rake handle that had caused him to trip. The sticks of wood that he had been bringing were scattered all over the carriage house. He started to pick them up and put them in a neat pile, but then he stopped. Why? It wouldn't make any difference to Maddie.

Putting on his shoes and his shirt, he let himself out of the door. He had a bounce in his step as he started across the dew-covered grass, when he heard the trill of a mockingbird. He found it perched on the top of the turret.

It was then that he saw the movement of a white curtain at the window. Looking back, he saw that his tracks across the dewy grass were clearly exit tracks from the door of the carriage house.

Only one of two possible people was at that window. Please let it be Diana. He could placate her.

Maddie slept much later than she had intended, and she jumped out of bed, yanking the first dress she could find off the pile. She had so much to do today, and Diana would be waiting for her. Without even attempting to control her hair, she ran down the steps.

And there she saw it. Wood scattered all over the carriage house floor.

She stopped and closed her eyes. How could Case not have been the first thing she thought of this morning? What he had done to her—no, what he had caused her body to do—had caused her to experience the most exhilarating feeling she had ever known.

For as long as Maddie could remember, her role in the family drama had always been behind the scenes. Diana was the star, and occasionally, Maddie got to be the supporting actress.

But after last night, that had all changed. Case had made her the star. She wanted to shout it to the rafters, but, for all her joy, it would be something she could only share with Case. For that, she was sorry.

Before she left the carriage house, she moved the wood to one side and stacked it neatly, knowing that the last person to touch each stick had been Case. Then, closing the door behind her, she walked slowly toward the house. Today, she had responsibilities. She had to get a tearoom going.

"Where have you been?" Diana demanded. "You're the one who said this place is going to open tomorrow, and nothing's been done. You have to decide what we'll serve, and as far as I can tell, we have next to nothing on hand. You have to go to the grocer's, and without Papa, I don't know how you're going to get there."

"I'll take care of it," Maddie said. "Has Mama been down this morning?"

"Yes, she has. When I came down she was in the parlor."

"In the tearoom, or the upstairs parlor?"

"The tearoom."

"Good. Did she say anything?"

"When I asked her what she thought, her only

comment was, 'It's come to this.' I don't know if she'll ever accept the tearoom."

"When Papa comes home, maybe he can convince her," Maddie said.

"If we don't get busy, he won't need to say anything. It will be closed before it gets started," Diana said. "Have you even made an effort to control your hair this morning? You certainly can't go outside looking like you do. No self-respecting woman would set foot in a business where the help looked so messy."

"I couldn't find my brush this morning. May I borrow yours?"

"I suppose so, but make sure you put it away. It's in the first drawer of my chest."

Maddie ran up the stairs and went into Diana's chamber. Finding the brush exactly where Diana had said it would be, Maddie quickly fixed her hair, putting it in her customary braid. There was a red ribbon in the drawer, and, picking it up, Maddie tied it around the end of her braid. She brought it to her lips and kissed it.

"This is for you, Case. Thank you."

Just then, she heard her mother in the hallway.

"My dear, would you fetch me . . ." Annabelle stopped when she saw that she was addressing Maddie and not Diana. Maddie had never seen such a look of hate on anyone's face, much less her mother's. Annabelle turned and returned to her room, slamming the door as she entered.

Maddie couldn't stand it. She followed her mother and, opening the door, entered her room. "Mama, I'm sorry." Her mother stood in the circular alcove that jutted out from her room. Her gaze was fixed on some indeterminate object in the backyard.

Maddie would have loved to go to her mother and beg her forgiveness, to tell her that if it was this painful, she would have the tearoom dismantled and the parlor returned to its previous state, but if the tearoom was going to have any chance of succeeding, she didn't have time. She turned away, leaving her mother staring through the back window.

Maddie took a quick inventory of the items they had on hand, and, checking through *Miss Beecher's Domestic Receipt Book*, found a myriad of recipes for tea cakes. She read several and then settled on one that looked good.

"Royal crumpets." Maddie thought of the line Case had used. *Diana's Tearoom is going to make it on its tea and crumpets.*

"If you think you can make them, that's fine with me," Diana said when Maddie made the suggestion.

"Then it's settled. I'm off to get the groceries."

Maddie started to walk to Main Street, but then she thought about Lucky. Case had told her the horse was hers to use, so, grabbing two apples, she went to the stable to get a bridle. Then, stepping into the enclosed pasture behind the building, she put two fingers in the corners of her mouth and whistled, just as her father had taught her. Both horses came trotting obediently to her, and she fed each of them an apple. Slipping the bridle over Lucky's head, she led her into the stable and soon had her saddled, then was on her way to the grocer's.

"Let's see," the grocer said as he checked off Maddie's list. "You got tea, flour, eggs, butter, sugar, saleratus, baking powder, yeast powder, molasses, and lemons. Is that it?"

"I think it is," Maddie said.

"You don't have any meat. Are you sure you don't need any?" the grocer asked. "A lot of teams arrived from the Bitterroot Valley yesterday—brought in twelve thousand pounds of choice bacon. Ever store in town's got it for sale, but I'm sellin' it for a penny less."

"No, thank you."

"What about some sarsaparilla or maybe some champagne cider? We got that, too."

Maddie laughed. "Sir, you're quite a salesman, but I think I've got all I can afford."

"I have to ask. What you plannin' on doing with all this here bakin' stuff? We've got more'n enough bakeries in town, and I hate to see you lose your money 'fore you get started."

"My sister and I are opening a tearoom."

"A tearoom? You mean like them they got down by Reeder's Alley? Them Chinese? Now they drink lots of tea."

Maddie immediately thought of their cups and tablecloths, which had indeed come from those very places.

"We like the colors the Chinese use, so we've tried to make our tearoom look like theirs," Maddie said, "but we want ours to serve only ladies."

"You don't say," the grocer said. "You think you'll make any money doin' that?"

"I hope so," Maddie said. "Would you mind if I put a sign up here to tell the women where we are and what we're doing?"

"Go ahead." He pulled out several sheets of paper and a lead pencil. "Puttin' up the signs is goin' to cost you fifty cents."

"Fifty cents?"

"Yes, ma'am."

Fifty cents was the cost the grocer charged to deliver the groceries, and she had worked her budget out to the exact penny. But how else was she going to let women know about the tearoom?

"Thank you, sir. By the way will you hold my order? I'll be sending a buckboard shortly."

"If it don't take too long. An order this big sittin' around gets in the way of my other customers."

After putting up her sign, Maddie left, leading Lucky the short distance to the Diamond R. She didn't know if she wanted to see Case this morning or if she wished he would be out of the office, but she had to find a way to get her groceries home.

She needn't have worried. When Case saw her, he came out to meet her, a broad smile spreading across his face.

"Good morning, sleepyhead. You look exceptionally beautiful this morning."

Maddie's face flushed. "Shh. Don't tell anybody."

Case chuckled. "Tell me, how can saying you're beautiful be telling anybody anything that they can't already see?"

Maddie suddenly grew serious. "Because I guess it's not something I'm used to hearing." She looked away, avoiding his penetrating gaze. "Case, I need your help."

"What's happened?" Case's thoughts went immediately to the moving curtain at the turret window. "Has Diana said something to you?"

"No, but she will if you can't help me. I need a wagon to pick up my order at the grocery store."

Case let out a long sigh, relieved that her problem was so simple to remedy. "That's easy to fix. Where should we go?"

"The Choice Family Grocery. When I arranged for the signs, I didn't have enough money left to pay for the delivery."

"And Sol wouldn't deliver it for free."

"I didn't ask."

"And I'm glad you didn't, because it made you come to see me this morning."

Case leaned toward Maddie and she thought he was going to kiss her right here in front of the Diamond R, so she moved backward until she ran into Lucky. Then, quickly, she swung up into the saddle.

"Thank you, Case. I'm going to put up more signs, and then I'm going to go see Annie."

Jasper Cline was in the wagon yard, and Case called to him to bring up a buckboard.

"That was the McClellan woman you was a talkin' to, wasn't it?" Jasper asked.

"Yes, I need you to go pick up an order from Sol Lampel's and take it up to their place. It's the big house next to mine."

"Yes, sirree, boss, I'll be happy to see that little

old gal again," Jasper said. "I ain't seen gams like that since Rosa lost her petticoat."

Case turned to Jasper and grabbed him by the shirt. "If I ever hear you say something like that about that woman again, you're fired. Do I make myself clear?"

"Yes, sir," Jasper stammered. "Yes, sir."

Case turned and entered the building, leaving Jasper behind.

"I think it's time to make us up a pool," Clyde Pell said as he stepped up beside Jasper. "It sounds to me like old Case has been bit by the bug."

"This is September. My bet is he's hitched by Christmas," Jasper said.

"Oh no, it'll be before that."

The next morning, a cheerful Annie Higgins came into the kitchen.

"This is so exciting—a tearoom, right here in Helena," she said. "I'm so glad you asked me to help, because it gets so boring at the hotel. What do you want me to do?"

"You'll be the waitress, but today, it shouldn't be that hard. Our cook only made one kind of tea cake," Diana said.

"Well, 'our cook' had other things to do, like get the groceries, put up flyers, and, as if that wasn't enough, I had to find plates that weren't all crazed," Maddie said. "Remind me to tell Ho Kwan we're going to need more napkins."

"Ho Kwan? Who's that?" Annie asked.

"He's Case Williams's houseboy," Diana said. "Maddie's been running back and forth so many times you'd think she lives over there."

"Is she going to see the houseboy or is she going to see the man of the house?" Annie asked.

"She says it's the houseboy, but it's probably the horse," Diana said as she picked up some candlesticks. "Now that you're here, I'm going to make certain everything's ready in the parlor. Oh, Maddie, keep the tea cakes in the warming oven, but don't let them get too hard."

Maddie did as Diana had suggested, and when Diana was gone, she turned to Annie.

"Speaking of man of the house, what's happened to Mr. White? Do you still intend to marry him?"

"Yes, he takes me to the Imperial every Saturday night."

"And that's it? He takes you to a restaurant once a week and he considers that courting?"

"You don't understand. There are more kilns opening all the time, and Mr. White thinks he has to stay out at Nelson Gulch. He's even built a cabin out there."

"And now he wants you to live out there."

"Yes. But Dale doesn't think I should," Annie said.

"Dale? You mean Mr. Hathaway?"

Annie nodded her head, as tears began to gather in her eyes. "Dale, he, uh . . ." She stopped, unable to continue the sentence.

"Oh, Annie," Maddie said as she sensed immediately what the situation was. "You've gotten yourself into a real predicament, haven't you?"

"What am I going to do, Maddie? Mr. White is such a nice man. He paid a lot of money to bring me here, and now he's spending more every day for me to stay at the hotel."

"You could—" Maddie stopped before she finished her sentence. She was going to say that Annie could stay with her but that wouldn't work. The thought of Case lying in her bed came to her mind. No, if she was going to be relegated to the carriage house, she didn't want a roommate. "Now that you're going to be making some money of your own, maybe you can find a cheaper place to stay."

"Dale and I have talked about that, but his office is right around the corner from the hotel. If I move someplace else he'll never be able to—"

"Come see you."

"Yes. Mr. Howe has been so good about everything. He lets Dale come and go through the back door," Annie said, as tears flowed freely down her cheeks. "Oh, Maddie, I'm just miserable. What am I going to do?"

Maddie enfolded Annie in her arms as she offered her what little comfort she could.

Case grabbed a handful of goodies as he left the house. The tearoom had been in operation for a little over a week, and every day more and more women were coming to call.

Maddie had asked him if he could get a few more tables from the Red Star, but Josephine Airey had balked when she found out where the tables were going. He had stopped by the Furniture Emporium, and he had convinced Richard Curtis that with so many women going to Diana's Tearoom, Richard could afford to supply a table or two for free advertising. Of course he had to agree to give Curtis and

Booker lower freight rates when their next shipment of furniture arrived.

Case smiled as he took a bite of one of the tea cakes. When he considered how much time he had spent getting the tearoom up and going, he decided these little crumpets were worth more than gold nuggets. Maddie and Diana both seemed to be pleased with how the business was growing, but he felt like Maddie had taken on the brunt of the work.

He stopped by every night, hoping that she would be able to go for a ride with him or perhaps go out to dinner with him, but she always had something that needed to be done. The tablecloths had to be ironed, or the sourdough had to be fed, or the floor had to be scrubbed. And it was always Maddie doing the work, never Mrs. McClellan or Diana.

He decided he was going to get Maddie a present. Quickly he sketched out a design, and when he reached the Diamond R, he went to the harness maker.

"Gus, how many hides do you have?" Case asked.

"I've got more than enough. What do you need?"

Case handed him the crude drawing. "Can you make something like this?"

Gus looked at the sketch and then back at Case. A frown crossed his face. "Oh, boss, I don't know. I ain't never done nothing like this before."

"You work with leather, don't you?"

"Well, yeah."

"This is leather. You figure out how to get it done."

FIFTEEN

The Wells Fargo coach pulled away from Bozeman on time, and Roy McClellan was aboard. He felt good about his first foray into the field. The siege by the Sioux had been negotiated, and a detachment of soldiers from Fort Ellis was now occupying Fort Pease.

If only his problems in Helena could be solved as easily.

He'd had time to contemplate a solution while he was away, and he had come to the conclusion that he would send Annabelle and the girls back to Washington. In his mind, he knew that only Maddie would be disappointed.

He smiled as he thought about her. She should have been a boy. Unlike Diana, she didn't appear to be fixated on finding a husband to take care of her, and he was sure she could make it on her own if circumstances demanded it.

How would Annabelle cope? The thought of living separately had crossed his mind many times, and if it would not be such an embarrassment, he would have sued her for divorce.

But on what grounds?

He couldn't claim drunkenness or adultery or willful desertion. What he could claim was extreme cruelty, but he knew he would never do that. To go into a courtroom and tell the world that he and his wife had not had marital relations for more than twenty years—no, no man needed that humiliation.

He took out his wallet and withdrew a folded piece of paper. On it was a pencil sketch of him and a beautiful young woman, she but a few years older than Diana. Written across the bottom was a note: *To my dear Roy, until we meet again, Lilla.*

He held the paper in his hand for a long time as he recalled every moment of this unexpected pleasure. Perhaps the Sioux Agency would require much of his time.

When Case walked up to the back door of the tearoom, he was surprised to find Dale Hathaway there with a keg of butter on his shoulder. He was trying to lift the door to the root cellar.

"Wouldn't that be a little easier if you set the keg down?" Case asked, as he pulled the door free.

"Thanks," Dale said. "Annie tells me you get all the cookies at the end of the day, so I thought I'd better come on up to get my share."

"You can have the crumpets, but not any of the new recipes," Case said. "Who would have thought this thing would take off like this?"

"I think it's because of Elizabeth Fisk. She makes

poor James put every little thing they talk about in the paper."

Just then, Roy came around the corner of the house, a grin on his face.

"What is this? I go out of town and when I come home, there are so many carriages in front of my house I have to walk a quarter of a mile."

"Professor," Case said extending his hand. "A lot has happened since you left."

"I can see that. Diana's Tearoom?"

"Yes, it was Maddie's idea."

"Of course it was," Roy said as he shook his head. "That girl is something."

"Well, as you can see, it's very successful. Annie's working here, too," Dale said.

"What does Mr. White think about that?"

Dale looked away, not meeting Roy's eyes.

"Annie's still living at the hotel," Case said.

"I see," Roy said as he arched his eyebrows. "Well, I guess I'd better go in and make my presence known."

"Papa, you're home!" Maddie said as she ran to meet her father.

"There's my entrepreneur," Roy said as he embraced his daughter. "These gentlemen tell me you've got quite a business going."

"It's not just me. Diana is doing a fantastic job entertaining the ladies, and Annie is running her legs off just keeping their teacups filled."

"And what about your mother? Is she enjoying the company?"

"That's the only bad part, Papa. Mama was against

this from the beginning, and now she barely speaks to me."

"Does she know how much money you're bringing in?"

"She doesn't care."

"Well, I'll have to have a little talk with her."

"I'm glad you're home."

Roy took a deep breath before he knocked on Annabelle's door.

"Are you in here?"

After a moment, the door opened and Annabelle stepped to one side to admit Roy. She returned to her chair in the turret alcove and sat down, taking up her tatting needles.

"My trip to Bozeman was most interesting. I met with the commandant at Fort Ellis and I believe the Sioux are pacified."

"I'm pleased that you were able to resolve the conflict." Annabelle's voice was flat and emotionless.

"So am I." Roy hesitated before he continued. "The tearoom is such an ingenious idea. Having women come for the afternoon must provide a lot of entertainment for you, Annabelle. It's so much better than having a boarder, and it gives the girls something they can be proud of. I thank you for supporting them."

Annabelle glared at Roy. "I'm sure Madelyn told you that what you're saying is not true. I'm not supporting them; I think having this go on under my very nose is an abomination."

"Serving tea and cookies? I hardly think that's offensive."

"Serving tea and cookies is not the issue. Serving up one's body is the issue."

"And what does that mean?"

"You'll have to ask your precious daughter. If you will, please close the door when you leave."

Ignoring Annabelle, Roy closed the door.

"Woman, I believe it's time you and I had a talk. I've been away for almost three weeks, and when you see me, all you can do is throw out some insane comment that makes no sense."

"Oh, it makes perfect sense. Your precious daughter invited Case Williams to her room, and she can't lie her way out of it."

"Did you ask her for an explanation?"

"I didn't have to. I saw it with my own two eyes," Annabelle said, as she glared at him. "That snake in the grass comes around here all the time, putting his nose in where it doesn't belong. And what does he do the first time he gets a chance? He beds your daughter."

"You know that for a fact."

"Why else would he be putting on his clothes while he's sneaking away from the carriage house at six in the morning? And to think, I once thought he was good enough for Diana."

"Well, for certain, we wouldn't want anything to happen to Diana, but if it's Maddie, we don't care, now, do we?"

Roy turned and left Annabelle staring after him as he slammed the door. Leaning against the wall, he closed his eyes as he rubbed his temples. What was he going to say to Maddie—or to Case, for that matter?

He thought of his trip to Bozeman and of the pleasure Lilla had provided him; he was no hypocrite. If what Annabelle had seen was indeed a tryst, he could only hope that Case Williams was an honorable man.

Over the next several days, the tearoom became even more popular, and one particularly busy day Maddie and Annie were in the kitchen. Diana had requested a choice between cream of pea or potato soup to be added to the menu along with a yeast roll, and she extended the hours, opening at eleven instead of one o'clock, and not closing until seven.

"Maddie, I don't know how you can do any more," Annie said. "I would think your mother or Diana would do some of the work."

"I'm just happy Mama has finally accepted the tearoom, and she's at least speaking to me again. Diana said she won the bridge tournament yesterday, so that was good," Maddie said. "I only wish you and I would have a chance to go in and sit down for just one day."

"I know, but that's not going to happen," Annie said.

Just then, the back door opened and Dale Hathaway stepped in.

"Dale!" Annie said, her face brightening. "What are you doing here so early?"

"If your boss will let you off, I have to take some papers out to Nave's ranch, and I thought you might like to come along," Dale said. "It's been a long time since you came on a carriage ride with me."

Annie looked toward Maddie. Several cups and

plates were sitting beside the dishpan, and the bread dough was almost ready to be punched down and made into rolls. Maddie was putting together a new batch of biscuits, and flour was all over the board.

"Go ahead, Annie."

"Are you sure?" Annie asked as she untied her apron.

"Of course, go ahead."

Annie and Dale had just left when Diana opened the door and called to Maddie.

"Where's the hot tea? And we need more cakes. Annie needs to get out here right now."

"I'll take care of it," Maddie said, leaving her task and grabbing the teapots.

When she returned to the kitchen, her father was there. He had taken off his jacket and his sleeves were rolled up, and he was standing at the dishpan washing teacups.

"Papa! What are you doing?"

"I'm washing dishes. It looks to me like your help has abandoned you and you could use a little assistance."

"Thank you, Papa," Maddie said, as she grabbed her apron. "It's been a long day."

Case hated it when he couldn't get away from his desk, and he gladly took the pouch of outgoing mail to the post office.

"Looks like you're drummin' up more business," Isaac Crounse said, as he took the mail from Case and began affixing stamps to the envelopes. "I'm glad you came in today. I got a registered letter for the Diamond R here. Let me get my registry book and you can sign for it."

When Case signed the book, he saw that the notation directly above the one for the Diamond R was a letter for Roy McClellan.

"Here it is," Isaac said. "Second one from the government I've handed out today."

When Case returned to the Diamond R he tore open the letter and began to read:

> *A representative of the freighting transfer company doing business as the Diamond R, located in Helena, Montana Territory, and executing contracts to and with the Department of Interior, with the express purpose of transporting freight and annuities to and from said Indian Agencies serving the following tribes: Piegan Blackfoot, Sioux, Assiniboine, Gros Ventre, Cree, Crow, and Nez Perce, is hereby summoned to Fort Shaw, Montana Territory, on September 24, 1875.*
>
> *Commissioner Samuel Walker, a duly appointed officer of the United States government, will be in attendance to discuss the alleged fraudulent contracts being entered into by said freighting transfer company and the Department of Interior.*
> *Signed,*
> *Columbus Delano, Secretary of the Interior.*

"Damn, Charles, do you know what this is about?" Case asked as he threw the letter on his partner's desk.

"I can't say that I do," Charles said after looking over the letter. "Alleged fraudulent contracts? Alleged by who?"

"It doesn't say, but whoever it is, they don't know this company. What other company hauls freight in the dead of winter? I don't see Kirkendall going to hell and back just to get supplies to some starving band of Indians."

"I'll bet McClellan knows something about this," Charles said. "You don't think he's the one who made a complaint?"

"I don't think so. We haven't spoken about this, but I noticed he signed for a certified letter, too. I'll go see what he knows."

When Case got to Roy's office, it was locked, so he headed up to the house. It was a good excuse to see Maddie, anyway—as if he needed any excuse at all.

It was close to four o'clock when Case got to the tearoom, where several horses hitched to cabriolets were tied to the hitching rail. He smiled, thinking it must be whist day.

"What kind of muffin do we have today?" Case asked as he opened the door. "Oh, Professor, I was looking for you, but I didn't expect to find you in the kitchen."

"If it's all the same, this will just be between you and me," Roy said, chuckling. "Annie's not here, and Maddie's been serving and cooking and cleaning all by herself. If she's going to be keeping a roof over my head, I figure putting my hands in the dishwater is the least I can do to help her. Now, you said you were looking for me. What do you need?"

Case pulled the letter out of his pocket. "I got a registered letter from Secretary Delano today, and as I read it, someone's accusing the Diamond R of cheating the government. Do you know anything about this?"

"Then that might explain a letter I got today. I've been called to Fort Shaw to meet with Sam Walker. The only thing my letter said was that the commissioner needs to discuss nonspecific irregularities."

"Are you supposed to be there this Friday?"

"Yes, the twenty-fourth."

"Then I suppose we can ride up together," Case said.

"That would be good," Roy said, thinking that during the trip, he might have an opportunity to feel out Case's intentions toward Maddie.

Just then, Maddie returned to the kitchen. She looked as bedraggled as Case had ever seen her, and her chin quivered as she worked to hold back tears.

"Hi, Case," she said as she literally fell into a chair.

"What's wrong?" Case asked.

"I'm tired. I'm so tired."

Case knelt beside her and began pushing strands of hair behind her ears.

"You need rest. Go out to the carriage house and lie down. Your father and I will finish up for you."

"I can't do that. I have to get ready for tomorrow."

"No," Roy said. "Case is right. You need to get out of here for a while."

The door to the kitchen swung open and Diana entered, followed closely by Annabelle.

"How could you do this to me?" Diana yelled.

"Look at these." She threw a biscuit at the table and it bounced.

"You cannot expect our guests to pay good money for items that aren't fit to eat," Annabelle added. "If you can't do any better than this, it's time we hired someone who can do the work."

"If you treat whoever you hire the way you treat me, they won't work for you for a whole day," Maddie said angrily, as she rose from the chair. She pulled off her apron and headed for the door, with Case following closely behind her.

"Yes, that's right, Mr. Williams, you go 'comfort' the little slut. Stay all night with her again," Annabelle said.

Case turned quickly and glared at Annabelle. "Don't you ever call your daughter a slut. She has more decency than—"

"I don't need to be lectured by the likes of you. Can you deny you've not spent the night with her in that . . . room she has over the carriage house?"

Diana gasped. "You spent the night with Maddie?"

"It was not what you thought, Mrs. McClellan," Case said.

"There's the proof," Annabelle said turning to Roy. "I told you I saw him leaving the carriage house, and he doesn't deny it. See to it that this bastard gets out and stays out of my house."

"This is my house, too, and I will not have my wife abusing a man who has been nothing but helpful and courteous to our family, and you will not defame my daughter."

"Mr. McClellan, you have two daughters, or have you forgotten that fact?" Annabelle asked. "Diana has been thoroughly humiliated before her friends. Just how do you expect to restore her reputation?"

"I don't intend to," Roy said. "Case, would you be opposed to Maddie accompanying us to Fort Shaw?"

"I wouldn't be opposed at all."

"All right, if you'll go tell her, I'll expect to leave at daybreak."

"You can't do that, Papa. Who will do my cooking?" Diana asked.

"Perhaps your mother will take over Maddie's tasks," Roy said, a stone-cold expression on his face. He turned toward Annabelle. "That is, if she hasn't forgotten every connubial duty a wife is expected to perform."

Annabelle burst into tears and ran from the kitchen.

"I suggest you either take care of your guests or else close the tearoom for the evening," Roy said. "When I return, you and your mother and I will discuss future plans for Diana's Tearoom, if there is to be a future."

"Oh, Papa, please don't make me close it. I've never done anything that I enjoy as much as this."

Roy smiled. "I'm glad to hear you say that. I'm proud of what my daughters have accomplished, but the two of you have got to stop competing all the time."

Diana laughed. "I think that may be easier now."

"Why do you say that?"

"Because Maddie won the contest."

"Did Case know he was the prize?" Roy asked.

"I don't think so. He only had eyes for her from the very beginning, because Maddie is genuine,"

Diana said. "I tried to show her the way, but I guess she showed me."

Roy embraced Diana. "Perhaps she did. All you have to do is be yourself and people will love you, but now you'd better get out there and pour some more tea. Your patrons are going to revolt."

Case had Maddie's present in his hand as he headed for the carriage house. Gus had done an excellent job of sewing, and Case was sure Maddie would appreciate his gift, especially under the circumstances.

"Maddie? May I come up?" Case called.

"You might as well. I am so sorry," Maddie said. "I've never talked to my mother like that. Will she ever forgive me?"

Case was glad Maddie had not heard the hurtful things her mother had said. It was just as well.

"Sometimes people say things in the heat of an argument that neither person means. Let's hope what was said tonight can be forgotten."

Maddie smiled. "It was funny, though, when Diana bounced the biscuit. I knew they were bad, but I didn't think they were that bad."

"Well, you're not going to have to cook for a while," Case said.

"Oh, did she mean it when she said she's going to get somebody else?" Maddie's expression was crestfallen.

"Not exactly. Your father and I have been called to Fort Shaw, and your papa thought you might want to come along with us. Are you up to riding that far?"

"How far is it?"

"It's not too far from the crossing. It shouldn't take us more than two days to get there."

"I would love to get away from here for a few days," Maddie said, as she threw her arms around Case.

"Be careful," Case said as he hugged her to him. "You know what can happen when we're in this room together."

"Shhh." Maddie held her finger to her lips. "Someone may hear us talking."

Case took her hand in his and lifted it to his mouth and kissed it. "I have a present for you." He handed her a bundle that was tied together with a strip of leather.

"What is it?"

"Untie it and see."

The gift appeared to be a tanned deerskin, but when she unrolled it, she realized it was a skirt.

"A leather skirt. Thank you, Case."

"It's not just a skirt," Case said. "Look underneath those panels. It's a divided skirt, and these panels can be taken off when we're out on the trail, and the skirt will act like trousers. Then when you want to look like a lady again, you attach the panels and no one will know you're wearing pants."

"This is the most practical thing I've ever seen. Where did you get this?"

"From my harness maker."

"He's not going to be your harness maker for long," Maddie said as she held the skirt up to her waist. "When someone sees me in this, they'll want to know where I got it, and your harness maker will have to open a factory just to make ladies' riding skirts."

"That could very well be. Tonight I want you to get a good night's sleep, because your father says we have to leave at daybreak. Take a coat, and try to borrow one of your father's slouch hats."

"I'll be ready."

Maddie's smile made his pulse quicken, and it was all he could do to keep from taking her to her bed and smothering her with kisses. He decided it was probably a good thing Roy McClellan was going on this trip as well, because if the opportunity arose, he was sure he wouldn't be able to stop himself with just a kiss. And then what would Annabelle have to say?

Maddie was overjoyed to be on Lucky again, and she took her through her paces, just to let the horse know she was in control. She hadn't realized how much she had missed being on a horse, and she relished every moment of the ride.

As when they had first come to Helena, they met and passed several coaches and trains coming and going from Fort Benton, with the majority belonging to the Diamond R. She supposed Case was a wealthy man, but he was the most unassuming rich man she had ever known. No matter who they met, he treated everyone the same, calling to them by name and taking some good-natured teasing, much of which seemed to result from her being present. If ever she was going to marry, she would want the man to be just like Case.

They reached St. Peter's Mission by midafternoon.

Maddie was pleased to be riding, and when they reached the lane, she slid to the ground and walked up to the church.

Mother Raffaella was sitting in a big circle, surrounded by the Indian children. When she heard the horses approaching, she looked up and, seeing Maddie walking up the lane, called out a welcoming greeting.

Maddie returned the wave.

It was then that four of the girls jumped up and ran to meet Case. He dismounted and opened his arms.

"Hold up, hold up," he said. "You're going to knock me over. One, two, three, four." He cocked his head. "I thought I had five girls. Here's Kimi and Nuna and Pana and little Koko, but one is missing. Who can it be?"

The smallest child, now laughing, said, "You know who it is, Uncle Case. It's Kanti. She's down by the river. She doesn't want to sew."

"Welcome to you all," Mother Raffaella said with a smile. "Kanti is just being Kanti. She doesn't know you're here yet, so I'll send someone to get her."

"Do you mind if I go get her?" Maddie asked, when she reached Case and the others.

"I think she would like that. The last I saw of her, she was sitting on the flat rock down by the river."

Maddie soon found the little girl, who was sitting cross-legged on the rock. When the child looked up, she had on one of the most forlorn expressions Maddie had ever seen.

"Do you mind if I sit beside you?" Maddie asked. "I'll bet you don't remember me."

"You came with Uncle Case."

"That's right. Do you remember my name?"

"Miss Maddie."

"That's it. Are you sitting out here so you can catch a fish?"

"No."

"Then why aren't you up with the other girls, sitting in the circle?"

"Because they're Indians."

"Oh," Maddie said, without any further comment.

The two sat silently for several moments as Kanti picked up small stones and threw them in the river.

"I don't want to make an old Indian dress," Kanti said at last.

"Is that what the other girls are doing?"

"Uh-huh."

"Did you know your Uncle Case is here?"

A broad smile crossed the little girl's face. She stood up quickly and began running back to the mission, in search of Case. She was wearing the same faded calico dress she had been wearing when Maddie had first seen her. Maddie knew intuitively that this child needed someone to love her, and she was sorry that she would be leaving for Fort Shaw in the morning.

A thought crossed her mind. It wasn't necessary that Maddie make the trip to Fort Shaw. Perhaps it would be better if she stayed at the mission and worked with Kanti.

When Maddie rejoined the girls, Case was listening intently to what they were telling him.

"He couldn't talk and he couldn't move," Pana said.

"So did you just leave him on the fish platform?" Case asked.

"No, we lashed the travois together and rolled him on top of it," Kimi said. "And then we pulled him up to the cabin, but we couldn't get him inside."

"I stayed with him all night," Kanti said. "He didn't die."

"You were all very brave," Case said.

Maddie saw a troubled look in his eyes.

"Did you tell Father Imoda what happened to your papa?"

"No, no," Nuna said. "Papa told us if we said anything, we couldn't come to school anymore."

"Well, I'm glad you're telling me, but now I want you girls to spend the night here at the mission. I'm going to asked Father Imoda to come with me to check on your papa. Will you do that?"

"He won't like it if we don't come home," Kimi said. "What will he have to eat if I'm not there to fix something?"

"Don't worry, little one. We'll take care of him. But now I need you to take care of Miss Maddie while I'm gone. Can you do that?"

There were several nods and smiles as the girls assured him they would.

"Good. See to it she goes to bed early, because she's got a long ride tomorrow."

Father Imoda and Case were soon on their way to Riley's cabin and Case was relating what the girls had told him.

"I can't be certain, but it sounds like he might have had an apoplectic seizure," Father Imoda said. "We used to call it a blood stroke, and that's exactly what it is—a hemorrhage in the brain. Did the girls say anything about his gait or his speech?"

"Yes, he was dragging a leg, and for a while Kimi said she couldn't understand much of what he was saying."

"Those are the classic symptoms," Father Imoda said. "If I could've gotten to him sooner, maybe we could have bled him and relieved some of the pressure on his brain, but it's too late for that. It's a miracle he survived."

"Is there a chance this will happen again?"

"Very much so. Whatever it was that caused this stroke didn't just get better on its own," Father Imoda said, as Riley's cabin came into sight.

Case took a deep breath. "I'm afraid I've got a very hard decision to make. Let's see what the old bird's going to say."

The girls had watched as Case and Father Imoda had ridden off, but when the men could no longer be seen, the children returned to the circle where Mother Raffaella was helping with sewing projects— all except Kanti, who stayed at the end of the lane.

Maddie walked down to her and, standing beside her, put her arm around the girl's shoulders.

"Is Papa going to die?" Kanti asked, holding back a sob.

Maddie was at a loss as to how to answer that question.

"I don't know, sweetheart. But Father Imoda is also a doctor, so I know your papa will get the best attention."

"Both of my mamas died."

"You had two mamas?"

"I had a mama when I was little, but she died. Then Badger Woman was my mama, and she died, too. When Papa dies, there will be nobody to take care of us."

Maddie's heart went out to the little girl, and she very much wanted to say that she would take care of the child, but she knew that wasn't practical. Instead, she bent down and pulled the child into her arms.

"Let's not think about that right now," Maddie said. "Your papa is still alive and your Uncle Case and Father Imoda have gone to see about him. And now, do you know what I think?"

Kanti shook her head.

"I'll bet Uncle Case brings your papa back to the mission. I think that's why he asked you and your sisters to stay here tonight."

"He wants us to take care of you."

"He did say that didn't he? Why don't we surprise him and you can teach me how to sew. Then you'll have a pretty new dress when your papa gets here?"

"They're making Indian dresses. I don't want to wear an old Indian dress."

Kanti's response answered Maddie's unasked question as to why the little girl was wearing a dress of faded calico.

"Why don't you want to wear an Indian dress?"

"I don't want to be an Indian. I want to be like Papa and Uncle Case." She crossed her arms and stuck out her lips.

"Honey, everybody knows Indians are noble people. You should be proud of your heritage."

"What does that mean?"

"It means all the traditions your people handed down to you. The songs, the clothing, the food—all the stuff that makes an Indian an Indian."

"Then why did the soldiers come to kill us?"

That question, coming from the mouth of this innocent child, stunned Maddie, and for a moment she was unable to respond.

"I don't know the answer," Maddie said. "But there aren't any soldiers here. Everybody who knows you loves you, so you don't have to be afraid."

Kanti hugged Maddie, and as she did so, the girl began fingering the soft leather of Maddie's new riding skirt.

"Is this an Indian dress?"

"Why, I suppose it is, in a way. It's made out of deer hide, just like Indians use," Maddie said.

"Then maybe it would be all right if I had one, too."

"That sounds like a good idea, but you'll have to show me how to make it."

SIXTEEN

Case and Father Imoda covered the ten miles to the old mountain man's cabin in about an hour and a half.

"Riley!" Case called. "Riley! Where are you?"

Case was a little concerned when there was no answer. He dismounted and walked toward the cabin.

"Riley, it's me, Case. I'm coming in, so don't shoot me, you old coot!"

The door opened before Case reached the cabin, and Riley stepped outside. Case noticed immediately that he was walking with a slight limp.

"What are you doin' in this neck of the woods?" Riley asked. Then he saw Father Imoda. "Why'd you bring him here? Has something happened to one of my girls?"

"No, they're all fine. Just worried about you, is all."

"So you brung this black robe out to check on me?"

"He is a doctor."

"I know he's a doctor. Who says I need a doctor?"

"Five little girls think you need one."

"Well, I'm fine, so take him back." Riley turned and went into the cabin.

Case and Father Imoda followed him in.

"Kimi said you passed out down by the river."

"Hell, that warn't nothin'. You ever been so bone tired you fell asleep and couldn't wake yerself up?" Riley asked.

"Only when I've had too much to drink," Case said, "and I can bet you weren't drinking when you were checking the fish pen."

"You got that right. I don't drink when I got my girls around."

"That's a commendable thing, Mr. Barnes. Do you mind if I examine you?" Father Imoda asked.

"Examine me for what? You can damn well see I'm just fine. I'm an old man."

"Let me look at your tongue."

"My tongue? What can my tongue tell you about me passin' out?"

"The color of your tongue can be a sign of apoplexy."

"Apoplexy?"

"Yes, have you ever heard of it?" Father Imoda asked.

"I've lived in these mountains for more'n forty years. Who in the hell is gonna tell me somethin' like that?"

"I think that's what has happened to you. It looks like you've got a partial loss of movement on your right side. Is that true?" Father Imoda asked.

"That ain't so."

"Here, hold this," Case said, as he handed Riley a cast-iron pot.

Riley dropped it with a clatter. "You surprised me, that was all." He leaned down and picked up the pot with his left hand and put it back on the hook.

"I think you should come back to the mission with me," Father Imoda said. "I'd like to observe you for a while and start administering some extracts of aloe and some calomel. That will work as a purgative for you."

"I'm not takin' any of your damn white man's medicine. If Badger Woman was here, she'd have medicine. Her medicine would work."

"Riley, don't be a cantankerous ass. You can't stay out here by yourself, not now. This could happen again at any time and you might not recover the next time. Then what do the girls do?" Case asked. "Do you really think Blackfoot medicine would cure you?"

"You're damn right. This fool said his medicine would work as a purgative. Now, I do know what that means, and you can't tell me that shittin' in the woods is gonna cure me of this apple . . . apple . . . whatever it is. Nope. I ain't gonna do it."

"Then that settles it. You're coming with me," Case said. "Do you remember Professor McClellan?"

"The one from Washington that come through here first of the summer?"

"Yes, he and I are on our way to Fort Shaw. If you and the girls will come with me, we'll go out to the agency and find out where White Calf's band is camped. Then you can see the medicine woman and she can give you the same thing Badger Woman would have given you."

"Case, you tricked me."

"No, I didn't. You're the one who said Badger Woman could have cured you. Now we'll go to the Blackfoot."

"I can't do it."

"Now why not?" Case was beginning to lose patience.

"The girls. They can't be ridin' with three men."

"The professor's daughter is with us. She'll take care of them. Now you tell me what you'll need, and I'll start loading the travois."

"I'll need Badger Woman's tepee."

Back at the mission, Maddie was enjoying the excitement all the girls showed as they held their finished dresses up in front of themselves for the others to see. And, to Maddie's surprise, Kanti was as excited as any of the others. Maddie had helped her with the decorative fringe that was applied to the dress, but the little girl had proved to be quite adept at sewing. She had a particularly good artistic eye when it came to working with the beads. Not only had Kanti selected the colors but it had been she who laid out the traditional Blackfoot designs for their application to the dress.

Like the other girls, Kanti held the dress up in front of her, smiling as she showed it to Maddie.

"It's beautiful," Maddie said as she felt the soft deerskin. "Mother Raffaella, do you think we could have a parade? I'd love to see all the girls in their new dresses."

"I suppose we could. Then you can wear your new clothes to vespers," Mother Raffaella said.

"Miss Maddie's skirt is Indian," Kanti said. "Can she be in our parade?"

"Of course she can," Mother Raffaella said.

When Case and Father Imoda reached the mission, they saw Maddie leading the children in a game of snake, as they were twisting and turning down the lane. All the girls were dressed in their new clothes.

Kimi was the first to see the horses approaching.

"Papa," Kimi shouted, as she ran to meet him. "You've come." But then she saw the loaded travois and a frightened look crossed her face. "Where . . . where are you going?"

"Not me, us," Riley said, as he slid off his horse. "It's about time you girls met some of your people. Case is takin' us up north."

"Do you mean to stay?" Pana asked.

"No, just for a visit," Case said, when he joined the group. "I have to go to Fort Shaw, and your papa thought it would be good if we all went."

"Will the soldiers be there?" Kanti asked.

"They'll be there," Case said, "but there are good soldiers and there are bad soldiers. Miss Maddie's papa is one of their chiefs, and he won't let anything bad happen to you, especially if the soldiers see you in such pretty dresses."

Kanti took Maddie's hand and held on tightly as they moved toward the chapel.

All the permanent residents turned out the next morning to see the travelers off.

Case and Riley led the little entourage, with Roy

riding slightly behind. The three men were followed by Kimi, with Koko hanging on behind her, and Nuna and Pana, who were also sharing a horse. Kanti rode alone, but her horse was dragging the travois. Maddie rode alongside her.

"Papa said we're going to stay at White Calf's camp for a while," Kanti said. "I don't want to do that."

"Oh, I think it will be fun," Maddie said.

"Would you stay with me?"

"I would love to, but I can't. I have to help my papa, just like you're helping your papa. Just look who he chose to drag the travois."

"Can I come live with you?"

Maddie was somewhat nonplussed by Kanti's unexpected question, and she wasn't sure how to respond.

"I'd love for you to do that, but your papa and your sisters would be so sad if you left them. Why, your papa would be so sad he would cry."

"Papa would never cry."

"He would if he lost you. Think about how sad he was when Badger Woman died."

Kanti was quiet for a long moment before she replied. "He was sad, but he didn't cry. Papa says Indians never cry."

Within a few miles they met a Diamond R train of at least ten or fifteen wagons.

"Is anybody hungry?" Case called from the front. "We'll stop while this train passes."

"What about us, boss?" a bullwhacker called. "You got enough to share?"

"I suppose we do," Case said. "Our grub came from the mission."

"The mission? We'll just keep rollin' on, if it's all the same to you. The last time we come through there, the Sisters was a pushin' that pumpkin soup and it ain't fit for a grown man to eat."

"Don't say I didn't invite you," Case said with a chuckle as he found a level spot among the rolling hills just to the west of Bird Tail Rock.

"Shall we find out what Mother Raffaella has provided for us?" Case asked, opening a skin pouch that was hanging from his saddle. "Looks to me like we've got grouse and biscuits."

"I like grouse and biscuits," Koko said.

When they reached the Sun River crossing, Case suggested they might want to cross over and see Jack Healey, but both Riley and Roy were against it. They wanted to get to Fort Shaw as soon as possible, and Maddie agreed. The girls had been wonderful travelers, but Koko had fallen asleep some time back. Case had deposited her in front of Maddie, and now Maddie's arm ached from having supported the child for so long.

When they reached Fort Shaw, the guard at the gate recognized Case and let the group pass on through.

"Riley, I think we'd better take the girls to the sutler's," Case said. "Koko's already asleep, and it looks like a couple others are all tuckered out."

"Do you still keep your place there?" Riley asked.

"I'm pretty sure I do, and if Cooper's taken it over, we'll just move him out."

They rode across the parade ground and stopped in front of the store, where Case took Koko from

Maddie. The little girl, who had to be close to seven years old, made a sound, and then she wrapped her arms around Case's neck as he carried her and led the others up onto the porch.

Inside, the sutler's looked like just about any other store Maddie had seen since coming west, though there were a few tables scattered about with a few soldiers sitting at one of them.

"Well, if it's not my long-lost partner," the civilian behind the counter called out when he saw Case. "Where'd you find this passel of Indians?"

Upon hearing the man's comment, Riley turned and stomped off the porch.

Case put Koko on a willow settle and went after Riley.

"Where do you think you're going? Will didn't say anything that should make you mad."

"You heard what he called my girls," Riley said. "We ain't staying here. We're going back to the crossing."

"He called them a 'passel.' That means 'a lot,' and five little Indian girls on an army base is a lot." Case turned quickly, dismissing Riley before the older man could make a comment. He went back into the store.

"I'm sorry, Case, did I say something I shouldn't have?"

"No, Riley's just sensitive where his girls are concerned. I need to let them all get some rest about now, and I want to put them in my room. Do you have anything in there?"

"Well, yes, I think I do, but it won't be that hard to move."

Will Cooper opened a door and Case stepped in. The room was piled with crates of all sizes. To one side was a stack of blankets.

"No need to move anything," Case said. "Spread out those blankets on some of these crates and the little ones can sleep anywhere. We'll let Riley have the bed if he can get to it."

Case went back outside, where Maddie was now sitting beside Koko on the settle, with the other girls standing close by. Riley was back on his horse, and Roy was engaged in conversation with a couple of soldiers.

"All right, girls, everybody inside. Mr. Cooper's got pilot bread and fresh-churned butter, and I think I saw some strawberry jam in there that's just for you. There might even be a can or two of peaches."

All the girls were smiling as Case herded them into the store.

"Humph," Riley said, as he slid off his horse and followed them inside.

Case returned to the porch and sat down beside Maddie. He let out a long sigh and reached for her hand. "Thanks. I may have bitten off more than I can chew here."

"Can you point me in the direction of the commandant's headquarters? I feel like I should make my presence known," Roy said.

"Of course," Case said, as he stood quickly. "I'm afraid I let a personal matter get in the way of my business. I need to see General Gibbon, too."

"Should I stay with the girls?" Maddie asked.

"No need, Riley will be here," Case said, "and Will's wife, Virginia, can help take care of them if he needs her. Oh—in all the commotion, I forgot to introduce you to my partner."

"I heard the man call you his long-lost partner, but I didn't know you really were his partner," Roy said.

"I am that. I don't get up here often enough to make sure it's profitable, but Will's a good man."

Case, Maddie, and Roy were greeted by the sergeant major when they stepped into the headquarters building.

"Sergeant Major, is the general available?" Case asked.

"Yes, sir, Mr. Williams." The sergeant rose from his desk and disappeared into an adjoining room.

A moment later, he reappeared. "General Gibbon will see you now, gentlemen—and lady," he added hastily.

Case stepped aside, allowing Maddie and Roy to enter first. A man at least six inches shorter than Case rose from his desk and came to greet them.

"Case," he said extending his hand. "I didn't expect you this soon."

"General, when a body gets a summons from the US government, I've found it's best to answer it as soon as possible," Case said.

The general laughed. "So true for all of us. And you must be the new field superintendent that Commissioner Smith has sent out here?"

"Yes, sir, Roy McClellan, and this is my daughter Madelyn. I hope it won't be an inconvenience for her to be here."

"A pretty young lady on an army post? An inconvenience? I think not."

"Thank you, sir. Everyone calls me Maddie and I'm pleased to be here."

"Mrs. Gibbon will be equally pleased. You'll be our house guests if Case hasn't made other arrangements."

"I have not," Case said. "I have Riley Barnes with me, and he's in my quarters."

"Oh dear, should I put on an extra guard just to watch out for him?"

Case laughed. "I think he'll be on his best behavior. He's been a little under the weather—and he has the girls with him."

"Very good. If you would, will you see to it that the McClellans get over to my quarters?"

"Excuse me, sir," Roy said. "I was under the impression that I was to meet a Mr. Walker. Is he here?"

"He arrived last week, but he's been spending his time out at the Blackfoot Agency with John Wood. I'll send a detail out to tell him you're here."

"Would you mind if Riley delivers the message?" Case asked. "It may be better for everyone if he's not on post."

"Certainly." The general sat down and began writing a note. "Have Riley give this to John. We'll meet at ten A.M."

Frances Gibbon made the McClellans feel comfortable as she invited them into her home. Maddie was impressed that she could accommodate houseguests without any advance notice, but she suspected many years as an officer's wife had schooled her well.

The table was set with what Maddie thought was Baccarat stemware. The china was of a dainty floral pattern, and the flatware was gleaming. Maddie smiled when she contrasted this with the service used at the tearoom. She had once counted the different patterns of her cups and saucers, and she was sure there were at least ten variations of the famille rose itself, to say nothing of the many butterflies, dragons, and landscape scenes that decorated other pieces.

Mrs. Gibbon was the consummate hostess, engaging everyone in conversation as she asked endless questions. When she found out that Roy had served in the Fifty-Fourth Massachusetts under Colonel Robert G. Shaw, the very man for whom Fort Shaw had been named, she was fascinated.

The tearoom was another subject she exhausted, suggesting that the officers' wives would be well served by a similar enterprise.

"Frances, you don't need another outlet for your energies," General Gibbon said. "You ride your horse almost every day, you organize chess tournaments, and you constantly have a theatrical performance in production. She even thinks she's going to give a cotillion as soon as she can garner enough recruits to learn all the steps to the dances."

"I'm very impressed. I had no idea there was so much activity at an army post," Maddie said.

"My dear, I've spent many years following the guidons," Frances said. "In the winter, when all the troops are in garrison and the temperature here in the Territory hovers around the zero mark, it's good to have some entertainment."

"I would imagine it would be most difficult for children to be so confined."

"Most do very well, but this winter may be a challenge," General Gibbon said. "One of our lieutenants has an absolutely incorrigible child. He doesn't intend to do bad things, but if anything happens that can't be explained, we find out if Jeremy was anywhere around."

"Jeremy—Jeremy Jackson?" Maddie asked with a broad smile.

"Don't tell me you've met this child," Frances said.

"I'm afraid we have," Roy said. "Lieutenant Jackson and his family were fellow passengers on the *Josephine* when we arrived, and Maddie hit it off quite nicely with the boy."

"Perhaps you would like to visit your friend in the morning while we meet with Mr. Walker," Case said.

"Oh, I would love to see Jeremy again," Maddie said, "but I'll be with the girls."

"Take them along. They've never been around a real boy, and I think it would be an adventure."

Maddie and Roy spent the night with the general while Case stayed at the sutler's store with the girls. The next morning, Maddie went out to the parade ground to watch the guard mount, and then to listen to the regimental band play a lively march.

"Miss Maddie!" someone shouted. Looking toward the sound of the voice, Maddie saw Jeremy Jackson running toward her. "I knew you would come," he said as he threw his arms around her.

"Jeremy! I've missed you," Maddie said, as she tousled his hair. "I think you've grown a foot since I last saw you."

The boy turned his head up inquisitively. "I think you forgot who I was."

"I don't think Miss Maddie forgot you, Jeremy," Lucy Jackson said as she and the other children approached. "We heard you were here."

"Now how could that be?" Maddie asked. "We just came yesterday."

Lucy laughed. "Nothing stays a secret at an army post. I thought I'd see you with the Indian children you brought with you."

"I expected to meet them here, but I don't see Mr. Williams anywhere," Maddie said.

"I saw him at the sutler's," an older child said.

"Then I'd better go find him. He and my father are supposed to meet with the general this morning."

"If you can, come by our quarters," Lucy said. "It's the third house down officer's row."

"Goody, goody!" Jeremy exclaimed. "You can have one of my baby kittens."

Lucy shook her head. "We do have kittens. Two mamas had babies."

"I can't wait to see them," Maddie said.

When Maddie reached the sutler's, Case had the girls all lined up. He didn't seem to be his usual good-natured self as he worked with one child's braids and then moved on to the next.

"Could you use some help?" Maddie asked as she approached the little group. "Where's the brush?"

"If we had one, it's on the travois and Riley took it with him," Case said as he raked his fingers through the tangles.

Maddie was amused as she watched Case, but then she realized what a trying job it would be for Riley to raise five little girls without a woman around. Even though the old man was fighting it, Case was doing the right thing in trying to get them all moved to the mission. She recognized that this visit to the Blackfoot camp was a diversion—a way to convince Riley that he had to leave his cabin, and that the best place for him was to be near a doctor, and the best place for the girls was at the boarding school.

"Ouch! Don't do that, Uncle Case," Koko said. "Let Miss Maddie do it."

"I think the first order of business is for us to go inside and buy a brush," Maddie said.

"Why didn't I think of that? I'll just go get one," Case said, as he started toward the door. "It's my store."

"We'll do that. You probably need to get over to your meeting. My father and the general left some time ago."

"You're right, but I have to find Virginia before I can leave."

"I'll take care of the girls. I saw Lucy and Jeremy this morning, and he said he has some baby kittens he wants to show us, so we'll be at the Jacksons'."

"Thanks, Maddie," Case said as he started toward the headquarters building. "I'll find you."

Maddie stepped into the sutler's store.

"There's my girls," Virginia greeted. "And Maddie, too. Case said Mrs. Gibbon laid out a fine spread for you—all the best crystal and china."

"She did, but now I need a brush."

"I'll say you do. What made Case think he could braid hair without one?" Virginia asked, as she moved to the back of the store, where a supply of feminine articles was kept.

As Maddie stood at the counter, waiting for Virginia to return with the brush, three soldiers came in. She glanced toward them for just a second, then turned away. But even as she looked away, she realized that one of the men had a familiar look about him. When she looked again, one of the soldiers was staring at her.

"Miss McClellan?"

"Sergeant Worley! Is that you?"

A huge grin spread across the sergeant's face. "Yes, it is! But what are you doing in the middle of Montana?"

"I came with my father. He's meeting with General Gibbon."

"Sarge, do you know this beautiful young woman?" one of the other soldiers asked, obviously surprised by the familiarity between them. "Yes, I do. I've never known a lady who could sit a horse like Miss McClellan."

"If you know me that well, you'd better call me Maddie—or is that name only used at Battery Kemble?"

"Is this the woman you said could ride Cyclone?" one of the soldiers asked.

"She's the one,"

"And who is Cyclone?" Maddie asked.

"He's the most cantankerous horse we have in the entire stable," Sergeant Worley said.

"Cantankerous? Or spirited?" Maddie asked.

Sergeant Worley chuckled. "'Spirited' might be a good way to describe him. Would you like to ride him?"

"You know, I would, but I can't right now. I'm going over to Lucy Jackson's house, but if you have the time, bring Cyclone by."

"I'll make time for you, Miss McClellan."

Roy and General Gibbon were already in the office when Case arrived.

"I expect John Wood and Commissioner Walker will be here very shortly," the general said.

"Just who is this man Walker?" Case asked.

"It seems there's a professor who's been raising a stink about the treatment of Indians, so Congress has ordered a commission to look into the problems, and Walker is one of the commissioners.

"The professor was in Dakota, but if there's a problem anywhere, then by extrapolation, they think there's a problem everywhere," the general said. "So here we are, wasting our time waiting on some government bastard to tell us how to do our jobs."

"Would that government bastard be me?" a man asked as he entered the office. "Samuel Walker."

General Gibbon jumped up as he extended his hand. "I'm sorry, sir. I was just engaging in a bit of army hyperbole there."

Walker chuckled. "I've been called worse, General."

"I don't believe you've met the new field superintendent, Roy McClellan, and this is Case Williams from the Diamond R Freight Company," General Gibbon said.

"And I'm John Wood, the Blackfoot agent." All shook hands and everyone was seated.

In the wake of the general's comment, the meeting started out on an adversarial note. Commissioner Walker laid out what the accusations against the army, the agents, and the freighting companies had been.

"This professor you speak of is Professor Othniel Marsh from Yale College. He is one of the world's preeminent scholars in the field of paleontology, and it is his belief that there are dinosaur bones located throughout the West. He has spent many months searching for these bones, and during this time, he has observed what he claims is fraud perpetrated against the Indians. He's reported seeing agents count cattle twice so that the government is charged for more cows than the Indians receive. He says that spoiled food is switched by the freighters for the good rations intended for the Indians. Then everyone involved—the agents, the suppliers, and the freight companies—divides the money."

"That may be true of some companies, but I can vouch for the Diamond R that we have not been a party to this," Case said.

"I'm not accusing you, Case," John Wood said. "But it has been happening."

"John, it was your reports that motivated Commissioner Smith to appoint me to the position I now hold," Roy said. "I assure you the Bureau of Indian Affairs takes these things seriously."

"I hardly think Secretary Delano does," John says. "The Department of Interior is rife with corruption."

"Be that as it may, the problem at hand is Professor Marsh's reports," Walker said. "They've reached the eastern newspapers, and now the allegations are public knowledge. If what the professor is alleging is true, what is happening is an offense to the decency and morality of the American people. And it could be the cause of the many lawless raids and killings that the Indians are perpetrating on the white settlers."

"I can attest to that," Case said. "We've had forty mules taken, and I know some of the stage stock has been stolen as well."

"From what I've been able to ascertain," Roy said, "the biggest problems are arising over on the Carroll road with Sioux raids. Can you confirm that, General?"

"Yes, it seems to be centered near Fort Ellis. You, I believe, were there for the negotiations with Major Pease," the general said.

"Yes, I just returned from Bozeman," Roy said.

"I hate to say it, but you can attest to this, John— the Blackfoot have become a very docile tribe. It may be we need another Major Baker," the general said.

"You mean to wipe out a friendly village of women and children?" Case asked. "If that's the answer, I don't want any part of this discussion." Case rose and headed for the door.

"Hold on there, Case. I wasn't suggesting that annihilation is the answer, but something has to be done about the Sioux. Just last month, there were eighty hostiles within a mile of Camp Lewis and they killed a fatigue party gathering wood. Then over at Box Elder, they took thirty-five horses, and a posse of citizens chased the Sioux all the way to Pompeys Pillar. Now the problem is, if there are friendly Indians in the area, the settlers could mistake them for Sioux and then attack them, and we really would have an uprising," General Gibbon said.

"Custer has been campaigning on the Yellowstone," John Wood said.

"The answer would be for him to take Sitting Bull in his home camp, and then send their families downriver. If he could do that, it would prevent us having to give the Sioux a sound thrashing."

"I have a suggestion," Walker said. "It sounds like most of the trouble in Montana is centered around Fort Ellis. A letter from a Mr. Bogert was passed on to me, saying that he anticipates trouble beyond the siege at Tongue River with Major Pease. I think it would probably be better if I moved my investigation there."

"Mr. Bogert? Would that be Vesuvius Bogert?" Roy asked.

"Yes, I believe that was his name. Do you know him?"

"I do. I met him and his daughter Lilla the last time I was in Bozeman. If you don't mind, I'd like to accompany you on this trip."

"And I'll provide a detail for an escort," General Gibbon said.

"Roy, haven't you forgotten something?" Case asked.

"Forgotten something?"

"Maddie. Do you want her to go with you as well?"

"Oh! I had completely forgotten about her. Would you mind taking her back to Helena with you?"

"Of course I don't mind," Case said. "But I promised Riley we'd go find White Calf. John, do you know where he is?"

"Right now he's on Gravel Bottom Creek, about eight miles from the agency. I think Mr. Barnes went on out last night."

"Do you think your daughter would be willing to visit an Indian encampment?" Case asked.

Roy laughed. "What do you think? This is Maddie we're talking about."

Maddie and Lucy were sitting on the porch watching the children play with the kittens.

"I can't tell you how much I'm enjoying your visit," Lucy said. "Case should bring you up here again sometime."

"He may be visiting more often—at least, he'll be coming as far as the mission. He's trying to get Riley and the girls to move there."

Just then, Jeremy jumped up and began running toward a soldier who was walking toward them. He was leading a horse.

"Oh dear," Lucy said. "It's Sergeant Worley. Jeremy loves that man, but I won't let him take the boy for a ride on that devil horse."

"Would that be Cyclone?"

"Yes, but how did you know?"

"I knew Sergeant Worley back in Washington, and I ran into him this morning. He told me about the horse—he said he was spirited," Maddie said.

Lucy rolled her eyes. "That's a kind word for that animal."

Maddie rose from her chair and went to meet the sergeant. "He's beautiful," Maddie said. "I can tell you take care of him."

Worley patted the horse. "He's got a bad reputation, but underneath he's a pussycat. I had a couple of men set up some jumps. Are you ready to ride?

Maddie smiled broadly. "You know I'm ready."

She called back to Lucy to tell her what she was doing, then swung up into the saddle and galloped out onto the parade ground.

"Damn, look at her ride!" the soldier who had set up the hurdles said. "I ain't never seen no woman that could ride like that."

"Sergeant Worley said she was good."

The girls and the Jacksons looked on as Maddie put Cyclone through his paces. She soon attracted the attention of several other soldiers.

"Ain't that Cyclone she's a' ridin'?" someone asked.

"It damn sure is."

The meeting in the general's office was over, and General Gibbon and Commissioner Walker followed Case and Roy outside.

"I see no reason why we can't leave today," the commissioner said.

"I'll be ready to go as soon as you are, Sam," Roy replied.

"Who's that putting on the riding demonstration?" General Gibbon asked, pointing to a rider out on the parade ground who was taking the hurdles with ease.

"Why, that's Maddie!" Roy said in surprise. "I had no idea she could ride that well."

"Really? I've seen her ride and this doesn't surprise me at all," Case said.

"I would be happy if one tenth of my cavalrymen could ride that well," General Gibbon said.

Case watched as, after she took the last hurdle, Maddie came over to the front of the headquarters building. Stopping in front of Case, and the others, she leaned forward and patted Cyclone on the neck.

"Have you ever seen such a beautiful horse?" she asked.

"That's Cyclone," General Gibbon said. "He can be difficult sometimes. I must say, you did a wonderful job riding him."

"How did you wind up on that horse?" Roy asked.

"Papa, you remember how I used to ride at Battery Kemble. Well, the sergeant who managed the stables there is here now. He's standing over by the children." She pointed toward the Jackson quarters.

"I know you're enjoying yourself, but Commissioner Walker and I need to go to Fort Ellis as soon as we can get ready. I'm leaving you in Case's capable hands." Roy looked pointedly at Case. "I expect you to be the gentleman I've come to know."

"Yes, sir." Case remembered the words Annabelle had said in the McClellan kitchen.

"Let me take the horse back to Sergeant Worley, and then the girls and I will join you."

Maddie rode Cyclone back to the Jackson house. Sergeant Worley had a huge smile on his face.

"I told 'em how good you were. I don't think they believed me, but they do now."

"My kitty cat wants to ride," Jeremy said, as he tossed the cat to Maddie.

The cat was startled, and it screeched as it landed on Cyclone's rump.

The horse took off like a cannon shot, galloping across the parade ground as the cat dug its claws into the horse's flesh in an attempt to hang on.

Cyclone started doing everything he could to get rid of the cat. He leaped into the air, arched his back into a bow, then came down on four stiff legs. That did nothing to dislodge the cat, but it jarred Maddie to her very bones.

It was all Maddie could do to hang on as the horse began caracoling wildly. She jerked Cyclone's head to one side, trying to prevent him from putting his head down. For a moment it seemed that she had him under control, but a sudden jerk pulled the reins from her hands. Feeling his freedom, the horse put his head between his forelegs and kicked his hind legs high into the air. With nothing to hang on to, Maddie was thrown from the horse.

Case ran out onto the parade ground as soon as the horse began bucking. Somehow he had to stop him before Maddie got hurt. But he was too late. He watched in horror as Maddie was tossed from the horse. When she hit the ground, she lay motionless.

"No!" Case yelled as he ran to her side.

He knelt beside her, paralyzed as to what to do to help her. Reaching for her hand, he felt for her pulse.

"Thank God, she's alive," he said as Roy and the general came up behind him. Her face was contorted with pain, and he saw that she was unable to breathe. "Maddie, can you hear me? Breathe! Even though it hurts, try to breathe."

"Do you think she broke her back?" Roy asked as he knelt beside Case.

"I hope not, but she's had the breath knocked out of her. She has to breathe."

Just then Maddie managed to draw a deep and audible breath, and when she did, she opened her eyes. She saw Case and smiled.

"I guess Cyclone and I put on quite a show."

"It's not one I ever want to see again. From now on, if I have anything to say about it, you'll be riding a draft horse," Case said, as he bent over to kiss her.

Maddie laughed. "Oh, that hurts."

"Don't move," a man said as he and Sergeant Worley approached the group. "I'm Dr. Taylor."

SEVENTEEN

Dr. Scott Taylor examined Maddie carefully as everyone else looked on. "I don't think there is anything broken," he said. "Try to sit up,"

Maddie was able to sit up without difficulty.

"Good for you. Are you breathing all right now?"

"Yes," Maddie said. "That was the strangest and most frightening thing. Why couldn't I breathe?"

"The fall caused all the air to leave your lungs, and it paralyzed your diaphragm so that you couldn't get any new air in."

"It's like I said. She had the wind knocked out of her," Case said.

Dr. Taylor nodded. "That was a good diagnosis."

Half an hour later, after consoling Jeremy, who was distraught because he realized that the accident had been his fault, Maddie told her father good-bye.

"How do you feel?" Case asked. "Are you up to riding?"

Maddie smiled. "Well, I don't want to put on any

jumping clinics, but if you're asking if I'm ready for a gentle ride on Lucky, then I can do it. Where are we going?"

"To the Blackfoot village to find Riley."

When Case, Maddie, and the girls reached a high ridge overlooking the Gravel Bottom Creek, they looked out over a beautiful landscape. To the west lay the towering Rocky Mountains, the serrated tops glistening with snow. A wide band of grayish-purple rocks separated the snow from the tree line. Over the mountains, a few fleecy white clouds floated high in the bright blue sky.

On a level plain just this side of the stream were about fifty tepees, covered by a haze of blue-gray smoke. Grazing horses were spread around the village, and young Indian boys, mounted bareback on ponies, rode around the herd, keeping watch. Here and there throughout the village were scattered groups of five to twenty-five, all involved in some activity. Maddie was impressed with the brightly decorated clothing everyone was wearing.

On this cool autumn day, three young men who were bare from the waist up came racing toward the visitors. All three were carrying rifles, with the butts of the weapons pressed into their hips, and the barrels pointing upward.

"Do you think we are unwelcome?" Maddie asked.

"No. I know one of them. They're just coming to see what we want."

Case held his right hand up, palm facing the approaching Indians.

"Chogan, it is good that my friend comes to greet us," Case said.

The Indian Case addressed held up his own hand, palm facing Case.

"You have not come to trade?"

"I have come in friendship. And I have brought new friends to the Piegan." He took in Maddie and the girls with a wave of his hand.

"Do you come to see Riley Barnes?"

"Yes."

Chogan spoke to the other two in a harsh, staccato-sounding language; then the two rode off, leaving only Chogan.

"Come," he said. "I will take you."

As they went farther into White Calf's village, several of the children came out to look at them, and they pointed in curiosity at the white woman and the five Indian girls. The children began laughing and speaking to one another in their native language, but they did not offer to speak to the newcomers, nor did the Barnes girls attempt to speak to them.

Maddie noticed that the tepees, obviously made of animal skins, were all laid out in perfect concentric circles. Each one was decorated with colorful pictures, of animals of all kinds, sunbursts, arrows, birds, and various other symbols.

"He is there," Chogan said, pointing to a tepee that was as gaily decorated as the others.

"Riley!" Case called.

Riley came out to greet them. He was dressed in new buckskin, all beaded and fringed. Had it not been for his beard, he would have looked no different from any of the other elderly Indians.

"Climb down and come inside," Riley said as a greeting.

The girls filed in through the flap quietly but did not show any affection toward Riley, which Maddie found strange. She had seen their reaction to him at the mission, and it was definitely different from this strained meeting.

Riley's tepee was one of the larger ones. He had a fire circle in the middle, in which a small fire was blazing. There was an iron tripod stretched out over the fire, from which was suspended a coffee pot and a kettle. Something was simmering in the pot, and a rich aroma permeated the tepee.

"I figured you folks would be here either today or tomorrow, so I started the pot," Riley said.

"I don't know what you're cooking, but it smells delicious," Maddie said.

"Venison and dumplin's," Riley said. "It's better with buffalo hump the way Badger Woman used to make it, but when you ain't got no buffalo, like we ain't got, then venison is passable."

Kanti was the first to speak.

"Papa, when can we go back home?"

"This is your home now," Riley said.

"I don't want to stay here," Kanti said.

"Well, here is where we're goin' to stay."

"I don't want to stay here either," Koko said. "They pointed at us and they laughed."

"None of us want to stay, Papa," Kimi said, her voice quaking.

Maddie put her arm around Kimi. "Honey, it's so beautiful. If your papa wants to stay, you should give it a chance. You might just learn to love it."

"Nobody likes us," Pana said.

"How can that be? You just got here," Maddie said.

"You didn't hear what those Indians were saying."

"You're right. I didn't understand them."

"They said we're white-man Indian girls, and we don't belong here," Kanti said.

"They said even our mothers and fathers ran away from us," Nuna added.

"Papa, they were right. We don't belong here," Kimi said.

"That's enough," Riley ordered, with a gruff voice. "No more talk of this,"

Four of the five children looked down without comment.

"Papa, I—" Kanti started, but Kimi looked toward her with an expression that effectively stopped her from continuing.

There was no more talk and the girls remained quiet until it was time to eat.

"Kimi, dish up the grub," Riley said.

Kimi picked up a gourd ladle and put the venison and dumplings on tin plates, then Nuna served Riley and Case before passing plates to the others.

In an attempt to relieve some of the tension, Maddie looked around the tepee and, seeing what looked like a rolled-up buffalo robe, inquired about the pelt. She reached toward it.

"No! Don't touch that!" Riley shouted, his words so loud and so sharp that they stunned Maddie.

She jerked her hand back, quickly.

"That's my beaver bundle."

"Your beaver bundle?"

"It belonged to Standing Bear, Badger Woman's Pa, but it's mine now. It's a medicine bundle."

Maddie looked as if she wanted to ask a question, but she held her tongue.

"Tell her what it is, Case," Riley said.

"A beaver bundle is a very private and precious possession that represents a person's spiritual life. It has medicine—we would say magic power—for protection, for good luck, for good hunting, and for a person's soul. And when one is handed down, the power passes with it."

"Do all Indians believe that?"

"Yes, they do, and so do I," Riley answered.

"But you're a white man."

"Not for much longer," Riley said. "After tomorrow, I'll be a full-blooded Indian. I know I'm an old man, and I'll be dyin' soon. But when I do die, I want to die an Indian, and White Calf has agreed. Tomorrow we'll have the celebration, and since you're here, you can come if you want to."

After the meal was over, Case invited Maddie to go for a walk, leaving the girls with Riley.

Maddie pointed to the decorated tepees, some small and some large.

"I think it's interesting the way the tepees are all in a circle. With all the designs and now with the light of the fires, it's like a work of art."

"It's more than that," Case explained. "The circle is a very important part of Indian life. A circle means that no person is more important than any other. When they sit in council, they sit in a circle, and this gives everyone an opportunity to speak and be heard. It also stands for family, and in a religious sense, it's the symbol for the survival of the soul: a circle has no beginning and no end."

"That's fascinating!"

Case chuckled. "It's also very practical. Whenever a village moves, everyone establishes their new residence in the exact same position within the circles, so their address stays the same. That way, visiting family and friends always know where to find each other."

"Well then, how did Riley know where to put his tepee?" Maddie asked.

"When he married Standing Bear's daughter, he became part of his family. When Standing Bear died, his tepee became Badger Woman's tepee, and his place in the circle became her place in the circle. And now it belongs to Riley."

Case pointed to a tepee that was much larger than all the others. The outside was very elaborately painted, and Maddie saw a brown bear pictured inside a circle, clutching an arrow in its forepaw. There was also a cross formed from a knife over a war club, as well as stripes, chevrons, and circles, and handprints of various colors.

"More than likely, this is where the beaver medicine ceremony will be held," Case said. "Not many white men are given this honor, but Riley's been a friend to the Blackfoot for many, many years."

"Case, you've never told me why the girls are with Riley. They all call him Papa, but I know he isn't their father."

"No, he's not, and none of the girls are sisters."

"Kanti said something to me one time about soldiers coming to kill them. Does that have something to do with this?"

"Yes."

"What happened?"

"It's not a very pretty tale," Case said. "Are you sure you want to hear it?"

"Yes. No. I mean, I don't think I want to hear it, but I think I should. I think I owe it to the girls to know what happened."

"All right, come with me and we'll find a place where we can talk. I'll tell you everything you need to know about the girls, and the stubborn, cantankerous old man who loves them as much as any father could possibly love his daughters."

Case led Maddie down to a wide, flat rock beside the creek.

"It was a little over five years ago."

As Case began to tell the story, he spoke in low, even tones, but the passion of his words provided impetus to the tale. The peaceful sound of the babbling brook was in stark contrast to the ghastly story he shared.

"The Diamond R had a contract to transport annuities from the Indian Agency to the Indian bands. And on that day, January 24, 1870, I was driving a sleigh, following alongside the Marias River, heading for the village of a Piegan chief named Heavy Runner. Riley was with me, and it was brutally cold. The mules were breathing heavily under the load, and their breath filled the air with clouds of vapor. I wasn't wearing gloves, because on this path, which was little more than a trail but considerably less than a road, I felt like I needed to feel the reins."

He chuckled. "My hands were so cold that I could barely move them."

Case told the story with such feeling, and such intensity, that time and place fell away for Maddie. It was as if she were present as the story unfolded, and though she wore a jacket, she shivered with the chill of that winter day, five years ago. She was no longer just listening to the story; she was a part of it.

"Want me to take the reins for a bit?" Riley asked.

"I thought you told me last time that your hands had frozen up and dropped off your arms," Case said.

"They did, but I picked 'em up 'n' put 'em back on," Riley said with a little laugh.

Married to a Piegan Blackfoot, Riley could speak Siksika, the Blackfoot language, and one of the ways he earned money was as a paid interpreter. Case often made use of that skill, and it was for that purpose that Riley was with him today.

There had been, of late, some difficulty between the Blackfoot and the white men in the area, but the village they were visiting was that of Heavy Runner, a chief who was friendly with the white men. Case had done business with him before, and he felt no anxiousness about visiting the village.

"Do you think Heavy Runner will have something warm in the pot?" Case asked.

"Ha! Ole' Heavy Runner always has somethin' warm in the pot. Why do you think they call him 'Heavy' Runner?"

"He doesn't look like he's missed too many meals," Case replied.

"He ain't missed none at . . ." Riley paused in midsentence. "I smell smoke."

"Well, I would certainly hope so. After this cold trip, I'm looking forward to sitting by the fire in a warm tepee."

"No. There's too much smoke for that," Riley said, the tone of his voice reflecting the expression of worry on his face.

By now Case, too, realized that this wasn't the normal smell of smoke one might expect when approaching a village. The Marias River curved to the left just ahead, and around that curve lay Heavy Runner's winter encampment.

Riley snapped the reins against the backs of the mules, and reluctantly they moved a little faster, though the increase in pace was barely perceptible in the snow. Not until they made the curve did the men see the village, or, more properly, what was left of the village.

Not one tepee was standing—all were collapsed, and many were blackened from fire. Smoke was drifting up from a dozen places where low flames still burned. There were also several human and animal forms lying on the ground, partially covered with snow.

"Whoa!" Riley said, pulling back on the reins.

"Riley, what the hell do you think happened here?"

"I don't know," Riley said. "In all my years, I ain't never seen nothin' like this."

"Would Mountain Chief do something like this? I

know he and Heavy Runner have been on the war-path."

Riley shook his head. "No, look at these bodies. Most of 'em is women 'n' kids. Mountain Chief is a mean son of a bitch, but not even he would do somethin' like this."

"Naahks!" someone called. The voice came from one of the lumps lying on the ground—an old woman.

"That's Walks Behind Him," Riley said, pointing to the source of the call. "That's Running Wolf's woman."

Jumping down from the sleigh, the two men hurried over to the old woman. She was lying on her back, a large patch of blood frozen on her chest.

"Walks Behind Him, what happened here?" Riley asked; then he repeated the question in Siksika

"Komap," the old woman said.

"A dreadful thing," Riley interpreted.

"Ainaki apo inita auki." The words were strained, and hard to hear.

"What? Are you sure?" Then, realizing that he had asked the question in English, he repeated it in the woman's own language.

"Aa," the old woman said.

"Riley, you want to tell me what she's saying?" Case asked, growing frustrated that he couldn't understand the conversation.

"All this," Riley said, taking in what was left of the village, with a wave of his hand, "is the work of white men. Soldiers."

"Soldiers?"

"Ainaki?" Riley repeated.

"Aa," the woman said again.

"Yes, soldiers," Riley translated.

"Was everyone killed?" Case asked.

Riley asked Walks Behind Him, and she responded, her words growing even weaker, until, with a last gasp, she died.

"She said some escaped," Riley said. "Some ran for the woods and some hid under the ice in the river."

"They're going to freeze to death if they haven't already."

"The bastards," Riley said, picking up a small bag, the contents of which had been scattered on the snow beside the woman's body. "They opened her medicine bag."

He picked up a feather, an acorn, two pebbles, a bird's claw, and some hair; then he put them back in the bag, singing a song that consisted of but three notes. He sang the song quietly, first in Siksika, then in English.

"What is life? . . .
It is the breath of a buffalo in the wintertime.
It is the little shadow which runs across the
    grass and loses itself in the sunset."

Very reverently, Riley hung the bag around the dead woman's neck; then he folded her arms across her chest.

"Kit Komozi, kit komota nizitapimix."

The words startled both Case and Riley, and they turned to see a girl of about twelve or thirteen standing a short distance from them.

"She says I know the people's ways, and she

wants me to save her friends," Riley translated. "Where are they?" he asked repeating the question in Siksika.

"Kono." She turned and walked toward the woods.

"She's going to take us to them."

The girl led Case and Riley to a cavity in the side of a bluff, where there was an opening that did not extend far enough into the wall to actually be called a cave. There, looking out from within the shadows of the natural grotto, were five children. Case didn't know if they were boys or girls, and he had no idea how old they were, but he would have guessed the youngest was about two, and the oldest couldn't have been more than seven. The girl who'd led them there said her name was Petah. She explained that these children, like she, had been orphaned by the action of the soldiers.

"And this child is taking care of all of them?" Case asked.

"Indian kids grow up fast when they have to," Riley said.

"Take them all back to the sleigh, and break out the supplies. We should have something they can eat. And find the blankets," Case said. "I'm going to look around and see if there are any others hiding close by."

Case looked for some time but could find no more who were alive.

"What should we do with these kids?" Case asked when he returned to the sleigh.

"I'm goin' to take 'em all back to Badger Woman," Riley said. "There ain't nothin' else I can do."

Case shook his head. "That's an awesome responsibility, Riley."

"Can you come up with somethin' better?"

"No, no I can't. But I can tell you what I'll do. I'll furnish what food and supplies you'll need to look after them."

"I ain't askin' you for nothin'," Riley said.

"I know you aren't. But we found them together, and if you're going to take care of them, I'm going to provide for them."

Riley nodded but didn't respond. "What do you say we get this sleigh on the trail?"

"Don't you think you should tell the girl where we're going and what we're doing?"

Riley told Petah, and tears began welling in her eyes as she burrowed the others and herself down in the sleigh.

After they were well away from the burned-out village, Case spoke.

"What's Badger Woman going to say when you show up with all these kids?"

"The onliest child we ever had died when she was still a young 'un, 'n' Badger Woman ain't never quite got over that. I reckon that, more'n likely, she'll be a-thankin' me," Riley said.

Case grew quiet, and the break in the narrative brought Maddie back to the present. The moon had risen during the telling of the story, and clouds were gathering, the gloom seeming even darker than normal because of the melancholy of the events just related. At first Maddie thought the story was over, but as they sat there for a long moment, the silence disturbed only by the babbling creek, she realized that Case was just gathering his thoughts before he continued.

"I learned, soon after that, that on daybreak of the twenty-third of January, Major Eugene Baker of the US Army had ordered four troops of cavalry and one company of mounted infantrymen to attack the village.

"At first, they may have thought they were attacking Mountain Chief's village, and if they had, that would have been justified, because warriors from Mountain Chief's village had been on the warpath, and they had murdered some whites, including some farm families.

"But it wasn't Mountain Chief's village, it was the village of Heavy Runner, and he was a friend to the whites; he even had a paper that said that, and when the attack started, he ran toward the soldiers, waving the paper to show them they were making a mistake.

"The paper didn't stop them. And when it was all said and done, one hundred seventy-three Indians were killed, most of them innocent women and children. Some, like Petah, ran into the woods. That young girl managed to keep the six of them together until we found them."

"And Riley took them back to Badger Woman?" Maddie asked.

"Yes, and he was right when he said Badger Woman would welcome them. She took care of them and loved them as her own, and when Petah left to marry a Canadian Mountie, Badger Woman was as proud as any mother of the bride had ever been.

"Then Badger Woman died last winter, and Riley's had to look after them all by himself. I don't know how much longer he'll be able to do it."

"Maybe here with White Calf is where they should be," Maddie suggested.

Case shook his head. "I don't think so. If something happens to Riley, there won't be anyone who'll take them in. They're girls, and when Riley's gone, even the young ones will be married off. And you can be sure I'm not going to let that happen. No, they can't stay here."

"Riley's not going to like that."

Case picked up a rock and tossed it into the creek. "No, he's not."

EIGHTEEN

Riley and the girls were already bedded down when Maddie and Case returned to the tepee. In the dim light of the low-burning fire, she saw that an extra pallet of buffalo robes had been laid out alongside the girls, and she knew that it was for her. Riley and Case were on the other side of the fire ring.

"Good night, Maddie," Case said quietly, "and thank you. I've never told the story of the Marias Massacre to anyone before, but it makes me surer than ever that the girls can't stay here."

"I thought of that. What horrible memories must have come back to them when they rode into this village."

Case reached for Maddie and held her close to him, not in a sensual embrace, but one asking for comfort.

Her heart went out to him. She could empathize with the emotions he was trying to juggle as he tried to do what was right for the girls without running roughshod over Riley.

"Tomorrow's going to be a long day. We'd better get some rest," Case said, as he released her.

She kissed him lightly on the lips as she turned toward her side of the tepee. "Good night," she whispered.

Sleep wouldn't come as she lay on the buffalo robes, watching the wavering gold reflection of the fire on the tepee walls. What these precious little girls had endured in their lives . . . How had they managed to build such a strong bond—how had they been able to create a family?

The answer was obvious. The crusty old man whose snores were filling the tepee had given them love, and Case, too, cared for them deeply. How was he going to maneuver through this complicated relationship?

She rolled over, secure in the trust that Case would manage. He always did. Wasn't it he who'd figured out how to get across the Sun River when no one else could, and wasn't it he who figured out how to get the tearoom furnished? She smiled. It was Case who'd figured out how she could ride a horse astride without exposing herself.

Case Williams. He was wonderful. And she loved him.

The next morning, before the sun came up, an Indian woman opened the flap of the tepee and entered. She was carrying a knife, and at first Maddie was frightened. Instinctively, she reached for the girls who, except for Kimi, were huddled together on her robes.

But she needn't have been concerned.

Riley welcomed the woman with a broad smile.

"Little Flower, you are here to welcome your sister's man."

"I bring food," she said as she withdrew a parfleche that was filled with fry bread and smoked fish. "And I bring two ponies for my brother's children, but now I prepare you to be Blackfoot."

By this time, the girls were awakening, and their eyes grew wide as they saw Little Flower approach Riley with the knife. Within minutes, she had cropped his beard short and had begun applying stripes of different colored paint to his face.

When she was finished, she smiled. "Badger Woman watches. By sunset, you will be white man no more."

When Little Flower had gone and the food had been eaten, Riley untied the strips of leather that held his beaver bundle together. He removed a carefully wrapped object, doing so very slowly, and obviously showing a great deal of respect for it. When he had it completely unwrapped, he held up a long-stemmed pipe, decorated with red ribbons and three eagle feathers.

"Case, will you smoke this pipe with White Calf, and with me?"

"I would be honored," Case said as he bowed his head, not knowing the significance of the pipe, but aware that it was an important relic.

"It is the pipe that Chief Sheheke smoked with Meriwether Lewis and William Clark."

"Riley, how did you come to have it?" Case asked.

"It was passed to Standing Bear, and when I became his son-in-law, it was passed to me. Standing Bear thought it would mean more to a white man."

Just then there was a call from outside the tepee.

"Come, Riley Barnes. Come." It was Little Flower, and she took Riley's hand and led him to White Calf's tepee, the largest one, located in the center of the camp. Case, Maddie, and the girls followed.

White Calf was seated opposite the opening, and he was flanked by other men. He pointed to the place where Riley was to sit, and Case took his seat alongside.

Little Flower indicated that Maddie and the girls should sit with the other women, all of whom were wearing beautiful buckskin dresses, which were heavily beaded. Several of the women had necklaces made of shells and animal teeth, and their moccasins were decorated with colored porcupine quills. Maddie felt somewhat underdressed in her riding skirt, but she was thankful it was at least made of buckskin, and she was glad the children had their new dresses for this ceremony.

When everyone was seated, the man beside White Calf stood and, with a forked stick painted red, took a live coal from the fire and put it on a piece of metal that was lying in front of White Calf. He withdrew what looked to be some sort of dried grass, and holding it up, he sang a few bars of unintelligible words. Then he placed it on the glowing coal.

Maddie had no idea what the dried grass was, but the smoke that curled up from it emitted a very pleasant aroma.

White Calf stood and began to sing, and the men

joined in, singing several songs, each song seemingly repeated two or three times. The whole time, White Calf swayed with the chants.

After about an hour, White Calf began to speak, and as Riley translated his words to Case, Kimi translated them to Maddie.

"I look upon you as my brother. I say, by the sun and the earth I live on, that I want to talk straight and tell only the truth.

"Today, in council, and by the power of the beaver medicine ceremony, you will be made one of us. From this day, when we speak of you, we will not speak of the white you. We will speak of you as one of the people."

White Calf sat down, and Maddie watched Riley remove the sacred pipe from its bag. Seeing it, everyone in the tepee began grunting in astonishment and respect.

"Azim akuinima!" several of them said.

"They say that it is a holy pipe," Kimi translated.

Riley moved to the center of the tepee and, lowering a stick into the fire, used the burning brand to light the pipe. Sitting in front of White Calf, he held it to the four points of the compass before taking a puff, waving the smoke from the bowl into his face as he did so. Then, holding the bowl in one hand, and the stem in the other, he handed the pipe to White Calf, who smiled in appreciation of the respect shown him.

"Mokamipohzi," several of the Indians said, and again, Kimi translated.

"Papa is a wise man."

Not until the pipe had been passed around to

all the other men sitting in council, including Case, did it come back to Riley, who took the final puff before sticking his thumb down into the glowing embers to extinguish it. Maddie knew that it had to have burned his thumb, but he gave no reaction to the pain. He moved back to take his place beside Case.

One of the other men produced a bag that held several gourds with pebbles in them. Handing the rattles to White Calf, he passed them out to the shaman, and all the other men, including Riley and Case. Riley then placed his own beaver bundle on the ground in front of White Calf. As the chief and the shaman began to sing, everyone present beat rhythmically on Riley's beaver bag, using the gourd rattles.

This went on for hours, with the singing, drumming, and playing of flutes, and it was impossible for Maddie or even Kimi to comprehend it all. They knew that there were songs to all kinds of animals, the most important being the beaver, and it was explained that many of the dances involved imitating the actions of the beaver: cutting trees, swimming with sticks in their mouths, building their dams, and even wintering inside their mounds.

At no time was there any talk of feasting, and Maddie knew that the girls had to be as hungry as she. During one break, Maddie led them back to Riley's tepee to get some pilot bread from her bag.

"Do we have to go back?" Kanti asked.

"Yes, it's very important to your papa that you are there," Maddie said. "It can't be too much longer."

"Why does he want to be an Indian?" Pana asked.

"Because he very much loves you and he wants to be what you are," Maddie said.

"If Papa can become an Indian just by all this singing and dancing, is there some way we can become white?"

Maddie smiled. "Yes, I believe there's a way. But you don't have to sing and dance. You just have to have some papers signed."

"Then that's what I want to do," Nuna said.

"Well, for now, we'd better get back before your papa misses us."

When they returned, more dancing was occurring—the elk, the moose, the antelope. When the last dance was over, White Calf rose, and in very solemn terms he inducted Riley into the Blackfoot tribe.

Maddie looked over at the little girls. Koko had fallen asleep, and many of the other children were being escorted out of the tepee.

"Can we go now?" Kimi asked. "Papa is an Indian, isn't he?"

"I think we can," Maddie said, as she started to stand.

"No, no, you stay," Little Flower said, as she pulled on Maddie's skirt.

"But the girls?"

"They go. You stay."

"Kimi, you go right to your Papa's tepee," Maddie said. "See if you can find something to eat for you and the girls. I know this can't go on much longer, but if it does, go ahead and go to sleep."

When the dancing continued, the men sat down and many of the women stood to dance. For the first time, except for retrieving the Lewis and Clark pipe, Riley's beaver bundle was opened. After each item was withdrawn—a badger skin, the head of a mallard duck, a prairie dog skin, a lizard, and a chew of tobacco, more songs and dances were performed.

How much longer could this day go on?

Maddie looked toward Case, and he smiled at her, knowing what endurance it was taking to celebrate this whole day, when they both could understand very little of what was happening.

But all at once, there was a definite change in the atmosphere. All the women began to titter among themselves as one woman and one man stood, the woman wearing a headdress with horns. White Calf handed out a separate string of buffalo horns and each man, including Riley and Case, took two.

Once it was established that they were imitating the buffalo, the dance took on a very sensual tone. The man and woman showed the others what to do, imitating the buffalo mating ritual, pawing at the ground in front of each other, hooking at each other with their horns, then the woman turned, and bending over, backed into the man, who, with whoops of laughter from the onlookers, simulated mounting her.

After that, many men and women began to dance together, and one of the Indian men came to get Maddie. At first, she was a little apprehensive, because she thought he wanted to dance with her. But, with a huge smile on his painted face, he took her over to Case and shouted something.

Case looked toward Riley.

"He said you are the bull, and you must mount your woman," Riley said.

"Case, no! Do we have to do this? In front of all these people?" Maddie asked, horror-struck by the idea.

"No, you don't have to do it," Case replied. "As long as you don't mind if the two of us are scalped."

"What?" she gasped.

Case laughed. "Come on, you don't want to make Riley lose face, do you? Anyway this is the grand finale."

Case pulled her out among the dancers, and the beating of the drums and the writhing of the others, the men and women—some of the women having hiked their skirts up to present their bare bottoms to their mates—had a most arousing effect on her.

The beating of the drums seemed to come from the beating of her own heart, and she worked up a sweat as she gyrated around, quickly realizing that most of the heat was coming from inside her body. She grew bolder and bolder still, pushing her derriere up against Case, feeling the very obvious rise in the front of his trousers, and delighting in the sensations it created. At first she wished they could be alone, but she soon realized that being in this situation, sharing this stimulation and this simulated copulation with so many others, heightened her arousal.

Suddenly she felt Case put his hands to either side of her hips and pull her to him, groaning as he thrust hard against her. She felt the lightning jolts of pleasure coursing through her body and looked around in quick embarrassment, wondering if anyone else knew what had just happened.

She needn't have been embarrassed. She realized at once that what had happened between her and Case had not been an isolated event.

The ceremony ended, and everyone stopped dancing. Now, in contrast to the drums, chants, and haunting melody of the flutes that had been so prevalent throughout the long day, there was only silence as the men and women walked together through the night to their tepees.

Maddie and Case consciously did not make direct eye contact, as if there was a mutual understanding between them that they would avoid each other after what had happened during the buffalo mating dance.

Riley was exhausted, but pleased over having been adopted into the "people," and while Koko and Kanti were already sleeping, the older girls were discussing the events of the day.

"Why did it take so long, Papa?" Nuna asked.

"Because these traditions are important. They've been handed down from one papa to another for generations," Riley said. "And now I can hand them down to you, so you won't be forgettin' what it is to be an Indian."

"What if I don't want to remember?" Kimi asked.

Case went to Kimi and put his arm around her shoulder. "Maybe right now you aren't proud to be an Indian, but when you get older, you'll look back and wish you knew more about your heritage. Your papa just wants you to have some good memories to help you wipe out the bad."

"I still want to go home."

"I know you do," Case said as he gave Kimi a hug. "We'll figure something out."

Maddie lay quietly on her buffalo robes, long after Riley's snores and the measured breathing of the girls told her that all were asleep. Then, in the dim light remaining from the low-burning embers in the fire circle, she saw Case rise from the dark shadows of the other side of the tepee. For a moment, she thought he might be coming to her, and she held her breath, waiting. But he didn't come. Instead, he slipped through the flap and went outside. She thought it might be a call of nature, but several minutes passed and he didn't return.

Her mind wouldn't be still as she recalled the events of the buffalo dance. In its own way, this had been more stimulating than when Case had come to her the first night she had stayed in the carriage house. Was a woman supposed to have such wanton thoughts? She would love to be able to ask someone—her mother, her sister, or maybe Annie, but she knew she wouldn't.

She thought about the Indian women, who were so carefree. They'd known what was coming in the buffalo dance, and they'd anxiously anticipated the movements that had brought them so much pleasure. Was she any different from an Indian woman?

Of course not. She could enjoy the pleasures a man could give her just as much as any Indian woman could. But would she enjoy those pleasures with any other man but Case Williams?

Maddie knew her relationship with Case was

at a crossroad. From here it could go one of two ways: it could proceed to a deeper commitment . . . or they would have to back away from one another. There were no other alternatives. And Maddie knew she wasn't in a position to call the shots. The next step, whichever direction it took, would have to be determined by Case.

Case was standing just outside the tepee, certain that Maddie was still awake. When he had first gotten up it had been his intention to go to her and . . . and what? He couldn't join her on her robes, not with Riley and the girls so close. Perhaps he could ask her to come outside. Yes, that was it. He would go back in and invite her to walk down to the water with him. There, they could discuss what was happening between them, decide whether or not they should . . . no.

If he went back inside and invited her to come to the water's edge with him, he knew she would do it. And he also knew that if she did, they would do more than just talk.

Case walked down to the little grassy table to look out at Gravel Bottom Creek. The water was breaking white over the rocks, making them nearly luminescent in the bright moonlight. Listening to the swiftly flowing stream, he thought this would be the perfect spot for a tryst . . . a tryst with Maddie. All he had to do was walk up the hill and she would be there. The thought of her lying in his arms caused him to feel the beginning of an arousal, and through force of will he dismissed it.

He wanted Maddie. He wanted her to be his wife,

and when they were back in Helena, he would ask her to marry him. But first he had to find a solution to the problem at hand. What would he do with Riley and the girls?

With a sigh of resignation, Case returned to the tepee. By now, the fire was completely burned down, so he had to pick his way through total darkness until he found his bedroll. He wondered if Maddie was still awake, and his first instinct was to go to her—to hold her, to ask for her counsel.

But that was the kind of conversation a man had with his wife.

The next morning Case was cutting out the new ponies that Little Flower had given Riley when he heard someone yelling.

"Uncle Case! Uncle Case! Something's wrong with Papa!"

It was Nuna, and she was running through the camp, her shouts arousing the curiosity of the other camp dwellers who were out attending to early-morning chores.

"What happened?" Case asked.

"I don't know. He was sitting there and then he fell over."

"Where's Maddie?"

"She's with him. She made him sit up, and now his eyes are open, but I don't think he can see. And when Maddie tries to talk to him, he won't answer."

"Crow Wing," Case called to one of the Indian boys who was watching the herd. "Take these horses back to the herd."

Crow Wing nodded, and Case and Nuna ran back to the tepee.

Case heard Riley's gruff voice complaining. "Get away and leave me be."

Case stepped through the open flap and saw Riley sitting on the ground with Maddie steadying him. Kimi was with him, but the other girls were hanging back.

"Get these women away from me. Can't a man have a bit of peace?"

"Maddie, what happened?" Case asked.

"I don't know. He was sitting there talking about everything that happened yesterday; then he just stopped talking and slumped over. I got him up and he just sat there with a blank stare. We tried to ask him what had happened, but he acted like he didn't hear us."

"Riley, was it like what happened on the fish platform?" Case asked as he knelt beside the older man.

Riley turned to Case. He was squinting as if he were trying hard to see. "My head hurts and I feel like . . ."

He began to reel and Case caught him.

"You've had another seizure," Case said, "and you have no choice. Either we go back to Fort Shaw or we go to St. Peter's. You have to see a doctor."

"Get the medicine woman. She'll take care of me," Riley said.

"I'll take you to Little Flower, and she can brew you some willow tea. But in the meantime, I'm going to strike the tepee."

"No, you go. We have to stay here," Riley said, his voice barely audible.

"Riley, I want you to be honest with yourself. You know you're in no shape to look after the girls anymore, don't you?"

"I have no choice," Riley said. "I have to."

"No, you don't. I'll take them with me."

"And do what with them? Leave 'em with the black robes? Make orphans out of 'em? These girls ain't orphans. I've looked after 'em for five years as if they was my own. They ain't orphans, and I'm not goin' to have 'em treated like they was."

"You can come. Father Imoda said you'd be welcome to stay there, too."

"I ain't goin' to live at no church, and that's all there is to it."

"All right, if that's the way you want it."

Riley nodded. "Now you've said somethin'."

"But the girls are coming with me." Case turned to Kimi. "Help your sisters get their things together."

"Case, no!" Riley's eyes grew moist. "Don't make an old man beg. Please don't take my girls away from me."

"You can come or not come," Case said. "But if you care anything at all for these girls, you know damn well they can't stay here with you."

"Case, please!"

Case looked at Riley for a moment, but he didn't reply. Instead he went outside.

Case was standing down by the water when Maddie approached him.

"Are the girls getting ready?" he asked.

"Yes."

"Good."

"Case, Riley is crying."

Case didn't respond. Instead he reached down to pick up a rock; then he threw it out into the water.

"Riley's the last person I ever thought I'd see crying. The thought of losing those girls is hurting him."

"He's a stubborn old fool," Case said. "He can come with them."

"I know," Maddie said. "And I know you're doing the right thing. Still, it breaks my heart to see him hurting so."

Case reached down to throw another handful of rocks into the water. "Then damn it, don't look at him."

Maddie was stung by the curtness of his reply, and she felt the burn of tears in her own eyes.

"I'll go help the girls," she said, starting back.

"Maddie?" Case called after her.

Maddie stopped, but she didn't turn back toward him. She waited for him to apologize, but he didn't.

"Tell the girls to hurry," he said. "I want to get to the mission before dark."

Maddie nodded, then continued on.

Not until Maddie was gone did Case dip water from the stream to splash on his face. He did not want her to see the tears streaming down his own cheeks.

It was at least another fifteen minutes before Case returned to the tepee. Maddie and the girls had their belongings ready to load on the horses.

"Where's Riley?" Case asked.

"He's inside with Little Flower and White Calf," Maddie said. "They're saying their good-byes."

"Their good-byes?"

"Papa's coming with us," Kimi said happily.

Case nodded. "Good."

A boy went to get the horses and within a short time, the tepee was down. Case thought it would be better if Riley rode on the travois, but he didn't ask him to. The old man's pride had been hurt enough for one day.

Nearly the entire encampment turned out to tell them good-bye, as the procession of eight horses headed out of the village. Many began to sing and beat on drums, while others shouted farewells.

"*Aakattsinootsiiyo'p!* We'll see each other again!" they added in English.

Riley neither answered nor gave any indication that he had even heard them. Instead, he continued to stare straight ahead as they crossed the Gravel Bottom Creek, then started south, with Heartbreak Mountain before them.

A more beautiful scene could not have been painted. The browning bunchgrass grew beneath the silver gray of the trunks of the cottonwood, which had bright yellow leaves still attached to its branches. The brilliant scarlet of the sarvis berry and wild rose made up the understory, while an adjacent thicket of the delicate purple of the alder bushes formed a complementary contrast. Off in the distance, the quaking aspens were changing to golden in groups that dotted the mountains.

They arrived at St. Peter's earlier than Maddie had expected, and the schoolgirls came running out to meet the procession. There was much animated talk, both in English and Siksika, as the girls were welcomed back to the mission.

Maddie mentally compared this greeting to that which the girls had received at White Calf's village. Riley was observing as well. The children who stayed here, though orphaned, seemed to be content, and by extrapolation, she hoped that Riley recognized that Case's decision had been the right one.

"Our travelers have returned," Father Imoda said as he came out to greet the group. "I trust that your visit was pleasant."

"It was," Case said as he dismounted. "Riley is now an official member of the Blackfoot tribe. It was a most impressive celebration."

"Wonderful," the priest said. "And how did you do, Mr. Barnes? No more incidents, I hope?"

Riley didn't answer the inquiry. Instead, he slid off his horse and slowly walked back to the travois. Case began leading the other horses to the corral, where he was met by Juneau, and the girls disappeared with their friends.

"He had another spell," Maddie told the priest and the mother superior, who had now joined them.

"Is he going back to his cabin?" Mother Raffaella asked.

"I don't know. I've not heard him say one word since we left this morning."

"Maybe he can't speak," Father Imoda said. "That sometimes happens with apoplexy. What do you think he intends to do with the girls?"

"Case has said the girls will stay here—that is, assuming you have room for them."

"Of course they can stay here, if Mr. Barnes will let them," Mother Raffaella said.

"I don't think Riley has any say in it anymore. Case has said they will stay here, and even if Riley doesn't agree, he doesn't have the strength to fight Case," Maddie said. "I'm worried about him. I've never known anyone who was as heartbroken as that poor man."

"Mr. Barnes can live here as well," Father Imoda said. "That way he'll be with the girls."

"Yes, that's what Case has told him. And although Mr. Barnes hasn't spoken to us, I would guess that's what he's decided to do."

Everyone except Riley went into the mission with Mother Raffaella. There was much excitement as the girls chose their beds. Nuna and Pana wanted to be next to each other, and Kimi had Koko next to her. Kanti, as was her usual habit, chose a bed as far away as possible.

"Why didn't Mr. Barnes come in?" Mother Raffaella asked.

"He probably has to get used to this idea on his own terms," Case said. "I'll go get him and let him see where the girls will be, and that will make him feel better."

When Case stepped outside, he was surprised to see the tepee erected. Juneau was gathering an armful of wood, and a thin, twisting rope of smoke was rising through the smoke hole in the top.

"What in the—now why do you think that thing is up?" Case asked.

"It looks like Mr. Barnes intends to stay," Father Imoda said.

"He can't live there," Case said as he started to go to the tepee.

"Wait, my son. Let the old man be. This may be his way of thinking things out."

"That may be," Case said, "but living in a tepee can't be the permanent solution. I have to go back to Helena tomorrow, and I can't leave knowing he's not settled. If he gets to feeling better, do you know how long it will take him to get back to that cabin? Even if he has to walk ten miles, he'll be gone before you can say Jack Robinson."

"Perhaps he'll join us for our evening meal," Father Imoda said.

"I doubt it. But if you don't mind, I'll take supper out to him."

"I think that would be good," Father Imoda said.

After the evening meal, Case walked out to the tepee that was set up next to the barn. It had grown dark outside, but he could see a splash of golden light projected through the open flap.

"Riley," Case called from outside. "May I come in?"

There was no answer.

"Riley?"

When there was still no answer, Case, concerned that Riley might have had another of his spells, set the bowl down and, abandoning all pretense of etiquette, bent over and stepped into the tepee. Riley was sitting cross-legged in front of the fire circle, staring into the flames.

"I didn't tell you you could come in," Riley said.

"I'm sorry. I shouldn't have come in without your permission, but I was worried about you."

"Humph. You don't care about me."

"You know that's not true. You're like a father to me."

"Iff'n you'd 'a been my whelp, I'd 'a held your head under water a long time ago."

Case smiled. "Now that's the cantankerous old bastard I know and love. I brought you some food. It's outside."

"Black-robe food?"

"The black robes did cook it, but I'm not sure ham and beans are exclusive to them. There's a chunk of warm cornbread to go with it. Shall I get it?"

"May as well. No sense in feedin' it to the critters."

Case stepped back to retrieve the food, then brought it in. He sat down beside Riley as the old mountain man began to eat.

"They're nearly all dead now," Riley said as he spooned some beans into his mouth. "The men I knew back then, the men I trapped with, went to rendezvous with, sometimes fought with. Jim Beckwourth, Kit Carson, Doc Newell, Angus Ferris—all gone now. Makes you wonder why I'm still hangin' around, don't it?" He finished his pronouncement with a bite of cornbread.

"Riley, why did you put up this tepee? Why don't you come inside? They have a room for you, they'll feed you, and you'll still be able to keep an eye on the girls."

Riley shook his head. "I ain't a-goin' to do it, Case. I been thinkin' about it, and I'm ready to admit that you're right about the girls. If I'm bein' truthful with myself, I know damn well I can't keep the girls with me. But that don't mean I have to stay here. I'm goin' back to my cabin."

"Riley, what if you have another one of these attacks and there's no one there to take care of you?"

"What's there to take care of?" Riley asked. "Either I die, or I don't. I've been around a long time, Case. I've seen lots of folks die—even caused a few of 'em to do it. Dyin' ain't no big thing. So if I'm about to die, I want to do it on my own terms . . . and that means I don't want to do it surrounded by a bunch of black robes."

Case was quiet for a moment; then he reached over and put his hand on Riley's shoulder and squeezed it slightly.

"All right, old man. Do it your way," he said. Case got back to his feet, but Riley didn't look up. He continued to eat his supper.

When he had finished, Riley put the bowl aside and laid out the buffalo robes. These robes were skins Badger Woman had tanned, scraping them, soaking them, and then working them back and forth with her fingers and sometimes her teeth, until the skins were soft. The buffalo were almost gone now, just as Badger Woman was gone. He knew it wouldn't be long before Kimi found a man, as Petah had, and then the little ones would grow up and leave him, too. Everyone would be gone and he would be alone. Maybe it was better to die. That thought gave him a heavy heart as he lay back on Badger Woman's soft furs and closed his eyes.

NINETEEN

Leaving the tepee, Riley began walking. He had no idea how far he had walked, or how long, but it was no longer dark. He heard laughter ahead and, following it, found himself at the edge of a river, the water sparkling with the sun jewels that danced upon the surface. Just on the other side of the river he saw three Indian women filling buffalo stomachs with water. Behind the women was an Indian village of many tepees. The village was covered by a low-lying cloud of smoke, and the aroma of cooking meat hung in the air.

Not wanting to frighten the women, Riley lay down his rifle, powder horn, and string of plews, then moved closer. One of the three was exceptionally beautiful. Her hair was as black as the midnight sky, but with flashes of blue in the midday sun. Her eyes were golden brown, and her copper-toned skin was smooth and blemish-free.

He looked closely at the beautiful woman. It was Badger Woman! But how could that be?

Seeing that he was startled, Badger Woman laughed, her laughter a soft, melodic sound, like the music of a flute.

"Don't be afraid, Riley," she said. The sound of her voice, the inflection of her words were as familiar to him as the whisper of a breeze through the leaves of aspens.

"Badger Woman, why are you here?"

"You are now one of my people. Do you not recognize a vision when you see one?"

Neither of the other two women seemed aware that he and Badger Woman were talking, nor were they even aware of his presence.

"Is this a vision?"

"Yes."

"But I didn't prepare myself for a vision. I have not gone without food or water. I have not injured myself."

"That is because you have not sought this vision; this vision has sought you," Badger Woman said.

"Why would the vision seek me?"

"I am here to tell you that soon, we will be together again. I have made a lodge for you, and I am cooking buffalo hump. The days are warm here, and the nights are cool for sleeping. There are many buffalo, and the water is sweet and cold."

Riley pointed across the river. "Here?"

"Yes."

Riley started toward the river, but Badger Woman held up her hand. "No," she said.

Riley stepped back.

"The mothers of our daughters are here with me. They have spoken. They are pleased that we saved their children when they could not. They are watching over you now, but they fear you will follow your heart and not your head."

"What should my head say?"

"Follow the wisdom of he who became our son. The girls should live in his house. He will find a good woman to be their mother."

"But what if Case won't do this? He says the girls should stay with the black robes."

"I will come into his heart. He will not know that I have done so, but his heart will be moved to do the right thing."

"I want to come with you," Riley said, and again he started to step into the river, and again Badger Woman stopped him by holding up her hand.

"No. Now is not the time."

"When will be the time?"

"It will be when it will be," Badger Woman said as she began to fade from view.

"Badger Woman, no, don't go, I want . . ."

A small gas bubble trapped in one of the burning coals burst with a loud pop, and Badger Woman, the river, the village, and the bright sunny day were gone.

Riley sat up and looked around the inside of his tepee. There was another pop among the glowing embers, and a small shower of sparks rose from the fire ring. Riley sat there for a long moment, trying hard to hang on to the vision he had just experienced.

But even while he tried hard to recall, the details drifted away from him as if being carried from the tepee on the column of rising smoke. He had no memory of the river, no memory of the village, no memory of Badger Woman. And now as he sat in his confused state, he was no longer aware that he was even trying to remember anything.

He was aware of only one thing, and that was the idea that came to him. The idea was so strong, and the solution so apparent, that he didn't know why he hadn't thought of it before. He would ask Case to take the girls with him, to live with him as if they were his own daughters.

"I'll take them on one condition," Case said the next morning.

"And what might that be?"

"You come as well. You and the girls all live with me."

"No!" Riley said, shaking his head adamantly. "You ain't goin' to get me to live in no town. Not now, not ever."

"Riley, I thought you loved those girls."

"I do. Why would you even question such a thing?"

"They lost their own parents in the massacre, they lost Petah when she left to get married, they lost Badger Woman when she died. And now you want them to lose you, as well."

"What do you mean, they're goin' to lose me as well?"

"If I take them to town without you, it's too far for them to come up here alone, and you know my trips are seldom. When would the girls ever see you again?"

"Well, I ain't a-goin' to live in no town," Riley said resolutely.

"Then I can't take the girls with me. At least if they stay here they can ride out to check on you from time to time, or you can come in to see them."

"Case, that ain't right, and you know it. You say you care about them girls, but when I want to give them to you, you turn your back on them. Now what's it going to be?"

"It's all of you, or none of you."

Uttering these words, Case felt like he was playing a high-stakes hand of poker. He knew that, in the end, he would take the girls with him, but if Riley was left behind, he would be dead before the month was out. He had to convince his old friend that he was doing the right thing.

Riley stared at Case with a pained expression on his face, but he said nothing as Case turned and walked away.

Now was when Case needed solace. He went to the mission looking for Maddie, but he couldn't find her. Seeing Mother Raffaella, he approached her.

"Good morning, Mr. Williams. How did Mr. Barnes fare in his lodge?"

"His health seems to be better, and he's speaking to me. In fact, he offered a proposal this morning, but I need to talk to Maddie. Have you seen her?"

"I believe I saw her walking toward the grotto. She may be there."

"Thank you."

As Case approached, he saw Maddie sitting on the bench in front of the pool. She seemed to be deep in thought, and he was hesitant to interrupt her. But he needed her assurance. He needed her to tell him that she understood what he was doing to Riley, and why he was doing it.

"How's Riley?" Maddie asked when Case sat on the bench beside her.

Case shook his head. "He's as stubborn as any mule that ever lived. This morning, he's concocted the idea that I should take the girls to Helena with me."

"Oh, I think that's a wonderful idea. What did you tell him?"

"I said no."

"No? Why not?"

"If Riley will come as well, I'll take them, but I won't separate them. He needs to come to his senses and live here—and not in that damn tepee, and not in his cabin."

"Do you think he'll ever agree to stay here?"

"No, I honestly don't think he will."

"If he asked you to take the girls, he must feel that's best for them and for him," Maddie said. "Helena is only a day's ride away, so it's not like they could never come back to see him."

"Suppose I do take them back? How am I going to take care of them? I'm trying to take some of the responsibility off Kimi, but if I get them to Helena, she'll only have more to do," Case said as he ran his hand through his hair. "I have a business to run and a partner who's tired of being left in the lurch. Julia's hounding Charles all the time, 'Take me to San Francisco,' or 'Take me back east,' but he can't go, because I'm not there."

"Why don't you marry me? I'll take care of the girls for you."

"Marry you? No. That's the most preposterous idea you've ever had. You really don't mean that."

"You're right. I guess I don't." Maddie rose from the bench without saying another word. She started running toward the mission.

"Maddie, wait!" Case called after her. "You don't understand!"

When Mother Raffaella stepped into the chapel, she saw that Maddie was crying. She said nothing, but went over to sit beside her until, finally, Maddie reached out so Mother Raffaella could take her hand.

"How does one become a nun?"

Mother Raffaella's gentle smile showed an understanding of the real reason for the question.

"The first thing you must do is pray long and hard. And through prayer, you will learn if you are truly going toward God, or"—she paused for a moment— "if you are running away from something else."

"If you're running from one thing, doesn't that mean you're running toward another thing?"

"No, my child, it doesn't mean that at all. It may be best if you tell me what is troubling you."

"I've made such a huge mistake. I . . . I asked Case to marry me, and he thought the question was—his word—preposterous. What a fool I am."

"Do you love him?"

"Yes."

"Does he know that? Have you told him?"

Maddie shook her head.

"Men are very complex creatures. Maybe he said no because the problem with Mr. Barnes and the girls is overwhelming to him."

"Or maybe he said no because having me as a wife is something he could never abide."

Maddie's mind flashed to the night he had come to her in her room. What had happened was breathtaking, but she intuitively knew there was something missing for him. Annie had intimated what it was like for a man and a woman, and Maddie knew that what she and Case had experienced together was not all that could be taken to the marriage bed.

She had hoped that Case would come to her again, or at least mention the night they had shared, but he never did. Maybe she didn't measure up to what he wanted in a lover, much less a wife.

Then she realized that she was sitting in a church. And she was sitting with a nun.

God would surely punish her for the thoughts she was having.

Maybe He already had.

Case didn't follow after Maddie when she left, because he knew it would only complicate the situation. When she said the words, *Marry me and I'll take care of the girls*, his first thought had been that she didn't really mean it, and his self-protection instinct kicked in. Over the last six years at least a dozen or more opportunities for liaisons had been presented to him by well-meaning friends, and some by the women themselves. But each time he had managed to extricate himself artfully.

What had just happened with Maddie was anything but artful.

On the other hand, maybe his comment wasn't

as out of line as he had at first thought. Maybe his comment was his psyche trying to warn him.

Marry me and I'll take care of the girls.

She had not said anything about him.

It was admirable that she wanted to help with the girls, but he could hire a governess to do that. If he was going to marry a woman, he wanted to be damned sure she loved him—at least as much as he loved her.

He had made this mistake once before. He recalled sitting with Mary Beth in a surrey as they watched a stern-wheeler steamboat make its way downriver toward St. Louis.

"I love you, Mary Beth. Will you marry me?"

"Yes, I'll marry you."

He had recalled that exact moment a thousand times since then. And each time he remembered the moment, he thought of something that he hadn't noticed at the time. Mary Beth had accepted his proposal, but she had not said that she loved him.

He was so confused.

Case was dreading the time when he had to start for Helena. Would he take the girls away from Riley or would he let them stay? This was the question he had wanted to discuss with Maddie. She had offered what she thought was a plausible answer, and he had thrown it back in her face.

He wished he could sit in this little quiet place for the rest of the day, but he didn't have that luxury. Taking a deep breath, he rose and went to face his problems.

∞

When Case came out of the copse of trees that hid the grotto, he met Juneau carrying lodge poles to the barn.

"Are those from Riley's tepee?"

"Yes, he's ready to go," Juneau said.

"Back to the cabin?"

"I don't think so. He told the girls he's going to Helena."

Case smiled. This was the first good news he had heard today. He hurried to find Riley.

"There you be, lollygaggin' around. Me and the girls and Miss Maddie was about to head out without you iff'n you didn't show your face mighty quick," Riley said.

"Do you have everything you'll need?" Case asked as he began going over things that were on the travois.

"I lived for a great number of years without somebody goin' 'round behind me, seein' iff'n I did it right. I reckon I can still take care of myself, no matter where I lay my head."

Case nodded in agreement. Then, seeing that Father Imoda and the mother superior were standing there, he spoke to them.

"Thank you, Father, for doctoring this old coot. And thank you, Mother Raffaella, for taking such good care of my girls."

"They're wonderful children, and I know they have bright futures ahead of them. And you, Mr. Williams, will have a happy family, if you can figure out how to do the right thing."

It seemed to Case as if Mother Raffaella looked pointedly at Maddie as she made that comment.

"I'll keep all of you in my prayers," she added.

The ride to Helena was strained. Case led the procession, followed by Riley, who rode in silence behind him. Maddie and Kanti brought up the rear.

The other girls were keeping up a lively conversation as they talked about what it would be like to live at Uncle Case's house, but Kanti hadn't spoken a word since they left the mission. Ordinarily, Maddie would have tried to draw the little girl out, but on this trip she was as introspective as Kanti. They stopped for lunch at one of the way stations, and while Case tried to act as if nothing had happened, Maddie answered his questions in as few words as possible.

It was shortly after dark when they reached Helena, and they rode directly to Case's house. Ho Kwan, hearing the horses, came out to meet them.

"You have visitors?"

"They aren't visitors, Ho Kwan. They've come here to live."

Ho Kwan's eyes grew large. "Where do we put them all?"

"We'll find a place. Maddie, would you mind helping get the girls settled?" Case asked.

"I'm sure that Ho Kwan can manage," Maddie said.

She felt terrible turning her back on the children, but she could not have the same kind of relationship she had enjoyed with them if their presumptive father didn't want her around. She dismounted and led Lucky to her stall, where she removed the horse's saddle.

"You've been a good girl, Lucky," Maddie said as she laid her head on the animal's neck. "And I've loved riding you, but I don't expect I'll be doing that anymore."

She hoped that by the time she left the stable, Case and the girls would be in the house, and they were. All the other horses, still saddled, were tied up to a long hitching rail.

Maddie dragged herself across the lawn to her own house, dreading what she would find there as she remembered her reason for making this trip in the first place. Where would she be this night, had she not accepted her father's invitation?

She knew the answer. She would be over at Case's house, tucking in the little ones. But just as there was to be no more Lucky, there would be no more girls. In that very moment, she decided that she would go back east.

TWENTY

Reluctantly, Maddie stepped up onto the porch and opened the door to the kitchen. She was surprised to see her mother standing in front of a dishpan, her hands immersed in the soapy water, and dirty dishes piled everywhere.

Annabelle looked up when the door opened, and when she saw it was Maddie, there was a genuine smile on her face.

"Maddie, thank God you're home."

Maddie furrowed her brow at her mother's greeting. "Has something happened?"

Annabelle lifted one hand from the dishwater and ran the back of it across her forehead. When she did so, she left a little streak of soapsuds.

"No, it's just that your sister is a regular Simon Legree. She never lets up."

Despite herself, Maddie chuckled. "Yes, that's how she is." Looking around the kitchen, Maddie saw that it was a mess. Flour was everywhere, and there were at least a dozen baking pans that needed cleaning.

"I'll finish this for you, Mama. Why don't you go up to your parlor and rest for a while. You look tired."

"I am tired. I had no idea how much Diana was asking you to do." Annabelle pulled a chair away from the table and sat down. "Where's your father?"

"He's going down to Bozeman and Fort Ellis with the commissioner. He said to tell you he'd be back within a couple weeks."

"I know it's going to be like this the whole time we're here. He'll be gone more than he's home."

"That's probably so," Maddie agreed.

The door from the tearoom opened and Diana came in. She stopped when she saw her mother sitting.

"Mama, what are you doing just sitting there? You know that six o'clock is our busiest time. Those dishes aren't going to wash themselves. We're going to need—" Then, seeing Maddie standing at the dishpan, she stopped in midsentence. "Maddie, you're back."

"Yes."

"Thank God you're back."

"That's funny. That's what Mama said."

"Well, it's true. Twice, we have run completely out of food, and then there were times when the crumpets weren't exactly right."

"But you got through it," Maddie said.

"You don't understand; this is a very critical time. More women are coming every day and if we can't handle them, they won't come back. Right now, I need a new batch of crumpets and we're running low on tea cakes. Mama can finish the dishes. You get started on the crumpets."

"Diana, your sister just got back," Annabelle said harshly.

"But Mama, I need . . ."

Annabelle stood up and pointed toward the tearoom. "What you need is to go out there and be the hostess. You're the one with the charm; use it to placate your customers."

Diana looked at her mother with an expression of surprised hurt; then she turned and went back to the tearoom.

"I'm sorry for what I said, Maddie. Can you forgive me?" Annabelle asked. She walked over to Maddie and embraced her. "I'm glad you're back."

"Thanks, Mama. I'm glad I'm home, too. By the way, where's Annie? Did Diana fire her?"

"Oh, that's right, you haven't heard. No, of course not, you couldn't have heard, because you've been gone. Annie got married."

Maddie smiled. "Then Mr. White finally convinced her to move out to Nelson Gulch."

"Hardly. She and Dale Hathaway ran off and got married. It's all any of the ladies in the tearoom have been talking about since it happened."

Maddie smiled. "Well, good for Annie," she said.

"Diana thinks it was a very foolish move on Annie's part. She gave up a good man who was positioning himself to become very rich, and what did she get? A lawyer who can barely rub two pennies together." Annabelle shook her head. "That girl will be sorry."

"Annie went with her heart," Maddie said. "I think she was in love with Dale."

"Pshaw," Annabelle said. "That's just a fairy tale. Don't stand around waiting for a Prince Charming, because, Maddie, he ain't gonna come."

Case had spent the evening getting the girls situated. He and Ho Kwan had carried bucket after bucket of warm water to and from the bathing room, because each of the girls had wanted to take a tub bath. By the time they were all settled down, in beds or on pallets, it was nearly midnight. Case was tired and his patience was running thin. Raising five little girls was going to be a real challenge.

And then there was Riley to contend with. He hadn't wanted to sleep in a bed, so Case and Ho Kwan had put a feather bed on the floor, and it had satisfied him.

When Case finally climbed into his own bed, he questioned what he had done. When he had suggested bringing Riley and the girls to Helena, he hadn't thought through all the ramifications.

That wasn't exactly true. He had thought Maddie would help him, and he was disappointed that she hadn't even come into the house with the girls. She had to know how hard it was going to be for them and for him.

But he had turned down her offer of help. When he thought about what he had said when she had proposed he was ashamed. No. *That's the most pre-posterous idea you've ever had.*

No, it wasn't preposterous. It was the most logi-cal way to handle the situation. He would ask her to marry him, and she would raise the girls. That was how it should be.

But he knew because of his own foolishness that could never happen.

Maddie wasn't like most women. If he had hurt her, she most likely would never forgive him.

But he had to ask.

Case loved her, and he would take her under any terms. Getting out of bed, he reached for his clothes and began to get dressed. He was going over to see her right now, in the middle of the night, and he was going to plead with her to forgive him.

He would ask her to marry him—not because of the girls' needs, but because of his own. Somehow he had to prove to her, in such a way that she was certain beyond a shadow of a doubt, that he loved her. And if she said no, he would try again. He was not going to let this woman get away from him.

Maddie made her way to the stairs to her room, so tired she was barely able to put one foot in front of the other. Even though she told herself not to do it, she looked toward Case's house. There was one room with a lamp still burning. She wondered if that was where the girls were, or was it Riley's room? Or was it where Case would be sleeping?

It was funny. She had never been in his house, and yet she had asked him if he would marry her.

And let her take care of the children. She had added that as a last caveat, just so it wouldn't seem so forward for a woman to propose to a man.

And her tactic had misfired.

Case Williams was not the type of man who could be pressured to take a woman as his wife, no matter the circumstance. And now he was lost to her forever. Mother Raffaella had asked her if she had ever told him she loved him.

No. She never had, and now she would never get the chance.

As she climbed into her bed, exhausted, she made a decision. She would stay in Helena only as long as it took to find someone to take her place in the tearoom. As soon as her father returned, she would leave. Where she would go, she didn't know, but it would be someplace where she would never see or hear the name Case Williams again.

As she lay in that twilight period between being awake and asleep, she thought she heard the door open downstairs. Quickly, her mind cleared, and she sat up in bed. It was well past midnight and she wondered who would be coming to her room at this hour.

"Maddie?" The voice was a familiar one.

She closed her eyes, not daring to hope that he had come to apologize. More than likely, there was some problem. Perhaps Riley had had another spell, or, heaven forbid, he had died.

"Maddie, it's me, Case. Are you awake?"

She lit the lamp.

"We need to talk."

Grabbing her wrapper, she walked to the door.

"Please, Maddie, let me come in."

Case stood just outside the door for a long moment. Then, with a sigh of resignation, he turned to start back down the stairs. That was when he saw a splash of light on the steps and heard the door open behind him. Maddie was standing just inside the room, her body silhouetted against a halo of light.

"Thank you, Maddie." Case came back up the steps and reached for her, intending to pull her into an embrace, but she stepped back, avoiding his arms.

"There," she said, pointing to a chair. "Say what you have to say. Then I want you to leave." She moved to the edge of her bed and sat down.

Case tried to think of what to say.

"Well?" Maddie asked when the period of silence grew longer.

"When you asked me to marry you, you scared me," Case said.

She laughed, a disparaging attempt to mock him. "You find the idea of marrying me scary? Case, that's rich."

"No, what scared me was . . ." Case stopped in midsentence, unable to put his fear into words. He ran his hand through his hair. "I think the time has come for me to tell you about Mary Beth Sullivan."

For the next half hour, Maddie listened as Case shared with her the humiliation of being left standing at the altar after his bride-to-be ran away with the man he had thought was his best friend. Hearing the story, she could sense his pain and his perception of betrayal, and her heart warmed. She could empathize, because, in her own way, she had felt rejection when he had said no to her marriage proposal. But at least hers hadn't been a public embarrassment. When he stopped talking, Maddie made no response. She really didn't know what to say.

"I know this story doesn't mean much to you, but I've lived with it for six years, and it's time to let it go," Case said, breaking the silence. "When you asked me to marry you, I said no out of hand, because that's been my pat answer for too long."

Case got up from the chair and looked toward Maddie, his eyes telegraphing his misery. "You don't have to believe this, because I know how much I've hurt you, but I'm going to say it anyway. I love you. Not because I need you to take care of the little girls, but because I need you for myself."

Case started toward the door, but before he reached it he stopped, then turned back toward her.

"Maddie, I've never known anyone quite like you."

He reached for the doorknob.

"You don't have to go," Maddie said, her voice barely above a whisper.

He didn't move, not sure he had heard what she said.

She went to him quickly and took his face in her hands, kissing him with a hunger she hadn't known she possessed. "I want to believe you, Case. I want so much to believe you. Tell me again that you love me."

Case drew back and looked at her, his eyes gleaming in the dim light.

"I do love you, Maddie. I will tell you that I love you as many times as it takes, and I will do all in my power to convince you to love me in return."

Maddie put her finger on Case's lips. "You don't have to say another word. I love you with my whole heart and soul. With or without a family."

When Case heard those words, he swept her up in his arms and carried her over to the bed. Putting her down gently, he began removing her clothes: first her wrapper, then her gown. She offered no resistance at all as she lay with longing in her eyes.

He stood before her and began undressing. When he shucked out of his drawers, she stared with unbridled curiosity, seeing for the first time a naked and fully aroused man. Unable to resist, she reached out with a trembling hand to touch him.

Quickly, it became more than just a touch of curiosity, as Case felt her hand wrap around him. He had not anticipated that, and though she wasn't the first woman ever to touch him there, hers was an innocent and curious exploration, and it sent a jolt of sensual pleasure through his body, so unexpectedly intense that his knees nearly buckled.

He climbed into bed and lay beside her, his naked body touching hers, his engorged penis positioned between her legs.

He began kissing her. These were kisses between a man and woman who had just declared their love for each other, and who were about to express that love in the most intimate way possible, by the total sharing, and melding, of their bodies.

Case enjoyed the sensation of his hand stroking the smooth skin, trailing across the flare of her hips, before dipping in to stroke that sensitive little nub, slickened by the moisture that had gathered there. He lowered his head, kissing first her neck and then her chest, where he began teasing the nipple with his tongue, until she thrust her breast upward, urging him to take it into his mouth.

Maddie reached up to run her fingers through the thick darkness of his hair.

"Case," she whispered through clenched teeth as his mouth, warm and moist, continued at her bare breast. She was thrilled not only by the physical pleasure but also by the realization that this was true love. Case loved her, and this was his way of showing her. She wanted to show him her love as well, and she would do that by being the most desirable woman he had ever known. She reacted with an abandoned recklessness she'd never known she possessed.

As he continued to kiss, nibble, and tease her breasts, her heart pounded in her chest. She pulled his head even more tightly against her, feeling the rough stubble of his chin against her tender skin.

He left her breast and rose up to sit on his haunches, his face showing hunger. Unlike before, when it had been his fingers that had aroused such pleasure, this time he wrapped his hand around his penis and used the head of it to begin stroking her.

"There's more," Case said in a husky voice. "Much more."

He repositioned himself to lie on top of her, naked flesh against naked flesh. His legs brushed against hers, and his chest hair rubbed on her breasts, enflaming her with desire. By now, she was cognizant only of an aching need. Then, when his legs parted her thighs, she felt the burning heat of him pushing against her core. She waited for it, eager for the next step.

When he started, he was gentle; then she gasped, as he thrust deeply into her. Maddie's entire body was alive with the most exquisite sensations she had ever felt. With every one of Case's deep, sensory-laden strokes, waves of ecstasy swept through her.

Then it happened, bursting over her like a lightning bolt, like during the buffalo mating dance, but unlike it in that this was so much more. She gasped at the sweetness of it, felt herself beginning to coast down; then, suddenly she was cresting again, lifted even higher this time than the first.

And now, feeling one final, shattering crescendo, she tossed her head from side to side as she called out his name. Her body convulsed and her thighs squeezed around that part of him that was making this most intimate invasion. Then she was aware that Case, with one powerful thrust, was experiencing his own release, and her body arched instinctively to prolong both his and her pleasure.

Pulling free, he collapsed on the bed, breathing hard, and she lay her head on his naked shoulder while he wrapped his arm around her, pulling her closer to him.

For a long moment, the only sounds were those of their breathing, the crackling of the fire in the stove, and the passage of a brisk wind outside. It was Case who broke the silence first.

"I love you, Maddie, and I want you to be my wife. Will you marry me?"

"No," Maddie said.

"What?" Case raised himself on his elbow and looked down at her in disbelief.

Maddie was smiling.

"I asked you first," she said.

Case laughed out loud.

"Yes, Maddie, I'll marry you."

EPILOGUE

Maddie was standing in Diana's bedroom dressed in plain white silk with a long train. Annabelle was fussing over the dress.

"It's not too late, Maddie. I can put this point lace over the corsage and let it drape down the front. Your dress is stylish, but don't you think it needs something? Some kind of decoration?" her mother asked.

"I like it just the way it is," Maddie said. "You did a beautiful job making it, and it doesn't need anything else."

"I have some grosgrain. How about if I tie some bows and let them hang?"

"Mama, she doesn't want anything," Diana said. "Help me attach her veil. I don't know why you had to wear your hair in a braid, but at least with it wrapped around your head, it'll stay neat."

"When Case sees it he'll think I look like a milkmaid," Maddie said with a giggle.

There was a quiet knock on the door and Diana called out, "That better not be Case Williams knocking. The groom cannot see the bride before the wedding."

"It's me, Kanti. It's all of us," Kanti called from the other side.

Diana walked over to open the door.

All five of the girls were wearing white dresses.

"Oh, how pretty you all look," Diana said.

"We have to look pretty," Kanti said. "We're all getting married today."

Diana laughed. "No, only Maddie and Case are getting married."

"Uh-uh, that's not true," Pana said. "We're getting married, too."

"Of course we're all getting married," Maddie said as she hugged each of the girls. "You look just like me in your pretty white dresses. Did your Aunt Diana fix your hair, too?"

"Yes, she did," Nuna said. "She said Pana and I look like twins."

"You do. Does anybody know what time it is?" Maddie asked.

"Papa says it's time. He said if we don't hurry, he's going to go back home and wait until the party is over," Nuna said.

"He can't go home; we couldn't get married without him. He's the best man," Maddie said.

"Well, Mr. Barnes is right," Annabelle said. "It is time. Are you ready, my dear?"

Maddie noticed her mother's eyes were shimmering.

"Mama, don't cry. This is a happy time."

"I know, but . . ."

"I'm just going to be next door."

Annabelle went first, and Charles Broadwater met her at the bottom of the stairs. He ushered her to a seat at the front of the parlor, where Mother Raffaella was sitting.

She looked around at the flowers that had been brought in on a special coach the Diamond R had sent to Corinne. Maddie had protested against spending the money for flowers that came all the way from California, but Case had insisted, and Annabelle was glad that he had. Everywhere she looked there were baskets of lavender and white flowers, and they complemented the red and black lacquer chairs of the tearoom.

Case had borrowed a piano from somewhere, and a gentleman was playing appropriate music as Father Imoda, Riley, and Case came in through the dining room to stand in front of the fire that was burning brightly in the fireplace. Case looked particularly handsome in a dark frock coat with a white vest and purple scarf. Riley looked particularly uncomfortable in his morning costume.

The music changed as Diana entered, wearing a dress made from lavender silk, and took her place in the front of the room. Coming close behind her were the five girls: Kimi, Nuna, Pana, Kanti, and Koko.

At last, the pianist started the wedding march, and Roy and Maddie walked through the small group of gathered friends. There were audible sighs as they processed to the waiting groom.

As Case watched Maddie come up the aisle, there were two thoughts on his mind: I have never seen anyone more beautiful, and, it's really happening this time.

Father Imoda began the brief marriage ceremony of the Romish ritual with a blessing of the bride and groom. When he had delivered a few well-chosen words, he offered his congratulations, and said the much-anticipated Latin phrase, *"Ego conjugo vos in matrimonium."*

Then Father Imoda made the announcement:

"Ladies and gentlemen, may I present Mr. and Mrs. Case Williams."

Case immediately kissed Maddie, and the guests stood as they applauded.

"When do we get married?" Kanti asked.

Many of the attendees laughed, but Case held up his hand to still them. "No," he said. "Today you came to witness not only the marriage of a bride and groom, but the marriage of an entire family. Judge Chumasero, would you do the honors, please?"

Some of those present knew what was about to happen, but the others sat down to watch.

Judge Chumasero came up to the front of the gathered friends, holding a piece of paper in his hand.

"Would the mother and father stand here, please?" he asked, putting Case and Maddie into position. "And, would the children stand beside them?"

"Kimi, Nuna, Pana, Kanti, and Koko, do you each and every one agree to be sisters, one to another, and to hold that relationship as sacred now, and for the rest of your lives? If so, say I do."

"I do," the girls said in unison.

"Do each of you agree to accept, honor, and recognize, not just in name, but in fact and in spirit, Josiah Case and Madelyn Jane Williams as your lawfully appointed mother and father, now and for the rest of your lives?"

"I do."

"Josiah and Madelyn Williams, I present to you these girls, Kimi, Nuna, Pana, Kanti, and Koko, to be your children. Do you accept them as your daughters, as much a part of your lives as any child as may be born to you, now, and for the rest of your lives?"

"We do," both Case and Maddie replied.

"Then as soon as I affix my signature to this document, you will be a family."

Again, there was a round of applause as Judge Chumasero signed the adoption papers.

Then Father Imoda stepped forward.

"Would this new family join hands and form a circle?"

The girls and Maddie and Case did as he asked.

"Father, don't we want the whole family?" Case asked.

Father Imoda smiled, and looked over toward Riley. "Indeed we do," he said. "Mr. Barnes, please join the circle."

With a broad smile, Riley came over and stepped in between Kimi and Pana.

"Mr. and Mrs. McClellan?"

Roy reached down to take Annabelle's hand in his. Lifting her hand to his lips, he kissed it. "What about it, Annabelle?" he asked so quietly that only she could hear him. "Would you marry me again?"

Annabelle blushed and smiled. "Yes, Roy."

Hand in hand, the two joined the circle.

"A circle means that no person is more important than any other. Never forget that in your dealings with one another. It also stands for family; a circle has no beginning, and no ending. Let this family keep the tradition of the children's Blackfoot heritage, and never let this circle be broken."

There were hugs and kisses all around.

Then Diana took over the celebration. She had Diamond R men move in the tables, and soon the red tablecloths and chairs were in place. She invited everyone for a wedding reception that featured perfectly made crumpets and tea cakes and a decorated wedding cake made by Ho Kwan, the newest employee of Diana's Tearoom.

"Are you really our mother and father now?" Kanti asked.

"We sure are."

"Does that mean we can't call Papa Papa anymore?"

"You know what? I always called my grandpa Papa," Case said. "You can call me Daddy, and call Riley Papa. After all, he's not going anywhere. He's going to continue to live right here with us. Right, Maddie?"

"That's right," Maddie replied, looking from Case to Riley. "From now on, we are just one big happy family."

Get email updates on

SARA LUCK,

exclusive offers

and other great book recommendations

from Simon & Schuster.

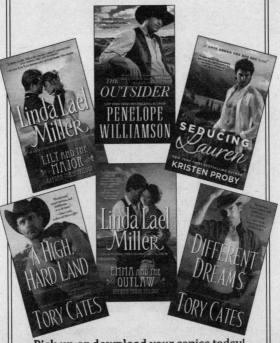